SUPERNATURAL LOVERS

With stories by
JC Grey
Marie Morin
Mandy M. Roth

Paranormal Romance

New Concepts

Georgia

Be sure to check out our website for the very best in fiction at fantastic prices!

When you visit our webpage, you can:

* Read excerpts of currently available books
* View cover art of upcoming books and current releases
* Find out more about the talented artists who capture the magic of the writer's imagination on the covers
* Order books from our backlist
* Find out the latest NCP and author news--including any upcoming book signings by your favorite NCP author
* Read author bios and reviews of our books
* Get NCP submission guidelines
* And so much more!

We offer a 20% discount on all new Trade Paperback releases ordered from our website!

Be sure to visit our webpage to find the best deals in e-books and paperbacks! To find out about our new releases as soon as they are available, please be sure to sign up for our newsletter (http://www.newconceptspublishing.com/newsletter.htm) or join our reader group (http://groups.yahoo.com/group/new_concepts_pub/join)!

The newsletter is available by double opt in only and our customer information is *never* shared!

Visit our webpage at:
www.newconceptspublishing.com

New Concepts Publishing
5202 Humphreys Rd.
Lake Park, GA 31636

ISBN 1-58608-712-6
© copyright 2005, JC Grey, Marie Morin, Mandy M. Roth

Cover art (c) copyright Eliza Black

NCP books are available at special quantity discounts for bulk purchases for sales promotions, premiums, fund raising, or educational use. For details, write, email, or phone New Concepts Publishing, 5202 Humphreys Rd., Lake Park, GA 31636; Ph. 229-257-0367, Fax 229-219-1097; orders@newconceptspublishing.com.

First NCP Paperback Printing: 2005

TABLE OF CONTENTS

DARKEST DESIRE

By
JC Grey

…and the great horned man-beast led his wild and ghostly hunt through the night sky….

Chapter One

His short ivory horns gleaming, a feral snarl on his lips, he drove his frothing horse forward. The stags, wild boars, wolves and snakes of the forest converged in his wake. Their howls and roars sounded louder now, and Morgan turned to look back in panic over her shoulder.

He was just two arm's lengths from her and she pushed herself on in frantic desperation, using every ounce of strength she could summon to try and elude him. She heard his harsh breath in her ear, the panting of his horse and then she stumbled over the hem of her long, white nightgown, tumbling into the bracken that carpeted the forest floor.

Stunned, gasping for air, she scrambled to all fours as the man-beast leaped from his horse. Then he was behind her, his teeth gripping her neck, hard hands pushing her nightdress up to her waist, brutally parting her legs as he prepared to mount her.

And the cries of the hunt quieted as the great man-beast overwhelmed his prey….

* * * *

In the silence just before dawn's first glimmers began to lighten the sky, Morgan McClellan's eyes opened wide in terror. Gasping for air, she lay face down on her bed, her black hair spread on her pillow, her sweat-soaked nightdress gathered around her waist. Between her legs, an unsatisfied ache throbbed, making her bite her lip against a moan.

Damn it, not again!

It was the third time in the last week that the dream had awoken her, so real that the

terror it evoked sent her hurtling from sleep to wakefulness in a fraction of a second, leaving her disoriented and so confused that she barely knew who or where she was.

Morgan looked at the old-fashioned alarm clock next to the bed. Just after five. She rolled over cautiously, wincing at the soreness between her thighs, raised herself on her elbows and looked around at the room. In the early morning gloom, the sparse furniture was dark and shadowy but familiar: the old armoire in the far corner; her grandmother's intricately-carved oak stool in front of the antique dressing table that was to be her next restoration project.

Methodically, Morgan reviewed her bedroom and assured herself that nothing had changed, that everything was right in her world. Her breath slowed and her pulse regained its natural rhythm. She slumped back down on her pillow and flung an arm over her eyes, groaning. Right now, she really needed an extra hour or two of sleep but there was no way she would be able to doze off again before her alarm went off at seven. Her job was exhausting enough at present but these early morning wake-up calls were killing her.

She lay in bed for a moment, going over all the things she had to do today. It was just eight weeks until the exhibition opened. She was at a stage where she needed to finalize the text for the displays and the accompanying catalogue. In some ways she hated this part of the job as much as she loved it. It required her to interpret the information about the significance of the exhibits in order to prepare meaningful and interesting context for the displays. The problem was that her passion for her subject often led her on speculative and highly personal journeys that tended to provoke controversy and leave her open for criticism.

Countless visitors to the exhibition would read her every word, and her text needed to be as accurate as she could make it, while saying something that would shed fresh light. With just six months at the museum, it was her first major project and she needed to make an impression to ensure her contract would be renewed. She couldn't afford a slip-up that would bring her own, or the museum's, reputation into question.

It was hardly surprising that she was feeling the pressure, but it was unusual that it should keep her awake at night. And, she thought, feeling her private parts continue to throb, it was most unusual for her dreams to feature such vivid sexual overtones.

While she wouldn't describe herself as frigid, Morgan was honest enough to admit she had little interest in sex, and none in screwing around. A couple of sweet but lukewarm experiences at college and in her early working days had failed to fire her imagination in the same way her job did, and for the past few years she hadn't bothered with intimate relationships at all. At thirty-one she supposed it made her a bit of an oddity in a world that seemed obsessed by the sexual antics of young upwardly-mobile urban women. Not that she cared at all. Most of the time she was absorbed in the romance of the far and distant past where the adventures of knights and ladies and other-worldly-creatures seemed more real to her than anything out of Sex and the City.

"Too real," Morgan muttered to herself, throwing back the quilt. If her recent dreams were anything to go by, she needed to restore some balance in her life.

Sighing, she shuffled her feel into the lamb's wool slippers under her bed. The chill dawn air quickly cooled the drying sweat on her body. In the bathroom down the hall, she hastily splashed water on her face and then sat on the curbed edge of the aged bathtub as she reluctantly lifted her nightie.

"Shit!"

Grabbing a face towel, she ran it under the hot tap for a few moments and then rubbed vigorously until the drying stickiness between her legs had disappeared. For a woman who prided herself on being so coolly controlled, it was embarrassing to admit to being brought to orgasm simply by a dream, but the evidence on her thighs was irrefutable. Momentarily she wondered if she should see a doctor but then discarded the thought. It wasn't the sort of problem one saw a GP about. What the hell would she say? "I'm having sexy dreams that make me come!" Anyway, the problem would resolve itself once she was through this stressful time, wouldn't it?

Pushing her thoughts aside, Morgan returned to her bedroom,

hastily slipping into a sports bra and panties before grabbing the hooded sweat top and fleece-lined running pants from her chair and pulling them on. With well-used running shoes laced firmly on her feet, she was ready for her morning jog. The floorboards creaked in the usual spots as she made her way down the rickety staircase of the old terrace house to the kitchen. She drank a long glass of water at the sink and gazed out over the large overgrown garden. The first fingers of sunlight were beginning to peek over the horizon.

At the front door, she tugged on a warm cap, tucking her hair underneath. While she hated rising early, Morgan loved pounding the pavements at this hour. The air smelled fresh and clean, and the streets were empty save for a few early joggers or dog-walkers. On the steps of her house, she stretched her cold muscles and jogged easily down the street, picking up pace until she joined the tow-path along the harbor. An early morning mist gathered over the still water, its ghostly presence obscuring the far side from view.

Its spectral presence brought the dream of the past few nights-- and the identity of the central figure, the ghostly man-beast who pursued her through the night--to the forefront of her mind.

The horned one.

Lord of the night hunt.

Cernunnos.

The great man-beast of Celtic legend was occupying not only her dreams, but all her work hours at present. Ever since the renowned archaeologist Hunter Riley had agreed to lend his latest find to the Southern History Museum's prestigious exhibition "More than Myths" four months ago, Morgan had thought about little except the lord of the hunt.

Riley's find in northern France was one of the few items ever discovered thought to relate directly to Cernunnos, a little-known Celtic god. He had unearthed the heavy, intricately worked silver torque--a necklet usually worn by a warrior--while on a dig in Brittany. The weight and craftsmanship of the piece indicated it was likely to be the ornament of a famous warrior but the thing that got the historians most excited was that it appeared almost identical to the torque worn by an engraving of Cernunnos on the famous Gundestrup Cauldron. The whispers among the academic fraternity began almost immediately. Could it be that a mortal was the inspiration for the divine figure?

From being a footnote in the exhibition, the lord of the hunt had suddenly become the star, with the torque featured larger than life on all the promotional material. Under wraps until the launch, it was the piece everyone wanted to see. Historians were openly debating the possibility that Cernunnos was more than simply a character of legend and the media were clamoring for expert opinions on the matter.

And if Riley approved of Southern History Museum's exhibition, there was talk that he might even donate the piece permanently to the museum. The museum board had almost slavered at the thought.

Morgan shivered as a sudden blast of cold air whipped across her neck, and she noticed her pace had dropped. She picked up her pace along the banks of the harbor as a watery sun gradually rose from its resting place, sending soft spears of light across the gloomy city. Her feet found their usual rhythm and gradually she blanked all thoughts from her mind but the thud of her feet on the path. After three-quarters of an hour, she branched off from the main towpath, circling round toward home, picking up the pace until she turned into her street.

On the steps of her house, she bent over with her hand on her knees, shoulders heaving for a moment while she caught her breath before she unlocked the door. It was barely six-thirty--still early. She could have a leisurely breakfast and still get to the museum shortly after eight. Hopefully it would give her an uninterrupted period to work on finalizing the copy for the Celtic section of the exhibition before most of her colleagues began arriving.

The museum was quiet when Morgan arrived at the staff entrance. As always, she took the long way round to her office, through the exhibition halls where the towering ceilings and exquisitely-tiled floors made her footsteps echo as though she walked in a prehistoric cave. She loved this time alone in the halls, wandering through the exhibits. She saw something new and fascinating every time, once a Roman coin with a face almost obscured by age, another time a section from the wall of an Egyptian tomb. She would press her nose to the glass as though she was five years old and imagine the piece whispering its story to her.

The front doors didn't open until ten, and most of the staff arrived around nine, although Augustus Waugh, her boss and Director of Displays--a title that conveniently allowed him to fuss over every small detail--was inevitably at his desk early.

Morgan waved good morning at him as she passed his office and got a cup of coffee from the machine before steeling herself to approach her desk. Awash with documents and books--three tomes even balancing precariously on top of her computer monitor--it filled the usually neat Morgan with dismay. She had worked so late last night that she hadn't been able to face tidying up her workspace before heading for home. It would have to be the first job on the agenda this morning.

As she filed papers and stacked books on shelves, Morgan didn't even notice the shabbiness of the cramped first-floor office. The window was tiny and the glass not particularly clean, letting just a sliver of gray light into the room, and the furniture had certainly seen better days. It was hardly surprising. The museum relied largely on a less-than-generous government grant as well as private donations and legacies to keep operating, and there was rarely spare cash to spend on furnishing the offices of staff. The only vaguely contemporary items were the computers and phones, and even they weren't new.

When she had first arrived from Great Western Museum, where she had begun her career, Morgan had been secretly appalled at the uninviting office. While she accepted the need to direct as high a proportion of the museum's funding as possible into new acquisitions and display projects, she saw no need for herself and her assistant to work in an office devoid of character. She needed color, inspiration around her. Morgan had immediately set to work on brightening up the space with posters and postcards, painting the bookshelves bright red and installing a glossy-leafed indoor plant. Now, at least it possessed some pizzazz.

She turned as footsteps sounded in the corridor outside her door.

"Good Lord, someone had a rough night." Augustus Waugh's slightly critical tone immediately set Morgan on edge. She looked at him as he tugged nervously at his short salt-and pepper beard. His hazel eyes looked worried, as usual.

"Thanks, Gus. You always know how to make a woman feel good."

"Sorry, but you look like death dished up. Are you sure the exhibition isn't getting to you?"

Gus had asked the same question all week and it was starting to irritate as well as worry her. She got the distinct impression that her boss was starting to question her ability to do her job without falling to pieces. Not that she took it personally. Not only was Gus a worrywart but he had a deep-seated and unshakable belief that women were likely to throw a hissy fit or burst into tears at the first sign of pressure.

Morgan couldn't say she hadn't been warned about Gus. When she had taken the job, her previous boss, Mary--who knew simply everyone in the field--had been up front about Gus's blind spot about women. Nothing he had done in the past six months had led her to believe that Mary had exaggerated.

"Gus, I'm just busy that's all." Morgan deliberately kept her voice calm, expressionless. "With the torque coming into the exhibition relatively late, it's meant a complete change to the thrust of it and a lot more work for everyone. As soon as we've finalized everything, I'll start to relax again, I promise."

"OK." Gus hesitated. "But if you need some support, just let me know."

Yeah, right, if she wanted a big black mark against her name-- woman who cracks up when the heat's on.

"Thanks but everything's under control." Morgan turned back to her desk and started gathering books into a pile for return to the library shelves. She hoped Gus would take the hint and leave her alone.

"Oh, by the way, about the meeting with Riley...he's finally back from France. I'll take him over the museum and show him the plans for the exhibition, and I really need you there to talk about the approach to the torque."

"Yes, it's in the calendar, Gus. Two-thirty, right?"

"Actually, he phoned late last night when he got in and asked if we could move it to eleven this morning. I said I'd check with you and get back to him if there was a problem."

Damn. She obviously wouldn't get as much work done prior to the meeting as she'd hoped, but maybe it was as well to get it out of the way this morning and then she might get an uninterrupted afternoon to work on her copy.

"Fine." Morgan nodded. "Just give me a call when he arrives."

"OK. Morgan...?"

"Yes?" Morgan raised her eyebrows at Gus. She wished he wasn't such a fusspot. Everything had to be discussed a million times before he was happy. It drove her crazy.

"Look, I just wanted to make sure you understand how important this is to the museum. If the exhibition is as successful as we hope, it has the potential to really give us the momentum to compete with the big boys." He paused to tug again at his beard. "The board is adamant that we keep Riley happy. They don't want any dramas."

Morgan nodded in sympathy at her boss. He was getting a lot of pressure from the board. After all, it was the biggest project the museum had ever undertaken, with a huge commitment in terms of resources at all levels.

"Yep, I know. I really do understand, Gus."

"Excellent. Well, I'll see you later."

His short, suited figure disappeared around the door and Morgan breathed a sigh of relief. Squaring her shoulders, she returned to tackling her desk, devoting the next half-hour to catching up on long-ignored filing and replying to critical emails. When her assistant Andrea arrived late at nine, she was reviewing the Celtic Exhibits file with a critical eye.

"Love the suit but the bags could do with some work." Andrea sat her plump behind in her chair and waved at the shadows beneath Morgan's gray eyes. "Someone didn't get much sleep last night." She raised her pale eyebrows and smirked suggestively. "Or perhaps you weren't allowed to get much sleep."

"If only," said Morgan, dryly. Andrea, at twenty-four, assumed everyone led as full a sex life as she did. Since Morgan had joined the museum, Andrea had waged an ongoing battle to uncover the "mystery men" in her boss's life, assuming that, as her manager, Morgan was just being circumspect in keeping her private life to herself. She would probably faint from shock if she knew the sad truth about Morgan's celibate life.

"Big day today," Morgan said, turning Andrea's attention to work matters. "Riley's coming in at eleven, and I really want to get our approach clear before then so I can talk to him with authority. Can you please answer my calls this morning, and just take a message if anything really critical turns up?"

"Sure, and by the way Morgan, that suit really does look great on you."

Morgan smiled her thanks and brushed her hands self-consciously down the tailored black pant suit, which she wore with a fine lavender wool scarf and high heels. Her long black hair was pinned neatly in a knot behind her head and she wore small pearl earrings. She had dressed carefully this morning, conscious of the necessity of making a good impression at her meeting, although God knew why. Hunter Riley would be far more interested in what she said than how she looked. His assistant, Suzie, had made it abundantly clear in their email correspondence over the past few weeks that, having loaned his find to the exhibition and considering making the donation permanent, he was expecting a rigorous approach to the museum's presentation of the torque and its potential links with the lord of the hunt. It was up to Morgan to convince him that she knew what she was talking about!

The next two hours flashed past as Morgan prepared notes for the meeting, and considered answers to some of the curly questions she was expecting from Riley, and by eleven she was as ready as she could be for the meeting. That didn't stop the adrenaline rush when Gus rang just after the hour to ask her to join them in his office.

Morgan quickly dabbed a little more concealer beneath her eyes, grabbed her files and her notebook and walked straight into Gus's office without knocking. Gus smiled at her as she entered, and indicated her presence to the tall man standing with his back to the door. Riley turned to face Morgan and shock waves resonated through her body as her gray eyes met his amber ones, framed by glasses.

"Ms McClellan?" He seemed as shaken as Morgan and hesitated for a moment. "Do I know you, perhaps?"

The faltering smile on Riley's handsome face was replaced with a frown as he reached to shake her hand, taking his glasses off to look at her intently. Morgan barely touched her fingers to his, but instantly an electrical pulse of connection seemed to arc between them. She did know him, but from where she had no idea. Withdrawing her hand quickly, she smiled up at him with as much serenity as she could muster.

"I'm not sure, Mr. Riley. Perhaps I just have one of those faces. But I'm very happy to meet the man responsible for bringing Cernunnos's torque to us, if that is indeed what it is. Either way, I've heard it's a magnificent piece." No point beating about the bush, Morgan thought. Whether or not the discovery of the torque indicated that the god had been a real person was something that needed to be discussed.

Riley's amber eyes studied her from a height of just under six feet. "I can't agree that yours is 'one of those faces'. You have a memorable face, Ms McClellan. Please, call me Hunter."

His eyes seemed to devour her, taking in every one of her features and recording it indelibly on his memory. Morgan knew she was reasonably attractive--her pale-skinned, black-haired looks were striking enough and her morning runs kept her 5'4" frame in reasonable shape, although she sometimes thought she was a little top-heavy--but Riley was looking at her as though he'd never seen a woman before.

Morgan blushed and looked away, glad when Gus finally intervened with a cough and motioned Riley to a seat.

"May I say again how thrilled we are, Hunter, to have the torque as the focal point of the exhibition?"

Morgan cringed as Gus's congratulation quickly turned obsequious. She tuned him out as he babbled on about how he hoped it was the start of a long association between the archaeologist and the museum, her eyes straying to the man who sat next to her. From where she sat, she could study him out of the corner of her eye while still appearing to be looking at Gus, and it was well worth the effort.

To her admittedly inexpert eye, Hunter looked like one of the rare men who had no idea of his own appeal. Dark brown hair flopped untidily over his brow and his well-won tweed jacket and cord jeans gave him a rumpled, academic appearance, but his warm, brown eyes, broad shoulders and low voice were seriously sexy. A very enigmatic package, she decided.

With a start, Morgan realized the two men were looking at her, Gus with bushy eyebrows raised as though expecting an answer to a question.

God! What the hell had they been talking about?

Morgan tried in vain to stop a pink tide of embarrassment from rising in her face as she desperately searched her mind for a sufficiently vague response that wouldn't reveal her as a complete fool.

"I believe Ms McClellan is prepared to stick her neck out and speculate that the lord of the night hunt may well have his origins in fact."

Out of Gus's line of sight, Hunter winked at Morgan. She could have kissed him for putting her on the right track, but she settled for a shy smile of thanks.

"Thank you, Hunter." Morgan moved seamlessly into the argument she had prepared this morning after re-reading her notes. "I certainly do feel it would be a wasted opportunity to ignore some of the more sensational implications of your find." She held up a hand to Gus, who opened his mouth to interject. It was high time some of the living fossils in the museum got a shake-up.

"Gus, I know your thoughts on this, but we need to adopt a position that history isn't about dusty old relics that sit in equally dusty glass cases. We have to breathe life into history, and the suggestion that this incredible part human-part beast deity was once a flesh and blood man...well, people will love the story.

"They will identify with a man much more than some mystical figure, especially if he was a warrior who, through his amazing feats of courage and skill, earned himself a place among the legendary figures of Celtic culture. People will be breaking down the doors to see the exhibition."

Gus choked on his glass of water. "Oh, the enthusiasm of youth." He looked at Hunter as though sharing a private joke about the impetuosity of young women in particular. "Morgan, I do appreciate your point, and we certainly want to do whatever we can to encourage the general public to visit the exhibition, even those who are not usually patrons of ours.

"However, I am concerned that the museum may be rather exposed should we stick our neck out too far on the matter of the origins of the find. It's still very much a matter of debate, you know. There's nothing that proves conclusively that Cernunnos was a historical figure.

"The last thing I--or the board need--is well-known historians claiming that we've taken liberties, or worse misinterpreted, the facts. Could be disastrous for the museum's credibility."

Morgan knew she needed to tread with care. It was a matter that very open to debate, and with discovery of the torque so recent, debate was ferocious as to whether Cernunnos was rooted in reality.

"My suggestion would be present both sides of the case." She spoke softly but confidently, her eyes bright with enthusiasm. "Show why the discovery of the torque has fired up so much excitement--but stop short of confirming any real-life links. Leave it as a mystery still to be solved."

Hunter nodded. "Good idea. People love a mystery." He looked at Gus. "I'm more than happy with Morgan's approach, Gus. The torque must have belonged to someone, presumably a high-ranking warrior. The Celts were famous for their warrior mentality, rushing fearlessly into battle. There could well have been a celebrated warrior who, over time, became worshipped as a god.

"It's a mystery that maybe future generations will solve. Every kid at the exhibition will dream that he or she might be the one to solve it."

Gus stood up, and shook Hunter's hand. "Well, as you're happy with Morgan's approach, I'll leave you in her capable hands. She can show you the plans for the exhibition and answer any questions you have."

Morgan closed the door to Gus's office behind them, and breathed a sigh of relief. She looked wryly up at Hunter. He smiled in sympathy, understanding her battle to make history passionate and exciting.

"I hope you'll be gentle with me, Morgan, now that Gus has placed me in your hands." He was standing so close she could smell the fresh, citrus scent of his cologne.

Morgan blushed again. She sure as hell wouldn't mind getting her mitts on the nice, sexy Hunter Riley, and if she did she wouldn't be at all gentle. But getting romantic with someone who was so closely connected with the museum was a recipe for conflict and wouldn't help her get her job done. She sighed. Life could be so cruel.

"I'm always gentle with our benefactors, especially one who goes out of his way to be so helpful." Morgan felt she had to get them back on a more professional footing. "Seriously, thank you for your support. I feel very strongly about this exhibition and particularly about the Celtic component, which is my particular area of interest, but I'm aware that I do sometimes get carried away so if you feel the need to disagree with me I'll try to keep an open mind." She indicated her office. "Would you like to see the plans?"

"Love to."

"Sorry about the mess." She shifted a pile of magazines from the visitor's chair and praised heaven that Andrea had gone out to lunch. Had her assistant been there, she would doubtless have flirted outrageously with the handsome archaeologist.

Morgan pulled out the diagrams showing where each of the key exhibits would be placed, and unrolled them on her desk. The exhibition was focused on Celtic legends and myths, but touched on links with other major cultures outside the key Celtic strongholds of Ireland, Scotland, Wales and France.

From time to time, Hunter nodded and asked questions as Morgan explained how each of the exhibits contributed to the program, and how they would be presented to the public.

Morgan raised her head from the plans to look at Hunter, a

question forming on her lips. At the same time he lifted his amber eyes to look at her and her question was never uttered. Their gazes caught and held, their breathing paused and deepened, and Morgan felt as though she was falling into a void, the office spinning wildly around her.

For as much as a minute there was silence, except for their breathing and the hum of Morgan's computer. Finally Hunter moved. Lifting his hand, he smoothed a loose strand of silky black hair where it had come adrift from the knot at Morgan's nape.

"I feel I know you," he whispered.

"Yes." The word was no more than a breath on Morgan's lips.

"How?"

Morgan shook her head. "I don't know, but I feel--"

The office door rattled and Morgan instantly tore her gaze from Hunter's as Andrea breezed through the office to her workstation. She looked at them, her pink lipsticked mouth open in surprise, her highlighted blonde hair windswept.

"Oops, sorry. I didn't know...I can make myself scarce if you're in a meeting. Would you like a coffee?"

"Uh, no thanks," Hunter murmured, straightening. "I have to get going, need to...uh, Ms. McClellan, I will need to approve the final captions and credits for the display. Perhaps you would get in touch with my office to discuss the timing?" He put a card on Morgan's desk.

Morgan's mind felt foggy. She couldn't think of a thing to say and watched speechlessly as Hunter left the office.

Andrea looked at her and raised her eyebrows. "Well," she said. "I did interrupt something, didn't I?"

Morgan composed her face into an expressionless mask as she met her assistant's inquisitive gaze. "Not really. Just going over the plans for exhibiting the torque."

"Sure. Anything you say." Andrea smiled at her disbelievingly and Morgan sighed, not surprised.

Andrea had definitely interrupted something, but just what that something was, Morgan had absolutely no idea.

Chapter Two

"So what do you think of our Mr. Riley?"

Gus straightened his bow tie in the mirror, his eyes on Morgan as he prepared for the latest in a round of board meetings. They were being held almost weekly at the moment as the board sweated on progress of the most significant, high-profile and expensive exhibition it had ever mounted. The anxiety that pervaded the museum was almost palpable in the air around the executive offices on the second floor, and for the past few days Morgan swore she could feel her nerves twanging whenever she arrived at work.

"What?" she said, startled, her eyes meeting Gus's in the mirror.

"Impressive fellow, don't you think? I hadn't appreciated he was quite so young."

"He's nearly forty," Morgan replied through stiff lips, wishing he hadn't raised the subject. She was finding it hard enough as it was not to think about the disturbing Hunter Riley. "Not that young." She had been a fervent admirer of Hunter Riley from afar since she had read a profile of him in one of the Sunday supplements years before. Since meeting him, she'd reread all the information she had on him. Three times. And stared endlessly at shadowed, grainy photographs. Not that Gus needed to know that.

"Young in terms of what he's achieved, I mean. Ted Farrell has one of the biggest reps in the field, but he was in his fifties before he scored that Roman find. And most of that was pottery. Riley seems to have a sixth sense for precious metal--always more glamorous!"

"Probably has a massive ego, as a result," murmured Morgan, though nothing she'd read or seen with her own eyes had suggested that. She was just being cautious, which was difficult when her heart beat so loudly every time his name was mentioned she thought it could probably be heard on Mars.

"Apparently not." Gus straightened his glasses and turned to face her. "Everyone says he's a hell of a nice guy. Prefers the hands-on stuff to publishing, which might not help his academic gravitas. But his media profile is something different. Doesn't hurt to have a reputation as a modern-day India Jones, and the dashing looks to match. Not that he seems to hunt magazine covers the way some do."

Gus wasn't particularly au fait with popular culture so Morgan didn't correct his mistake, she simply smiled and hugged the information to herself. A nice guy. Hopefully sexy nice rather than boring nice. No, he definitely wasn't boring, that she could tell with her own eyes and ears.

"Took rather a liking to you, Morgan." Gus glanced at her before picking up his briefing papers from the desk. "Not surprising that a fellow like him has an eye for the girls. Can't hurt in the museum's quest to get that torque as a permanent exhibit."

Morgan stared at him agape. Had her play-by-the-book boss all but instructed her to flirt with Hunter Riley for the museum's advantage?

"I hope you didn't mean that the way it sounds, Gus." Her voice sounded stiff, and she tried to smile to lessen the brusqueness of her words.

"I simply meant that it makes your job a little easier, that's all," he blustered.

Makes your job of securing the torque easier, you mean, Morgan thought, but she kept silent except to wish him luck for the board meeting. He gave her a harried smile and brushed past her to hurry to the meeting.

Morgan ate lunch at her desk, reviewing the documents she had prepared for Hunter Riley's approval. She had stayed late every night for the past week and put in numerous hours at home trying to get them exactly right. She didn't feel confident about anything right at the moment, and dreaded the thought of him seeing her work. It was crazy, but she felt as though she had poured herself into the captions she'd written for the displays. She hoped they reflected her fascination for the exhibits, for this intriguing slice of history, but it was always so hard to judge someone's own work.

Gus had just read the material, sniffed and handed the captions back to her with a brief "fine", but Marshall, the curator had been complimentary. Still, she wouldn't be happy until Hunter had seen and approved them.

She read the captions one final time, decided that no more fussing could possibly improve anything, and before she could change her mind again, she sent an email to Hunter's assistant Suzie, attaching the captions for Hunter's approval within the next few days.

Morgan felt better when her computer confirmed that the email had been sent. If nothing else, it meant she could now concentrate on other long overlooked aspects of the exhibition that needed her attention, not to mention reviewing the licensing arrangements for postcards and other items of stationery that were out of stock in the museum's shop and required reprinting.

When the phone rang, she was absorbed in checking the copyright documentation for the exhibits and works that appeared on the museum's postcards.

"How's it going, hon?" The strident voice of her mentor and former boss crackled in Morgan's ear and she smiled to herself. A former New Yorker, Mary Wilsden was as loud as she was open-hearted. She and the more reserved Morgan had been slow to hit it off but over time had become firm friends, and Mary remained a champion of Morgan's career, going out of her way to encourage and promote her.

"Oh, you know how it is when an exhibition is coming together," Morgan said lightly, aware that her museum and Mary's were now competitors. It wouldn't do to admit progress was slower than everyone had expected. "A daily dose of drama that has me tearing my hair out, but it's coming together slowly."

"I heard that you got the torque," said Mary. "Hell, everyone's talking about it. How did you do it?"

"Well Hunter Riley's been very supportive throughout," Morgan replied, wishing that his smiling amber eyes didn't appear in her mind every time his name was mentioned. "I was surprised at how easy it was to secure the torque for the exhibition considering he's archaeology's golden boy at the moment and the torque is in such demand. Apparently when the French government decided not to make any claim on it, Hunter was keen for it to be displayed for a while at some place that has a major focus on Celtic history and mythology, like Southern. The timing of the exhibition is perfect."

"So have you met the golden boy yet?"

"Mmm, just a few days ago. Gus and I had a meeting with him."

"Nice isn't he?" said Mary probingly.

Morgan wrinkled her nose. "Nice enough," she said carelessly. "If you go for his type."

"What's not to go for?" said Mary, laughing. "C'mon, you'd have heaps in common and he's a real sweetie."

"Oh, he's just a bit of a flirt, that's all," said Morgan vaguely. "Anyway, I didn't realize you knew him."

"I don't really. Just made small talk with him a couple of times at various functions. But he seemed nice."

"Why does everyone keep using that word," Morgan muttered, feeling vaguely irritated, though she wasn't sure why."

"Maybe because he is. Anyway, I wouldn't have minded jumping his bones." Mary laughed.

"I'm just glad he's cooperative about the exhibition. I'm not looking for a relationship with the guy." Liar, liar, Morgan's inner voice screamed until she told it to shut up.

"Hon," sighed Mary. "I know how hard you've worked for your career, but you have to get a personal life sometime. Why not Hunter Riley?"

"You sound like Gus," Morgan muttered. "It's just not a good time, and anyway, I can't imagine being involved with a celebrity." She made the last sound like a dirty word. "Paparazzi, gossip columns. No way."

"I hardly think our Hunter's in that category. Anyway, what do you mean 'like Gus'?

Don't tell me that old nervous nellie has been telling you to get a life. I thought he'd be only too happy to let you chain yourself to the museum twenty-two hours a day."

"Well, this morning he seemed to think it was in the interests of the museum for me to get it on with Hunter," blurted Morgan.

"Seriously? The old fossil said that?" Mary sounded amused rather than angry on Morgan's behalf, which only increased Morgan's frustration.

"Well, he didn't quite put it like that, but he certainly couldn't resist dropping a few hints about how it would be to my advantage if Hunter took a shine to me. And this is the guy who constantly yaps about standards and professionalism to our junior staff." Morgan's voice was tart.

"Well, I don't want to railroad you into anything, but most people would consider Hunter a darned good catch."

"Well, I've never been interested in fishing," replied Morgan dryly. "All I want is for the exhibition to be a success and still to have a job at the end of it all."

"OK, OK," Mary said, laughing. "I won't nag anymore. I just always have your interests at heart, as you know. Now, when are we going to catch up? It's ages since I saw you and I want to hear all about hunky Hunter first hand."

"Sure...."

"There's a lecture at the Library on Saturday about Ancient

Greek mythology. Wanna go?"

They made arrangements to meet at Morgan's home before ringing off. Morgan realized how much she missed talking to her friend on a daily basis.

Shaking her head, she returned her attention to her computer monitor. She was actively pursuing her dream of doing interesting work for a prestigious, if relatively small, museum and she was prepared to do whatever it took to make a success of it.

* * * *

Morgan peered into the protective case that held the torque. The heavy antique silver gleamed dully from inside, the twisted strands marked with the dark deposits of time and wear. The masculine necklet was no delicate piece of jewelry--the metal had been worked to form a silver rope, melded to a bulbous end, and the piece was far weightier than other torques of its era. This was the symbol of a warrior and a nobleman who had walked the earth before even the Roman Empire had reached the peak of its power.

She closed her eyes. She could imagine the torque around the man-beast's neck, the weight nothing to the proud, strong warrior. His dark hair flowed to his powerful shoulders, his jaw covered by a short beard, face marked with the blood and grime of battle. As he raised heavily muscled arms to plunge his short sword into the unfortunate victim before him, he opened his mouth in a cry that raised the delicate hairs on the back of her neck.

"It's exquisite," she murmured to herself. She instinctively reached out a hand, wanting to touch the metal but then quickly withdrew it. The torque had yet to be inspected, cleaned and dated. Only authorized personnel were allowed to handle it and she wasn't one of them.

It was late afternoon and she had escaped to the storage room to take another look at the torque after interminable hours spent with Andrea's curious eyes upon her. Every time Morgan lifted her head from her work, Andrea was looking at her, a question on her lips about what she thought she might have seen last week between Morgan and Hunter Riley. At first it had been amusing, and Morgan had batted aside her queries and suggestive comments with glib responses. But after six days--and most particularly after her conversation with Mary yesterday--it was irritating in the extreme particularly when there was so much work to complete in the final weeks before the exhibition opened. Eventually she had snapped at her assistant and her verbal missile had ensured a cool atmosphere in the office ever since.

Morgan knew her short temper was in part due to her own frustration. She had no idea what exactly had happened between her and Hunter and it was driving her crazy. At times she thought she must have imagined the electrical current that seemed to pass between them when their fingers touched in a handshake, imagined the intensity of his whisky-colored eyes, even her own attraction to him. It had been so long since she had been seriously interested in a man that she distrusted her own judgment, although Andrea's reaction to what she had seen or sensed gave her a little confidence that she wasn't confusing fantasy with reality.

She wondered whether Hunter had received the email she had sent him yesterday. In an effort to maintain a professional façade, she had phoned his office this morning to ensure he had received the display captions for approval. When she found him away from his desk, relief warred with disappointment inside her as she had spoken with his assistant Suzie, who confirmed that he had the captions and would get back to her within the next few days. Perhaps it was meant to be. Speaking to Hunter would only have her in turmoil again, so things were better handled electronically. It was more efficient and allowed no opportunity for things to get personal.

"I was told I would find you here…."

Morgan drew a startled breath and turned around to find Hunter Riley looking at her oddly. He wore jeans and the same tweed jacket he had worn before over a dark shirt. Five o'clock stubble grew on his chin and made Morgan want to reach out and run her palm across it.

"Stop it!" she muttered to herself.

Hunter frowned. "Are you ok?"

"Yes, sorry. You startled me is all." Morgan felt her hand shaking slightly. His melting drawl sent liquid heat curling through her body and she tightened her muscles as though to resist it.

"Do you mind me turning up like this?"

"Of course not. I just…wasn't expecting you. I was anticipating an email from you about the captions within the next day or so."

"I know," said Hunter. "Suzie said you'd called for me. I was on my way back from a late lunch and I thought I'd drop in."

Morgan didn't know what to say. One thing she had learned during her six months in the city was that virtual strangers didn't just drop in on one another.

Hunter looked at the torque in the case. "Hard to believe it may have lain untouched for thousands of years, isn't it?

"How did you come to find it?" Morgan had read everything she could about the find but was eager to hear the real story first-hand.

"Funny really," he shrugged "We weren't even looking for Celtic items. The dig was in an area that had previously turned up Roman artifacts, and I wanted to see what else could be uncovered. We did find a few Roman coins and jewelry, some ceramics, bits and pieces. And this." He nodded at the torque.

"It was wrapped in a cloth that had mostly disintegrated, tucked behind rocks in a cave on the coast. The kind of place someone would hide something, planning to retrieve it later. Perhaps a Roman. Who knows?" He shrugged. "Maybe someone in Roman times recognized its importance just as we do, and they hid it carefully meaning to come back, but for whatever reason they never retrieved it. That's just a theory, though.

"When I saw the design and felt the weight of it I was pretty excited, but I didn't really know its significance until it was cleaned up and a French lab did prelim dating tests."

"It's one of the most beautiful things I've ever seen," said Morgan. She looked away from the torque to Hunter.

"Yes," he said but he was looking at her.

God, she wished he wouldn't do that. His intense glances had a way of turning her into a trembling fool when she needed to maintain a business-like façade. She squared her shoulders and tried to maintain a professional focus.

"Are you trying to evade the issue?" he asked softly, his head lowered towards hers. Morgan swallowed and her hands gripped the seams of her skirt. She felt suddenly hot. Very hot. And flustered.

"Um, no, of course not," she stammered, deliberately misunderstanding his words. "Ah, thanks for coming in today but you didn't need to. Have you had a chance to look at the text I sent? I'd like to get the captions finalized but I know how busy you must be."

Hunter backed off a little, frowning as he looked intently at her, trying to gauge her body language. Finally he nodded. "It's excellent...enthusiastic, colorful. I imagine you had a bit of work to do to get it past Gus and the board."

Morgan sighed. "Our curator seemed ok with it, but Gus didn't say a lot and the board weren't exactly bowled over. It's a problem I encounter a lot. People see history as something that belongs on the page of a book or behind glass in a museum. They want it to be clean and neat, and nicely packaged but it's not like that. It's full of blood and sweat, and love and tears..."

"And sex...." said Hunter. "Especially when it comes to the Celts."

"Um, that too," she said, wishing he hadn't mentioned sex. But I think Gus and the board would love to believe that all deities were completely sexless. They weren't of course and Celtic mythology is particularly carnal. I've carried out considerable research on Cernunnos over the past few weeks, both popular material and the more academic sources. As you know, there's quite a disparity of views, but my feeling is that Cernunnos was a very earthy creature. Extremely sexual. The horns are incredibly revealing. In fact, I think they are symbolic of his lascivious nature."

Morgan blushed. Oh Lord, she didn't really want to be talking about the sex life of a centuries-old divinity with this man. But she couldn't think of how to climb out of the pit she had dug for herself so she did what she always did when she was nervous-- talked more.

"I see him as a very potent force. Invariably he is depicted with the antlers of a stag, and that's very significant in terms of the information it gives us." She lifted a slightly unsteady hand to bat away a loose strand of hair.

"The horns?" asked Hunter.

"Yes. I mean, I know opinion varies here and that some see him as more of a passive, earth-father icon, but I believe the antlers are intended as the outward sign of his stag-nature. Cernunnos is a wild, virile creation. To me, he symbolizes male sexual prowess and fertility, and that's the way we would like to present him in the exhibition. Well, the way I would, anyway."

Morgan's rush of words stopped abruptly as she realized that Hunter's gaze was fixed on her mouth. She suddenly found it hard to breathe, and looked down at the floor.

Hunter laughed. "What you're saying is he was a horny little devil."

"Sorry," she muttered. "I didn't mean to sound as though I was lecturing a bunch of history students. You must know all this as well as I do."

"Your enthusiasm for your subject is infectious. Don't apologize for it," said Hunter, smiling.

Morgan blushed. "Well, I do think that the presence of the horns is intended to represent the carnal appetites of men...their baser desires, if you like. There are also the serpents that he holds. You could draw an analogy with the serpent in the Garden of Eden--a symbol of temptation, and of sexual power. In fact, some sources draw parallels between Cernunnos and the devil, his links with the underworld."

Morgan looked anywhere but at Hunter as she spoke. Talking about carnal desires, even those of a mythical figure, wasn't a good idea with a man you fancied the pants off and who had a habit of looking at you as though he hadn't had sex in a million years.

She felt a sudden heat between her legs and tightened her thighs, which just made it worse.

"Um, anyway, as you've seen from the script I emailed to you, the copy for the display will speculate on the origins of Cernunnos and his various guises, one of those being the noble warrior with an element of raw sexuality."

Her words conjured an image of the warrior god pursuing her through her nightly dreams, hunting her down with his pack of wild animals, and then falling on her. Her breath shortened, her heart began to thump wildly and her legs felt shaky.

Hunter didn't move for long moments, and Morgan finally dared to look up at him hoping her arousal wasn't as obvious to him as she felt it must be. He took off his spectacles and put them down on the table before putting out a warm, callused hand, circling it around her neck and pulling her gently toward him. His amber eyes locked on hers.

"Apparently the Celts believed Cernunnos appears whenever a person acts with wild abandon...."

Morgan gulped. "I read that somewhere, too," she said.

"D'you think it's true?" His warm breath rushed across her face, stirring the hair at her temple. A large callused hand pulled out the butterfly clip that held her hair up, and black waving strands spilled across the neckline of her white striped shirt. Then he undid her top button, his knuckles rough against the skin of her neck, and dipped his head to press a delicate kiss to the hollow in her throat. Morgan knew in part of her brain that she should stop him, but she seemed to be stupefied, awaiting his next move.

"I've wanted to do that forever," he breathed. Morgan's legs felt weak and wobbly and she put her hands on Hunter's shoulders to steady herself. Her eyes drifted shut as his head lowered again, this time to her forehead, and then her eyelashes, working his way down her face until his mouth hovered over hers. So close.

At the last moment, Morgan turned her head away and took a step back. She wasn't ready for this. He was too overwhelming. Too damn sexy. And she had an exhibition to prepare. Any distractions would be her undoing. But she didn't want to piss him off, either. That wouldn't make Gus happy.

"Morgan?" His voice sounded hesitant but the underlying yearning in his question almost brought her undone. Oh how she wanted to be incautious, irresponsible, but she just couldn't shake the habits of a lifetime.

"Um, I have work to do," she said, turning towards the door. "If you would confirm in writing that you have approved the text, I'd appreciate it."

"Did I get it wrong?" Hunter asked quietly.

"I'm sorry if I misled you." She smiled faintly, trying to ease the situation and cause the least embarrassment for both of them, but he continued to frown at her. "Perhaps you confused my passion for my work with something else."

"I don't think so," he said, straightening, his eyes cooler than she had ever seen them. "I didn't imagine the way you looked at me a moment ago, did I?"

"I...no. I'm sorry. It was a mistake." Morgan met his stern gaze. "I was carried away and it was wrong. I don't want to compromise the exhibition by introducing a conflict of interest. It's so important to us. To Gus. To the museum, I mean."

Hunter's normally open face was now full of angles and planes, shadowed as the last of the evening light was lost. Finally, he released the tension in his shoulders.

"I'm sorry, too. I probably came on too strong but I've been thinking about you since...you know."

Morgan smiled at him gratefully. "Thank you," she said, relieved. She didn't want any tension between them.

"Don't thank me yet," said Hunter, replacing his glasses. "I didn't say I was giving up. I'm just giving you a bit of space to breathe and myself some time to think." He stalked to the door and looked over his shoulder, his look intense. "And myself some time to think. I'll be back."

The door shut softly behind him, leaving Morgan alone and stunned by the way she had come so close to falling into his arms.

What on earth was happening to her?

* * * *

The door of his office slammed and Hunter Riley was alone. That wasn't unusual for him. In fact, it seemed like his natural state. Perhaps it was something to do with his background.

Orphaned at fourteen, he'd spent most of his adolescent years split between boarding school and the houses of kindly friends and responsible relatives. Today, he appreciated their generosity in putting a roof over the head of a dorky kid who'd rather spend his days in the museum poring over dinosaur bones than play basketball or chat up girls. He'd been a pretty handy football player, which had saved him from excessive geekiness, but still he'd always been aware of being slightly different from other kids his age.

As soon as he'd begun archaeology studies at university, he'd signed up for as many field trips and digs as he could, happiest when he was covered in dust from his hat to his boots. Financial freedom--thanks to his parents' considerable estate--meant that even as a young man he'd been able to join several overseas digs. He was still a novice when he had scored his first significant find--a bronze Roman coin. He knew at that moment that he belonged in the field, rather than poring over thick tomes in a library somewhere or preparing lectures for half-interested students.

It wasn't until he'd been in his early thirties that he'd begun to pay much attention to his personal life. He hadn't been a monk but the casual free-spirited love affairs that he witnessed on digs weren't for him. Nor was he interested in the groupies who occasionally hung around dig sites, lured there by the press attention and glamorous aura that sometimes followed the team.

Being away from home for months at a time put major brakes on a relationship--not that he'd recognized how much until Erica Fallows. Because Hunter had no problems sustaining a long-distance relationship, he had assumed that his fiancée felt the same way. But at that stage he'd thought she loved him and not just his profile as an archaeologist with a growing international reputation.

When her real motives had emerged from the disastrous collapse of their engagement, Hunter had buried himself in his work. In truth, it had been his pride that took more of a battering than his heart. Secretly he felt he'd had a lucky escape but he'd also been bitter that Erica had so casually trampled his trust and loyalty into the mud. For a couple of years he hadn't gone near another woman but time heals all wounds and recently he'd had the occasional date or casual sexual encounter.

On an increasingly rare trip home, he'd been visiting one of his favorite old university lecturers. Sitting in her secretary's office waiting for her to finish a student tutorial, he'd been idly flicking through an archaeology magazine when an item on the news-in-brief page had caught his eye. Or rather a picture.

The photo was of two women; one of them, Mary Wilsden, he knew vaguely from various luncheons and lectures, but it was the other that struck him a blow somewhere about the solar plexus. The impact had been so sudden, so immediate that he'd nearly gasped out loud.

Serious gray eyes framed by straight dark brows had stared out from a pale oval face. Straight dark hair was held back from her face by a clip and her slim figure was clad in a conservative grey pant suit. Elegantly attractive without being stunning, Morgan McClellan certainly looked the part of the Southern History Museum's new Publications Manager, but it was the faint sense of vulnerability that had caught Hunter's eye.

Morgan McClellan's lush lower lip was pinned between sharp white teeth as though she was nervous of the new responsibility she'd taken on. There was no reason for her to be if the qualifications and experience outlined in the brief news piece were accurate. She had a good degree and six years with Great Western, and her credentials were highly thought of in the museum world.

By the time Professor Janssen arrived back from her tutorial, Hunter had neatly removed the page and folded it into his breast pocket. For the rest of the day, the girl with the most luscious kissable mouth he'd ever seen had stayed close to his heart. She was still there when he made the Cernunnos discovery in France.

On his return to his office months later, a waiting letter from the Southern Museum had caught his eye. The Museum had approached him, as a local son, for permission to feature the torque as the centerpiece of its forthcoming exhibition, 'More Than Myths'. The slightly old-fashioned, hokey tone of the letter had made him smile wryly but he had met the board and Gus Waugh, the director of displays, and been impressed by the scale of the exhibition the museum was preparing to mount.

He'd feigned a particular interest in the captions and catalogue material for the exhibition, and Gus had immediately arranged for him to meet Morgan. Even thought he had engineered the meeting and thought he was prepared for her, the first sight of her expressive grey eyes and lush mouth had blown him away.

Somehow he had known that she would feel the strange and overwhelming connection between them; and their first meeting didn't prove him wrong. Her teeth had loosed their nervous hold on her bottom lip, and her tongue had darted out to lick away the dryness. She had wanted him. Hunter didn't have an egotistical bone in his body but he knew sexual desire.

Since that day though, Morgan had deliberately applied the brakes. In the store room he'd felt scorched by their mutual desire but when it threatened to sweep them away, Morgan brought them to a screeching halt. It was frustrating and it sure as hell was painful.

If Hunter had his way, he would have taken her to bed that first day. Once he'd been inside her, he felt she would find it impossible to detach herself emotionally. She wasn't the sort of woman who fucked simply for recreation or release. She wasn't that simple; which was good, even though right now it was damn uncomfortable.

Hunter's mouth twisted ruefully as he stared out of the oval window of his third-floor office. Right now he wished she was the type of woman who fucked for fun. At least if they had already been intimate, he wouldn't feel the kind of surging in his groin that brought him out in a full body sweat every time he thought of her. Which was approximately every five seconds. On the other hand, perhaps he would. One time with Morgan McClellan was unlikely to be enough.

His rampaging hormones made him feel like the sixteen-year-old boy he hadn't really been when he was sixteen. All he thought about was going to bed with Morgan, and if he didn't get inside her soon he thought he might die. Perhaps he should simply tell her that, he mused. She might take pity on him.

Hunter was certain of one thing: it would happen sooner or later. And when the opportunity came he would ensure he loved her so well and so long, she would find it simply impossible to withdraw from him.

Chapter Three

Morgan woke gasping, tangled in the sheets and the wreckage of her pajama pants. Her head spun with the remnants of her dream, like the mother of all hangovers, but after long moments she dragged herself sluggishly from bed and wobbled unsteadily to the bathroom where she surveyed the damage. Leaning heavily on the vanity, she looked into the mirror to see her flushed oval face staring back at her, her mouth dry and darkly-lashed grey eyes shadowed with fatigue.

She pulled off her ruined pajamas, hands shaking. If it was merely a dream, why was her clothing wrecked? She took off her pajama top to find finger-like blue bruises around her upper arms, and when she titled her face up, an obvious beard rash roughened the tender skin of her jaw.

"What's happening to me?"

Morgan sank naked to the cool tiled floor, her back propped against the side of the tub while tears of weariness and frustration tracked silently down her face. For long moments she sat there, her slim shoulders shaking, legs folded into her body as she vented her confusion and despair.

Eventually the chill morning air of the bathroom began to penetrate her skin. One shiver followed another until she pulled herself to her feet and wrapped a towel around her body. She turned the shower on, waiting until the water was steaming hotly from the shower head before she shed the towel.

For more than ten minutes she stood unmoving under the spray, her head raised as water coursed down over her hair and body. Finally she found the energy to wash herself. She rubbed hard at her body, as though if she took off the top layer of skin, she could shed the remnants of the dream that wrapped silkily around her like a spider's web. Finally the water ran cold, forcing her from the shower. She dried slowly, wrapping her hair in a towel as she dabbed moisturizer on her face and slathered her sore body with a soothing lotion.

In her bedroom, Morgan drew the drapes, sending morning light skidding across the dark room. Outside, a stiff breeze sent russet and gold leaves skipping across the street. Autumn was definitely here.

She looked at the clock. Nine. She must have slept longer than she thought, although she felt like she hadn't had a wink all night. She rubbed her eyes tiredly. She needed coffee. Badly.

Morgan shrugged into a cozy robe and slippers and stumbled downstairs to the kitchen where she brewed a pot of extra-strong coffee, gulping down a large mug of the nearly scalding brew at the old pine table. She felt a little better. At least it was Saturday and for the next two days she vowed not to think about work or about sex-crazed man-beasts or about Hunter Riley. She would enjoy Mary's company and the lecture they had planned to attend, and then she would spend the afternoon working on restoring the old kitchen dresser she had discovered in a flea market. It had been sitting accusingly in her kitchen for nearly a year now and she hadn't progressed beyond stripping the top layer of varnish. Manual labor was precisely what she needed to empty her too-crowded mind for a few hours.

With that decided, Morgan felt her weariness lift. She dressed warmly in jeans, tee-shirt and a dark green hooded knit her mother had made. One sleeve was slightly longer than the other and the buttons weren't quite straight, but it was warm and comfortable. She started to feel hungry and, after a trip to the nearest shopping center, she cooked a big breakfast of eggs, bacon and toast slathered in butter.

Feeling comfortably full, she tidied up the house and put a load of laundry into the washing machine. There was still twenty minutes before Mary was due to arrive so Morgan decided to drop in on her neighbor as she often did on a Saturday.

The elderly, house bound woman had been a long-time friend of her grandmother, and Morgan had known her since she had been a child. Thelma Wick's house adjoined Morgan's, but its paint work was shabby and sections of trim were missing. It wasn't the only house in the row that showed signs of neglect. As the old folks like Morgan's grandmother died, young singles and families were buying them up and gradually returning them to their former grandeur.

"Mrs. Wick? You at home?" Morgan knocked loudly on the door to ensure the sound reached the old lady's one good ear.

The front door finally opened and crack and Mrs. Wick's pointed face peered out. She was notoriously worried about break-ins, despite the relatively safe area.

"Oh, it's you dear. Can't be too careful these days. Come in."

She opened the door just enough for Morgan to enter although she had to turn her body sideways and slide in.

"You OK, Mrs. Wick? I just wanted to check on you after that fall the other week." Morgan looked enquiringly at the elderly woman who looked frailer by the week. Her scalp was visible though her thinning hair and, conversely, bristles sprouted vigorously from her chin. But she was as smart as a tack and refused to even discuss the prospect of moving into sheltered accommodation.

"Oh, that was nothing, dear. Just missed my step. Bit of a bruise but it's nearly gone now." She peered up critically at Morgan through eyes made glassy by cataracts. She was waiting for an operation which would restore her sight. "You look peaky, though. Boyfriend troubles?"

"Oh, no. Just a few problems sleeping soundly, that's all." Morgan shrugged her shoulders. "I've been frantic at work. The new job is taking its toll."

"Hmm. Come and sit down, dear." The old woman ushered her into her parlor, where heavy brocade drapes shut out most of the natural light. Well-worn floral carpeting and heavy, ugly furniture made the large room seem small. She sat opposite Morgan and took the younger woman's hands into her own palms where blue veins showed beneath the translucent skin.

"Oh, Mrs. Wick. You know I don't believe in that sort of thing…."

"The hands never lie, dear." She murmured. "They're a mirror into the soul if you know how to look for what's revealed there. Gift was passed down to me by my mother, but she had much clearer sight than I do. Now let me see …"

She studied Morgan's hands for long moments although whether her cataract problem allowed her to see anything at all was in question. "Well," she said at last, "I can see you're troubled. It's because you try to turn away from your fated path, child." She smoothed Morgan's hands with hers. "There is a tall, dark man …."

Morgan choked back a laugh and the old woman's face peered up at her accusingly.

"Yes, it sounds like a cliché but I see a man, tall and dark. Not exactly handsome but he has lovely eyes. And, let me see…there is someone else. A shadow—oh…."

She stopped abruptly, dropping Morgan's hands as though they scalded her.

"What is it? What did you see?"

"Well, there's a man who wants you." Mrs. Wick visibly composed herself, plastering a polite smile on her face. "There was something else but I'm not sure what. Powers are about as good as my eyes these days, I'm afraid."

She got to her feet and showed Morgan to the door with a little more haste than usual. Baffled, Morgan didn't even think to resist and found herself suddenly on the steps, the door shut behind her with an audible thump. Morgan shook her head in amusement. Usually the old lady rabbited on and on endlessly, and Morgan would almost have to fight her way to the door when she wanted to leave. It was odd but Morgan didn't take it too seriously. After all, it was Mrs. Wick who had once told her that she was destined for the stage. As if!

Morgan returned to her own house and had just laid the fire for later when she heard a knock at the door. She opened it to reveal Mary's friendly, freckled face, which instantly looked concerned when she saw Morgan's tired features.

"You look like you need a good --"

"Mary!"

Morgan tried to look shocked but couldn't keep it up and laughed at her friend who stood on the doorstep. She motioned her in and closed the door against the dreary day.

"Seriously, you've lost weight and you're one of the few people in this country that doesn't need to. How much have you dropped?"

"Oh, not much. I'll put it on when the exhibition is open and hugely successful."

Mary frowned at her. "Don't put it off. You look like you need to get a life, kid. All work and no play...well, you know what I'm saying."

"That I'm dull?"

"Well, at risk of it."

"Thanks." Morgan decided to change the subject. "You're just trying to draw attention to the fact that you look stunning."

"That's what regular sex does for a girl. Nothing like it for burning the calories and making your skin glow."

"Well, I'll have to take your word for it," said Morgan wryly. "In fact, I can barely remember what it's like."

"Hon, you need to get out more. Take up tennis, party a bit...you never know where your knight in shining armor will turn up. Look at Drew and me--"

"Yeah, well, I don't think I'll be taking up rollerblading any time soon."

"Don't you go turning up your nose at rollerblading. You bump into the most interesting people."

Mary's eyes sparkled with happy memories of her first encounter with her partner of two years, Drew Smith, who she'd quite literally knocked off his feet while rollerblading in the park.

"Any sign of a ring yet?" asked Morgan. Mary had been hoping to make the big announcement for more than a month now. Every time, Drew suggested a romantic dinner she held her breath. But she was still waiting.

"Any moment," she said confidently. "And if the idiot doesn't get on with it soon, I'll buy the damn rings myself and just send him the wedding invitation so he knows when to turn up."

They drank fresh coffee in Morgan's large, airy kitchen as Mary regaled Morgan with tall tales of the subtle hints she'd rained down on Drew's head for the past few weeks, trying to prompt him into popping the question.

Mary stared around the old-fashioned kitchen enviously. "Lord, I'd love for Drew and I to be able to move into a place like this when we're married, instead of that ridiculous apartment."

"There's nothing wrong with where you live," said Morgan. "You have great views of the city."

"Yeah, it's ok but it's expensive and it belongs to someone else. Why can't someone leave me a lovely old place like this?"

"It needs work."

"It's damn gorgeous, and you're damned lucky to have such a kind--and dead--grandmother."

"Thanks, I think."

They were both eager to walk to the city library and assumed a brisk pace through the suburbs, arriving flushed and still chatting forty-five minutes later. There was something about Mary's sunny personality that allowed Morgan to shed her natural reserve without even thinking about it. A small crowd had gathered outside, most rugged up in woolen scarves and hats against the chilly morning air.

They took their seats in the grand old lecture theater to listen to Professor Dorothy Dwyer discuss some of the less well-known Greek myths. It was fascinating stuff if one overlooked the professor's dry rendering of the tales. Why did historians have to be so earnest, thought Morgan, not for the first time in her career?

"That woman needs a dose of excitement pills," murmured Mary. "She's about as thrilling to listen to as the washing machine."

Morgan choked back a laugh and turned to nod discreetly at her friend. A slight movement caught her eye and she peered past Mary across the aisle. A familiar pair of amber eyes appraised her warmly, and a mobile mouth widened in a smile of recognition that made her skin prickle and her pulse begin a slow, lazy throb. Hunter Riley was most definitely sexy nice not boring nice.

Mary looked at her, frowned and glanced in the same direction. Her eyes widened slightly and then she smiled knowingly.

"Has the Hunter found his prey?" she whispered to Morgan.

Morgan compressed her lips, turned away from Hunter and forced her mind to return to Professor Dwyer, who continued to drone.

It was impossible to concentrate, though. Morgan could feel his eyes burning across the space that separated them. She shifted uncomfortably in her seat and flicked agitatedly through the printed program. In the end she could bear it no longer and lifted her eyes to glance across the lecture theater. She wished she hadn't.

Hunter Riley's gaze still sought hers, but there was no smile on his lips, nothing remotely frivolous or flirtatious about his expression. If anything he smoldered, his eyes dark, his chin set in a determined line that seemed to reiterate the last words she'd heard from him. I'll be back.

A wave of polite applause caught her off guard and Morgan turned startled eyes to the podium where Professor Dwyer was smiling proudly and nodding to the audience, seemingly satisfied that her audience was hanging on her every word. Automatically, Morgan brought her hands together but her mind was still on Hunter Riley. He wasn't going to miss this opportunity to confront her. His look had made that perfectly obvious.

"Mary, I'm going to make a run for it," she muttered beneath her breath. "I'm avoiding Hunter Riley at the moment. I'll call you, ok?"

"Wait," hissed Mary urgently, but Morgan was off, her loosely-tied black hair swishing like a silken tail behind her. Her slim form disappeared out the front door of the museum ahead of the crowd. She dashed around the corner, slap bang into a hard chest.

"Sorry, I...oh!" Morgan looked up, straight into the cool eyes of Hunter Riley, whose large, capable hands at her shoulders held her steady.

"Are you all right?" he said calmly. He wore a cord jacket above a pair of jeans worn almost white at the knees, and an unreadable expression.

"No, I'm damn well not," she said in a low, irritated voice. "Are you following me?"

For a split second, her thoughts ricocheted to another pursuit, this time at night, when the man chasing her had long dark hair and the spine-prickling howl of a ferocious beast.

"Don't be silly," he said, mildly. "How can I be following you when you ran into me?"

"That's splitting hairs," she said, her eyes spitting silver darts at him. "You were lying in wait," she accused.

"Hardly. I was on my way home when I remembered I'd left my umbrella under my seat in the library." He let go of her shoulders and Morgan felt the sudden cessation of warmth. "It looks like it's going to rain."

Morgan glanced up at the sky where ominous clouds gathered. Damn! Why hadn't she through to bring an umbrella? She looked around at the emerging crowd for Mary and saw her dashing down the street to the nearby bus stop just ahead of an approaching bus. At least she would stay dry. Mary turned back towards the library as she stepped onto the bus, saw she had Morgan's attention and gave her a wave and a cheeky lift of her eyebrows before she disappeared.

The first drops of rain splattered down on Morgan and Hunter, and the purple-green clouds gathered in intensity. It was going to be some storm. Before took in what was happening, Hunter was flagging down a cab and holding the back door open for her. Morgan hesitated for a second just at the point the heavens opened, drenching her woolen jacket within moments.

"Come on," urged Hunter above the roar of the rain as it sheeted down. Drops trickled down his glasses and his brown hair was plastered to his scalp.

Morgan didn't have to be urged twice, darting into the back seat before he could change his mind. Hunter's solid body slipped in beside her, and then he was giving the driver her address, and the cab lurched off through the murky downpour.

The cab was warm inside and the damp conditions outside soon steamed up the windows, shutting out the rest of the world. Morgan tried to peer through the steamy windows, but she couldn't make out a thing. Water dripped from her hood down her neck, and her jeans stuck clammily to her legs, making her shiver despite the heated interior.

The next thing she knew, a warm arm settled around her shoulders, pulling her close to the side of the male body sitting next to her.

"You can snuggle up against me," Hunter murmured. "I'm always warm."

Morgan stared at him, trying to detect a double-entendre in his expression, but he was straight-faced. She pulled away slightly leaving the tiniest sliver of space between them but didn't remove his arm. It felt kind of nice. Comfortable.

"Thank you," she said, avoiding his eyes. "And for sharing your taxi with me."

"Always willing to help a lady in distress."

"Not exactly in distress, just a little er...damp."

Morgan hadn't meant to be suggestive with that last word, but it seemed to hang between them, steaming up an already warm and heavy atmosphere. She hoped he wouldn't say anything corny in response and he didn't. He was silent in fact but only verbally. His right thumb brushed seemingly casually along her neck, eliciting another shiver. This time it was nothing to do with being cold.

He flicked his thumb along her nape for a second time and suddenly she was damp. There. Between her thighs. How could he make her respond like that? With just one touch. He must be some sort of demon.

Morgan thought again of the wild creature who inhabited her night terrors and glanced up at the genial, rumpled archaeologist who sat beside her. They were nothing alike, but something...oh! She was being ridiculous.

"Nearly there," he whispered against her hair. Morgan realized that the space she'd subtly created between their bodies had just as subtly disappeared. She was now pulled tight against his side, his warm, lemony scent seeping into her pores, his scratchy chin against her forehead as though it belonged there.

Morgan felt unable to move, unable to talk. A great tidal wave of lethargy swept over her body, leaving her unwilling to do anything but just sink against Hunter. She felt his devious thumb against her neck. Did he know it was a woman's most sensitive point? Or was it just random? He didn't look like a man who was a great connoisseur of women. His appearance was charming, haphazard. He wasn't dressed to impress, and he had nothing of the playboy about his manner. Still, without much seeming effort, he had her in a warm clinch and had moistened her panties in a way no other man had done for years. If ever.

The cab drew to a splashing halt at the curb outside her old terrace house. Morgan turned her face to thank Hunter but he was handing the driver a bill, and before she had time to gather her thoughts, the door was open and she was being dragged along beside him. They sprinted up the narrow tiled steps, gasping for breath as they reached the partial shelter of the porch. Hunter's big body crowded hers as he stood behind her, taking the brunt of the rain as it fell relentlessly, waiting patiently as she fought with her slippery front door key.

At last they were inside, breathing heavily and dripping wetly on the floor of the tiled foyer. Morgan shed her wet knit, hanging it on the old-fashioned coat rack. Hunter followed her lead, shrugging out of his coat to reveal a long-sleeved navy tee-shirt stretched tight across his broad chest.

The cool air of the hall drifted across Morgan's chilly skin and she shuddered slightly. She looked down at herself, seeing her nipples pucker against the damp fabric of her top. She looked up and saw Hunter had noticed them too. She moved to fold her arms defensively across her chest and her tongue emerged to wet suddenly dry lips.

Morgan's action unwittingly turned Hunter's attention from her breasts to her mouth. She watched transfixed as he raised a hand to her mouth, running his thumb along her bottom lip.

"Did you know you chew your lip when you're nervous?"

"Um, no...I...." She stopped as he touched a rough spot on her lip, the roughly callused pad of his thumb tenderly soothing the sore skin. "Hunter...."

"You do." His voice was little more than a breath; his attention fixed on her mouth. "Every time you worry your lip, I want to touch you here." He ran his thumb back the other way.

Morgan felt her breath catch in her throat and her knees weaken from his roughly tender caress. Her thoughts turned to mush and she opened her mouth to tell him to stop but nothing emerged. She tried again.

"Don't," she said and brought her hands up to his wrist, not sure whether she wanted to pull his tormenting thumb away from her mouth or keep it there.

"Do you want me to stop?" He said it politely as though it didn't matter to him one way or the other.

Morgan was irritated with him for asking her to make a decision. She wanted him to continue but she didn't want to have to admit it. When she didn't say anything, Hunter pulled her forward into his arms, his hands loosely on her shoulders.

"Morgan?" he prompted.

"I don't know," she breathed, staring at his chest. "I can't think."

"Either you do or you don't," Hunter replied, his hands moving to rub circles into her shoulders.

His body sent of waves of heat, like a force field, sucking her into his orbit. Morgan's blood sizzled and all she could process were his harsh breathing and her thundering pulse. Speech was beyond her and she shook her head to tell him.

Hunter stood still for a brief moment, unsure if it was a denial and she meant to put an end to it, but instead she lifted her mouth the final fraction of an inch to meet him, their lips settling together in a soft exploratory kiss.

He was warm as a blazing furnace, his arm around her shoulders was secure without being possessive and the male scent of him was so seductive that Morgan propelled herself further into their embrace, raising herself to her toes and wrapping her arms around his shoulders, the fingers of one hand twisting into the thick brown hair at his nape.

She moaned as he deepened the kiss, his lips sliding across hers, his tongue darting out to stroke her softness and, when she opened her mouth to take a deep breath, pushing inside to meet and mate with hers. As their tongues pursued their erotic exploration, Hunter's arms slid from around her neck down her back, stroking in broad circles, pressing her closer to his solid body.

For some reason Morgan hadn't appreciated the hard strength of his body. His clothes hid the muscular power developed during long days spent outdoors engaged in physical work but when her hands gripped his arms, she could feel the tension and steel in his biceps.

He moved one leg to brace himself for her weight and Morgan's body moved naturally between his thighs, her groin pressing against his. She felt his penis, pushing at her through the layers of their clothes and she moved herself against it, pressing hard as his tongue curled around hers. The dull ache between her legs suddenly became insistent, making her cry out in anticipation.

One of Hunter's hands descending to press against her rounded bottom, holding her in place, the other smoothed up her body until it reached her waist. He tunneled under the soft cotton of her tee-shirt, his hand stroking around to the soft warmth of her belly.

"I want to see you. All of you." He pulled his head back for a moment, gasping for breath.

Morgan felt the white tee-shirt lifted over her head and float to the ground behind her as though in slow motion, her bra-clad breasts exposed to his gaze. It didn't seem real that this was her, straight-laced Morgan McConnell, half-naked in her dark hall with a man she had met just twice before. She wished briefly that she were a little less voluptuous up top and wondered whether he was thinking the same thing. Then he lifted his eyes and she saw that amber had turned a molten gold with passion.

"You're so perfect," he told her. "A goddess." He released her to touch trail the tips of his fingers across the lacy fabric of her bra until they reached the pink-brown crests jutting against the lace. He acquainted himself with their softness, bringing them to stinging, rigid life and then dropped his mouth to the left one. He took it deeply between his lips and teeth, tugging on it powerfully, making Morgan cry out and her body twist against him in passion. His tongue lapped at the little nub through the lacy fabric, pulling on it until it hardened almost painfully. He turned his attention to the other one, and Morgan pulled his head more tightly against her skin, the short coarse strands of his brown hair abrading her breasts as his head moved against her.

Outside, a car door slammed and Morgan shot up straight, wrenching herself away from Hunter. Oh God, what the hell was she thinking! She barely knew this man sucking on her breasts. Heaving air into her lungs, she grabbed her tee-shirt from the floor and wrenched it on. Her fingers were shaking so much she could get her arms into the sleeves.

She glanced up to watch Hunter sink against the support of the wall behind him. Her damp tee-shirt twisted as she pulled it awkwardly over her head and she swore with frustration.

"Shit!" She pulled it roughly down, the wrinkled fabric unpleasantly damp against her.

Hunter turned slightly away, his jeans uncomfortably tight against his swollen flesh. Morgan couldn't help watching as he rearranged himself discreetly. She wondered how it would feel to touch him with her hand and blushed fiery red at the thought.

"I suppose you want me to apologize again?" Hunter turned back to her.

"No...I just...I'm sorry but I'm just not...it's best if you leave," she muttered. She couldn't even look at him but he grasped her chin in his hand, lifting her face so she couldn't avoid looking at him. It made her feel slightly better to see the red line along his cheekbones. At least she wasn't the only one embarrassed by what had happened.

"Look, Morgan. I don't know what you're thinking but if you're worried that all I want is a quick fu...a fling--"

"Please. I really don't want to discuss it now." Or ever. Morgan looked away from his probing eyes. She felt tears well and she never cried.

She felt more than heard Hunter sigh. "I want to see you, Morgan, away from work. I'm not involved with anyone else, in case that's worrying you. In fact I haven't been involved with anyone seriously--"

"No...I....Look it's a bad time, OK. The exhibition opening is just around the corner. It's my first big project for the museum since I moved there from Great Western and...."

"Don't make excuses." Hunter grasped her shoulders, gently shaking her. "I don't think you would have reacted like that if you weren't as interested in me as I am in you. We're adults. So let's just see where it takes us, huh?"

Oh, God. She didn't feel capable of making any sort of rational decision at the moment; she just wanted to be alone for a minute to get her act together. She pulled away from Hunter's hands and put a hand up to cover her thumping heart.

"I can't think right now...."

Hunter looked at her assessingly. "If there's someone else...?"

"Uh, no...I just...." Morgan came to a stuttering halt, realizing almost immediately her mistake. If she'd implied there was someone else, Hunter might have backed off. Too late now.

"I want to see you, Morgan." His voice was low but firm.

Morgan looked desperately around the shadowy foyer, desperate to find an escape route. She felt her mind warring with her wanting body. Her head told her to back off, while her body yearned for more of Hunter's caresses. If he pushed her, she would succumb, and she didn't feel ready to indulge in an intense sexual relationship with him.

She wanted him to leave so she could think rationally and with her usual calm about her predicament. She heard the rain drumming on the roof of the house and knew he would need a taxi to get home. He --

Morgan frowned as something flitted through her mind, something she'd missed at first. She lost it and then it floated past again and the second time, her brain grabbed it and brought it to ground.

Her mouth parted and she raised confused eyes to Hunter's, whose own glittered as he observed her from against the far wall.

"How...how did you know where I lived?"

Hunter took a breath. "What?" he said casually. Too casually.

Morgan gnawed on her bottom lip. "In the taxi, you knew what address to give to the driver." Her voice was flat. "How did you know?"

Hunter shifted uncomfortably, his eyes not meeting hers. "Uh...I found out."

"Found out? How?"

"The phone book." He shrugged and tried a casual smile. "Does it really matter? I was interested in you so I ..."

Morgan stared at him, hard. "What? Checked me out?" She felt uneasy at his blatant interest. No other man before had been so interested in knowing about her life. "So you know where I live. What else do you know?" Her voice rose accusingly. She hated her privacy being invaded.

"Nothing!" Hunter raised his hands in supplication. "I was interested in you from the first moment I saw you in your boss's office--before in fact--and so I found out everything I could about you. What's weird about that? Morgan, listen--"

"Before?" she started to ask, then shook her head. "It doesn't matter. I can't...I'm sorry, Hunter. This isn't what I want." Morgan tried to make her voice sound firm, final, while inside she felt as though she was a quivering mass of indecision.

She watched Hunter shrug his jacket on and bit her lip until she tasted blood.

"I'll phone a cab for you," she started to say but he shook his head.

"I want to walk."

"But it's raining and your umbrella's still at the...." Morgan broke off as she met Hunter's sardonic look. "You didn't leave your umbrella at the library did you? You were waiting for me outside. You knew I'd try to avoid a confrontation with you."

Hunter's mouth twisted self-deprecatingly. "OK, you got me. Sorry." He didn't sound it.

"It's not funny."

"No, it's not." He indicated the front of his jeans where the fabric still fought a battle with his aroused flesh. "It's fucking painful, right at the moment."

Morgan's eyes flared at the realization that she could affect him like that. She felt guilty and delighted in equal measure. "I'm sorry," she lied

"You could kiss it and make it better." He was smiling at her, flirting, but his words held an edge of seriousness that made Morgan look at him in shock and blush like a virgin schoolgirl.

"No? Oh well, another time, maybe, when we know each other better."

"Hunter…."

"Deal with it, honey. I'll leave you alone now but this isn't the end. I've said it before and I'll say it again. I'll be back."

The front door slammed behind him and Morgan watched through the window as he walked briskly down the street. He didn't look back.

Morgan let her breath out before she was aware she'd been holding it in. For one seemingly sweet, easygoing archaeologist, Hunter Riley sure had a temper, not to mention a streak of persistence a mile wide. Usually men found her reserved, prickly nature too much trouble and quickly went in search of easier prey, but she suspected that Hunter would not be quite so easily deterred. That made her mind flash to the dream warrior who hunted her at night and she shivered before pushing the thought aside. Right at the moment, she had bigger problems with one very determined flesh and blood man. Hunter had made it quite clear he was coming after her, whether she liked it or not. What was not so clear was what the hell she was going to do about it!

Chapter Four

"Absolutely impossible, Morgan."

Morgan pushed a loose strand of hair from her pale face and

pressed her lips together. Her boss was in a particularly difficult mood. And since she'd arrived in his office nearly twenty minutes before, he'd turned downright obstinate. In contrast to her own pale cheeks, his were ruddy with frustration and--dare she say it--temper. Yes, Gus was about to lose it. Big time.

"Gus, just listen for a moment. We can handle this professionally and smoothly if--"

Spittle foamed on Gus's lips and a speck hit her face. He was absolutely apoplectic.

"Morgan. What don't you understand about the word no?" He ran an exasperated hand through his thinning hair. "The absolutely crucial thing at this stage is Riley's support. We haven't yet secured the torque as a permanent part of our collection and until we had the deal signed and sealed I will not even contemplate messing him around."

"But Andrea--"

"Andrea is doing very well but she's inexperienced and has a tendency to rush in. She certainly is not up to establishing and maintaining the kind of rapport with Riley that the museum needs to get the torque on a permanent basis." Morgan opened her mouth to speak but he held up a hand. "I haven't finished. Apart from that, I do not want to change the contact arrangements. Riley likes you. He trusts your judgment."

"You don't know--"

"But I do. Riley has made it crystal clear how much he values your involvement. My dear, the man was so complimentary about you last time he was in my office that he could have been your PR agent."

Yeah, well, she knew all about what Hunter had been up to last time he was in her boss's office.

"Gus, there's a conflict."

"What conflict, for heaven's sake?" Gus boomed.

"I just feel uncomfortable. He makes me feel uncomfortable." Morgan flushed and flicked another strand of hair behind her ear. "I think a more professional approach would be to have someone else handle the day-to-day contact with him. I'll still be doing everything behind the scenes as I've always done."

"Morgan, I've listened but the answer is no. We have just a few weeks left until the start of the exhibition. There is a lot of work for everyone--you especially--to get through in the time remaining in order to guarantee a smooth opening. Any number of things could go wrong without us setting up a situation that we know is certain to cause us grief."

"I can --"

"No. And you have always known that I will not under any circumstances risk upsetting the man who has the power to make or break the museum's immediate future. We need that torque in our collection and I couldn't live with myself if I permitted a situation that led to the piece going elsewhere. Relationships are everything in this business, Morgan."

For a brief second, Morgan shut her eyes and imagined she was somewhere else, a leafy glade with a waterfall trickling gently in the background. It was her retreat when things became crazy. But she couldn't focus, her eyelids trembled and she opened her eyes to meet Gus's implacable brown ones.

He tugged on his beard. "Morgan, I hope you understand what I'm saying, I really do...for all our sakes."

Morgan nodded mutely. She did understand Gus' position and knew he was right. That wasn't the issue. When she'd finally plucked up the courage to knock on her boss's door after minutes hesitating on the threshold, she'd been ninety percent sure that he would turn down her request to remove herself from the liaison role. It was part of her job description so she had no rights to expect any flexibility unless there had been an extraordinarily unusual circumstance. There wasn't. Unless she could think of something fast, she was stuck with him.

Gus merely grunted as she left his office, no doubt glad to get rid of his least favorite member of staff. Morgan racked her brains to think of an alternative solution that would have the same effect of moving her out of Hunter Riley's sphere but, if there was one, it eluded her.

She walked slowly back to her own office and slumped down in her chair. Andrea looked up from her desk where she was reviewing the invitation list for the launch that the PR office had sent down earlier. Morgan wanted to ensure they didn't accidentally twist someone's nose out of joint by omitting them from the launch, particularly not one of their key patrons or associates.

"Hey boss!" Andrea smiled broadly at her. Morgan scowled back, wondering grouchily how the girl managed to stay so goddamn perky all the time.

Andrea raised her eyebrows. "Gus at it again?" she said sympathetically. "Don't worry, he's on everyone's case. You know how anxious he gets before big events."

"It's not that," Morgan muttered. "I asked him if you could handle Hunter Riley for the time being. I'm up to my neck and--"

"Oh, Morgan. I'd love to. I've been here two years and he's never trusted me to do anything important in all that time." Her mouth turned sulky. "He even called me an airhead once. To Marshall."

Morgan hid a smile. "Sorry, Andy. He said no. Wouldn't accept any of my arguments. But I take your point about giving you some added responsibility and I'll look seriously at it. You need to progress in your role."

Now it was Andrea's turn to scowl. "That's too bad. I wouldn't have minded looking after Mr. Sexy Riley." She glanced cheekily at Morgan. "As long as I wasn't stepping on anyone else's toes, that is."

"Well, Gus says--"

"Hey!" Andrea interjected. "Does stuffy old Gus need to know? I mean your next meeting with Riley doesn't even involve Gus. There's just Marshall but there's no reason for him to go blabbing to Gus about who was and wasn't there. I'll take the meeting, report back to you and you brief Gus. Simple."

Oh, if only. "Well, it could work but I hate to put you in this position."

"What could go wrong? As long as you cover all bases in your brief, it'll be fine."

Morgan wasn't so sure but it did provide some respite. She didn't want to have to confront Hunter in a professional setting again tomorrow. It was too soon. She knew it wasn't a long-term solution but she was so, so tempted to agree to Andrea's suggestion.

Should she, shouldn't she? The debate swirled endlessly around in her head, ensuring another sleepless night. At least it kept her dark pursuer from her dreams. She was no more decided at the break of day and arrived at work exhausted and fraught. In the end, she prepared a full and detailed brief for Andrea and talked her through it before the meeting. Just in case. And then she worried the issue some more. It wasn't simply that she was defying her boss's strict instructions--in itself probably an offense that warranted an official warning--it was that she felt like the biggest coward alive.

Morgan sat rigid at her desk for the full two hours that Andrea was in the meeting. She couldn't even answer the phone when it rang. By the time Andrea returned, a tension headache was forming across her brow. Even when Andrea told her everything was fine, that Hunter had signed off on everything and hadn't had a problem with her absence, Morgan still couldn't relax. She'd always prided herself on being the ultimate professional and now she was backing off from her usual standard because the guy had kissed her once. Apart from letting herself down, she was still anxious that Gus might find out and blow a fuse. Not that she would blame him but it sure wouldn't make their working relationship any easier. As to what might say to her the next time they met--well, she refused to even think about that.

* * * *

Damn her to hell!

Hunter threw his battered briefcase on the desk and glared at Suzie through the glass partition. She hastily returned her attention to her work, not looking like she possessed even the remotest inclination to ask her boss how the meeting went. It was a wise move, thought Hunter. If anyone said a word to him, he would explode into a tirade of vile abuse about womanhood in general and one woman in particular.

Part of him was ticked off in a very male way that Morgan wasn't following the plan. Meet. Fall into bed. Fall in love. Simple except he'd somehow managed to achieve stages one and three at approximately the same time, and stage two seemed as remote as ever. He drew a hand over his stubbled jaw. He'd been relying on the fact that, even if she refused to see him socially, she had to see him professionally. Now she'd found even a way around that. How the hell was he supposed to convince her of his credentials as a bed and life partner if she would even see him?

For the first time since he'd met Morgan, a vague sense of doubt drifted across Hunter's mind. He was just about to hit forty, for shit's sake. Forty. He wanted a partner. He wanted a family. The decision should have been the hard part, not the execution, but he'd reckoned without his chosen woman being more stubborn than the proverbial mule.

From the moment he'd seen her photo, he'd perceived Morgan McClellan as some vulnerable creature that needed taking care of, and himself as her rescuer. Now he had to admit that his image had been rather two-dimensional. Yes, she was vulnerable but she was also passionate, volatile, determined, independent, ambitious and stubborn as hell. And scared.

Hunter's expression brightened as he grasped the significance of that last thought. If she didn't care, she would have turned up at the meeting.

She was running scared.

Hunter's smile grew broader.

* * * *

Andrea finally packed up her desk and left at five, and Morgan let her shoulders droop under the accumulated pressure of the day. When her phone rang, she hoped it was Mary. She needed a heart to heart. It wasn't. It was Hunter.

"I expected more from you," he said quietly.

"Hunter, I--"

"What did you think? That I'd leap across the table and try to ravish you?"

"No, of course not. I've just been swamped." It sounded lame, even to her own ears.

"You're a coward, Morgan McClellan," he gritted. "Too scared to reach out and take what you want."

That was precisely the problem, thought Morgan tiredly. She wanted everything. But admitting to her desires was something else.

"I'm sorry--" she started to say but the flat dial tone at the end of the line told her he'd ended their call.

Slowly Morgan lowered her head until it rested on her arms on the desktop. She couldn't have screwed things up worse if she'd tried. "What a mess!" she said to herself, wondering how on earth she could straighten things out and get back on top of her responsibilities. The minutes ticked by and the hour hand of the clock rotated. Finally it was close to half past six and still she sat there. The only thing that came to mind was the mantra that had seen her through every tough situation she'd encountered so far.

Tackle it head on.

Morgan raised her head and stood up, squaring her shoulders. She'd had tough situations in the past, but she'd always summoned up the courage to deal with them openly. This was different because it involved not only her professional responsibilities but her emotions and, well admit it, her body.

She flicked quickly through her contact book as she shrugged her black woolen coat over her lavender jersey dress and wrapped a silky scarf around her throat, making a note of Hunter's office address which she stuffed into her bag. She had no idea whether he would still be there but she had to try.

* * * *

Hunter's assistant, Suzie Green, smiled quizzically at her and motioned her to a vinyl seat that looked like something from a rummage sale. If Hunter had money he sure didn't spend it on furniture. Or clothes, she smiled inwardly. For some reason she had associated the Riley name with wealth, but perhaps not. Then it came back to her. It had been mentioned almost in passing in one of the article's she'd read that Hunter's mother was from old money. Virginia and Declan Riley, both anthropologists of repute, had been killed in a plane crash in a remote part of Zambia when Hunter was a teenager. There was a substantial inheritance that had allowed him to pursue his passion for archaeology.

"He's due back shortly so you won't be waiting long. Will you tell him I said goodbye? My boyfriend has tickets for the theater tonight and I can't be late." Suzie dragged a woolen hat over her curly brown hair and said goodbye.

"Sure. Enjoy the show." Morgan smiled politely at the girl as she dashed out towards the stairs.

On the third floor of an old red brick building in a seedy area of town, Hunter's office was cluttered with the detritus of years of haphazard filing and an outdated catalogue system. Books, files, ceramic and bone fragments--even a complete skull--crowded the shelves and most of the floor space.

Morgan sat for a few minutes on the battered chair trying to wriggle into a more comfortable position. She stared at the shelves where papers, files and books seemed to stuffed any which way, and bit her lip. She really shouldn't touch Hunter's working space but her inner neat freak urged her to at least get the books into alphabetical order. It was no easy task. Many of the titles meant little to her and she had to guess at the content in some cases. She found a small step ladder and was busy stacking books on the top shelf when the door opened.

"What the hell!"

Morgan gasped. The step ladder wasn't high but the sudden noise made her over-reach with the pile of books. She listed precariously, dropping the books and flailing for a hand grip on the ladder when strong arms seized her around her hips and dragged her against a hard male body.

"Idiot," he muttered and then Hunter's hot breath was mingling with hers as his mouth came down on hers. With an effort she pushed away from him, her hands against his shoulders holding him at arms' length. He stood there his chest moving up and down with the force of his breathing, and Morgan sensed a volcano was about to explode.

"I wanted to tell you...."

"I don't give a damn what you wanted to tell me. It never makes sense." Hunter's voice was cold but his eyes were hot.

Morgan took a deep breath and reached out a shaking hand to steady herself on the back of the chair. Her knuckles showed white where her slim fingers gripped the torn vinyl.

"I'm sorry about the meeting today. I panicked. I'm not good at this."

"You can say that again." Hunter's mouth was a straight line, giving nothing away.

"I know it. You don't have to say it again." She was bitterly ashamed. She knew what he was thinking. "I know what I did was cowardly. I should have faced you."

"A person's actions speak louder than words." Hunter watched her speculatively. Morgan had the sense he was goading her.

"I--"

"I'm not playing your games, anymore." He pulled the glasses from his face, setting them down on his desk, and rubbing the bridge of his nose tiredly with his fingers. "Look I'm tired. It's been a hell of a day, one way and another."

"My games? What about yours? The umbrella thing, the way you knew my address," Morgan shot back at him. "And I'm tired, too. That's why I'm all over the place. I'm not deliberately jerking your chain, believe me."

"Well from where I'm standing you're behaving like a first-class cock tease," he told her crudely. "Morgan, I'm forty in March, not some pimply seventeen-year-old for you to test your wiles on. I don't doubt you have every man in the vicinity wanting to get in your pants but I'm through flirting."

Morgan felt her cheeks heat at his words. "Hunter, you've got it all wrong. I'm not trying my wiles out on you. I've never been like that."

Hunter stared at her, disbelief written on his face. "Yeah right," he said sarcastically.

"It's true," Morgan said. "In fact, I've never had men chase me at all. I've always been the serious type that men avoid." She sighed and looked away from him. "To tell you the truth, I'm not very experienced and I haven't dated at all since I joined the museum. I'm just nervous around you. Nervous and confused."

"I can't believe you don't have the men flocking around you." Hunter's voice softened. "You're the most stunning creature I've ever seen in my life."

"Yes but...." Morgan smiled and indicated the table where his spectacles rested. "You're blind. Admit it."

"Mad, maybe. To think I might have a chance with you." His smile was whimsical. A little sad.

"Hunter. You're a really nice guy. I like you...a lot. I just need time to think."

His harsh laughter cracked the quiet room like a gun shot. "That'd be right," he said tightly, his fury only just contained. "Good old Hunter. Shame he never gets the girl. He's just too nice."

Morgan winced. She had used that word, nice. But she'd meant to insult him. He was nice. Sweet and funny. And very sexy.

Hunter saw her expression and misinterpreted it.

"I'm right, aren't I? You thought I was nice. Not someone you could ever have strong feelings for." His tone was bitter. "Great to have as a friend but not as a lover. God forbid!"

"Hunter, no!" Morgan was astounded. "I admit I think you're one of the sweetest guys I've ever met. I haven't known you long but everything I've seen so far tells me you're warm-hearted, witty and charming."

"But not exactly Valentino, huh?"

"Hunter!" Morgan came towards him and laid her hands on his shoulders, looking deeply into frustrated golden eyes. "You're incredibly--"

"Sad about old Hunter," he interrupted, his voice bitter. "Did you hear about his bitch of a fiancée? They were engaged for two years but she kept shying off from the final commitment, till one day she finally said yes. And then told him she was pregnant.

"Good old Hunter was delirious with joy thinking he was going to be a husband and a dad until he did the calculations and worked out that he couldn't possibly be the father. Poor bastard had been away on a dig at the time of the conception. Turned out she'd been screwing another guy, and he'd had no idea. He never even thought about cheating on her and just assumed she felt the same way."

Morgan was shocked into silence for a second before reaching up a hand to stroke the hard plane of his face. "I'm sorry, Hunter. You didn't deserve that."

Hunter brushed her hand away angrily. "Yeah, well, I'm not messing around. What you see is what you get so make a decision. If you want me then prove it. Take me. Now. Otherwise get out."

"Hunter, I...." She didn't want to lose him from her life; she just needed time.

He shoved one hard hand between her legs in an uncharacteristically crude gesture, his fingers gripping her crotch.

"How much more plainly can I put it? If you want sex then you can stay, if you don't, then get out."

Morgan stared at him, frozen by his hostility and aggression. Where was the sweet, kind Hunter she knew?

"Too late." Her hesitation wasn't overlooked by Hunter who pulled her roughly to him, one hand reaching out to curve roughly around her breast. She gasped as his thumb glanced against a nipple.

"Hunter, wait!"

"No, I'm through waiting. You had your chance to run and you didn't take it."

"Hunter, please. Not like this."

"Exactly like this." His voice was deep, harsh. His large hand cupped the back of her head, spilling her hair free from its barrette. He pulled her head to him until she felt his breath, warm and heavy on her face.

"Hunter. I do want you. You must have felt it."

He shook his head. "I thought you felt it too. But every time we touch, you pull back."

Morgan's eyes pleaded with him. "We need to talk about this."

"No more talk. Just sex. Right here. Right now." His voice was husky as he lowered his mouth to hers. Despite his words the first touch of his lips was delicate, like butterfly wings against a flower.

For some reason, the sinful sweetness of his lips scared her more than the intent of his words or his hands at her breasts. Panicked, Morgan pushed away from him and turned towards the door, but he came after her, an arm hooking around her waist. Her left foot tangled with his in the rush and Morgan cried out as his bulk propelled her heavily to the floor.

Morgan's cheek was against the carpet. It should have smelt old and moldy, but instead she caught the scent of the forest, the aroma of damp leaves and the sound of the breeze in her ears.

And somewhere in the peripheral senses, she heard the clash of stag antlers, the snuffle of a boar and the howl of a lone wolf.

Then the weight of Hunter came over her and she was hurled back into reality. He pinned her to the floor as though he expected her to struggle, his hands pushing up the fine wool of her dress to her waist, pulling off the panties and stockings underneath. Her shoes came off with her underwear, and then cool air washed over her skin.

Morgan didn't struggle, didn't even want to. Her control, her will was gone. All she wanted was to surrender to this man and let the tide of passion take her where it wished. She lay half dazed, crushed beneath him, feeling nothing but his heat and weight against her, the hardness of the linoleum-covered floor beneath her.

He grunted with satisfaction as he spread her legs apart, his hands moving over her skin and between her thighs. She moaned as his fingers parted the tangle of her pubic hair, stroking abruptly against her soft flesh until she felt a scalding rush of heat well up in her lower body. His fingers teased her sensitive clit making her breath freeze in her throat. Then his deft touch moved to her vulva and the well of moisture that had been building in her body was released with a sudden rush, flooding her body with liquid arousal.

"Oh, God," she moaned as she felt the scalding liquid leak from her body, flooding Hunter's fingers. She felt him dip inside her again and then his hand was gone for a second. She heard his murmur of delight.

"You taste of woman," he said and Morgan realized he was licking her fluid from his fingers. She couldn't see but the image of it sent a trembling tide of passion through her body, making her bones soften, her sinews lose their tension and her flesh feel as if it was melting away. "When I come inside you, I'll let you taste us, mixed together," he whispered, his hard mouth close to her ear.

Morgan shivered at his words. There was no doubt of his intention to have sex with her. None at all. An image of her lusty warrior ghost rippled through her mind. He would have sex like this, she thought. Rough. Untamed. Like a rutting animal. She shivered.

She was wet enough to take Hunter now but he didn't seem in any hurry. He gathered her long hair into his hard fist and pressed a wet kiss to the pale, bare nape of her neck. She cried out then and he laughed with satisfaction at her response.

"Look in the glass," he said and Morgan lifted her upper body from the floor, turning her head to see herself reflected sharply in the glass divider between Hunter's office and Suzie's workspace.

She was Morgan and someone else at the same time, a woman completely given over to her instincts, her desire. Black hair framed her oval face in untidy waves, her mouth was swollen from his kisses and her eyes were sleepily sensual. She could see their bodies twisted together, his hard limbs covering her softer curves. He pushed two fingers abruptly inside her and made her lift her head to watch her own reaction in the glass, mouth open, eyes closing in dazed desire until they were nothing more than a slit. The wide boat neck of her dress exposed generous amounts of creamy bosom. Hunter slipped a hand inside, reaching for the nipples of her breasts and finding them stiffly erect. He ran a warm palm over them, making them tighten into almost painful buds and then he pinched them roughly and again made her watch herself as she flinched.

Wordless with desire, Morgan pushed her body back against his, needing to feel the pressure of him at the juncture of her thighs. He let her buttocks find the hard ridge of him expanding beneath the rough cord of his pants. The he released himself, pushing his cock between her legs, rubbing it roughly into her sensitive mounds, making her squirm with desire.

"Open your legs wider," he commanded, and Morgan had no thought but to obey his words and the urges of her own body. She moved beneath him, spreading herself until her inner thighs ached. She felt his penis replace his fingers at the entrance to her body, pressing past the tight muscles he found there, ignoring her whimper, until he was lying poised at her threshold to her body.

"You feel tight," he whispered smokily against her cheek.

"I haven't...not for a long time," she said, her voice trembling. "It's OK." But she wasn't sure if she was reassuring Hunter or herself.

Withdrawing a fraction, he shoved his cock forward, his lips against her nape as she tensed and arched her neck in a gasp of discomfort. His thick length pressed full-length into her, stretching her sheath to its full extent so that she felt she must split under the pressure. He withdrew and plunged again, cleaving his way into her, forcing her unused muscles to accept him. He moved fast and hard, driving into her with his fullest extent every time until her body began to soften and accept him.

His pounding rhythm echoed in her pulse, her blood thundered in her ears and she began to gasp in time with his thrusts. It was primeval, it was devastating, and she wanted more.

"Hunter!"

He seemed to understand without words, one hand dropping down to tease her softness where his body became one with hers. His fingers circled around her stretched opening again and again, then drifted up to her clit, touching, tempting, taunting. Morgan felt the pressure building inside her, release just outside her reach, taunting her, tantalizing her. She muttered words even she couldn't understand but Hunter seemed to understand what she needed, focusing his attentions on her clit, moving on it and around it until she was thrusting her hips in abandon, searching for that elusive moment. And still the pressure built in them both until he was slamming into her in response, and she was gasping and then screaming, and then there was a moment of stillness and her body took flight as the pulsations gripped her. She rode the waves of her convulsions, dimly aware that Hunter was gripping her buttocks, thrusting ever more aggressively into her through her orgasm until he was unable to escape the tight grip of her climaxing muscles. He tensed for a long moment, and then his release roared through him and, shuddering, he spewed his ejaculate into the liquid depths of Morgan's body.

For endless moments, their joined bodies continued to rock with the force of their pleasure. Slowly, finally, they stilled. Supported on trembling muscles, Hunter let himself collapse onto Morgan, his face buried in her shoulder as he heaved air into his lungs.

When their breathing had quieted, Hunter released himself from her body and pulled them both upright, swiveling their bodies until they were sitting in front of the glass. Quickly, he stripped off her dress and bra, and his clothes so that she felt his furred chest damp with sweat along her bare back, his thighs spread along side hers. Her hair hid the curve of her breasts but the nipples poked through the strands, glinting pinkly.

She looked like herself and not like herself, as though she'd been stripped to her core. The business clothes, the neatly-pinned hair, the prissiness and protocol banished. She was just a woman.

Morgan twisted her head to peer up at him cautiously. He looked down at her enigmatically, saying nothing but his hands pulled her legs apart until Morgan could see her body in the reflective glass open to Hunter's gaze. Blushing, she tried to close her legs but he wasn't having it, forcing her legs to part further and then lifting her knees until her intimate flesh was fully exposed. She moaned and tried to look away.

"Morgan, I want you to look at yourself." His deep baritone voice was firm in her ear.

"No." She twisted against him but he held firm. "I feel so exposed," she whispered. "Stripped bare."

"Don't be afraid," he murmured. "You're beautiful, Morgan. Look at yourself. See how you respond to me." Hunter's hands moved beneath her thighs to her vulva, his fingers plucking tenderly at her moistness. The pulse began again between her legs and she moaned closing her eyes.

"I'm depraved!"

"You're not. You're just a woman uncovering her sensual side. Open your eyes."

She did as he asked, whimpering as he pushed two fingers into her wet opening, probing her. His fingers emerged wet with the juices of their pleasure, and he brought them up to her mouth, running them around her lips.

"Open," he whispered and with volition her lips parted and he touched his fingers to her mouth letting her taste the dark essence of their orgasm. She twirled her tongue around his fingers, capturing the tantalizing drops, then taking his fingers inside her mouth, sucking them deeply in a parody of penetration.

In the mirror, she forgot herself, forgot her inhibitions, her attention focused on her lover. She watched his eyes deepen from light amber to burning gold, witnessed the blood rise, dark and red along his cheekbones, the breath coming in gasps between his lips. She stroked her hands up the hairy, muscular thighs that lay alongside her smooth ones and against her back, she felt his male sex rise again, prodding demanding and hot against her back.

Instinctively Morgan reached back, taking his cock in her hands, stroking along its increasing length, circling its expanding thickness. She cupped the weight of his testicles in her palms, juggling them, stroking them, making him moan. And then she turned to face him, her hands returning to his penis, firmer now, less experimental as she grew in confidence, understanding through touch what moves made him grit his teeth and which caresses drove him right to the edge. She held him firmly close to his body, her other hand moving, squeezing along his length, then pumping powerfully until he was crying for her to stop the torment.

But she didn't. She continued her motions, faster and faster until he was poised on the knife-edge. Then, at the final moment, she rose up, held herself poised above him for a brief second before sinking down to impale herself on the stiff cock beneath her. No gentle taking this, but a frenzied coupling as she lifted then sank down in a powerful rhythm as her body gripped and released him. She heard her own panting breath as if from afar, felt his mouth open on her shoulder in an agony of anticipation, and then her body was tightening around him, muscles clenching in ecstasy forcing him to join her on her tumultuous ride of passion.

Chapter Five

Morgan arched her back and rolled her head wearily in large circles. The letters on her laptop screen were a blur and the day had barely begun. She had come into the office early in an attempt to get a head start. There were less than six weeks to the opening. Six weeks into which she would have to pack about four months work if the exhibition was to be the success she desperately hoped it would be. Once it had opened without any dramas she would be able to relax again, and maybe get a full night's sleep.

Sleep. Just the thought of it made her salivate. Until she had begun this project, she had had no idea of how essential sleep was to sanity, and how sleep-deprivation could affect the rational thinking of even the most sentient being. Most nights she managed little more than five hours, and even those were disturbed with dreams.

Sometimes the ghostly horned god appeared and the dreams were inevitably erotic, laced with excitement and fear. At other times, she saw nothing but just felt as though she were standing on the edge of an abyss, about to plunge off into space of her own volition. And then there was Hunter.

Hunter. Sometimes he was kissing her, at other times just smiling his sweet smile or holding her hand. Then he would turn cold and angry. He would turn and walk away while she called to him, disappearing into the mists where she couldn't find him.

She hadn't seen him or heard from him for two days since that night, when the overwhelming carnality he'd inspired in her had sent her running from his arms.

"For God's sake, Morgan, what were you thinking?" Gus's furious voice shattered Morgan's reverie. She turned, startled, to see him standing at the door to her office. Someone had evidently given the game away about her absence from the meeting with Hunter. She wondered if it was Hunter himself who had complained.

Gus obviously didn't expect an answer to his rhetorical question and Morgan didn't give him one. As far as he was concerned, there was no rational answer, thought Morgan as she watched him impassively. She felt like a five-year-old being blasted by the principal for playing hooky in the lunch break. And she probably deserved it.

"What the hell kind of message do you think you were sending to Riley? To send your assistant--a girl with less sense that God gave a sparrow--to take a critical meeting because you were too busy...! Well, all I can say is I'm very disappointed in you. It was the height of rudeness."

"Did he call you?"

"No, of course not. He hasn't said anything. He's far too courteous, which is more than I can say for you!"

"Is that everything?" Morgan couldn't remember the last time she had been hauled across the coals for a lack of professionalism. She just wanted him to get it out of his system and leave so that she could lick her wounds in private.

'No it is not! I've been at great pains to stress to you the importance of making Riley feel like he is the most important person in the world. Negotiations are still ongoing with his lawyers regarding a long-term home for the torque. Other institutions have also expressed their interest, and I want nothing, I repeat nothing, to jeopardize the claims of the museum. Do I make myself clear?"

Morgan nodded. "I apologize, Gus. I was out of line. There were some things I'd been neglecting that I needed to take care of and I felt it would be a good experience for Andrea to handle the meeting. Marshall was there too, of course."

"I know Marshall was there. Our curator was the one who enlightened me about the situation. He's no happier about it than I am."

Morgan hung her head. "It seemed like the sensible thing to do.

Andrea has been keen to take on more responsibility, and I was up to my ears...."

"Look, Morgan, I don't deny that you've been working hard on the exhibition, but you look exhausted. I hate to say it, but perhaps the pressure is affecting your judgment. If you're finding it all too much, perhaps we need to look at alternative options. It's no reflection on you."

Morgan averted her face to hide the red tide of anger that rose to her cheeks at his words. "Gus, I'm coping fine. It was just a misjudgment on my part. I'll sort it out with Mr. Riley, Gus. I'll apologize and make sure there are no negative repercussions."

"Do it." His tone made it clear he wouldn't tolerate any further undermining of his authority. "Another instance like this, Morgan, and I shall have no alternative but to put you on an official warning.

"It would be a great shame if that was to happen, Morgan. You have a lot to offer this museum but I cannot have you simply countermanding my instructions because you think you know better."

"I know, Gus." She sighed and met his eyes.

Gus tightened his lips and pulled at his goatee. "Just do your job, and keep me in touch. I want to know everything that happens. Every communication between you and Riley I want to know about. Is that clear?"

"Crystal." Morgan nodded, thanking her lucky stars his rule wasn't retrospective.

When Gus turned on heel and stalked back to his own office, Morgan almost ran to the bathroom where she covered her face with her hands. She glanced in the mirror and saw a woman whose eyes grew daily more shadowed and whose cheekbones were prominent in her once softly rounded face. She'd barely eaten in two days, had no appetite for anything except the sexual desires that taunted her since that night with Hunter Riley.

He had pushed her to the edge during the night, denying her every attempt to draw back from him. After steaming up his office, they had taken a taxi to a small, impersonal hotel in the city, registering under Hunter's name. In the lift up to the third floor they had averted their eyes from each other, each afraid to be the one to suggest pressing the emergency stop button and test out their fantasies about having sex in a confined space. They just about made it clothed into their room before falling into the huge bed, clutching each other.

There, he whispered to her about all the things he would like to do to her, and then he did them, one by one, raising her from one peak to another with his mouth and hands, driving her on until he finally took her, braced on his elbows over her, his face set in hard lines as he pushed further and further into her. Grinding himself into and against her, Hunter raised her up again and, when she was on the brink, he left her there while she begged for completion. But he refused to finish what he had started, holding her arms when she would have pulled him against her. When she had descended from the brink a little, he began the process all over again until she was panting, begging, cursing him.

On the third time, Morgan tried to push him away as he began arousing her all over again, and this time he tied her hands over her head, looping his belt around the bedpost. She tried to kick him but he took her slim legs in his hands, lifting and parting them until they were draped over his shoulders, her core at his eye level. She flushed and moaned with embarrassment, her feet drumming ineffectually on his back as she twisted to avoid his all-seeing gaze.

For long moments, he just looked at her, arousing her with his perusal, dissecting her most intimate parts with his eyes. By the time he put his mouth on her, Morgan felt about to explode, the touch of his tongue and lips all but driving her over the edge. When he knew she couldn't hold off her orgasm any longer, he lowered her legs to circle his waist and penetrated her the way she wanted, his huge cock breaching her swollen entrance, this time driving into her twice, three times as she cried her release against his lips.

Hunter stayed hard within her during her climax, not yet ready for his. When the tumultuous storm had passed, Morgan asked Hunter to release her hands but he refused, telling her he wasn't done with her yet. He held her legs apart and began thrusting again but she was too dry and swollen, crying out as he drove into her. For a moment, his weight disappeared from the bed. She felt him dressing in the dark and thought her refusal had driven him away. She called out to him, promising not to deny him again, but he brushed a kiss on he forehead and told her he would be back.

Morgan lay in the dark for long minutes, wondering if he would return or if this was some sexual game of his--for the maid to discover her tomorrow, tied naked to the bed, humiliated. She pulled half-heartedly against the belt but could feel little give in the leather, not enough to be able to slip her hands free. It seemed an age, but it was probably less than ten minutes, before she heard the click of the door and then he was there, embracing her, kissing her, reassuring her. She heard rustling in the dark and a soothing coolness between her thighs as he lubricated her inner tissues with his pharmacy store purchase. Then he was unfastening his jeans and probing her entrance again, easing into her and driving her up, and up again, until they peaked in unison, wrapped in each other's arms.

Opening her eyes, Morgan shook the memories of that night from her head. She splashed water on her face and redid her make-up before venturing into her office where Andrea observed her curiously but didn't say anything. Andrea had picked up on the tension emanating from Morgan and had trodden warily around her boss, avoiding personal comments or questions and sticking closely to work topics.

Morgan felt she owed her some sort of explanation and, without implicating Marshall, told Andrea that Gus had discovered their ruse. Andrea's mouth formed an O of dismay, and Morgan tried to reassure her that there was no blame associated with her.

"Gus is mad at me," she said, a wry smile twisting her lips. "It doesn't reflect badly on you and, when he calms down, I'm sure he'll realize what a great job you did."

* * * *

As soon as Morgan sat down at her desk, the phone rang. It was Mary, her voice brimming with excitement.

"Long time no hear, hon," Mary drawled as guilt welled up in Morgan. She should have phoned her friend after her sudden disappearance from the lecture at the weekend. Morgan had meant to but things had just gone from complicated to outrageously convoluted since Saturday afternoon and she hadn't had a chance.

"Mary, I'm sorry. It's the job," she lied. "It's just all-consuming at the moment."

"Liar! You just want to keep secrets from me about the sexy Hunter Riley."

Morgan gave an unwilling laugh. "You know me too well."

"So?" As always, Mary cut straight to the chase. "Tell me everything. I assume you've fucked him."

"Mary!"

"So you have done it. From the look on your face and his that day, I thought you would have by now. Wow, you two looked like you were about to go up in flames in the street outside the library." She giggled. "That would have given the lecture crowd something to get excited about after Dottie Dwyer's drab delivery."

"Mary, I…."

"So what was it like? From what I've seen of Hunter, he's very tactile--always the sign of a magnificent lover."

"How do you know that?" Morgan laughed.

"Experience, Morgan. Experience."

"Actually, it's a bit of a mess at the moment." Morgan lowered her voice realizing Andrea was watching interestedly. "I can't really talk, though."

"Oh, my. This sounds too juicy. When can we catch up?"

"You're supposed to be concerned about me," Morgan breathed, "not salivating."

"Call me shallow but gossip makes my world go round."

They arranged to meet after work later in the week and Morgan breathed a sigh of relief. She needed a friendly ear. As she put the phone down she noticed that the light on her phone was flashing indicating a voice mail message. A low ache in her gut told her it was Hunter. A sense of dread settled deep in her stomach. She didn't want to deal with it so she ignored the flashing light and hoped it wasn't an urgent work-related query. It seemed no-one was happy with her at the moment.

She looked at her diary. A full day of meetings with the museum's department heads beckoned, and she knew Allison, the museum's PR, also needed time with her. Picking up the phone, Morgan made an appointment with her to discuss a press release on the exhibition and spoke to the catalogue printer about the quality of paper stock. It had begun curling noticeably on the catalogues already delivered and everyone was on her case about it. Morgan was conscious of Andrea's eyes on her, and when she finished her call, she looked up at the blonde.

"They're looking into the problem and expect to have an answer by the end of the day," she said to Andrea. "Can you make a note to retrieve the unsatisfactory catalogues from the warehouse?"

"Sure. I'll get on to the warehouse guy straight away." She hesitated for a moment. "I'm really sorry Gus found out about the meeting. Hunter didn't seem to mind at all. He's such a sweetie."

Little do you know, thought Morgan, nodded at Andrea absentmindedly. A real sweetie. It was everyone's first impression of him--an endearingly absent-minded academic type with warm brown eyes and a gift for digging up old things. Who just happened to be the very devil in bed.

God, he was extraordinary. Morgan ached just thinking about what they had done together. Some of positions he had prompted her to try made her blush to the roots of her hair just thinking about them. When she had awoken in the middle of the night, for a moment she hadn't known where she was, the strange surroundings of the hotel room, the warm arms and steady breathing against her rumpled hair confounding her in the dark.

For a moment she had simply lain there amid the bunched and tangled sheets as the events of the previous evening replayed in her head. Lord! Could that uninhibited creature with Hunter in his office and then later here in the hotel bed really have been her?

It seemed impossible, a mistake. She was Morgan McClellan, the one her old workmates had once called the Ice Maiden after she'd turned down three prospective suitors in a row. Even her best friend had accused her of being dull. Well nearly. Could she really have spent the past abandoned night with Hunter Riley, a man she barely knew? Have let him come inside her endless times without giving a single thought to contraception? At least she was already on the pill to control her monthly cramps so she was safe from an unwanted pregnancy, but that didn't make her feel any better about her lack of control when it came to Hunter Riley.

She moved her head fractionally to check he was still asleep. He was. Thank God. Morgan didn't think she could face him when he woke. What did people say after having screwed like rabbits through the long, sweaty night?

Frozen with panic that rose in her like a chill tide, she lay stiffly in his arms, her eyes darting frantically towards the shadows in the room. How the hell was she going to get out of here without his waking? Morgan knew she simply couldn't face him. Not now. Not after the carnal impulses that had consumed her.

Hardly daring to breathe, she had slowly untangled her naked body from the arms and legs wrapped around her, freezing when he twice murmured in his sleep. Eventually, she had extracted herself, sitting rigidly on the bed as Hunter rolled heavily away from her. Only when he didn't wake did she dare begin breathing again. Edging to the end of the bed, she fished around with her foot, eventually locating enough of her strewn clothing to dress herself. Her bra seemed to have completely disappeared, and one boot she finally discovered lurking in a chair. Her bag was on the small coffee table and she picked it up as she let herself stealthily out of the room.

For a moment, she had leaned against the wall outside the door, breathing deeply, before she had made her way down the fire stairs, not game to go through the lobby under the scrutiny of the night concierge. In the dim light of the car park at the back of the hotel, and she looked down at herself, nearly groaning at the sight she made. Her coat buttons were unevenly fastened, her stockings bagged at her ankles and her hair hung uncombed about her face. She looked like she was a mugging victim, or a candidate for a serious style makeover. Or like a woman who had been well and truly loved.

The thought that Hunter, disturbed by her departure, might wake and come after her sent her scurrying from the hotel grounds and out into the street. Despite the soreness between her thighs, she ran like the very devil was on her heels, all the way to the intersection where she turned left. There were precious few taxis at this early hour of the morning, and those that did cruise by took one look at her disheveled appearance and drove right on by. Dispiritedly, she walked towards home, feeling alternately like a coward and an impostor. For a while she flagged every cab that passed but when it was clear that none was prepared to stop she gave up. It was nearly three am when she finally dragged her front door key from her bag and let herself in. As heartsore as she was footsore, she pulled her clothes off for the second time within hours and slumped exhaustedly into bed.

Morgan became aware that she was sitting unseeing at her desk as she relived the events of the night before last. That night, or early morning really, she had barely slept and last night she had managed only fitful sleep, arriving late for work and completely unprepared to face Gus's wrath. She felt as though her organized, controlled life was slowly unraveling, and wondered desperately how she could get it back on track.

For a moment, her shoulders drooped. Then she straightened at her desk. She knew exactly how to handle the situation. By steadfastly plowing through her work and refusing to entertain any disruptions, that's how she had always got through tough times in the past.

Determinedly ignoring the voice mail alert on her phone, Morgan gathered her work diary and her to-do list, and carefully plotted out the rest of the week, allocating time for all essential tasks and meetings. When she was done she felt a little more in control of her professional life at least. She was gathering the files she would need for the afternoon's meeting when Andrea headed towards the door, telling Morgan she was going out for a quick lunch and offering to bring a sandwich back for her, which Morgan refused. She thought she would be sick if she tried to eat anything right now.

When she had gone, Morgan checked the office door was tightly shut. Then she picked up the phone to retrieve the voice mail message. Her gut wasn't wrong. It was Hunter, sheer rage underlying his attempt at a calm and measured tone.

"Morgan, it's been two days. I hoped you would have phoned me by now." Morgan heard a faint voice in the background and Hunter's terse reply saying something she couldn't quite make out except that it didn't sound polite. "I wanted to be calm and understanding when you explained to me why you ran out in the middle of the night but I'm still fucking furious, Morgan. How could you--" OK, OK, she heard him bite out to someone else. Then the message cut out. His 20 seconds was up.

Moaning, Morgan held her head in her hands. He was all but spitting venom and quite within his rights to do so. She had run out on him without a word, leaving him lying in a hotel room that just hours before they had nearly ripped apart with their passion. But should she trust her heart, or her instincts? Morgan pressed the button to replay the message, shriveling inside at the harshness in his voice. She knew Hunter deserved an explanation, or at the very least an apology. But right at the moment, she suspected he wasn't in the mood to listen--even in the unlikely event she managed to come up with an explanation that was worth listening to.

Morgan ate the sandwich Andrea brought back for her even though she didn't feel hungry. It tasted like sawdust but she knew she needed to eat. She had lost more weight over the last week, and the drawn face she saw in the mirror did little for her confidence.

The afternoon passed in a blur of almost continuous meetings. Her print supplier had promised to reprint a batch of unsatisfactory catalogues which soothed many of her colleagues, and she concentrated acutely on the other matters that demanded her attention to ensure that neither Gus nor any of the other department heads could catch her unawares. Fortunately no-one raised the issue of a permanent home for the torque, which right now, given her relationship with Hunter, could be looking more than a little iffy.

By the time the last meeting ended it was nearly seven but she felt more in control. She returned to her office to see her voice mail light blinking steadily and her heart sank. Reluctantly, she listened to the recordings. One was from a photo agency confirming the fee for using an illustration of another piece in the exhibition. The second was from Hunter.

"Damn it, Morgan. Aren't you ever in your office? I need to talk to you and it's urgent. Just call me. OK?"

Oh God, she didn't want to call him but refusing to speak to him was just compounding her sins. Heart in her mouth and with no idea what she would say to him, Morgan picked up the phone and began to dial his office number. After four digits, her fingers froze and she hung up. She couldn't do it.

His anger wouldn't be pleasant, she knew, but that wasn't the real crux of the problem for Morgan. If she spoke to him she would have to face her actions of the night before and she just wasn't ready to face up to the dark side of her soul.

Morgan hoped that her home would be a comfort to her. Whenever she had problems in her life, she had always found an evening snuggled up on the sagging old couch with a glass of wine would soothe her worries. But tonight was different.

The house seemed empty when she arrived home. Usually she loved the space and peace that the rambling old terrace afforded her but tonight it felt too big for her. Lonely. It was a generously-proportioned old Victorian, designed to house a family. It needed parents chatting about their day while they prepared dinner for two or three rough-and-tumble kids who raced through the rooms at top speed, yelling and laughing.

Morgan shrugged out of her coat and made her way upstairs to change into warm sweats. When she came down, she lit a cheery fire and cooked a pasta dinner for one. She picked at her dinner and finally gave up. The silence seemed oppressive so she switched on the TV and flicked through the channels, but nothing caught her interest so she switched it off. She wandered aimlessly through the rooms in search of a place to settle, reminding herself of restoration projects she needed to begin or finish, and wished she had someone to discuss her plans, her passions with.

She wished Hunter were with her. She wanted him entwined with her on the shabby couch or up in the big king bed, and wondered what he was doing tonight. Whether he was thinking of her and cursing, or whether he'd already put her from his mind. She felt dread sitting heavily in her chest, made worse by the fact that she had no-one to blame but herself.

Chapter Six

The cotton sheets twisted around her body as she tossed from side to side, fragments of memories and dreams rushing through her mind in a frenetic whirl. It was as though she was spinning through time and space. First Hunter's earnest face appeared in her restless dream, and then his strong jaw softened and faded, the glasses, short brown hair and tweed jacket slowly disappearing. Only the eyes remained, turning from amber to a burning gold, the eyes of a wild animal.

Morgan whimpered in her sleep, her head thrashing from side to side as the shadow moved, darkened, solidified behind her eyes, morphing into another man shape, looming over her as she backed away in panic.

"No," she whispered and turned to run, twisting on bare feet, the legs of pajama pants slapping against her ankles. A rough, scarred hand shot out, taking her arm in a bruising grip. She came to a shuddering halt, crying out as his fingers tightened mercilessly. Slowly she turned to face him and shuddered in terror.

His molten eyes bored into hers, a lascivious smile twisting his lips as he forced her closer and closer. Long dark hair hung to his shoulders and sweat beaded his broad brow.

"Let me go," she screamed, trying to wrench her arm from his steely grip but inexorably she was dragged forward until she found her face almost buried in the rough smattering of hair that covered his naked chest. He smelled of fresh male sweat, and his chest heaved with exertion. A droplet of sweat clung to his throat. A rush of heat enveloped Morgan's body and she wanted to lean into him and scoop up the droplet with her tongue.

A palm cupped her chin and then his mouth swooped, taking

her mouth savagely, forcing it open to permit entrance for his marauding tongue. Morgan tried to pull her mouth from his but his hand pressed harder against her face, forcing her to accept him. His other hand left her arm to curl around her waist bringing her up tight so she could feel the tension in the broad muscles of his legs. He pulled her between his open-legged stance, pressing her softness against the rising hardness at his groin.

With a last surge of energy, Morgan flung her head from his, raking her fingernails down his cheek as she pushed away. Her calf muscles propelled away from him across the chilly, straw-hewn room for no more than half a dozen steps and then he was on her, roaring in fury, pushing her down to the ground at his feet. She looked back at him, a plea falling silently from her lips as she saw the tiny ivory horns protruding from his hair.

Morgan found her voice then, a hoarse scream of fear mingled with excitement tore from her throat as the creature tore apart her pajama pants. She heard him panting, his hands probing inside her, something huge and burning pushing demandingly between her buttocks.

"Noooo…"

She sat bolt upright in bed as her own very real cries of fear awoke her, the dream fleeing as consciousness chased sleep away. When her terror began to subside and frustration took over, she turned her face into her pillow and sobbed.

* * * *

Morgan stared at the phone for a long time, summoning up her courage, before dialing Hunter's office number. She had no idea what she was going to say to him if she did reach him. How did one apologize for running out on him in the middle of the night as though he was some demon rapist? Would he even believe her if she told him that she was running, not from him but from herself? Would he even be prepared to listen, let alone give her a second or was it third chance?

He'd made it clear he wasn't prepared to play games and who could blame him. Morgan mentally cursed the bitch who had strung him along and then tried to foist another man's child on him. It was hardly surprising he didn't want to waste time on someone who didn't know what she wanted.

Her teeth nibbled at her bottom lip as she tapped in his number. A second later she replaced the receiver quietly without saying a word. Neither Hunter nor Suzie was there and she couldn't leave a message on the machine. Too impersonal. Too open to misinterpretation.

Shaking her head, she tried to get a grip on the workday ahead. The countdown serious had begun with the exhibition just a few short weeks away. She scrolled down her emails, answering those that required immediate responses and putting others into various files. A new email flashed up from Gus, asking her to come to his office as soon as she was free. God, she hoped nothing else had gone wrong. She had enough on her plate as it was.

Morgan walked briskly down the corridor, wanting to hear whatever Gus had to say and then return to her desk so she could start making some headway in her work. It was still one area of her life that she still had control over. Sort of.

The door was ajar and from the voices inside, it was clear Gus had company. She went to knock, but then a baritone rumble brought her up short. Hunter.

Immediately her breathing seemed to quicken, her pulse picked up pace and a slow-burning heat ignited in the pit of her belly. What was he doing here? Gus usually kept her up to date with meetings and he'd said nothing about a visit from Hunter.

"….so I must apologize, Hunter, for Morgan's actions. She has been under a huge amount of pressure, as I'm sure you understand, but that is no excuse for what occurred a few days ago.

"Our curator Marshall Beasley filled me in on the fact that Morgan--against my express instructions, I might add--failed to attend a meeting with you. I'm sure you must have been most insulted, however generously you've tried to excuse her behavior."

"Please, Gus, there was no harm done." Hunter's voice was pitched so low, Morgan had to strain to hear it.

"No, really, Hunter, you must let me apologize. I would hate in any way for you to think that I or the museum have endorsed Ms McClellan's behavior. In fact, as soon as I heard about what had transpired at the meeting, I had very serious words with Morgan with regard to her absence at the meeting and I believe she understands just how badly she misjudged the situation. She assured me that she would put the situation to right immediately."

Morgan stood horrified, realizing how Gus's words might be misinterpreted and willing him to silence. It did not work.

"Hunter you have been more generous in allowing the museum to undertake the first public showing of Cernunnos's torque. As you know, the museum has made no secret of the fact we would love to have the piece as a permanent addition. Morgan knows how crucial this is and I have made it clear to her your satisfaction is our greatest concern. She assured me she would do whatever it took to reassure you of our, I mean her, commitment. She will be here shortly if you have any questions or concerns."

"Thank you but no. I think everything is quite clear." Hunter's words were coated in ice. Not that Gus seemed to notice.

Transfixed with a sense of impending doom at Gus's unfortunate choice of words, Morgan didn't realize that Hunter was about to leave until he came around the door. He stopped short when he saw her frozen there, a look of horror on her face. Morgan didn't have to ask him how he'd interpreted Gus's words. It was plain to see.

His mouth twisted and he brushed past her, striding down the corridor towards the exit. For a moment, Morgan remained rooted to the spot, and then she tore after him, her heels clattering on the stone tiles.

"Hunter." If she didn't stop him now, she feared she might never see him again.

"Forget it, Morgan."

"Just listen. What you heard just now--"

"Was the first reasonable explanation to your behavior I've had in days." He looked down at her contemptuously and continued walking towards the door.

"I didn't--"

"What? Didn't fuck me like you couldn't get enough of me? Or didn't fuck me to get what Gus told you to get?"

"No, it had nothing to do with the torque." Her voice wobbled precariously. "I would never use--"

"I wonder if Gus knows what a little treasure he has. Someone who'll open her legs to tip the negotiations in his favor, no questions asked," he spat. "I have to admit I admire you. You know you've got quite a bargaining chip there."

"Hunter, please don't. I made love to you –"

"Love? Don't ever use that word to me," he spat. "It was sex. Nothing more."

"How could anything that passionate not be making love?" she whispered, reaching out to touch his arm. He shrugged it off, intent only on hurting her as he'd been hurt.

"You don't need to worry." Light brown eyes bored coldly into her gray ones, and his mouth twisted as though at an unpleasant memory. "I know how distasteful it must have been for you. Did you grit your teeth the whole time? Must have been sheer hell for you, worse than that, to make you run like that. Under cover of darkness."

One of the store room staff wandered by at that instant and looked curiously at them but didn't say anything. Morgan realized they could be overheard by anyone walking by and pulled Hunter into an empty specimen room. He leaned casually against an unused display cabinet, folding his arms. His expression said that he cared for nothing she had to say.

Morgan bit her lip, searching for the right words before she spoke. "I was scared, Hunter. I should have woken you and told you, but I was scared and I ran."

"Scared of what? What have I ever done to make you fearful of me?" He raised his eyebrows in disbelief.

"It wasn't you I was scared of. It's what we become together. It was so...erotic. I become someone I don't recognize. Completely taken over by sex." She shuddered for a moment, recalling the feel of him inside her. "I don't know how far I'd go if you asked me and it frightens me."

Hunter looked at her sardonically, hands resting casually in his pockets, but his features were stiff with anger. "Well I'm not exactly into whips and chains, honey. But in any case you don't need to worry. You're off the hook. I've already decided the museum should house the torque permanently so there's no need to sacrifice your body for the cause any further.

"Of course, should Gus decide there's something else I have that the museum wants, I might be open to offers. I can't deny you're the hottest piece I've ever had." His eyes slid over her body suggestively, insultingly.

Morgan felt humiliated beyond despair. She knew he was hitting out at her because he hurt, but it didn't excuse anything. Tears brightened her eyes, and her mouth trembled violently.

"Do you really believe I'd use you that way?" Her voice broke and she couldn't go on.

Hunter shrugged. "What else am I supposed to think? Every time I come on to you, you respond then back off. Teasing, flirting, keeping me hanging on. Then your boss tells you to keep me happy and suddenly we're in bed fucking like there's no tomorrow."

"He didn't--not until after we had been together and in any case...." Morgan's voice trailed off. It was like talking to a brick wall and, anyway, she did not sound believable--even to herself.

Hunter's face was shuttered. "What does it matter? Even when you did finally come to me, you ended up running." A smile twisted his lips but didn't reach his eyes. "That's what I don't get. The bed virtually went up in flames from the heat we generated. I could have sworn you were with me all the way, and yet when I wake up, you're gone. Without a word."

Morgan hung her head. "I wasn't running from you."

"So you keep saying. Well, honey, there were only two of us there," he said, pushing away from the cabinet and striding towards the door.

"Hunter--"

He turned, his hand on the door handle. "I want a woman who knows her own mind. I want a woman who isn't afraid to reach out and take what she wants."

The door swung closed behind him and Morgan stood there in the silent dusty room. The brown walls were faded where old furniture had once sat. Dusty Venetian blinds let streaks of late afternoon sunlight into the room. It seemed incongruous somehow that the first sunny day the city had seen for weeks was also the worst day in Morgan's life.

And as she stood there, her work, her love, her life unraveling around her, the tears began to fall and wouldn't stop.

* * * *

The phone was a welcome distraction, Hunter thought as Suzie signaled him from her office. Anything to take his mind off the infuriating Morgan McClellan.

Nearly twenty-four hours had passed since the scene in the museum and still he felt the angry surge of frustration, as much with himself as with her. He'd gone off half-cocked and all but accused her of prostituting herself for her employer. He hadn't meant it, of course. He hadn't really thought she was guilty of ingratiating herself, even when Gus Waugh had inferred it was part of her brief.

But he'd been royally pissed off with her for coming to him and then disappearing, and when he'd seen her standing there outside Gus's office, he hadn't been able to hold back from verbalizing the rush of bitter disappointment. He'd been confident that once they made love, all her fears would simply disappear, but instead of being reassured she had run. Hunter cursed to himself. He was too old to play the flirting game. He wanted to know where he stood with her, and her indecision drove him crazy.

Ah, but he should have listened, Hunter thought. She'd looked so distressed, as though she was barely hanging on to her composure. He knew he was a sucker but when she looked at him with that luscious, trembling mouth, he wanted to take her in his arms and reassure her everything would be all right. But if he did, he would still be the one making all the moves and what he wanted--more than anything--was for Morgan to come to him freely.

Nothing like being caught between a rock and a hard place, he mused without much humor. Adding insult to injury was he was in the office on the brightest weekend morning since the leaves had begun to take on their autumnal hues.

Abruptly he became aware that Suzie had put the call through and a tinny voice was talking frantically at the other end of the line.

"What?" Hunter frowned as he tried to make out what was being said. The line was scratchy and the time delay pissed him off. "Francois? Is that you?"

"Oui, Hunter." As the French accented voice of his French colleague continued, Hunter suddenly understood what he was trying to say and felt suddenly sick. He asked a few questions to make sure he had heard right. He had and it was bad. Very bad.

* * * *

In the unbroken stillness of night he came to her. The last embers of the fire in the grate threw up ghostly, flickering shadows on the walls of the chamber. The shadows lengthened and deepened, and from them stepped a figure. Man or beast, Morgan couldn't tell at first.

Her eyes riveted on him, he approached the huge bed where she lay amid the warm furs. He was naked but for the heavy silver torque of a high-born warrior.

"Cernunnos," she breathed, her eyes rising up along his tall form. His hair hung long, partly obscuring his features, but she had the impression of hard chiseled features, jutting cheekbones and sensual lips. He came closer and his hair parted, exposing tiny ivory horns. Morgan's eyes met his, burning like molten metal through the darkness of the room.

He snarled then, softly, the beast in him coming to the fore as he approached the bed. Morgan gasped as he rose over her and scrambled back against the wall. A flitting movement in the far corner of the room caught her attention. For a moment, she thought there was someone else with them, hidden in the shadow of the huge fireplace. But with the naked creature bearing down on her, she had no time to consider anything but the threat of the man-beast.

Trapped against the wall, she could go no further and she huddled there, naked under the furs, like small, soft prey awaiting the cruel grasp of talons and teeth. But his hand when it touched her was human as it pulled her back down the bed, the fur sliding away to reveal her palely naked form. He ran his hands roughly over her breasts and thighs for his own pleasure. Morgan didn't get the impression that it was to arouse her. When he moved to part her legs, she cried out and dived away, across the bed and towards the door.

Roaring with lust, he sprang after her, eating up the distance to her in a flash. His hands wrapped around her waist and she was picked up and flung her face down across the bed as though she were a rag doll. Her breath coming raggedly through her teeth, she braced herself against the furs as the man-beast grabbed her hips, pulling her legs up and apart.

His desire for her sent the blood thundering in Morgan's ears and a reciprocal passion permeated her body, making her nipples throb and sexual liquid drench her core. The creature stopped and sniffed the air. Morgan looked over her shoulder in terror. He could smell her, could tell that she was ripe for rutting. He smiled then, an utterly carnal movement of his lips, and she knew there was no escape even if she had wanted.

Still she screamed as he reached between her thighs, probing roughly inside her with his long, hard fingers, feeling the wetness that flooded her. And then he was withdrawing his fingers, dragging them up towards the crease in her buttocks. He circled the tightly-puckered hole hidden between the pale globes of her bottom, his fingers dipping in and out, around and around.

Morgan froze as she recognized what he was about. Oh God! He was preparing to mount her there, where she had never before felt a man's possession. A frisson of anticipation hummed through her body and then she felt a powerful force, there, at that tiny entrance. Pushing, forcing. And as her scream of terror and desire rent the air, her world shifted and grew misty. The shadows faded and disappeared, the fire in the grate shriveled and died, and there was silence. She was alone.

* * * *

A whimper escaped Morgan's throat as she hurtled up from the depth of dreamland and then her eyes were open, darting frantically around her bedroom. From the door, to the armoire, the beautifully carved chest and to the window where the old rocking chair sat.

She forced herself to take long deep breaths but it was minutes before she was calm enough to realize she was alone in her own snug bedroom, in her house. She shivered though she was warm in her flannel pajamas. Almost too warm. Perspiration clung to every pore on her skin, her hair in damp rats-tails about her face. She moved her legs cautiously and felt her own stickiness dampen the crotch of her pajama pants.

With one arm, she reached out and turned on the lamp. The bulb sent tendrils of gentle light across the room, illuminating all but the darkest corners. Her clock-radio read six. Dawn should be brightening the eastern sky, but the gloom of approaching winter blocked out the early rays.

It was said that the Celts believed Cernunnos was the god of autumn, appearing as the year moved inexorably towards its close. The dying time, Morgan had heard it called. Then, he would make his annual descent into the underworld. Was that it? Was this his dying time? And what was his purpose with her? Did he plan to take her with him?

Morgan felt consumed by his flame as it licked outward from her dreamland into her real world. His ferociously carnal instincts set her alight, transporting her from her restrained solitary existence to a world where impetuosity and passion burned long and hard. As soon as Hunter had entered her orbit, he had been sucked in to her flame, precipitating her unconscious sexual awakening.

She felt alive, as though the flame of the great man-beast, the leader of the night hunt, burned passionately within her, driving her to explore her deepest, darkest desires. As she made her way slowly downstairs, she paused on the stair that creaked, thinking of the dream that had passed.

Despite her terror at falling once again into the clutches of the man-beast, she had thrilled in his desire for her. He had made her blood run hot, even as it chilled her veins. She wanted him to do his will with her, to penetrate her every orifice, to spill his seed where he would. She thought of him pressing there in that forbidden place and knew she had wanted it and would want it again. Reality had intruded before he could consummate his depraved desire but he would return. Morgan could see that clearly now. He would return and she would follow him into his underworld of sexual abandonment.

Morgan drank heavily from a bottle of chilled water in her fridge, and then pulled on her running clothes, wincing as her clothes touched the bruises on her hips and buttocks. She ran, quickly finding her rhythm, her mind blank of anything but the steady thud-thud of her feet on the track. The early morning gloom had lifted, and across the harbor, apartments and offices were coming to life, as the inhabitants of the city rose to make breakfast and the early worker bees sat behind their desks. The street lights were still on and cars rumbled through the streets. Morgan was oblivious, though. She lost all sense of time as she ran, and was surprised when she found herself opening the door to her house.

Hungry, she cracked two eggs into a bowl and made an omelet, and then scooped coffee into the pot. She felt strangely calm as she ate. Admitting to her dark sexual desires in her life had lightened the oppressive burden she had been carrying for the past few weeks. She felt free to explore and reveal herself without fear.

Morgan showered and then dressed carefully in a sleek black dress, with a wide neckline that emphasized her delicate shoulder bones. Pale stockings and black high heels complemented the look. She pulled her black cashmere coat around her and caught the bus to the museum. As she got into the lift, she heard heavy breathing behind her and turned to see Andrea running towards her. Morgan held the doors open for her, and smiled.

"Made it." Andrea caught her breath and gasped the words out.

"You beat the clock." It had become a departmental joke that Andrea was always late, although usually only by a few minutes.

"It's my New Year's resolution."

Morgan frowned. "It's not New Year's."

"I'm getting some early practice in."

The phone was ringing when they entered their office.

"No rest for the wicked," said Andrea.

"Morgan, we have a disaster on our hands, I'm afraid." It was Gus, and he sounded as worried as she had ever heard him. "I need to talk to you. It's about Riley's torque."

Chapter Seven

Heart in her mouth, Morgan rushed down the corridor to her boss's office. Gus was all anxiety, wringing his hands together as he told her that the latest dating tests done on the torque suggested it was much more recent than originally thought.

"But, I thought…?" Morgan knew that the original results had shown it to date from the fifth century BC, at a time when the Celts were only starting to become established in Europe.

"Yes, I know, but it seems there may have been a stuff-up somewhere, possibly at the French end but maybe here. They're now saying that contamination may have affected the original results and that the torque's more likely to derive from the period around the birth of Christ." He sighed heavily. "They've apparently just had the other artifacts back from the lab and they're definitely Roman, which would suggest first century BC."

Morgan looked at him in shock as he paced up and down his office. This news undermined the whole thrust of the exhibition, which had Cernunnos at center stage on the basis of the torque and other recent finds.

Until very recently, the horned god was thought to be a just one of hundreds of divinities worshipped by the Celts. Their rich and complex culture had been filed with the adventures of legendary humans and deities. Even King Arthur had never been proven to exist, despite the longevity of his legend and a link to England's very real Tintagel and Glastonbury. Historians continued to debate the matter, some claiming it possible that there had been a supreme ruler by the name of Arthur to give substance to the legend, while others simply pointed to the lack of evidence.

Cernunnos, by comparison, was far more obscure. While Arthur's legend first arose around 500 AD, Cernunnos was centuries older. More than sixty depictions had been found of the god but just one identified him and, until recently, all the icons that had emerged--including the one from the famous Gundestrup Cauldron--were from around the first and second centuries BC, relatively late in Celtic development. Indeed, so mysterious had Cernunnos been that until last year just one of the artifacts had clearly identified the horned god by name.

But then two discoveries had shed new light on the mystery. At a dig in northern France, the ornate tomb of an early fifth century BC warrior had been discovered. It had been disturbed at some stage, the bones and military accouterments dispersed and fragmented but for a near-intact shield bearing the visage of a warrior wearing a heavy necklet. Except for the absence of antlered horns, its resemblance to later representations of the horned god was uncanny. Shortly afterwards, a cave in Italy had yielded a series of ancient cave paintings bearing the same figure, on horseback, brandishing a sword as an army fell in behind him. They were dated from around the same time as the shield and seemed to be telling a story about a legendary warrior, with none of the mystical elements that had surrounded later Cernunnos finds.

Though the evidence was still not conclusive, historians had begun to embrace the possibility of that the ghostly leader of the wild hunt was based on a flesh and blood man. And then Hunter's discovery of the torque had set the archaeological world alight. No other necklet had been discovered to compare with it. It was clearly the mark of a great and noble warrior but was it the torque of Cernunnos?

As fiercely as the debate raged, most historians knew the question might never be answered. The problem was that the Celts had never made a written record of their history and mythology. Though the Druids, the Celtic priests, were learned and knew Greek and Latin, they were forbidden to record their knowledge. The only records were in the tales passed down through the ages, and in the artifacts that survived the passage of time.

Morgan suddenly became aware that Gus had stopped pacing and was talking to her. "I'm sorry." She looked at him quizzically. "What did you say?"

"Riley." Gus glanced briefly at his watch. "He left for France on the weekend to try and sort things out. He's taken the torque for a final, and hopefully conclusive, test. I'm just concerned about the timing." He pulled off his round glasses and rubbed his eyes. "I think we should delay the opening of the exhibition."

"God, Gus, we can't delay." Morgan was horrified. The museum would never recover from such an embarrassment. "It's too late--we have only five weeks until it opens. We've been advertising it, promoting it everywhere. We have guest lecturers booked. The catalogues and postcards are printed." She pushed a strand of dark hair from her eyes. 'What does the board think?"

"We're talking at noon." He looked frazzled at the thought. "I don't know what to tell them. I've discussed it with Marshall and the others. And with Allison...from a PR point of view it's a disaster, of course. No-one can agree on the best course of action. The board will expect a point of view from me and I simply don't know what we should do for the best."

He pulled at his little beard and looked so desperate that Morgan almost felt sorry for him, despite the difficult time he'd given her. Canceling or postponing were no solutions at all in her opinion. In fact, she thought Gus was over-reacting. Even if the torque turned out to be more recent than originally thought, they would simply change the focus. It would be difficult to do in the time available, and the replacement captions would have to be makeshift but they would be able to do something.

One thing she definitely didn't want to do was pre-empt the results of Hunter's trip. Just because the other items found at the site were more recent, didn't mean that some Roman hadn't hoarded away his or her ancient treasure with contemporary items for safe-keeping, much in the way a modern day collector would, just as Hunter had speculated. Her problem was that Gus was already panicking and his anxiety might influence the board to jump the gun. She had to convince Gus to calm down and plastered a reassuring smile on her face.

Gus looked at her accusingly, pulling at his beard. "I should never have let you talk the board into approving your slant on the torque. It was all highly speculative. No real evidence that Cernunnos was anything but one of many Celtic gods."

Morgan's mouth twisted. Her boss's reaction didn't surprise her. He was the type to look for someone to blame rather than a solution. Resolutely she squared her shoulders and looked him straight in the eye.

"Look, I think we need to say calm. Let's wait to hear from Hunter. I'm sure he's as anxious as we are to have this resolved. We may get prelim results from the tests within a few days, and we can make a decision based on that." Morgan hesitated and lifted a hand to fiddle with her pearl earring. "Um, did Hunter leave you a number?"

"No. Just an email, sent from the plane I believe. Even his assistant's gone with him so we'll have to wait for them to respond to us."

"Uh Gus, I'll try and reach him in France." If she did get an email through to him, his reply might clue her in as to whether he had calmed down. "Ask him to get to get back to us with any news. And if you can convince the board not to make any hasty decisions that would probably be for the best. If we do have to rework some aspects of the exhibition, we'll just have to work day and night to get it done. I'll get the back-up captions ready just in case although I think there's a good chance we won't need to use them."

She smiled reassuringly at her little ferret of a boss who nodded uncertainly. "Very well. I'll take your advice. We had just better hope it's the right thing to do."

In her office, Morgan's heart fluttered as she typed a message to Hunter. She debated for some time on what to say and how to say it, writing and rewriting until she was happy with it. Knowing that there was always a chance Gus would ask to see it, she excluded anything personal.

Dear Hunter,

Gus has explained the problem to me. Everyone here is very concerned, as I'm sure you'll understand.

Please touch base as soon as you have any information about the dating of the torque as it will have implications for the exhibition, as you know. We hope not but we do need to know.

Morgan

Her hand hovered for agonizing minutes before she pressed the button to send, and then it was gone, winging its way into the ether. She hoped desperately that it reached him, and even more desperately that he didn't misconstrue the business tone of the email. Morgan ached to see him, to tell him about the decisions she had come to about her life and that she wanted to talk to him about his wants and desires. She recognized she knew little about his work, how much time he spent in the country, even what he liked to do in his private hours.

The day crept by, agonizing in its slowness. A thousand times Morgan checked her inbox for a reply. There was none. She knew that there was a time difference of several hours but, by the end of the day, she was feeling anxious and defeated in turns. Now she had resolved so much about her own life, she was eager to turn her decisions into action. Her energy and desire to do something, anything, curdled into a hard nervous ball inside her, churning her guts so that she jumped every time her phone rang or someone spoke to her.

In the end she packed up early, worked out at the gym for an hour to try and relieve some of the stress she felt, and then headed out for drinks with Mary. Despite her workout, she felt drained and wan, and would rather have gone straight home to a hot bath and bed but she owed Mary an explanation for her odd behavior.

As it turned out, she didn't need to say anything. She walked into Bernie's Bar to find Mary sitting at a window seat. She immediately spotted the new addition to her left hand, and her mouth opened in shock. A diamond that sparkly would have been damned hard to miss.

"When?" she got out at last.

Mary beamed as though she'd swallowed the sun whole. "Tuesday."

Morgan thought back. "But we spoke on...you didn't say a thing!"

"Sorry, I wanted to but it didn't seem like the kind of announcement you make over the phone. Anyway, he hadn't bought the ring at that stage. Just as well he waited for me to choose it." It was a known fact that Mary didn't have a high opinion of Drew's taste when it came to, well anything really.

"So when's the wedding?"

"Probably 2027," sighed Mary, "seeing as it took him two years to propose, I'm thinking it'll be decades before he decides he's ready to marry."

"He might surprise you," Morgan laughed. Mary's company always cheered her up.

"Yeah, well, any time before the end of the decade would be a pleasant surprise." She looked enquiringly at Morgan. "So, I take it your world isn't one of pleasant surprises. What's up, kid?"

"Oh, nothing. Work problems but I can't really talk about it because things are still being resolved."

Mary gave her a long, probing look. "Girl, work problems don't give you that look like your heart's about to bleed all over the table. Now tell me the truth about hunky Hunter and you. What happened after the scene at the lecture when he caught you fleeing the scene?"

Morgan smiled wryly at her friend. She had missed her sense of the ridiculous. Not to mention her caring. "Oh, Mary, I don't want to talk about unhappy stuff when it's such a fabulous time for you."

Mary flapped an arm to wave away an approaching waiter. "Don't be silly, hon. I'm nearly a boring old married woman. I have to practice living vicariously through my still-single friends."

Morgan fiddled with the cocktail menu. "It's complicated." She smiled weakly. "Aren't all man-woman things?"

"Go on." Mary prompted, leaning forward.

"I stuffed up big-time, if you want to know the truth. And right now, I haven't the faintest idea what to do."

"Hmm, sounds like you got a few questions rattling around in your brain. When did you last see him?"

"Uh, a few days ago."

"And what happened then?"

"He was pretty mad. Furious, actually."

"Well I know you can drive people crazy," Mary said. "What did you do?"

"We...ah...well we...I kind of left him in the lurch after we'd...you know. Then he got the wrong idea from something Gus said. He thinks I slept with him just to win a favorable outcome on a matter the museum's negotiating with." Morgan looked ruefully at her friend. "He practically accused me of being a whore."

Mary's face registered astonishment, and then she burst out laughing.

"Sex for sale at the Southern History Museum!" she chuckled. "If it wasn't so ridiculous it would be damned funny." She paused briefly. "Actually it is damned funny. Does Hunter understand who he's accusing. I mean you are still known as the Ice Queen by the guys in the packing room out at Great Western."

"Still?" Mortified, Morgan sank her head into her hands. Was she the only discriminating woman in the city?

"Don't worry," said Mary cheerfully. "It's just their juvenile way of dealing with the fact that none of them got in your pants."

Morgan grimaced. "Funny, I was at the Museum to work. Not indulge in sexual liaisons."

Mary shook her head. "Well, anyway, that's in the past. I'm interested in how you're going to kiss and make up with Hunter Riley."

Morgan shook her head. "I don't know, Mary. He's had to fly out to France at short notice and maybe it's for the best he's overseas at the moment. At least it gives us some space so he can calm down and I can work out how I'm ever going to make it up to him."

"Well, an apology would probably be an appropriate place to begin," Mary replied wryly. "Apart from anything else, it's pretty bad behavior to run out on someone just after you've...you know. Unless they're truly bad in the sack, of course. He wasn't was he?"

Morgan shook her head. "He was...it was...." The rosy blush on her face was detail enough.

"What's your problem, then?" Mary looked mystified. "Let me tell you, girl. If you find a stud that truly lights your fire, you want to hang on to him. There aren't many good ones around."

"I know, it's just...."

"Just what?"

"Just overwhelming. I've no reference points for feeling the way I do."

Mary's freckled face looked sympathetic. "Hang on in there, hon. You'll have your day in court, and if he doesn't want to listen, just pin him down and show him!"

Now that sounded like one way to convince Hunter she was serious, thought Morgan, as she waited for the bus home. If he would only give her the chance.

* * * *

Morgan had thumbed it so often that the comprehensive guidebook to world legends opened automatically to the section on Cernunnos. The illustration was of the exquisite Gundestrup Cauldron--the inner surface of which contained the most famous of all depictions of the horned god. A warrior torque was fastened about his neck, another clasped in his right hand. In the other dangled a long serpent.

Morgan shivered and closed the book. Was the serpent symbolic of the temptation, the overwhelming urge to abandon every caution and take a bite of the forbidden apple?

Either way, she had taken more than one bite. Had chewed, swallowed, digested and found the forbidden fruit much to her palate. She wanted to indulge again and soon. Every time she thought of Hunter, her breasts felt heavy and her core began to throb in expectation. At night, she was able to bring herself release but it did little to assuage her more fundamental need for his hard cock thrusting inside her, spurting his seed against her womb.

Six days and still no word from Hunter. Gus got more anxious by the hour, more panicked by the day. He had taken to roaming the corridors and at regular intervals would appear in her office asking worriedly if there was any news. Morgan knew the board was on his tail, wanting to know the implications for the exhibition and how things would be resolved. Edwina, the museum's director had begun giving local media interviews about the launch and, while she had been briefed to discuss the exhibition in a general sense, it had been impossible to avoid some of the more detailed questioning without seeming evasive. Now the media was on the scent of a story, and Gus was falling apart.

Well, there was no point sitting at her desk worrying into the night, especially on a Friday. She had new captions for the displays mocked up and ready to go if the news wasn't good and the torque turned out to be from the wrong era; there was little more she could do tonight. She just wished Hunter would call.

On her way out of the museum, Morgan swung by Gus's office but he had already left. She left the latest progress report for her department on his desk and walked out the door. Just as she turned to head down the corridor, the phone rang. She picked it up without thinking.

The line was faint, the static loud but she could just make out Suzie's voice at the end of the line asking for Gus.

"Suzie, it's Morgan. Gus has left for the day. What's the news?" Morgan felt adrenaline rush through her body. A combination of dread that she was phoning with bad news and anticipation that the developments were positive.

Suzie sounded jubilant. "It's good...testing not complete but...soil...looking good"

"Suzie, the line's not good--"

"...field phone, poor...Hunter.... "

"The line is really bad, Suzie, can you just tell me, yes or no, if you are confident for us to proceed with the use of the torque in the exhibition along the agreed lines?"

"Yes, ok to proceed"

Morgan took a deep breath. "Suzie, is Hunter there? Can I speak with him?"

"Sorry...already in the air...tomorrow afternoon.…"

"What time is he due in, Suzie? Suzie?" Morgan repeated the question but the connection broke and then died altogether.

Morgan replaced the receiver, the blood thundering in her ears. Tomorrow. Hunter would be back home tomorrow….

She got a grip on herself. She needed to ring Gus to tell him the news but she couldn't find his cell or home numbers anywhere. Well, perhaps the director would have it. Morgan had only had cause to speak to Edwina twice before, but she felt certain that the director would want to share in the good news. She climbed upstairs to the executive suite but the director's office was closed. Looked like Morgan was about the last person in the museum.

Morgan stopped at the desk of Edwina's PA when she noticed the correspondence book. Jubilant, she flicked to W and there was Gus's name, address and home phone. She rang him there and then but no-one was home so she left a message with the good news.

Unconsciously her fingers flicked to R in the address book. There too was Hunter Riley's name and his home address. She felt guilt settle low in her stomach. Morgan knew she shouldn't be doing this but in one glance she had memorized the address. She knew the area he lived in, and old suburb of big lots and rundown mansions. But what should she do with the information? That was the question.

* * * *

Hunter's ears popped as the 747 continued its laborious descent towards its destination. It hadn't been a good flight. Delays out of Paris had made everyone grouchy; the leg room seemed to shrink as the flight progressed and overweight business executive next to him was snoring her head off--right in his direction. He let his head slump against the headrest and, almost unconsciously, he thumbed the creases between his eyes. It was the appropriate end to a tough week. Hellish.

The stress of waiting for the results of the tests had been bad enough--if the torque had been proved conclusively not to originate from the 5th century BC, it would have taken much of the gloss off the find--but, simply, he didn't want to be in France.

But the tests were almost certain to confirm the original finding and thus the mystery would remain. Whether it belonged to a warrior who later became deified as Cernunnos, or to some other great fighter, would probably never be known. Maybe it was better that way. At least the exhibition could continue without changes and Morgan wouldn't have to suffer the wrath of Gus that she'd no doubt been subjected to over the past few days.

Morgan.

During the last week, the stress and long days hadn't allowed

Hunter much time to consider the disaster that his personal life had become but in a few hours he would be back home and he would have to decide what to do about his relationship with Morgan. If he still had one.

In the brief moments he had had to himself, he had thought a million times of phoning her from France but to say what? That he wanted her and needed her? That he was sorry for pushing her too far too fast? That he regretted accusing her of using him? All of that and more?

He had been ready to phone and spill his guts before that cold little email had arrived. He didn't know what it meant, if anything, but as much as he read and reread it, he could squeeze no ounce of passion or feeling from it.

He had deleted it without responding but when he closed his eyes he could still see the brief, businesslike words burned into his brain. If Morgan was ready to come to him then she hadn't given anything away in her email. More likely she had come to the conclusion their relationship was going nowhere and had already moved on.

Hunter rubbed his face wearily. Depression sat like a dead weight around his neck while a sense of impending doom pressed around him like a shroud. Maybe things would seem different after a good night's sleep. Right at the moment, though, and not withstanding the loss of his parents and his broken engagement, he felt as disheartened as he had ever felt in his life.

* * * *

Just as Morgan was slipping the key into the door lock, a quavering voice called out to her from the other side of the wrought iron railings that separated Morgan's house from her neighbor. She peered around the side of the porch to see the old lady standing there, dressed in a warm-up suit.

Despite her tiredness, she smiled at the old woman. "Hi Mrs. Wick. How have you been?"

"Can't complain dear, but I was wondering if you would come in for a moment."

"Is something wrong, Mrs. Wick?" Morgan slipped her house key back into her pocket and hitched the strap of her laptop case back onto her shoulder as she walked around to take a closer look at her neighbor.

"Oh no, dear. I just found an old photograph of your grandmother that I thought you might like. I won't be around too much longer, you know."

Morgan stepped into the musty house, reaching down to pet the old cat that twisted itself sleekly around her ankles. Mrs. Wick had a soft spot for neighborhood strays. She hoped it didn't have fleas.

Mrs. Wick rummaged around in the deep drawer of a heavy Victorian dresser, finally pulling out a sleeve of photographs. She sifted through them with hands that trembled slightly until she found what she was after. She moved awkwardly across the room to sit beside Morgan on the lumpy couch.

A gnarled finger, twisted with arthritis, stabbed at a tattered sepia photograph of three pretty young women in their late teens or early twenties, arms around each other and smiling.

"Your gran, Maeve, with me and my sister Bessie." Her filmy eyes grew dreamy with nostalgia. "Lookers we were in those days. You wouldn't believe how the boys swarmed all over us."

"Maeve was the choosy one. Bessie and I were long married when she settled on her boy, John. A lovely fellow, quiet. But still waters run deep, as they say. He was your grandmother's soul-mate."

"I haven't seen this photo before," murmured Morgan. "I have others of gran at that age but not this one of the three of you."

"I have another one, so I want you to have this," said Mrs. Wick. Her veiny hand pressed the photo into Morgan's smooth one.

"Thank you." Morgan's voice was soft as she looked at the photo. "I miss her."

While she loved her parents and step-brother, she had always been closer to her grandmother. A forceful and independent woman, Maeve, had been the one she'd always turned to at times of youthful crisis. Maeve had always counseled her to trust her instincts.

Mrs. Wick reached out to pat her hand comfortingly. Wrinkled flesh met smooth for a brief second before the old woman's eyes flared and she gasped, withdrawing her hand as though stung.

"What is it?" said Morgan, hurriedly. "Is it your heart? I'll call a doctor."

The older woman grimaced as she shook her head. "My heart's as strong as a bull's, dear. It's you."

"Me?" Morgan was mystified. "What did I do?"

Mrs. Wick chuckled nervously. "I got quite a charge when I touched you. You're putting out a very powerful force at the moment."

"A force?" Morgan hoped the woman wasn't about to begin spouting more of her mumbo-jumbo.

"Your emotions must be in turmoil at the moment. Such a charge you gave me." The old woman's blue eyes stared into hers. "Did that nice-looking man ever come into your life?"

Morgan frowned as she thought back, her confusion clearing when she remembered Mrs. Wick's vision the last time she'd seen her. She smiled sadly. "Yes but things haven't run smoothly."

"Don't worry, child. Things weren't always smooth between Maeve and John, either. Both too strong-willed. You need to give a little."

"It may be too late."

"Never too late, dear. You just tell your young man what's in your heart. He'll listen." She hesitated. "Morgan...."

"What is it, Mrs. Wick?"

"Morgan...the last time, I read something in your hands. Something that frightened me a little..."

"Mrs. Wick, I don't mean to insult your gift but--"

"Listen, dear, I saw something, something in you. And I have to admit it scared me." She looked intently into Morgan's confused grey eyes. "You need to face it."

"I've been...troubled, Mrs. Wick, but I'm trying very hard to sort out my life. Maybe that's what you saw."

"Maybe." The old lady spoke cautiously. "If you're honest with yourself, you'll be able to face what you must. Don't be afraid."

Deep in thought, Morgan left her neighbor's house. At home, she pulled a heavy photo album from the bookshelves in the sitting room and carefully slotted the old photo of her grandmother into a space, smoothing the plastic sleeve over it to hold it in place. She did it mechanically, scarcely aware of her actions. All her thoughts were on Mrs. Wick's words of advice.

Morgan stood for long minutes staring unseeingly at the old photo of the three spirited young woman. Finally, decided, she pushed the album back into its place on the shelf. Face what you must. She would do it. And she would do it tomorrow.

Chapter Eight

A dog howled in the distance and the fine hairs on the back of Morgan's neck stood up as she pushed open the rusted iron gate. It grated on the old hinge as it swung open and then closed behind her. In the dark, she picked her way along the shadowed drive-way. Overgrown shrubs and weeds spilled from the plantings alongside the crumbling stone drive, brushing her legs with their long damp leaves. She shivered.

Guided only by a faint light from the porch, Morgan was making her way to the front door when she heard the faintest panting breath behind her. She frowned and turned, wondering if Hunter had a dog. She peered into the gloom but could see nothing. She picked up her pace. The front entrance was still a way off but she continued steadily down the path. The rhythmic pants were now off to the side but still coming closer.

Trepidation sent a clutch of fear to her heart and she turned again, standing stock still in the dark. The damp seeped through her canvas shoes, and her hair clung clammily to her face. Tendrils of mist hovered eerily over the grass obscuring her view of the house. The worst of the mist passed but, as much as Morgan strained to see the porch light, she could no longer make it out.

In the mist, she realized she must have strayed from the stone path that led to the front door. She spun around in panic trying to find a point of reference, the gate, the house, but succeeded only in disorientating herself further. The trees were closer than she remembered, their flimsy branches reaching out like the arms of lost spirits, pleading, beseeching.

One caught her arm and she gasped, thinking a human hand held her. She stopped to release herself, and it was then she heard the animal again. That strange savage panting was closer, more frequent, overlapping. With a start, Morgan recognized there must be more than one beast but the moon and stars were obscured by cloud and she could see nothing but the dark night.

She heard them sniffing then, not far away. The animals, whatever they were, let off a chorus of howls, more like wolves than dogs. Morgan's blood congealed in her veins. They had scented her.

A cry of fear rose in her throat as she took to her heels, striding out through the damp forest. The wind sighed through the trees and shook the branches so they slapped against her face and tangled in her hair, slowing her progress.

The panting gasps of the pursuing pack were coming closer now. There was the sound of horses' hooves, the sense of something vaguely human. Morgan could almost feel the hot breath against her neck, her back as she sprinted through the gloom. Hard hands reached out, grabbing her around the waist and she cried out, struggling. This time, it was no tree ensnaring her but unyielding male hands. A scream rose up in her as images of the horned pursuer of her dreams flooded her mind.

"Let me go," she yelled. Her flailing fist connected with skin and muscle, her nails raking flesh. She heard a male grunt, an intake of breath and then the hands around her waist lost their grip and she was dumped unceremoniously on the ground. She sat there panting, staring up at the figure in front of her.

"Hunter?" She whispered as she recognized the shock of brown hair. He wasn't wearing his customary spectacles and his eyes were shadowed, his face etched with tiredness. She had never seen him look so grim. "Hunter, I...." She turned her head to look behind her into the forest but the trees had disappeared and she could no longer hear the panting of the animals behind her.

Silently, he reached down a large palm. Morgan stared at him for a moment before clasping his hand and letting him pull her to her feet. When he would have set her free, she clung to his hand, her long fingers entwining with his broad ones. She moved closer to the security his broad frame offered, and turned her head to scan the forest.

"Hunter, we need to get out of here. There's something in the trees." Morgan's voice shook and she took a deep breath before continuing. "I think they were tracking me, following my scent. Like hunting dogs."

Hunter remained silent, staring at her grimly. Morgan looked away from his intent gaze, and wiped damp blades of grass from the rump of her jeans. "And I heard a horse, and something human, I think, coming closer and closer...chasing me."

"I heard nothing except you." His voice was terse.

Hunter shook free of her hand and turned on his heel without saying a word, striding towards the porch of his house, where a welcoming light shone brightly, leaving Morgan to trail after him.

"Hunter! Wait!" Morgan grabbed him by the arm, forcing him to stop and face her.

"What are you doing here?" His voice was expressionless.

"I thought we could...talk."

"I don't have anything to say to you." He evidently hadn't softened his stance during the time he'd been away, his body language rejecting her unequivocally. "It's cold out here," he said. You should go home."

"No." Morgan felt a strange urgency grip her body. Somehow she knew that if they didn't talk now, the chasm between them would grow and bridging it would become impossible. "I'm not going."

Hunter looked impatient then "Look, Morgan, I'm tired. It's been a hell of a week and I'm just back from France a few hours ago."

"I know. I need to talk to you…"

"If it's about the torque, everything's fine. We can talk on Monday."

Shaking with fear, not knowing what she was letting herself in for but determined not to be dismissed, Morgan strode to the open front door and stepped inside.

Her eyes moved around the shabby hall. Remnants of its magnificence remained in the ornately plastered ceiling and richly hued rugs remained, but a sense of neglect hung heavy in the air.

The door slammed behind her and Morgan spun to see Hunter leaning against it. She had a brief sense of a fly lured and then trapped in the spider's web.

"Umm, I came to...." Morgan gulped. "I wanted to see you, to apologize. And to--"

"Apologize about what?"

"The way I left that night. It was wrong. Rude." Morgan couldn't meet his eyes. "I'm sorry."

"I'm not interested in your apology."

"I wanted to speak with you about it, but you sounded so angry when you left the museum that day."

"What the hell did you expect?" Hunter growled at her, eyes stormy. "I'm human and I hate not getting what I want as much as the next guy."

"Meaning me?"

"Yes you! I'd made it pretty fucking obvious what I wanted."

Morgan felt an irritated flush sting her face--one of the disadvantages of having such a pale skin.

"Yeah, you made it pretty obvious from day one that you

wanted to get me in bed!"

"It wasn't all I wanted!" Hunter threw back. "You knew I wanted a relationship with you."

"Yes, but on your terms. You seemed to want to sweep me off my feet--regardless of what I wanted. You didn't give me a moment to think about things," Morgan fumed. Damned if she was letting him have it all his own way.

Hunter shrugged helplessly. "How the hell was I supposed to know what you wanted? Every time, I thought we were getting somewhere, you backed off."

"I told you I had a problem with the timing." Morgan glared, her grey eyes shooting silver sparks. "I had other considerations like the exhibition. I can't just drop my life because I'd...." Morgan came to a shuddering halt as she realized what she'd been about to say.

"Well, I didn't realize you had a fucking schedule in place for this sort of thing?" Hunter shoved his hands in his pocket and stalked past Morgan into the drawing room.

Morgan followed him. "It wasn't like that. I had commitments, for God's sake."

Hunter spun back to face her. "Commitments that you wanted me to fit around like I was some kind of afterthought!"

"You were never an afterthought. In fact for days I thought of nothing but you." She told him hotly. "My days were consumed by you, and my nights...." She paused and looked away, not sure what to say.

Hunter smiled slowly, sensually. "You were saying about your nights?"

"Nothing," Morgan murmured. She wasn't quite ready to share the erotic details of her encounters with the warrior of her dreams.

"Well, if they were anything like that night, then I sympathize," said Hunter. "If it makes you feel any better then my nights have been pretty shitty, too. Wanting you next to me, beneath me." His voice lowered.

"Don't!" Morgan slapped her hand against the ancient upholstery of an old couch. "Don't reduce it all simply to sex."

"Well, at least I'm not pretending that it wasn't the best night of my fucking life," Hunter roared, his eyes a furious molten gold.

"I'm not pretending," she blazed.

"Well, you haven't mentioned one word about it voluntarily, in case you hadn't noticed." His lips were a flat angry line. "It's like you'd prefer to pretend it never happened."

"No! Never that." Morgan's voice softened. "I was just scared of wanting you so much."

"And now?" asked Hunter, his voice expressionless.

Morgan stared at him mutely for a moment before she spoke again. "This might take a while. Could I have a glass of water, please?"

"There's wine." Hunter struck a match and held it to the open fire, waiting until yellow and blue flames erupted, before pouring her a glass and topping up his from an open bottle on the table.

She sat on the couch across from him, sipping the wine at first, then gulping greedily until it was empty. He was there ready with the wine bottle, pouring her a second glass before she even asked. The mellow red warmed her, curling through her belly, loosening her tongue.

"What do you want of me?" Hunter's voice was low, weary. "I've given you everything. The torque is the Museum's and I'll sign anything to that effect. You don't have to sleep with me."

"For God's sake, it's nothing to do with the torque." Morgan's frustrated voice burst loudly in the quiet gloom of the house. "I know what you think Gus said...." she looked at Hunter's implacable face. "Damn that man to hell," she muttered.

At last Hunter smiled. A tiny twist of the lips, admittedly, but Morgan was willing to see it as a step in the right direction.

"I don't blame you for hating me." Morgan's anger subsided as quickly as it had erupted. "Your fiancée was...well, she wasn't the best advertisement for trust. And I haven't exactly given you good reason to believe in me."

"I don't hate you." His low baritone rumbled. "I just don't understand. I thought we had something. After we...I dreamed of you all night and I wanted to wake up next to you and know that it wasn't all a figment of my very creative imagination. But," he raised a mystified hand, "you'd gone. And I still have no idea what you really want."

"I want everything." Morgan's voice was soft, sure. "I want to explore you."

"And how far are you prepared to go?" His tone was dark

Morgan's eyes locked with his. "Wherever it takes us."

Hunter smiled then and stood, holding his hand out to her but, although Morgan rose, she didn't go to him. Instead she slowly unwrapped the scarf from around her neck, sliding it down her body. She smiled at him, and then drew her jacket off, letting it, too, slide down her body until it pooled at her feet.

Morgan went to remove her T-shirt but Hunter was there pressing his face into the glossy strands of her hair and inhaling its scent.

He pulled her close to his muscular body, breast-to-breast, thigh-to-thigh, letting her feel his heat and arousal. His eyes studied her upturned, yearning face for long seconds as though searching for answers there, before finally his mouth descended to hers.

A series of soft, tantalizing kisses taunted Morgan as Hunter teased her with his mouth, withdrawing and then settling again on another spot. Quickly tiring of his game, Morgan reached a hand behind his head, pulling him against her hard, taking control of their kiss, her tongue demanding entry to his mouth. Hunter complied and their lips touched, tasted and then tangled ferociously as their passion mounted.

"I've wanted you for so long," he murmured into her mouth.

"It's less than two weeks since you had me."

"Not just sexually. You always responded to me sexually but I wanted you to want me in your heart and mind as much as your body."

"I do want this now. I've never wanted anything so much in my life." As she spoke, Morgan knew it was true.

"When I woke up in that hotel, I nearly died when you weren't there. I'd thought I'd found heaven with you, and then it turned to hell." He looked into her eyes. "Did I do something to make you run?"

"No, not unless you count making me feel things that I'd never felt before." She blushed. "I did things with you that I've never even thought about with anyone else. It seemed so carnal, so sexual. I woke in the dark, hearing you breathing and I was horrified by the things I'd done and, at the same time, I wanted to wake you and make you do them to me all over again."

Hunter groaned at her words, his mouth growing rougher and more impassioned against hers--twisting, savaging and arousing desire in both of them that flooded every cell of their bodies. Morgan pressed closer and closer to his hard body as though trying to imprint his body on her own. Frustrated with the clothes between them, she tugged at off his jacket and tee-shirt, while he kicked off his shoes, before turned their attention to Morgan's clothes.

Finally they stood naked, not touching, just drinking in the sight of each other's bodies. Hunter raised a hand to her face, curving it around her head and enfolding her body with his as he pulled them both down to the thick rug in front of the fire. He lowered his head to her breast, tugging the hard peak of her nipple into his mouth, licking, laving, sucking, nipping, sending tendrils of liquid desire through her body, moistening her womanly parts.

As he lavished equal attention on her other nipple, Morgan spread her legs, allowing him to settle his hips between them, his hardening penis pushing demandingly against her softness. She touched him intimately, stroking the length of him, circling his girth with her fingertips, feeling the dampness at the head of his cock as he grew even larger in her hands. She reached her hand further down, gently massaging his testicles until he groaned enough, pushing her hands away.

Morgan spread her legs wider as she felt the coarse hair of his groin against the softness of her inner thighs, her feet against his buttocks, hands against his shoulders as she massaged his maleness with her femininity. Her movements inflamed him as much as her and he pulled his mouth away from hers, breathing harshly as he hovered above her.

"I can't wait much longer."

"Why wait at all?" breathed Morgan.

"Once my cock is inside you, it won't take much for me to...I want you with me and you're not ready yet," Hunter muttered. "I want you hot, and wet, as aroused as I am."

"I am, oh!"

Morgan gasped as Hunter's hard, blunt fingers discovered her intimate lips, tickling along the crease, parting her and stroking upwards. He found the hard nub of her desire, manipulating it until she moaned, arching herself into his hand. With his palm hard against her pubic bone, he delicately spread her labia, opening her, sliding two fingers inside her. Morgan jerked upwards him as she felt his fingers probing her vagina, his nails scratching delicately against the inner surface. He introduced another finger, stretching her inner cavity to its limit until Morgan moaned, closing her eyes as Hunter forced her body to accept this extra intrusion.

With his other hand holding her spread wide, Hunter withdrew his three fingers as she arched beneath him before roughly penetrating her again, simulating the movements of intercourse with his fingers until Morgan was twisting against him, her eyes glazed and unseeing.

He began pushing his fourth finger into her tight opening, her inner muscles tensing in sudden pain.

"Too much," she gasped, looking up into his desire-hardened face.

"Try it, babe. Just relax and take it."

Morgan wanted to tell him that she couldn't but he was making her, thrusting his fingers beyond the protesting muscles of her entrance, making her cry out. His mouth curved in satisfaction as he forced his fingers deep and then deeper, in and then out, until her body began to soften and her rhythm matched his.

"Hunter, I'm...oh God, I can't. Please.…"

"I know, darling," he said, feeling her body begin to throb and shake. "You're nearly there, just a second more."

Morgan felt her body rise and rise, finding its crest in the moment of stillness that always preceded the storm. She felt Hunter release her with his fingers and then he was lifting her up to meet the savage thrust of his cock. She was flying, her body shuddering with release as he thundered into her again and again until the powerful contractions of her body caught him in their grip and he arched his neck, shouting his climax to the heavens as he spurted his milky essence into receptive depths.

Hunter sprawled in her arms, sweat-damp, his damp hair against her breasts, body heaving as she stroked his back languidly. So cataclysmic had their release been that Morgan felt like she could lie still with him like this for a hundred years and still feel no urge to move. He still lay semi-rigid inside her and Morgan could feel his semen dripping down her inner thighs and pooling beneath her.

When he withdrew slickly from her body and rose to his knees over her, she moaned, feeling the coolness of the air replace his heat between her legs.

"No," she murmured to him, reaching out to pull him back against her.

But Hunter wasn't finished with her. Rolling her over onto her stomach, he pushed her hair back from her nape, touching his tongue to her sensitive spot just there between her shoulder-blades. Morgan moaned as he dropped little butterfly kisses down the length of her spine till he reached the crease of her buttocks.

Reaching out an arm, he pulled two cushions from the couch, laying her head on one. The other he used to raise her hips until she was on her knees. Fitting himself over her, his groin to her buttocks, he levered her thighs wide apart with his legs. His tumescence was expanding again and he pushed it between the crease in her bottom, working himself against her roughly.

Morgan could feel the slap-slap of his testicles against her skin as he moved against her, the blunt head of his engorged penis closing in on her vaginal opening. But he didn't enter, just continued to move sexually against her.

At the edge of her vision, she caught a faint movement, but with Hunter's weight over her, she couldn't turn her head for a better view. Was there someone else in the room with them?

"Hunter?"

She tried to raise her neck to see the room better, but he pushed her back down to the floor. He moved his hand beneath her, squeezing her distended breasts and pinching her nipples until she gasped. His hand moved down her belly, tunneling through the dark hair at her thighs until his fingers found the taut nub. Morgan caught her breath as he pressed hard and she felt her sexual moisture flood her body anew, dampening her passage and mingling with the last of his semen as it dried on her.

She felt his fingers probing inside her vagina, taking her moisture on his fingertips and smearing it upwards to the crease in her buttocks. One wet finger circled the secret dark hole between the globes of her bottom, distributing her liquid, probing tentatively inside her. She jerked at his touch and felt his breath hot against her ear, telling her how beautiful she was.

Then she felt a rougher touch on her, a harsher heavier breath against her body. Morgan gasped and looked up. She could sense another presence at her side, just beyond her range of vision. Tall, powerful but hazy. Her sub-conscious nudged at her awareness. A memory of a shadowy figure who disturbed her night.

"Hunter, who…?"

"You know, darling. You've been calling to him."

Her breath caught. Cernunnos?

"But I don't understand. What does he want?"

Hunter kissed her ear tenderly. "He has been watching, Morgan. Watching you and now he's hungry for you."

"But I want you, Hunter. Only you." Panicked, she struggled helplessly against him but he held her down.

"Shhh, darling. He is waiting to mount you."

"I don't--"

"You must service him, my love, for you have called to him. For weeks he has been watching, waiting for his turn upon you."

Oh, God, was this what her dreams had meant? That subconsciously she had been calling to the depraved man-beast to satisfy her basest desires?

"No, Hunter, please."

But he was drawing from her and a darker, heavier form crouched over her, his skin hotter than Hades, his breath rasping. A tongue darted out to lick her ear and pointed teeth caught at her nape. Morgan struggled against him but hard arms and thighs kept her body pinned and spread beneath him.

A blunt force gathered at the apex to her anal opening, something intruding savagely into the delicately protesting flesh as Morgan screamed with excitement and terror. One brutal thrust and he was in to the hilt. Morgan caught her lip between her teeth, trying not to cry out as the man-beast took her fragile flesh. Again and again, huge, harder than anything she felt before, he rocked against her. One hand pulled tight around her belly, making her accept the full force of his thrusts as his fingers tweaked her clit, giving her pleasure to match the pain. His other hand anchored them to the floor, their only stability in a frenzy of animal mating.

Morgan tried to twist to see him but he growled angrily, increasing the force of his thrusts until she cried out. And there in front of her was Hunter, grasping her chin in one hand as his other placed his engorged cock inside her lips. And he was encouraging her mouth to pleasure him as her anus was pleasuring the lord of the hunt. And in a flash of awareness, Morgan understood they were one and the same. Hunter and the man-beast, love and desire.

And as the thought crystallized in her mind, the beast fucking her from behind roared as if in answer, his thrusts pounding into her as he approached his climax. Hunter's movements were matching him in a devastating counter rhythm, and Morgan closed her eyes, seeing in her mind's eye a vision of them coming inside her simultaneously. The image was so arousing that Morgan felt her inner tissues swell as a scalding tide of passion rose inside her. Her vagina clenched strongly in orgasm just as the beast reached his climax, flooding her passage with his liquid as Hunter jetted his release into her mouth.

Morgan cried out as the trio reached the pinnacle. She heard her voice as if from a distance, and then the heat and the sweat and the passion were fading, she saw the room as if it was an antique sepia photo spilled from an old photo album. She felt as though she was drifting into a strange unconsciousness. Her eyelids fluttered and she slept.

* * * *

Morgan stirred, one cheek against a soft pillow, her body soft and relaxed. She felt a kiss at her temples, not much more than a breath of air, and then a faint voice in her ear.

"Sweet dreams, beautiful one. Be happy with your Hunter. Call for me when you feel the desire and I will come for you."

Morgan moaned, her eyes tightly shut. She could sense the voice but couldn't really hear or it or tell from which direction it came. Then there was a rush of air, the heavy curtains drawn tight over the window fluttered in the morning breeze and it was gone.

She lay for a long moment as reality seeped back into her. She was curled on her side, a hair-roughened leg thrown casually over her hips below the sheet and a hard arm across her shoulder, half-smothering her. Morgan felt deliciously warm and secure. Hunter's regular breathing told her that he was still asleep and she let her mind wander back to that glorious night of pleasure.

She snuggled closer into Hunter's arms, thankful that he had given her another chance with him. He muttered something under his breath, something that sounded like I love you. Morgan smiled and stroked his arm, and he went back to sleep.

After his flight back from France, Hunter slept late but as the weak sun of early winter began its shallow arc across the sky, Morgan rose and took a shower. She had packed--more in hope than expectation--a change of underwear in her bag, and she dressed warmly in the jeans and thick jumper she'd arrived in yesterday, padding downstairs to the kitchen wearing clean but too-big socks from Hunter's closet.

The big old house was gloomy and Morgan went into every room, drawing the heavy drapes to let the morning light in. Despite the cold, she opened several windows to release the musty smell of a house shut up for several days.

The house had a mournful atmosphere as though it had been too long without an owner, but the generous proportions of its rooms and the exquisite plaster work and tiles gave it a unique character. Morgan wondered whether Hunter was simply renting the house as a place to stay between digs or whether he owned it.

She made a mental note to ask him when he woke.

She had explored the kitchen cupboards and was making breakfast when Hunter finally put in an appearance. His hair was mussed and his eyes still filled with sleep as he wandered in, dressed in shabby sweats.

"I feel like it should be about four in the morning," he said, yawning widely as he came over to drop a kiss on her lips. He held her close for a moment."

"Hungry?" Morgan nodded at the pan. I'm making eggs but there's no bread for toast."

Hunter looked at her warily. "You don't have to do this," he said. "I don't expect you to take on the domestic duties just because you're a woman."

Morgan laughed. "Don't worry. I'm just cooking because I'm hungry." She put a plate of eggs in front of him and poured coffee for them both before sitting down.

"Strong. Good." He sipped the coffee and smiled. "Hell, I can't believe I feel so wiped out."

"That's jetlag for you."

"Not to mention a wild woman who found her way into my arms last night, exhausting my energy reserves." He winked at her. "I hope you aren't expecting the same performance every night."

"You mean you put on a show just to reel me in and now you think I'm hooked, the real Hunter will emerge?" Morgan mocked him.

"What do you expect from the real me?"

"Oh at least four times a night and an encore every morning."

Hunter groaned. "Well, I'll do my best--but you'll have to pull your weight. I'm not Superman."

"I'll try," agreed Morgan. "Especially as I think we'll find that we're on our own from now on." She thought of the brush of air she had felt this morning, the feeling that she had said goodbye to her night-time apparition.

When Hunter didn't respond, she looked up from her breakfast to find him frowning at her.

"What do you mean?"

"I mean, you know...." she stopped suddenly, realizing from Hunter's blank look that he had no idea what she was talking about. She thought quickly. "Just that we can get on with our relationship without my hang-ups intruding."

Hunter nodded, apparently satisfied and went back to his

breakfast. Morgan stared at his dark head for a moment, still stunned. Could it really be that he had no recall of the other participant in their wild lovemaking the night before?

Hunter looked up and caught her watching him, and he smiled his warm smile. Morgan smiled back and leaned across the table to plant a kiss on his mouth. What the hell did it matter anyway? Now she had made peace with the passionate side of her nature, she no longer needed help from the other side to release it.

"I feel like I need a few more hours in bed." He stroked her hand suggestively. "Wanna come tuck me in?"

Morgan stood up and walked into his arms. "As long as there's no sleeping involved."

"I think I can guarantee that."

Epilogue

Letting out a long sigh of relief, Morgan sank into her office chair, letting it spin under her weight. Under the desk, she kicked off her black spike heels. After an entire evening of standing in those torturous things, her feet ached, matching the throbbing in her head. Too much champagne and no more than a couple of bites from the finger food the caterers had supplied made her feel light-headed. And she had talked to so many people--friends, colleagues and strangers had all approached to congratulate her on the exhibition--that her throat felt raw.

Still, it had been a success, a surprising success. The torque had proven a marvelous centerpiece for the exhibition, and guests had crowded around it, marveling and asking questions. Compared with other highly ornate pieces, it was simple and spare, but its weight and age were obvious even behind the glass. It exuded a strange mystical pull that had held everyone in its thrall.

The other elements of the exhibition--the legends, the divinities, the heroes and heroines of old--told their stories through ancient manuscripts and artifacts, interpreted by Morgan. She had held her breath, waiting for some strait-laced historian to haul her over the coals for daring to deviate too far from the accepted version. So far, though, all she had received were compliments, with David LeMaire and other leading historians complementing her for her thoughtful and imaginative approach to the exhibition.

The director and the curator had both made speeches introducing the exhibition, and Hunter had been invited to follow them with a few words about the torque. His wry and amusing anecdotes about his experience on digs had amused even the conservative crowd, and he had winked at Morgan during his speech, making her blush and then laugh.

She knew that life with Hunter wouldn't be all glamorous openings and parties. When Hunter was on a dig, they might be apart for months and they had discussed the possibility of Morgan freelancing at the museum so that she was available to travel with him some of the time. The fluidity of life and work with Hunter would sometimes prove frustrating, Morgan knew, accustomed as she was to a more clear-cut routine, but she felt calmer and more able to deal with changing plans.

"So, you two are the talk of the town now," said Mary, pushing open the door and sinking into the visitor chair in Morgan's office and running a tired hand through her blond-streaked bob. "Everyone's tongues are wagging about the handsome archaeologist and his raven-haired beauty."

"Typical." Morgan's mouth twisted wryly. "They never mention the woman's professional competence--only her looks."

"Still, can't hurt to get you noticed. You just have to make sure they don't try to mark you down because you've got where you are based on sex, or because you're Hunter's partner. You know what it's like. The gossips can be as cruel here as anywhere else."

She stood up and hugged Morgan. "Anyway, I'm happy for you, hon. You always were a star even if you didn't know your own worth half of the time."

"Thanks, Mary. Everyone should have a friend like you."

"So…." Mary drawled the word and Morgan knew she wanted the juice on Hunter. "You never did tell me how you made up with the handsome Hunter."

"Oh, you know," Morgan waved a hand vaguely. "An apology...and a lot of sex did the trick."

Mary chuckled. "Don't you love men--so simple!" she looked at her watch. "Talking of men, I'd better round mine up before he demolishes everything the caterers have to offer. He's had the wedding tux fitted so he can't afford to pile on the pounds. You should go rescue Hunter, too. Last I saw Edwina and Gus had him in their clutches and he had a glazed, rather terrified look in his eyes."

Morgan reluctantly found her shoes and the two women walked into the grand hall, which was emptying fast as guests decided to take to advantage of a break in the rain and make for their cars. Morgan said her good-byes to Mary and other guests that she knew personally, before making her way over to Hunter, Edwina and Gus, who were deep in discussion with Marshall, the curator. Standing close to Hunter, she discreetly reached her hand towards him, her fingers entwining with his.

"Well done, my dear," said Edwina. "I've been discussing your work with some of the more eminent names in the field, including Ted Farrell. They were most intrigued by your approach to some elements of the exhibition. In fact, David LeMaire even suggested that you might want to touch base with him about a book he's working on." Eileen touched her arm. "Between you and me, I think he might want help jazzing up a Celtic history tome he's been writing for years. But make sure you get due credit--push him for a co-authorship."

Morgan shook her head and started say something but Edwina said, "Nonsense. It would be good for you. Get your name out there."

"Good for the museum, too," Marshall muttered under his breath.

"Well, let's hope tomorrow's newspapers publish something about the exhibition itself and the launch isn't just consigned to the society pages," said Gus shrewishly, glancing at Morgan's backless red sheath dress.

"Oh, Gus, don't be so stuffy!" Edwina reprimanded him, while Hunter ran his hand gently down Morgan's back, making her nerve-endings prickle. "A veneer of glamour is just the thing this musty old place needs.

"In fact, I want to talk to you all in the next few days about where we head next. Even if More than Myths is a success beyond compare, we can't afford to rest on our laurels. We need always to be thinking one step ahead. I have a few ideas about where we go next, and I want you all to bring some suggestions to the table too."

Edwina excused herself and Hunter told Gus he was ready to take Morgan home unless she was needed. Slightly surly after the put-down from Edwina, Gus wished them goodnight and headed over to admonish the caterers who had accidentally chipped the corner of an exhibition wall with a drinks tray.

Morgan watched him bustle off, knowing she was going to

have to work hard to win her boss over to her way of thinking during the next few months. Regardless of Gus's old-fashioned attitude, she felt for the first time a sense of belonging at the museum, and confidence in the respect her colleagues felt for her expertise and contribution.

"You were wonderful tonight." A large callused hand touched her nape where tendrils escaped from her upswept chignon. Morgan felt a shiver ripple down her spine as the memory of sharp teeth nipping her there rippled through her mind. Then she looked up into the loving visage of her mild Hunter, his warm amber eyes smiling proudly down at her.

"The history and archaeology buffs loved you. Usually they get some moldering, middle-aged professor type with thick glasses and bad teeth--or a scruffy young thing in jeans with thick glasses and bad teeth. They're not used to sexy young goddesses wearing red silk, and with compellingly radical ideas of her own about Celtic mythology."

Hunter leaned down to her, his lips touching hers. Morgan's mouth opened for the sweep of his tongue as his lips met with hers. He tasted her for a moment and then pulled her upright into his arms to deepen the kiss. Finally Morgan pulled away, gasping, resting her head against Hunter's chin.

"I think we'd better continue this later when we have more privacy," she said.

"Is that a promise?"

Morgan reached a finger up to touch his lips.

"Your place or mine?"

Hunter considered the question. "Hmm, mine then. It's nearer and I don't think I can wait long to have you in my arms again."

Though they hadn't formally decided to live together, it was rare that they spent a night apart, unless Hunter was away. They had discussed which house would be their primary residence but hadn't yet reached a conclusion. Morgan loved her old townhouse, its rooms filled with the furniture she'd inherited from her grandmother or discovered in dusty antique stores and restored with love. It felt like home. But Hunter's gothic mansion--which he had bought some months before but had barely lived in--was starting to grow on her, too. She knew if they had children, the space that Hunter's house offered, made it a better option. At the moment, though, they stayed wherever best suited them.

Morgan smoothed the tie at Hunter's neck. Though the launch

was formal he'd flat-out refused to wear a tux, although he had agreed to ditch his old cords for the event, and the beautifully cut charcoal suit and dark red tie gave him a dashing elegance.

They had turned heads when arriving at the launch and the bored press photographers had suddenly swung into action at the first sign of glamour. Morgan knew that Gus and some of the more conservative members of the board wouldn't be too happy but if she and Hunter helped add a sexy edge to history that helped bring the exhibition exposure and--more importantly--visitor numbers, they could hardly complain. She was pleased that Edwina evidently concurred.

Morgan and Hunter walked slowly back to her office where she collected her evening bag and wrap from her desk. On Monday, she would have to pack all her research materials on the horned man-beast away and begin working on new ideas. As the turned to leave, she caught her foot against the corner of something sticking out from underneath her desk. It was a book about Celtic mythology that she hadn't found time to delve into. A silky bookmark was tucked into a page near the end and a phrase caught her eye.

....so the story goes, an apparition of the horned god appears in the dreams of those who act with wild abandon, or people who burn with passionate desire....

She smiled as she remembered Hunter saying something similar in the early days of their relationship.

As they walked down the empty corridor of the museum and out into the damp night, she looked up at her handsome archaeologist and smiled at him.

"What?" he entwined his fingers with hers.

"Oh, nothing really," she smiled up at him. "Just thinking that all my dreams have come true."

The End

THE DJINN

By
Marie Morin

Chapter One

It had a strange, pungent odor. It wasn't unpleasant, just powerful, particularly considering the phial appeared to be empty. Elise Beauchamp wrinkled her nose, jerking away from the tiny bottle she'd just opened and waved beneath her nose.

"Some love potion," she muttered under her breath. Not that she'd believed any of that malarkey the vendor had spouted. It had sounded good, though, and it wasn't as if the old trinket had cost that much.

Still, she didn't know why she'd bought it. She didn't particularly care for jewelry. She'd only picked it up to study it because of the tiny, cunningly wrought, glass bottle secured to the chain like a charm. Noticing her interest, the vendor had immediately begun to weave tales about it's history, asserting finally that there was a love potion inside the bottle that would bring her true love to her.

That alone had almost been enough to make her put it right back, because she'd already found her true love--and lost him, but she supposed, maybe, in the recesses of her subconscious, hope still dwelt that she was not destined to live the remainder of her life alone, and she hadn't been able to leave the charm because she couldn't leave hope behind.

She'd brought very little money with her and had had to resort to counting the last of her change just to pay for it. She'd told herself that she would just wander around and check out the wares the flea market merchants were hawking, just so she didn't have to sit at home and think about the fact that today would've been her second anniversary...if John had only stayed home that day, instead of rushing off to work...or if they hadn't overslept...or if they'd only slept just a few minutes later.

It tortured her almost as much to think life without John could be counted in minutes as it did having to learn to live without him. If he hadn't arrived at that particular intersection at that particular moment....

Sadness filled her, but the tears had all been cried long ago.

Slowly, the memories receded and she became aware of her surroundings once more, aware that a dark shadow had fallen over her. She looked up. Comprehension wasn't immediate. Sluggishly, her brain assimilated the fact that there was a person standing before her--a man.

Her first impression was 'naked'. He wasn't, of course. Just the next thing to it.

Must be some displaced Yankee, she decided. They might be in Florida, but natives still considered February winter and dressed accordingly. They certainly didn't go around in public places bare chested.

It was Gasparilla, though, not nearly as wild as Louisiana's Mardi Gras, but some people went a little overboard.

He wasn't even wearing pants! Not what she'd call pants, anyway. It looked more like those filmy things belly dancers wore, fitted at the waist and ankles, but baggy everywhere else. Since she was sitting on a bench and he was standing, his 'package' was practically nose level.

It was an impressive package.

It occurred to her that she'd been staring at 'it' transfixed for several moments. Even as her gaze jerked upward in the direction of his face she felt blood begin to pound in her cheeks.

She forgot all about being embarrassed, however, when her gaze reached his face.

He didn't look at all pleased. His lips were drawn into a tight, thin line, his dark brows arched but pulled into a sharp v above the bridge of a noble blade of a nose.

It wasn't the scowl on his face that stunned her, however. It wasn't the wicked looking, neatly trimmed 'Fu Manchu' that framed his hard mouth. It wasn't even the scalp lock of silky black hair fluttering from the crown of his head, or his eyes,

more gold than brown, glittering with intelligence, curiosity--
animosity.

The moment she gazed up into his face, it was almost as if
she'd been struck a physical blow. A shaft of pure animal lust
shot through her, right down to her toes, something so alien to
her that she wasn't even certain of what had happened at first. It
was almost as if she'd been struck by a bolt of lightning.

She noticed his lips were moving. It took an effort to still the
quivering in her belly in response to those lips. Frowning, she
tried to hear past the clamoring din her heart was making in her
ears and discovered she still couldn't understand a word he was
saying. "What?"

"What is your wish?"

Elise stared at him uncomprehendingly. "Look. I'm sorry. I
don't know what you're selling, but I'm not interested."

He looked surprised and then irritated. "You summoned me. I
have offered to grant a wish."

Elise gaped at him. *She* had summoned him? Of all the nerve!
She'd been sitting on the bench, minding her own business,
completely oblivious to everyone around her. How could
anyone, even the most obnoxiously conceited male, interpret that
as a come on? "I did no such thing!" she said indignantly. "Now,
go away, or I'll call the cops."

"This is your wish?" he demanded, sounding as indignant as
she felt. "That I go?"

"Didn't I just say so?"

He frowned. "You must be more precise. Where am I to go?"

Elise gave him a look, tempted to tell him to go to hell, and
then cast a glance around to see if there were any cops nearby.
Not a glimmer of a uniform, and wasn't that always the case?
Fail to come to a complete stop at a stop sign and there was a
damned cop right on your tail. Need assistance, and there wasn't
one of them in sight. "What do you want?"

He crossed his arms, studying her thoughtfully for several
moments. "To give you what your heart desires."

Pain, unexpectedly sharp, lanced through her. What her heart
desired? John...but no one could bring him back to her. The pain
cost her her patience. "Who do you think you are, anyway, Santa
Claus?"

He frowned. "I am the djinn, Raheem. My patience grows thin,
Mistress. Tell me your wish and I will grant it most gladly so that
I may return to my own concerns."

Elise glared at him. "Your patience?" she echoed. "Look, mister. I don't give a damn who you are, if you're expecting to get something from me, just don't hold your breath."

He frowned. "Why would I do that?"

"What?"

"Hold my breath?"

Elise rolled her eyes. She would've gotten to her feet and stalked away, except that he was standing so close it unnerved her. He'd said, though, that he was anxious to go about his own concerns, he just had to hear her wish before he could go.

He was a lunatic, of course. But if it was the only way to get rid of him, why not? "If I wish for something, you'll go away?"

Something gleamed in his eyes, something wicked. "Yes, mistress," he said, a slow, tantalizing smile curling those lips in a way that made her heart trip over itself.

Elise wished she could ignore the effect he had on her, or at least convince herself it was fear that made her heart hammer with excitement at the sound of his voice, the curl of his lips, the gleam in his eyes. She'd never been terribly good at self-deception, however.

She pasted on a smile, though she was neither amused, nor tempted to flirt with the man. "Fine. Good! I *wish* you'd go away!"

His lips tightened with annoyance. "I must have a destination."

Elise pursed her lips. "Fine! Go find Santa Claus and tell him I want him to bring me back what I lost Christmas before last," she said tightly, wishing he *could* bring John back.

The Djinn frowned, but, to her relief, he straightened, as if prepared to leave. "Where would I find this Santa Claus?"

"North pole," Elise said with a cold smile, then turned away, reaching for her purse. If he wasn't going to go away and leave her alone, she decided, she would leave, and if he tried to follow her.... To her surprise, when she looked up again, the strange man had vanished. She glanced around, expecting to see him striding away. She didn't, which was really odd considering the bench was set in a very open area.

Frowning, she got to her feet, looked around again and finally shrugged. Who'd have thought a man that big could move so fast?

Shaking off the strange encounter, she tucked her 'love potion' into her purse and headed for home. There were just too many weirdoes out for her peace of mind.

* * * *

Wind driven sleet pelted Raheem from head to toe the moment he materialized. Shuddering, he looked around, narrowing his eyes against the blowing ice crystals. He had never cared for this world, but, as bad as much of it was, within sixty seconds he was convinced that he had discovered the worst it had to offer. There was no dwelling within sight. He would have been surprised if he had seen one. As simple as humans tended to be, they didn't seem so witless as to choose to live in such a place as this.

The female had said he would find Santa Claus here, however.

Summoning a cloak of heavy animal hide, he wrapped it tightly around him and began his search. After two days he was forced to conclude that the female was either wrong--which would not surprise him in the least--or she had sent him upon a fool's errand.

He laughed aloud at that thought, though there was no humor in it. No puny man of the species had ever outwitted a djinn, and certainly no weak minded female could do so.

Finally, deciding she was probably just too ignorant to know where the person lived, he summoned the winds and moved through the skies, searching for signs of human habitation. He was many miles from the north pole when he at last spotted a tiny community.

Materializing on the ground once more, he looked around and finally strode towards the building from which music emanated. It appeared to be a tavern. Thrusting the door open, he strode inside and looked around as he shook the snow from his cloak. All conversation had ceased at his entrance. He ignored the curious stares of the humans. He was accustomed to such.

The man behind the bar was the only person present who's mind seemed unlikely to be fogged by spirits. Raheem strode to the bar.

"Can I help you?"

Raheem nodded. "I have been sent to seek out Santa Claus. Tell me where to find him."

The man sitting on the stool beside him snorted in his beer, then commenced to coughing. Raheem glared at the oaf. The men grinning beside him lost their smiles and returned their attention to the beverage in their mugs.

"You missed him by a couple of months, buddy. He won't be back until next year," the bartender offered, struggling against a grin.

Raheem's eyes narrowed. "How many days until this man returns?"

The bartender scratched the whiskers on his chin. "I never was too good at math. He comes around every December, though, regular as clock work...you're a foreigner, aren't you?"

Raheem frowned. Time meant little to him--in the way of things--but he had no desire to cool his heels in this place for months. "I can not wait that long. I must know where to find him."

"Try the north pole," someone called from across the room and then snickered.

Raheem turned, his gaze zeroing in upon the man. "I have been there. No humans dwell there."

"Well, he ain't exactly human," someone else volunteered. "I think he's an elf."

Raheem looked at the man. "Elves are woodland creatures. No elf would dwell in such a wasteland as this."

The bartender cleared his throat. "Don't pay him any mind. He's just teasing. He ain't real, you know."

Raheem turned to look at the man again. "Who is not real?"

"Santa Claus. I don't know who sent you to find him, but there ain't no such thing. He's just a holiday myth...for fun, you know."

Rage filled Raheem. "This is the truth? The man does not exist?"

The bartender shook his head. In the next moment, however, the doors to the tavern burst open in a swirl of mist and ice. By the time the patrons had managed to close the doors again, the mysterious stranger had vanished.

* * * *

Mondays were always the worst, Elise reflected as she sank into the hot, pounding water of her whirlpool. It felt heavenly. Singing under her breath along with the song playing on her headset, she settled back to enjoy her soaking massage. She had just begun to drowse when an icy cold wind brushed her bare shoulders. Her eyes popped open.

She would've screamed, but she couldn't seem to find her voice.

Chapter Two

Raheem glared at the woman as he swiped the snow from his face, flicked it to the floor and then began brushing it from his cape. "There is no Santa Claus!" he snarled furiously. "I am the djinn, Raheem! Do you dare to toy with me, woman?"

Elise gaped at him, too stunned to do anything else.

Several things occurred to her almost simultaneously.

She was naked.

There was a dangerous looking man standing over her.

And she knew damn well she'd set her alarms.

At that thought, she glanced at the bathroom door. It was still closed, still locked. She whirled to look at the stained glass window--the only window in the room. It was still intact.

Abruptly, anger replaced her fear--or fear spawned the attack mode per her survival instincts. She wasn't sure which and she was in no mood to try to figure it out. Snatching her headset off, she snarled back at him. "What the hell are you doing in my house?"

The man looked slightly taken aback. Though his scowl remained firmly in place, something flickered in his eyes. "I am the djinn of the phial. You are my mistress. Whither thou goest, I may follow."

"You may not! Get out! NOW!"

He glared at her, folded his arms and promptly vanished.

Elise gaped at the spot where he'd stood only moments before. She might have thought she was losing her mind--except that there was a puddle of melted snow where he'd stood only moments before.

She was shaking...sweating from the heat of the water, but still shaking like a leaf. Weakness washed through her in the wake of the adrenaline rush.

It was the man from the park several days earlier. Stunned as she was to look up and find him standing over her--again--she had recognized him immediately.

He must be a madman.

Djinn? As in genie?

Now that she thought about it, he did sort of remind her of Mr. Clean--what was she *thinking*?

With an effort, she climbed from the tub, turned the jets off and popped the drain. So much for relaxing in her bath.

Maybe that was it? Maybe she'd relaxed too long and the heat had gone to her head? The problem was, she knew she hadn't been in the tub that long.

She turned to study the puddle on the floor. After a moment, she moved toward it, lifted one foot and stuck her toe in. Hot as she was from having just emerged from the tub, the icy water sent a shock wave through her, making her jaw clench.

She wasn't hallucinating the temperature of that water. He'd brushed snow from his clothes. She'd seen it. The water was cold enough to be melted snow.

Maybe she'd suffered a psychotic break?

Was it possible she could do that and still be able to consider it as a possibility?

Shaking her head, she decided to fix herself a drink. She didn't usually drink alone. She'd been so devastated by John's sudden death, she hadn't trusted her self-control in finding relief in drugs. At the moment, however, she felt like she needed something to steady her nerves.

Drying off, she wrapped the towel around her and left the bathroom.

The bar, she discovered, was bare. She looked at the two lonely bottles and realized they were from that last party. She had never finished cleaning up after the police had arrived at her door with the terrible news.

Abruptly, unexpectedly, a knot of misery gathered in her throat.

She'd thought she had gotten over this part--the part where she had only to look at something that triggered a memory to immediately burst into tears.

Taking a deep breath, she gathered up the empty bottles to dump them in the trash. As she turned, however, HE was standing right behind her. This time, she had no trouble finding her voice. She screamed like a banshee.

When she sucked in her breath, her towel fell to her feet.

His eyes widened, his brows arching upward in astonishment.

She wasn't certain if the jolt of surprise reflected on his face was because she'd just screamed at him or if it was the 'unveiling.'

Pitching the bottles at him, she grabbed her towel from the floor and clutched it to her breasts, trying vainly to grab the ends and wrap them around her with her free hand. "What are you doing here?"

He frowned. "I am the djinn...."

"Will you stop with that! Jesus Christ!"

"I am Raheem."

He wasn't joking. Elise stared at him a long moment. "You're not here to...uh.... How did you get in, anyway?"

He cocked his head to one side. "I entered," he said slowly, as if he were speaking to a half-wit.

Elise's lips tightened. "I know you 'entered', damn it! I asked how you managed it. I locked the doors. I turned on the burglar alarm. It is the very latest in home security. How did you bypass it?"

Frowning, he clasped his hands behind his back and walked around her, studying her, Elise thought, as if she were some sort of alien creature. She clutched her towel more tightly, finally managed to draw two ends together and, she hoped, covered her ass. She felt a chilling breeze back there, though, that made her more than a little uneasy.

He was built like a body builder. If he meant her harm, she didn't have a chance in hell...unless he was slow. But then she remembered how quickly he'd vanished.... She frowned. "How did you do that trick in the bathroom while ago?" she asked when he'd finished his inspection and faced her once more.

"Trick?"

"The vanishing act."

"I am the djinn...."

"For God's sake! Don't start that again!"

He frowned. Anger snapped in his eyes, but curiosity as well. "This world has changed much since I was last summoned. Women were not so...outspoken."

"Summoned? *This* world." Elise pointed at the floor. "You don't honestly expect me to believe you're an alien...from space. I could believe you're an illegal alien from...somewhere."

His brows rose. "This language. It sounds curiously familiar, and yet your speech is almost incomprehensible. What place is this?"

Elise backed away a cautious step. When he didn't follow her, she relaxed fractionally. "Look. I see what the problem is now. You're not from around here. You're confused. You've made a mistake...got into the wrong house. Why don't you just go now and I won't even call the police. I swear!"

"What is po-lice?" His arms were clasped behind his back once more, his feet slightly spread. It looked like the 'at ease' stance of a military man, ramrod stiff, but Elise found it difficult to picture him in a uniform. He'd discarded the fur cloak somewhere and was once again wearing nothing but the loose breeches of before, not even shoes. The breeches rode low on his hips--she hadn't noticed that before. She wished she hadn't noticed it just now, because the bulge right below the waist band riveted her gaze for about two seconds too long.

"Cops. You know. The guys that drive the cars with the scary blue lights on top that throw you in jail?"

"Authority?"

"Uh...yeah."

He shrugged, waving one hand as if he was chasing away a pesky fly. "I have no interest in them. They have no authority over a djinn."

She hadn't really thought he would scare that easily, but she'd figured it was worth a try. "I don't suppose it'll do any good to ask you to leave?"

He frowned, anger filling his eyes. He pointed a finger at her. "You sent me to the north pole to find a man who does not exist! This is jest to you?"

Elise gaped at him. "What are you talking about?"

"I offered to grant your wish...."

Understanding dawned, but Elise didn't really want to discuss that with him, particularly since the subject seemed to be a sore point. "Could I get dressed?"

He looked taken aback. "Are you not dressed?" He reached over and took hold of the towel. For several nerve wracking minutes, Elise feared he would snatch it from her. Instead, he merely seemed to be examining the fabric.

"No, I'm not. This is just for drying off."

He nodded, made a dismissing gesture. Elise took it as permission and beat a hasty retreat to her bedroom. Slamming the door behind her, she scrambled for the phone, punching in 911 with shaking fingers. When she turned to check the door to make certain he hadn't followed her, he was standing at the foot of her bed. Letting out a shriek, Elise dropped the phone from suddenly nerveless fingers.

He glared at her. "Woman! Have I grown two heads? Cease shrieking at me!"

Elise nodded jerkily, discovered she'd dropped her towel again and snatched it up.

He frowned, stalked toward her and snatched the towel off, tossing it across the room.

Elise was still staring at him with her jaw at half cock when he turned back to look her over. Instinctively, she wrapped an arm across her breasts, covering her pubic thatch with her other hand. "You took my towel!"

"It is useless. You scream. It falls to the floor."

"I happened to be covering myself with it!" she said indignantly.

He cocked his head to one side, waving a hand dismissively in the air. "Not well. In any case, you are a beautiful woman. You have no need to hide yourself." The comment seemed to give him an idea. He studied thoughtfully for several moments, a look of cunning coming into his eyes. "If you but ask it, I could adorn you with jewels...the finest silks. Diamonds, I think. And pale silk to set off your golden hair."

This time Elise was taken aback. "I don't see how jewels would cover me," she said uneasily. "And...uh...I'm allergic to silk." Grabbing the edge of her bedspread, she pulled it up to cover herself, then wished she hadn't directed his attention to the bed.

He hadn't seemed to notice it before. Now, he looked it over with interest and moved toward it, launching himself at the mattress, where he landed with a bounce...on top of the bedspread. Elise gave it a tug, but she knew she wasn't going to be able to pull it out from under him. He must weigh every bit of two hundred fifty pounds, maybe more, all muscle... except, unfortunately, his head. He rolled onto his side, propped his head on his hand and studied her. "This is much improved from the sleeping mats used before."

Elise smiled weakly, gave the bedspread another surreptitious tug and finally gave up. Faintly, she could hear a voice on the phone at her feet. She stared down at it with longing for several moments until an idea popped into her head. "You asked what this place was when you broke into my house while ago," she said loudly. "It's 13489 Fletcher Avenue."

Raheem frowned, scooted across the bed. Elise jumped back. "Don't hurt me!" she yelled. "Please, don't hurt me! Take anything you want! Just go!"

Raheem stared at her as if she'd lost her mind, looked down at her feet and reached for the phone. Elise's heart did a back flip as he picked it up, examined it and finally put it to his ear.

"911. What's your emergency?"

"I have no emergency," Raheem said shortly.

"Sir, are you the party who called?"

Raheem gave Elise a long, hard stare. "You are the po-lice?"

"I can get them for you, sir. What's your emergency? Is there an injured woman? I thought I heard a woman's voice."

"No," Raheem said and placed the receiver very carefully back onto the cradle. To Elise's dismay, exactly as it should have been, disconnecting. She felt like stamping her foot in frustration.

Grabbing the cover, he gave it a yank, jerking Elise, who was too surprised to let go, across him. He rolled, tossing her to the bed and ending up half on top of her. Elise squeezed her eyes closed, holding her breath, trying to ignore the bare chest pressing so tightly against her breasts. When nothing happened after several moments, she opened her eyes a fraction and peered at him through her lashes. He was studying her thoughtfully. "This is a very strange world. It has changed much since I was last summoned."

"You said that before," Elise pointed out, deciding it was useless to play possum. "Where are you from?"

"My world."

"Oh. That's so helpful," Elise said sarcastically.

"I could explain, but the human mind is far too simple to grasp the concept," he said, touching a finger to her head.

She jerked away, frowned at him. "Try me."

"Another plane...elemental."

Elise gave him a skeptical look. "Ah. Right. Can I get up now?"

A faint smile curled his lips. "Mortal females were not so...interesting when last I was here." He looked her over speculatively.

A frisson of something that was part fear and part pure excitement went through Elise. She didn't want to examine it. "You really believe you're a genie, don't you?"

His brows rose. "I know I am djinn. You are asking for proof?"

"No. No! That's OK. If you say so, that's good enough for me."

He frowned, studied her face for several moments. "You fear that I will ravish you."

It wasn't a question. "I hadn't thought about it," Elise lied.

He leaned back, ran a curious, possessive hand along her body from her neck to her thighs and then upward again, sending quivers of something that should have been fear, but wasn't, all the way through her. "Alas, it is not possible. I should like to taste this little pink berry here," he said, lightly pinching first one and then the other of her nipples. "But, it can not be. It is...forbidden."

Fighting to draw in a calming breath, Elise looked at him in surprise, and not a little hope. "No?"

"No."

She wiggled out from under him and sat up. "What a shame."

Something gleamed in his eyes. One corner of his mouth tipped up slightly. "You agree? Indeed. I am tempted to make an exception."

"Oh no! I'm sure it's for the best," she said quickly, then scooted to the edge of the bed and, when he didn't stop her, got off. Backing toward the tall chest of drawers across from the bed, she began to fumble blindly for something to cover herself. Finally drawing out a pair of lacy panties and a bra, she bent to step into the panties. When she straightened to pull them up, he was standing within inches of her. She jumped reflexively, dropping the bra. Leaning down, he lifted it with one finger, studying it curiously. Elise snatched it from him and put it on. "How do you do that?"

His brows rose in a question.

"Move so fast? Without making a sound?"

"I am elemental...a djinn. As the wind."

Elise crossed her arms over her bare stomach, nodding. She felt marginally more comfortable with her underwear on, but not much, particularly when his gaze roved over her with interest. He ran a finger along the elastic waist of her panties--the inside. Elise felt her belly quiver at his touch. It took an effort to remain still, but she didn't want to appear too disturbed by the man. It might encourage him to do worse. At the moment, he seemed more curious than anything else. "What is this...garment?"

"Panties." It seemed absurd. Surely, regardless of his charade, he had to know what they were.

To her relief, he removed his finger. In the next moment, however, he'd flattened his palm over her, cupping her sex. Her eyes widened. "And this fabric?"

Elise moistened her lips. "Nylon, I guess."

"It grows?"

For one horrifying moment, Elise thought he might have noticed the dampness his nearness had produced, but then she realized he was still discussing the panties.

"Manmade."

He nodded and turned his attention to her bra, examining it as he had her panties. "You certainly are curious," Elise commented shakily, tempted to slap his hands away except for the fact that he was a foot taller than her, at least a hundred to a hundred fifty pounds heavier...and she strongly suspected he was mad as a hatter.

"This disturbs you?" He paused, studying her face.

Elise had a feeling that he knew damn well his touch disturbed her, and not altogether because he unnerved her. He'd noticed she was physically attracted to him. She knew he must have. He was toying with her. She wasn't certain why, but she had no desire to give him the satisfaction of acknowledging his suspicions. "Since you're neither my husband, nor my lover...yes," she said stiffly and retreated several steps.

He shrugged. "Dress yourself. I am interested to see the strange clothing mortals adorn themselves with now."

Folding his arms, he levitated right before her eyes, crossing his legs Indian fashion and sitting on nothing but air. Elise was so stunned she didn't move or blink for several moments. Finally, she shook herself and peered above his head. It was completely impossible that he could've rigged something in her room to manufacture the illusion--but far more unbelievable that he was actually floating. Seeing nothing, she waved a hand beneath him.

There was no question about it. He was floating.

Chapter Three

Raheem gave her a look that was both amused and faintly contemptuous.

Elise's lips tightened. Turning away abruptly, she snatched the drawers open, grabbed a pair of jeans and a knit top and dressed herself. The man had a serious superiority complex. She supposed, upon reflection, that it was warranted, at least somewhat. She certainly couldn't float on air, or walk through walls...or do anything he, apparently, could.

He seemed to consider djinns far superior intellectually, as well.

She didn't believe for a moment that he was a genie, though.... Did she?

She realized she was beginning to. It might be crazy, but if she wasn't and he was really doing the things she thought he was doing, then he certainly wasn't just an average house breaker.

Of course, he could just be a figment of her imagination, but she found it was far easier to believe he was something--not entirely human--than to believe she was hallucinating. She considered that she possessed a great deal of imagination, but she wasn't prone to hysteria and she wasn't prone to imagining things.

If she wasn't imagining him, then he had to be real. He hadn't claimed to be a ghost--strange that it occurred to her that she would've had an easier time believing that! The truth was, though, that he was not Caucasian--not any race known to man-- or to her. His skin was brown, but it was no tan. He spoke English well, but it was not his native tongue, for his speech was heavily accented.

Genies were myths from the middle East. She'd never really been 'in' to middle eastern myths. Just about everything she knew about genies arose from the few re-runs she'd watched of the old TV show about a man that had found a bottle on the beach that held a beautiful blond genie, and she had a sneaking suspicion that the TV show had taken a LOT of liberties with the old myths.

So, where did that leave her?

With no clue of how to get rid of him.

Genies were compelled to grant the wishes of the owner of the bottle, weren't they? Sort of became a slave to whoever possessed the bottle? She looked at him speculatively for several moments, but, not in her wildest imagination, could she picture this man as a slave...of any description.

She almost smacked her forehead when she remembered the 'charm' necklace she'd bought. Then she frowned. It was certainly a tiny bottle. She rolled her eyes. As IF they made bottles big enough to hold a giant like him!

The bottle must be like a gateway, or something. Elemental or not, she simply couldn't picture him being trapped in that tiny thing through the ages. At any rate, if he had been trapped, wouldn't he be glad to be freed? Not pissed? Because he'd look really pissed about the idea that he had to grant her a wish. She must have done something like trip an alarm when she'd opened it, and he'd been 'summoned.' It made sense in a nonsensical kind of way. He'd said she'd summoned him. How was she supposed to get him back in the bottle, though?

She looked around, wondering where she'd left her purse.

"What are you looking for?"

"The bottle," she said distractedly.

"Why?"

She looked up at him in surprise. He floated down, settling when he was eye level with her. "Uh...to send you back?"

A scowl descended over his features. "You can not."

Elise gave him a look. "Why?"

Something unidentifiable flickered in his eyes and was quickly hidden. "I have been summoned."

"Well, you can go back," Elise said reasonably. "I thought it was a.... Anyway, it was an accident. I'm going to send you back now."

"You thought it was...?"

Elise's lips tightened. "Don't tell me you don't read minds!" she said sarcastically.

His eyes narrowed. "Only those equal to my own," he said coolly.

"And mine is so inferior?" she demanded, her hands on her hips.

He nodded, smiling coolly.

"Pity. But good for me." She gave him a saccharin smile.

He looked disconcerted.

Turning, she left the bedroom and went into the living room. Her purse, she discovered, was on the table in the foyer, where she'd left it when she came home from work. Grabbing it, she moved back into the living room, sat on the couch and upended the purse, emptying the contents on the seat of the couch. Disentangling the necklace from a tube of mascara, she clutched it in her fist. When she looked up, the djinn, Raheem, was seated on the opposite end of the couch. She jumped reflexively, but she was beginning to grow accustomed to his abrupt appearances. Pulling the tiny cork from the neck of the bottle, she held the phial out. "Here you go!"

He gave her a look.

She didn't particularly like that look. He'd said he was the genie of the bottle. Well, he either had to show her by going back in, or cease the charade. "You have to get back in the bottle."

His eyes narrowed. He folded his arms. She waited, but he didn't disappear, or levitate...and he didn't go back in the bottle.

"Don't be stubborn now! You acted all pissy about me 'summoning' you. Go home!"

"What is this word, pissy? I do not believe I care for it."

"Too bad."

His eyes narrowed. "You are a sarcastic wench. Have a care. I can do things...most unpleasant."

"More unpleasant than your unwelcome presence?" Elise said, wondering even as she said it why she was being deliberately provocative. She should be afraid of this--man? Genie?

"Infinitely," he murmured, lifting a hand and crooking one finger at her--as *if* he had only to crook his finger and she would go to him!

She found herself on his lap.

With one arm around her shoulders to support her, he caught her chin in his other hand, his eyes narrowed, dangerous as he studied her face.

Elise swallowed with some difficulty, feeling a shudder race down her spine that was only partly fright. "How did....?"

"How? Or why?"

She licked her dry lips. His gaze followed the movement. "What?" she asked vaguely, unable to connect the words with any meaning in her mind. A rush of excitement had filled her at his nearness, his touch. She couldn't seem to think of anything except her body's reaction to him.

"Tempting," he murmured, his head drifting closer until his lips were so near her own she thought she could feel them, just brushing hers. Her lips tingled, itched for more intimate contact.

When he did nothing more, she found she couldn't bear the suspense, couldn't bear to allow him to pull away again without kissing her. She couldn't remember ever wanting anything nearly as badly. Allowing her eyelids to drift downward, she leaned closer, brushed her lips against those so tantalizingly close to her own, touched her tongue to the smooth, hard surface. A sound, like the rumbling growl of a bear escaped him. For a moment, she thought he would yield to her touch.

Abruptly, he moved away, his eyes narrowed still, though something else flickered in them now. He looked at her a long moment. "Enchantress," he murmured and vanished.

Elise blinked as she landed on the couch with a gentle bounce, then looked around, but she knew he was gone, for all the warmth and excitement had died and gone as well.

* * * *

"You should wish for a palace."

The words brought Elise wide awake. Blinking her eyes against the light streaming into her bedroom, she looked around in search of the speaker. Raheem, she saw, was pacing her room, his hands clasped behind his back, a look of contempt on his face as he examined her abode. Flopping back against the mattress, Elise pulled the covers over her head. "You again. Am I being punished or something?"

He didn't respond and after a moment, Elise lowered the covers again to see what he was doing. He'd paused by the bed and picked up the framed picture of John. A shaft of anger went through her. She snatched the picture from him, clutching it against her chest.

He lifted his brows at her. "Who is this man?"

"My husband, John," she said stiffly.

His brows rose. "Where is this husband?"

Elise looked away. "Gone," she said flatly and scooted to the edge of the bed. Pulling the drawer of her bedside table open, she carefully placed the picture frame inside and closed the drawer. When she sat back and pushed her hair from her eyes, she saw Raheem had extended his hand. Without a whisper of sound, the drawer slid from the night stand and levitated, hovering before him. He examined the contents curiously while Elise gaped at him with a combination of surprise and irritation. Before she could demand that he put it back however, he reached inside and pulled a plastic packet out. "What is this?"

Elise blushed to the roots of her hair. "Birth control," she mumbled, trying to snatch it from him.

He ignored her, opening the packet and tossing the wrapper aside, then held the condom up and looked at it. "How is this used?"

Elise's lips tightened. She got up abruptly and headed for the bathroom. "You're so smart, you figure it out."

She slammed the door behind her.

Much good it did.

He appeared before her, a look of smug satisfaction on his face. Elise wasn't looking at his face, however.

He was wearing the damned condom...and absolutely nothing else.

"Aren't you the clever one?" she muttered a little weakly, tearing her gaze from the unnerving member and moving past him to the shower. "Do you mind?" she asked, tossing a glance at his face.

He waved a hand.

"I want to take a shower now."

He nodded.

"Go away!"

"Where?"

"Mars might be far enough."

He vanished and Elise relaxed fractionally, relieved herself, then tossed her night clothes aside and got into the shower. The hot water revived her but it did nothing to calm her jittery nerves or her aggravation. If she couldn't get rid of the damned genie, they were at least going to have to come to terms with the bathroom issue.

When she wiped the water from her face, Raheem was standing directly in front of her, scowling. "It is a barren world."

Elise gaped at him. "What are you doing in my damned shower!"

"You are an ill tempered wench!"

"You should talk!" Elise said, planting her hands on her hips.

He stepped closer, until their bodies were nearly brushing. "You have not seen my wrath!" he growled.

Elise's eyes widened. Abruptly, she remembered she was naked and covered herself. The washcloth was woefully inadequate, however.

Distracted by her movements, he looked down, his eyes narrowing. "You cover yourself from my sight."

"Don't look and I won't have to," Elise said shortly. "I really, really prefer to be alone when I'm in here."

A gleam entered his eyes, banishing his ill temper. As abruptly as he'd appeared, he disappeared. Elise felt more than a little uneasy about that gleam in his eyes, however.

* * * *

Elise told herself, at least a dozen times, that she was relieved. She hadn't seen Raheem in days. She didn't know what she'd said that had finally convinced him to remove himself from her life, but she was glad. She'd been surprised, but relieved, when she returned from work and found him absent. She'd almost overslept the following day because she'd more than half expected him to wake her and he hadn't. When two days passed with her expecting him to reappear at any moment and he didn't, she began to relax and fall back into her normal routine.

The little stopper was still in the bottle, however.

She was fairly certain he couldn't have gone back to his own world when the gateway was blocked to him.

The third day after her final encounter with the difficult djinn, Raheem, Elise decided, for no particular reason, that it was time she collected John's possessions and packed them away. She'd left everything pretty much as it had been since they'd moved into the house. She hadn't wanted anything else in her life to change. The house, at least, must remain comfortingly familiar.

Now, however, she felt a restlessness for change.

She decided it was spring fever...a little early, perhaps, with spring still weeks away, but undoubtedly that was it.

She started by emptying his closet. Despite her resolve to pack away the memories with John's things, she found she couldn't resist sniffing his clothes for any telltale scent of him that might linger.

She was disappointed. The clothing merely smelled of laundry detergent and dust, but she refused to allow her disappointment to get a firm grip on her, dismissing it, busying herself collecting everything except the picture in her night stand and packing it up to take to charity.

As she was bending over to set the last of the boxes in the hallway, the sleeve of her T-shirt fell off. Elise stared at the wedge of cloth, and then down at herself in stunned surprise. The threads hadn't even seemed loose. How could it just fall off?

Frowning, she picked the piece of fabric up and examined it. There was no sign of rot. Apparently, the thread in the seams had just given way.

How very odd! "That'll teach me to shop at discount stores," she muttered, clutching the fabric in her hand as she started to her room to find another shirt. She'd reached the door of the room when the side seam of the T-shirt gave way. The remains of the shirt slid down her arm, bringing her to an abrupt halt. "Thank God I didn't go out in this," she said, leaning over to retrieve the scraps of fabric and wadding them into a ball. Crossing the room, she pulled a drawer out and found another shirt. As she turned, slipping her arms into the shirt, then lifting them over her head to pull the new shirt on, her shorts fell to her feet.

Aborting the attempt to pull the shirt over her head, Elise gaped at her shorts on the floor uncomprehendingly.

A deep chuckle brought her around with a jerk.

Raheem was sprawled across the foot of her bed, his head propped in his hand. As she watched, he lifted his hand, pointing at her, then wiggled his forefinger.

Her bra fell off.

She gasped, covering her breasts with the shirt she still held in her hands.

It was at that point that her panties dropped to her ankles.

When she looked up again, Raheem had vanished.

Chapter Four

Elise did not delude herself into believing Raheem had vanished for good. Two days passed without him, with her jumping at every creak of the house, checking each room for him when she came in in the evenings--dressing, or changing with frantic haste.

She'd made a serious mistake in making it so obvious that nudity unnerved her. She'd given Raheem the means to revenge himself upon her for sending him off to the north pole on a wild goose chase.

The devil.

She hadn't even had the chance to 'wish' that he would not intrude on her privacy in the bath. Not that she was at all certain that he would honor the wish, but she'd like to think she could brush her teeth, bathe and...pee without an audience.

She spent a good deal of time trying to think of a wish she could make that would permanently remove him from her life, that he couldn't twist into something unpleasant.

Finally, after nearly a week of restless sleep, she came in from work and fell asleep on the couch in front of the TV.

It was a chill breath of air that woke her. Disoriented, she sat up, rubbing her neck, glancing around sleepily to see if she could figure out where the draft was coming from. When she first saw the mound of clothing on the floor at her feet, she merely looked at it blankly, wondering when and why she'd left laundry on the floor by the couch.

Her bare legs came into focus just about the time the clothing began to snake across the floor toward her bedroom as if they were alive. Reflexively, she jerked her feet off the floor, thinking, at first, that something was under the clothes. When her bare knees made contact with her bare breasts, however, everything fell into place.

"Raheem!" she shouted, jumping to her feet.

He didn't answer, but her clothing continued to slither in the direction of her bedroom. She darted for them, trying to catch them before they were completely beyond reach, but each time she reached to sweep them up, they jerked beyond her grasp.

"This isn't funny!"

The only answer was a splash from the direction of the bathroom.

Stalking toward the door, Elise flung it open.

Raheem was lounging back in her whirlpool, a wicked smile curling the corners of his lips.

Elise plunked her hands on her hips, but, to her chagrin, she couldn't think of anything to say.

Lifting a hand, he crooked a finger at her.

Elise grabbed frantically for the door frame.

She landed on his water slick chest and slid down it. Scrambling frantically for purchase, she finally managed to lever herself up, but before she could leap from the tub, Raheem grasped her firmly about the waist and settled her on his lap...straddling him. A hard ridge of flesh rose to snuggle between her spread thighs, nudging against the crevice of her body.

Wide eyed, she looked up at Raheem.

He wasn't smiling anymore.

Elise's heart was thundering in her chest until she could hardly catch her breath. It should have been fear. It wasn't.

If she'd harbored any misapprehensions that the djinn was a dangerous...entity...she could no longer delude herself. She was certain that that was the main objective of the little demonstration he'd just given her, that he could be anywhere and she would not know it, do anything. She was fortunate he hadn't decided to do anything really unpleasant.

The rational part of her mind knew all of that. The sensory part of her mind was flooding her body with the natural chemicals of pleasure, making her skin hypersensitive in anticipation of pleasurable stimulation. She didn't know whether to be glad, or further unnerved that Raheem was no more able to control his body's response to her than she to him.

Djinn or not, she could see that Raheem had snared himself by snaring her. His erection was proof enough of that, but desire shown in his darkening eyes, as well, his pupils dilating with need at their proximity.

Inwardly, she struggled against the compulsion to give in to her clamoring body, to throw caution to the wind and push him past self-control. To distract herself, she said the first thing that came to mind. "Why did you call me enchantress before?"

She blushed the moment the words were out. It sounded as if she was fishing for compliments. She knew, though, that he hadn't meant the comment as a compliment. She thought for several moments he wouldn't answer.

"You are not?"

"Something like a witch?" She shook her head. "Why would you think that?"

Instead of answering, he frowned, looked down at her, studying her body in a leisurely fashion that threatened her self-control. "It is written that evil will befall those who yield to the temptation of the flesh. I have not...been tempted before."

Biblical, and yet she didn't believe he meant it quite that way. "If the djinn should yield to the temptation to...lie with a mortal, you mean?"

His gaze returned to her face. After a moment, he nodded ever so slightly.

She should not have been so pleased that he had admitted he found her as tempting as she did him. He'd left her in no doubt of how very dangerous he was...and he was not of her world...and she was not the sort of woman to whom casual sex appealed, which meant that, even if the curse of the djinn did not touch her, she was still in danger of having 'evil' befall her if she yielded to temptation.

"It's emotional as much as physical...."

A scowl descended over his features. "The djinn does not suffer the weakness of emotion. We are far too superior to be vulnerable to human weaknesses."

Elise's lips tightened with anger, but she knew very well that it wasn't his superior attitude so much as the fear that he spoke the truth, that he was immune to those emotions that could so easily devastate her. "You suffer from temper and conceit!" she snapped. "If that's not emotion, I'm damned if I know what is!"

"You are only human. You can not be expected to comprehend."

"No?"

"No," he said coolly.

Elise studied him a long moment and leaned toward him. A wary look came into his eyes, but he did not move away. She brushed her lips lightly across his, then gently kissed the corner of his mouth. "I think I understand far more than you do," she whispered.

She felt a tremor run through him. For a moment she thought that she had pushed him too far. His hands slipped upward from her waist to just below her breasts, his fingers tightening as if he fought a round with himself as to whether to push her away or pull her closer.

Abruptly, he vanished. Elise, who'd been leaning toward him, nearly lost her balance and landed in the tub face first. "Coward!" she growled at the empty air.

He didn't respond, but she didn't believe he'd gone far. "Fine! You don't want to be tempted--I wish that you will never come into this room again when I'm in here! You hear me? Or take off my clothes!"

"That is two wishes. I will only grant one."

The voice came from no where and everywhere at once. Elise's head whipped around, but he had not materialized again. "Fine! The first one, then. But if you're so damned worried about temptation you should seriously consider NOT taking my clothes off or touching me! It's a damned sight easier to resist temptations of the flesh when you're not rubbing naked body parts!"

The encounter spawned such vivid erotic dreams that Elise would have wondered if they had actually happened except for one crucial detail. When she awoke, her body was on fire with unfulfilled desire. Exhausted as she was from such troubled sleep, she realized almost immediately that the nightclothes she'd gone to bed in had disappeared. Struggling up on one elbow, she looked over the side of the bed. Sure enough, her gown and panties lay in a heap beside the bed.

In her dreams, she'd taken them off and tossed them onto the floor, but she didn't believe for one moment that she'd done it in reality. Sure enough, even as she reached for the gown, it slithered across the floor. She stared at the creeping bit of lingerie dully and finally flopped back onto the bed, arms spread wide. "Have it your way!"

Despite her irritation, exhaustion almost got the best of her. She was drifting to sleep once more when she became aware of a presence. Opening her eyes, she saw without much surprise that Raheem was watching her.

She glared at him. "What did I do to deserve having you worry the hell out of me?"

"You breached the gateway."

Elise sat up abruptly and looked at him. He was lying on his side, his head propped on his hand, but he hovered above the bed by more than a foot. "The bottle's a gateway?"

"You had surmised as much."

"So you're the djinn of the gateway? Not the bottle?"

"Guardian."

Elise studied him a long moment and finally got out of bed and went into the bathroom. To her relief, he didn't follow her. She supposed that meant that she'd used up another wish and wondered how many more she would have to use up before he would leave forever and allow her life to return to normal.

The thought brought a lump to her throat. Normal. Boring, lonely--

She shook those thoughts off. It was her own fault that her life was boring and lonely. She'd chosen to avoid relationships since John's death. She could choose *not* to avoid them and sooner or later, surely, she would meet someone who would make her happy.

No one could replace John, but she neither wanted nor needed a replacement. She needed someone else.

As far as that went, she was an adult. She could seek the entertainment available to adults. She could make new friends, reacquaint herself with old friends, go out and do things. She didn't have to confine herself to the day-to-day drudge of work then home then work again.

It was dangerous even to consider how much she would've liked to have Raheem around indefinitely, when he couldn't stay indefinitely even if he wanted to. Sooner or later, once he'd done what he came to do, performed whatever ritual it was that he had to perform to seal the gateway once more, he would return to his own world and his own concerns.

She decided she must have a streak of masochism. Raheem aggravated her endlessly. Why would she *want* to have someone around who went out of his way to tease and torment her? He was handsome in a purely male way, exotic even. He had a gorgeous body--any red blooded female would lust after a man than looked like Raheem.

But, of course, the problem was, he wasn't a man. He just looked like one--felt like one--acted like one most of the time. It was an illusion--an illusion that had made her feel alive for the first time in almost two years.

It occurred to her quite suddenly that, just as she'd revealed a weakness he could exploit, he had revealed one. He lusted for her. He didn't dare act upon it--which was a pity, but still a safety net for her.

She could torment him as much as he tormented her.

A wicked smile curled her lips as she stepped out of the shower and dried off. She hesitated. Her acute modesty was no act. She had never really gotten comfortable about being completely naked around her husband--not in the sense that she felt at ease strolling around the house undressed.

On the other hand, there was no time like the present to rid herself of inhibitions. She tossed the towel aside and, with as much unconcern as she could muster, strolled out of the bathroom and into her bedroom.

Raheem, she saw from the corner of her eye, still hovered over her bed. Ignoring him, she selected her clothes and dressed at leisure, like a strip tease in reverse.

When she dared a glance at him finally, the glitter in his eyes unnerved her, but it also sent a shaft of need through her, making it patently obvious that she could no more tease him in such a way with complete impunity than he could her.

* * * *

Elise was a long way from being independently wealthy, although her friends seemed to think she was. She'd invested most of the money from John's life insurance and earned a modest, supplemental income sufficient to survive in reasonable comfort whether she worked or not. He'd had life insurance on the car and the house as well, and those had been paid off after his death...which to the average American, was virtually the same as being wealthy.

She would've rather had John.

Nothing in life was more certain, however, than that one could never have everything, or even mostly have, what one wanted most.

She worked part time as an EMT. She'd wondered if she'd lost her mind when it had first occurred to her to take the training, because she would be exposing herself almost daily to the same tragedy that had cost her her happiness.

There was comfort, however, in being there to help others, in thinking that she might make a difference for someone else...if she was fast enough in reaching the scene, and skilled enough to save those she went to help.

Tired as she was when she finished her shift, she was also tense. Instead of going directly home, she decided to stop by the library and see what she could find out about the djinn.

She found several books. A good bit of the information was conflicting. The djinn was an evil being; the djinn was mischievous, a trickster, rather than the personification of evil. The finder of the vessel could call forth the genie and the genie, a slave to the master of the lamp, or whatever, was forced to grant wishes. However, the genie, having been summoned and not too pleased about it, had a tendency to twist the wishes. If someone wished for a million bucks, they didn't get a million dollars. They got a million bucks.

She thought about Raheem. There was no doubt in her mind that he was dangerous, but evil?

She realized she didn't want to believe that he was, but did that mean, deep down, that she'd sensed he was? Or that he wasn't?

An hour later, she had assured herself that there was nothing at all in the books about sex between a mortal and a genie--She hadn't even realized she was looking for a reference to it until she'd drawn a blank.

A blush climbed her cheeks and she looked around guiltily.

Raheem was sitting cross legged on the library table across from her.

Elise gasped, clutching the book to her chest as her heart lurched painfully.

"What have you there?"

The blush that had scarcely died, flashed into her cheeks in a tidal wave. "Nothing," she said quickly. "Really."

He opened his hand and the book flew from her fingers and into his grasp. He fanned the pages and handed it back to her. "This is not correct."

"Which part?"

He waved his fingers in the air dismissively. "What would you like to know?"

Elise looked at him suspiciously. "Could I trust you to tell the truth?"

He gave her an affronted look. "I have no reason to lie."

"Except that you might want to," Elise countered.

A gleam entered his eyes. His lips twitched. "You are surprisingly astute for a mortal...particularly a female."

"You're sexist!" Elise gasped, outraged.

"I do not know this word. What does it mean?"

"It means you assume superiority based on gender!"

"Ah." He laid down on the table, propping his head on his elbow. "These are enlightened times?"

He was baiting her. She crossed her arms over her chest. "I might have known you would be...you are from the dark ages, after all."

"Where were these dark ages?"

She shrugged. "I'm not a historian. A thousand years ago, at least...I think."

He frowned, apparently studying over it. "When last I was summoned, a mortal by the name of Attila was raping and pillaging Europe. That was...." He stroked his beard, contemplating.

Elise's jaw dropped. "Attila...the Hun, you mean?"

"He is known here?"

"Good God! You can't be that old!" Elise exclaimed.

He chuckled. "Age is a concept of mortals. I am as I have always been, as I will always be. This form you see is no more than a manifestation of my...spirit, if you will. The djinn exist without form."

Elise stared at him in dismay. It was almost the same as saying he was merely a ghost. Was that to be her lot in life? Always to be chasing ghosts?

That thought, erupting from her subconscious without her even having been aware of the emotion behind it, stunned her. Until that moment, she had not acknowledged, even to herself, that she was drawn to the djinn in ways that should never have occurred to her.

It had seemed harmless enough to acknowledge a physical attraction to him--it was impossible to ignore, at any rate--but it didn't really matter whether it was something that could, or should, be acted upon. She'd been sexually attracted to men who were unattainable more than once in her life. Just like most everyone else, there'd been models, movie stars...singers, even men she'd met in her day to day life, that she'd daydreamed about, knowing it would never be anything else. It was a harmless form of excitement so long as one didn't allow it to get out of hand.

She'd been secure from any more heartache, though, because she still loved John. She could not allow herself to become emotionally attached to yet another 'ghost' or she was dooming herself to a life of loneliness, and here she was, already well on her way to just that.

Abruptly, she began to close the books that lay open around her on the library table, gathering them up. She was aware of Raheem's frowning observation, but he said nothing and she wasn't about to volunteer answers to questions that had not been asked.

A gasp behind her distracted her and she turned to see one of the librarians come to an abrupt halt at the end of the aisle behind her. "What...are you doing? You must get down at once!"

Elise glanced from the woman to Raheem, who'd sat up and was staring at the woman in dawning fury. Even as she watched, he lifted a hand and pointed a finger at the woman. Without thinking, she leapt to her feet and grabbed his hand. "Don't! Please don't!" she whispered anxiously. "She's a nice lady. Don't do...anything to her."

Raheem stared at her angrily, then glanced at her hands for a long moment. Something flickered in his eyes. Abruptly, he nodded at her and vanished.

"What...where did he go?" Alicia Chaney asked, bewildered.

Elise glanced at her. "My...uh...friend, you mean?"

"That...He was a friend of yours?"

"Well...more of a new acquaintance, I guess," Elise said, smiling faintly. "I asked him to wait for me outside."

Alicia frowned, still looking more than a little confused.

"What in the world was he doing up on the table?"

Elise shrugged, smiling wryly. "He's a...uh foreigner. He's not used to the way things are here. It won't happen again."

The librarian was still looking around, as if she expected momentarily to see Raheem. "No. We can't have that. He could fall, get hurt. You must explain to him."

"I will, but I won't bring him back again. Anyway, I think he'll be going home soon."

Chapter Five

Elise had more than half expected to find Raheem lounging on the couch when she reached the house. He wasn't. Her sixth sense told her even before she'd searched the house that he was not there at all, but she looked anyway.

She was disappointed when she found he wasn't. The disappointment was dismaying. She hadn't even known him a month ago. She should not be expecting, or looking forward to, finding him in her house.

It was her fault. Her friends had been trying to get her to circulate for more than a year. Even her mother, while acknowledging that grief was something that only time lessened, had pointed out that, at twenty five, she was far too young to withdraw from life, that she needed to socialize, give herself the chance to meet someone...consider having a family. She'd thought she was reasonably content. She had no desire to settle for less than she'd had before, and no belief that loving another man even nearly as much as John was a possibility.

Obviously, she was far more lonely than she'd acknowledged to herself. If not, she would not have been so susceptible to the first 'male' who refused to be ignored, would she?

Sighing, she glanced disinterestedly through her mail and tossed it onto the hall table. Restless, she decided after several moments to cruise the web for a while. She wasn't hungry and it was too early in the evening to find anything, except the news, on TV. Booting the computer, she went into the kitchen to find a cold drink and then returned to her small home office and connected to the internet.

There was more junk mail in her mail box than anything else. After cleaning out the junk mail, she answered the few personal messages and checked out a couple of her favorite chat rooms.

Without much surprise, she saw that only a few people were in the rooms, none that she generally 'visited' with.

Losing interest, she went to a search engine and pulled up pages referencing genies. Three hours later, she had a headache and was no wiser than before. The djinn was believed to be a being, or spirit, that existed on another plane--as Raheem had told her.

Leaving the desk, she found the charm she'd bought and settled on the couch with it. If she simply removed the tiny stopper and left it, would Raheem return to his own world? Or would she be 'inviting' others to emerge from the tiny gateway?

She wasn't really surprised when two legs appeared before her, but her heart did a little double trip. Determinedly, she put it down to surprise. She looked up slowly. Raheem was standing before her in his 'at ease' stance, studying her.

"You are a curious creature."

Elise frowned. "That's so flattering."

He cocked his head to one side. "Have you decided upon a wish?"

She sighed, then bit her lip as a thought occurred to her. "I asked you to give a message to Santa for me ...."

He glared at her ferociously, but there was a gleam of amusement in his eyes. "You must wish for that which exists."

Sadness filled her at his words. She nodded.

"I could give you wealth beyond imagining," he said coaxingly.

Elise smiled faintly. For a moment, she allowed her imagination to run wild; thinking of yachts, mansions, designer wear...trips around the world. But they were all material things, things that would bring enjoyment for a little while and then cease to bring any joy at all. Who would she share them with? People whose only interest was in acquiring material things for themselves? Who had no real interest in her? Or, worse, who would plot to knock her off just so they could have the things for themselves?

"You don't have the power to give me what I really want," she said finally.

He frowned. "The man whose image appears beside your bed?"

"In the picture," she corrected, nodding.

"He has passed into the dark world?"

"That's one way of putting it. He no longer exists, except in my memory."

He snapped his fingers. Abruptly, a man appeared next to him. The man looked stunned, confused and more than a little angry.

Elise was equally stunned. She stared at the man uncomprehendingly for several moments, then slowly, like someone sleepwalking, stood up and touched the man. He jumped and began to speak to her in a language she didn't recognize.

She didn't need to understand his language to know what he was saying, however. It was obvious the man was as stunned and unnerved to find himself in her living room as she was to see him. He was not John. He resembled him a great deal, but it was most definitely no more than a similarity.

She turned and glared at Raheem. "Send him back!"

The djinn chuckled. "He is what you wished for."

"He is NOT!" Elise snapped angrily.

The djinn walked around the man, studying him closely. "He looks much the same."

Elise threw the charm at him.

No one was more surprised than she was when the charm struck him just above one of his wickedly arched brows. She gaped at Raheem, horrified. He looked at her as if she'd grown horns. The stranger looked at both of them as if he'd found himself in a lunatic asylum.

Abruptly, both Raheem and the stranger vanished. Elise found that she was shaking. She stared down at the tiny charm that had landed on the floor, fighting the temptation to walk over to it and crush it with her shoe.

Instead, she scooped the charm up, studied it for several moments and finally went into her room and tossed it into her lingerie drawer.

After pacing for a time, she decided, maybe, she was just going stir crazy. Pulling her address book from her purse, she thumbed through it until she found the number of one of her coworkers. She'd gone out with Lonnie a couple of times, but had discovered by the end of the first date that there simply was no spark. All the same, Lonnie seemed more than a little interested in her.

She called him and asked him out to dinner.

* * * *

"You look good enough to eat!" Lonnie said with a grin when he met her outside the restaurant.

Elise smiled with an effort. It was a compliment...not particularly to her taste, but well intentioned. "Thanks!"

He crowded close, pressing her back against her car. She slipped away. "We should go in before the place gets too crowded."

He shrugged, grinned and fell into step beside her. "I was surprised when you called."

"Sorry. I know it was short notice."

"No problem. It's just that, after what you said about not dating coworkers, I didn't expect to hear from you again."

Elise was saved from answering immediately by their arrival at the hostess' station. Unfortunately, she still hadn't come up with a good explanation by the time they were seated. "I still don't think it's a good idea...but, we *are* friends," she said a little hopefully. "I figured, even if we weren't actually dating, there was no reason why we couldn't go out...as friends, you know."

He frowned. He was studying the menu, but Elise didn't delude herself into believing the frown was from concentration. His smile, when he looked up at her, was a little strained. "I'm not really 'in' to having female friends."

She supposed she should appreciate his honesty, even if she didn't particularly care for his bluntness. There were plenty of guys, she was sure, who would've been willing to go along with the suggestion that they were 'just friends' until they got the chance to jump her bones. Before she could think of any comment, his smile broadened to a grin.

"Now, if we're talking fuck buddies, I could deal with that."

Elise gaped at him, feeling blood flood her cheeks, then glanced around quickly to see if anyone had overheard him. Thankfully, there was no sign that anyone had. "That's a little hazardous these days, isn't it?"

He shrugged. "That's part of the excitement."

The statement gave Elise cold chills. How could she have forgotten that the main reason she'd stopped seeing Lonnie was because he was a class A jerk? She forced a smile. "I've never been one for 'Russian Roulette' myself."

He looked her over and shook his head. "That's the part that really surprised me about you. To look at you, nobody'd ever guess you were such a tight ass."

Elise cleared her throat, looked up uncomfortably at the waiter who'd appeared beside the table just in time to hear the remark. The polite smile she'd plastered on her face froze.

It was Raheem.

He was dressed like all the other waiters in the restaurant, but it was hardly a disguise.

The rest of the evening passed in a blur. She had no idea of what she ordered, or ate, or what Lonnie said...until he suggested they go back to her place and his glass mysteriously tipped over the edge of the table, filling his lap with beer.

That ended the evening abruptly and she and Lonnie parted company.

She supposed she should have been angry, but the truth was she was relieved that she wouldn't have to try to fend off Lonnie's determined efforts to get laid.

* * * *

It was the worst wreck, bar none, that she had seen since she'd begun working as an EMT. There were times when she'd thought she was growing numb to the carnage, but every time she thought so she was called out on another wreck and discovered she was far from numb.

A truck driver had apparently fallen asleep at the wheel. The semi had jackknifed, taking out three cars and killing or maiming everyone inside. The car directly behind the semi had burned a streak of rubber in the pavement at least a hundred feet long, but still hadn't been able to stop. They'd gone under the truck. They'd been wearing their seat belts, pinned to the back of their seats so that the truck took their heads off. The girls had been in their teens.

A family of four had been driving the first car to hit the careening truck head on. The young mother and the toddler were dead, the father probably vegatized--the infant had come off almost unscathed...orphaned, but uninjured.

Elise had done her best to calm the screaming infant, but she wasn't used to babies. She didn't know what to do to. Despite her best efforts, tears of helpless frustration and pity filled her own eyes as she walked and bounced the baby, cuddled it, patted its back...nothing seemed to work and she knew it was because the baby wanted its mother.

She'd moved away from the highway, on the other side of the van from the traffic, hoping the quieter spot might help her to calm the baby. Raheem appeared abruptly and she looked up at him helplessly.

"I can't get her to stop crying," she said, her chin wobbling.

Raheem studied her a long moment and reached for the baby, bouncing it above his head. Unnerved, Elise moved closer, fearing he'd drop it. To her amazement, the baby stopped crying, staring at Raheem in open mouthed wonder...hiccoughing, but too frightened of him, or too stunned, to cry. Settling the baby in the crook of his arm, he pointed a finger, moving it in a tiny circle. Sparkles of dancing lights appeared, rainbow colored, swirling. The baby gaped at the swirl of light and color, fascinated. After a moment, she offered up a coo of appreciation.

Elise was as fascinated as the baby...though not with the light show. She would never, in her wildest imaginings, have thought that Raheem could be so gentle, so...good with a baby.

For the first time, she wondered if he had a woman, and children, of his own.

"You have children?" she asked tentatively.

He glanced at her, surprise evident in his features, then frowned. "No."

"But...how did you do that? She stopped crying the minute you took her."

His eyes gleamed with amusement. "Women find me irresistible."

Elise laughed. "They must."

He looked past her, as if he saw, or heard something she hadn't. Handing the child back to her, he vanished.

Elise looked around in time to see a police woman rounding the end of the van. "Your partner needs you. I'll take the baby. We're going to carry her down to family and children services until we can locate relatives...could be awhile. They were from out of town."

Elise handed the baby over, watching with a mixture of guilt, relief and sadness as the police woman walked away with the confused baby.

"This is no work for women."

Elise glanced sharply toward the sound of his voice, not particularly surprised to see that Raheem had reappeared.

"It's no work for anyone. Someone has to be willing to help, though."

His eyes narrowed. "It is easier for some than others. You are too empathetic to the pain of others."

"I wouldn't want to be lying beside the road dying and have someone who didn't care helping me."

He cocked his head to one side, studying her. "You can not undo the past."

Elise's head snapped around. "No...." A thought occurred to her quite suddenly, however. "You could. Couldn't you? Take me back so that we could get here more quickly? The baby's mother...she died before we reached the scene. If we'd been here sooner ...."

Raheem's lips tightened as he studied the pleading in her eyes. In all the time that he had been guardian of the gate, he had never once questioned whether it would be wise, or right, to grant a wish demanded. It had certainly never occurred to him to warn the unwary. He found, however, that he could not simply do it without warning her. "What you ask is...impossible. I can not grant it."

Elise stared at him in stunned dismay, but something in his eyes told her he was lying to her. "Can't? Or won't?"

"You can not change the past," Raheem said angrily.

"Why? If I had another chance ...."

"It would be the same. It was meant to be or it would not have happened."

Elise's lips tightened. "I don't believe in manifest destiny! We have choices. There wouldn't be any point to even try if nothing we did made any difference."

"You do not understand your own world--it is balanced, carefully maintained balance. When something is taken from here, then something must be taken there, or there. Balance must be regained."

"You've asked me what I wanted, over and over. I made a wish!" Elise said angrily.

Raheem shook his head. "It is one that will bring you regret."

Before Elise could say anything else, she found herself in the EMT van once more. In surprise, she looked over at her partner, who was driving like a madman, whipping around cars, weaving in and out between stopped vehicles.

"Where are we headed?"

Alan, her partner, threw a frowning glance at her. "The crash on the freeway."

Elise gulped, her leaping in her chest. "I meant, what route?"

"The Fowler exit's closest."

"They said it was near the Busch Boulevard exit. Why don't we cut across to Busch? The traffic on the interstate is bound to be backed up."

He frowned, but shrugged. "You might be right."

The scene looked different approaching it from the opposite direction. The moment Alan parked the van, she was out the door and racing to the back to help with the equipment. "This car!" she shouted when Alan turned toward the car wedged beneath the tractor trailer. "I think I hear a baby."

They ran to the car as fast as they could carrying the heavy cases of equipment and medical supplies, but when they arrived at the car, Elise came to an abrupt halt. The car was crushed in on both sides. It hadn't been like this before. She remembered. The driver's side had been crushed in, but the passenger side hadn't had nearly so much damage. With an effort, she forced herself on, reaching the car as Alan leaned through the broken window to check the driver, then shown his flashlight around the rest of the car. He shook his head. "I think we're wasting our time here. Looks like they're all dead."

Elise stared at him. His voice was barely audible, as if he were yelling at her from a great distance. "They can't all be dead!"

Numbly, she watched as he moved around the car, checking each for any sign of a pulse.

"Over here!" someone shouted. "We've got some people over here."

Elise turned as Alan rushed away. The policeman was standing beside the car the two teenage girls had been driving.

Elise stared after him. "This isn't right. They died. The baby lived. Raheem! Put it back the way it was!"

He appeared beside her. "You choose the baby?"

Elise stared at him. "It's not my choice!"

"It is not."

Elise swung the heavy case at him. It missed him, but the momentum of her swing carried her off balance. She should have fallen. Surprisingly enough, she didn't. Raheem righted her, steadied her. "Go away!" Elise said angrily. "Just get out of my life!"

Chapter Six

If Elise had been in any frame of mind to think, she would have realized that she was not in the best of conditions for driving. Numbness had stolen over her while she'd worked with Alan to stabilize the two girls for transport. Both were in critical condition, but expected to pull through Alan had told her when she'd clocked out. She'd nodded.

She was glad...happy for their families.

She couldn't get the baby's tiny face out of her head, though.

She'd held it, comforted it.

One life was not, should not be, more important than another.

She had helped to save the lives of the girls. She should feel euphoric. If she had not gotten her wish--if she had simply done her job and ignored the rest--

She was fortunate that it was late and the traffic light. She was not paying as much attention to her driving as she should have.

Raheem was sitting on the couch when she came in the front door. She stared at him a long moment, then dropped her purse on the floor and went into the bathroom. Filling the tub with hot water, she turned on the jets, disrobed and climbed in. The hot, pounding water eased the tension from her. After a few minutes, she covered her face with her hands and cried until she couldn't cry any more.

Exhausted, she climbed out of the tub with an effort, dried off and dropped the towel on the floor. It took an effort to walk from the bathroom to the bed and climb in. She didn't bother to turn out the lights. She wasn't tired enough to sleep...or, more precisely, she wasn't weary. She was heartsick.

Sitting in the middle of the bed, she wrapped her arms around her knees and stared at nothing in particular, willing her mind to go blank so that she didn't have to remember, or think.

She was aware of Raheem, but she ignored him.

Maybe, she thought, he'll get tired of being ignored and go away.

No such luck!

It didn't take Raheem long at all to grow tired of being ignored. He began to pace back and forth beside the bed. "You must cease this!" he growled finally.

Elise looked up at him dully. "I'm not doing anything."

"Exactly!" He'd stopped directly beside her, his legs spread, his balled fists planted on his hips.

She frowned at him, feeling the first stirrings of emotion once more. She didn't particularly want to feel anything and it made her angry that Raheem seemed determined to make her feel. "Go away!"

"You are being childish!"

Elise glared at him, the anger rushing through her like a tidal wave of acid. "Why did you do it? She was a precious little baby. How could you have done that after you'd held her? Played with her?"

To her surprise something curiously akin to pain flickered in his eyes. "I warned you," he said angrily.

"But you didn't have to twist it like that! I wanted to help them, not make it even worse!"

He caught her upper arms in a bruising grip, dragging her toward him until she was on her knees on the edge of the bed, facing him. "That was not my doing!"

"You made it happen differently!" Elise yelled at him.

"I allowed the past to replay itself. I warned you! There is always balance! If you change something, everything changes!"

Elise stared at him a long moment, feeling the fight go out of her as everything she'd done differently played through her mind. It didn't seem logical, when she was not even involved in the wreck itself, that anything she might have done could've changed anything, but then, she'd intended to change everything, hadn't she? What had made her stupid enough to think that she could outsmart nature, or whatever force it was that kept the world and everything in it in balance? "It was my fault, then."

He studied her a long moment, looking as if he was tempted to shake her until her teeth rattled. Instead, he pulled her roughly against his chest. Threading his fingers through her hair, he tugged her head back and bent to cover her mouth with his own in a kiss that was both angry and possessive.

Elise stiffened at the punishing assault, but the sensations that rushed through her were anything but unwelcome. He had pinned her arms to her sides and she could do nothing but wrap them tightly around his waist, opening her mouth to the marauding invasion of his tongue.

He released her so abruptly, she fell backwards on the bed, staring up at him with a mixture of surprise and desire as pain and disappointment slowly took their place. He was breathing raggedly, molten desire in his eyes, but confusion, as well.

The urge to cry washed through her again. Her eyes filled with tears that cut trails along her cheeks.

Raheem frowned. "Woman! Do not weep at me!" He scrubbed a shaking hand over his face. "This can not be. I am a djinn. I can not be as you are without being mortal, as well--to feel all that a human feels is to *be* human."

Nothing he said made any sense to her beyond the fact that he had made it clear he would not offer her comfort. She shook her head slowly, sniffed, mopped the tears from her cheeks with her hand. "I just...don't want to think about what happened. I can't stop thinking about the baby, can't put her little face out of my mind."

Abruptly, he bent toward her, scooping her up, pulling her roughly against his chest and wrapping his arms around her. Elise buried her face against his chest, sliding her arms around his waist gratefully. All she'd really wanted was to be comforted. "I wish I could just forget all of it," she mumbled, bursting into fresh tears.

Raheem pulled slightly away from her, tugged her chin up so that she was looking up at him. After a moment, he brushed his fingers lightly over her face. "As you wish, myska."

Elise blinked, found her eyes were filled with tears and blinked again. Finally, Raheem's face came into focus. "What does myska mean?"

He released her abruptly, frowning. "It is what you call...pesky. Like the fly."

A faint smile curled Elise's lips. "Liar."

Raheem glared at her for a long moment and finally folded his arms and vanished.

Elise glanced around the room and frowned. She felt strangely disoriented and realized she couldn't remember how she'd come to be in Raheem's arms. More disturbingly, she had no idea why she'd been crying.

She was in bed. Maybe she'd fallen asleep and had a bad dream?

Shaking it off, she got up and dressed, then went into the kitchen to look for something to eat. She was starving, as if she hadn't eaten all day.

She knew she had. Vaguely, she remembered that she and Alan had pulled into a fast food joint between a run that had proven to be a false alarm and the trip to the nursing home.

Dismissing it, she puzzled instead over the incident with Raheem and the things he'd said...and not said.

He'd called her myska. She might not know his language or the precise meaning of the word, but she was no fool. The meaning behind it had been crystal clear. It had been an endearment. The question was, what kind?

He'd made it clear he considered the djinn far superior to mortals. Did that mean it had been an affectionate term for...well, like a pet? Or a child? Or a woman he desired?

Plainly, he desired her and just as evidently the consequences of yielding to it were too dire for him to consider it. He'd said that to feel human was to be human. Had he meant literally? Or figuratively speaking?

She thought it over and finally came to the conclusion that he'd meant it literally. Nothing else made sense. He'd alluded to the 'evil that would befall' before, which meant, true or not, he believed that being with her as a man would make him one, that he would no longer be the djinn, no longer be immortal. He would be trapped in her world, powerless.

She felt a little sick at that thought. It was possible, of course, that the warnings of dire consequences were like a lot of the warnings parents gave children--exaggerated.

What if it wasn't, though? What if, by continuing to tease and torment him until he yielded, she was enticing him to give up everything that he was? Wouldn't he hate her? Could she live with herself, for that matter? In essence, she would be luring him to his death. As a mortal, he would, at least eventually, die.

She felt nauseated at the thought. She was only twenty five. Ordinarily, she probably wouldn't have given a thought to the dark future that awaited her. John's death had changed that, torn away the rosy, youthful fantasy of immortality. It had also forced her to see that immortality wasn't something she really wanted. She was in no hurry for death. She hoped to have a long life, but the thought of going on forever, of struggling and suffering endlessly, was worse even than the thought of dying.

She knew, even though she couldn't completely grasp what his world was like, that Raheem, nor any of his kind, experienced pain, suffering, sickness--any more than they experienced death.

There could be no such thing as casual sex between them, nor physical comfort, or even something more meaningful. It would be just as reprehensible for her to entice him from his world for love as for nothing more than a whim...worse, really.

She was going to have to figure out how to make him go back before one of them did something really stupid and, just as importantly, she had to protect herself from becoming any more attached to him than she was already.

There was no sense in lying to herself and pretending she wasn't becoming more attached than she had any business doing. That wouldn't protect her from being hurt when he left. She had to focus on someone else, someone from her own world.

* * * *

"Why don't we order?" For lack of a better distraction, Elise had decided to try once more with Lonnie. She'd been a little nervous about going out with him again, not because of Lonnie, but because Raheem had joined them the last time.

Raheem had been gone for days, though.

After spending the first fifteen minutes darting glances around, certain he would appear at any moment, she dismissed her fears and concentrated on Lonnie.

He was an ideal candidate as a distraction, actually. Physically, he appealed to her. On an emotional level, he left her cold. She wasn't even remotely likely to come away from the encounter emotionally damaged, but he would certainly do as a lover.

It wasn't in her nature to simply decide to engage in a purely physical relationship. She was as much an 'old fashioned girl' who believed in hearth, home and family, as she was the feminist who believed she had every right to a career to enrich her life and that she was just as capable of making logical decisions as any man.

She realized, however, that she was not immune to physical need. She desired Raheem. It was as simple, and as complicated, as that. If he'd not been djinn, she would have taken a chance with a physical relationship, hoping an emotional commitment would follow. He wasn't and she couldn't, but she had to get the fire out of her blood somehow or she wasn't going to be able to resist trying to entice Raheem.

For both their sakes she needed a serious distraction.

Lonnie would do. He was certainly more than willing to have a casual fling with her.

Lonnie, she saw when he didn't answer, was giving the waitress a once over that had her all aflutter. Irritated, Elise ordered a mixed drink, thinking he might at least be gentleman enough to pretend to give her his undivided attention while they were on a date. Men like Lonnie, however, always on the prowl, never considered how incredibly rude such behavior was, or, if they did, just didn't care.

Mentally, Elise shrugged. It was precisely because Lonnie was a player that she'd chosen him. Surely he had enough sexual experience to be a decent lover--she hoped. It didn't necessarily follow that, just because a man was a pure whore, he was actually adept at his favorite pastime. As often as not they were too self-centered and conceited to actually learn anything from their many encounters. They expected their 'oh so beautiful' self to be a turn on enough.

By the time their dinner arrived, Elise had polished off one drink and was working on a second. It occurred to her that she might be just a little too relaxed--Lonnie's banter had become amazingly witty--but she dismissed it.

She was a little surprised when she discovered she'd finished off her second drink. She never, ever, had more than two. Two mixed drinks were enough to go to her head. She realized she'd just eaten, however, and that that probably had offset the alcohol. It probably wouldn't hurt to have just one more.

"You're drunk," Lonnie said after a while, grinning.

Elise smiled back at him. "No...OK, well, maybe a little."

"I should take you home. I don't think you should drive."

Elise frowned. "What about my car?"

"I'll bring you back in the morning to pick it up."

That sounded reasonable enough. Elise wasn't entirely happy about leaving the car, but she decided he was probably right about her not driving. She'd had three drinks, after all, and she wasn't used to drinking. "I couldn't impose! I can just call a taxi."

Lonnie got up and helped her to her feet. "We can talk about it tomorrow."

Elise nodded, leaning against him and giggling because it took her a couple of minutes to get her balance. "I think I drank too much," she confided in him in a loud whisper as he guided her out the door and into the parking lot once more.

He chuckled. "Think so?"

"Two's my limit. I shoulda stopped at two." She was a little confused when he helped her into the front seat of his SUV. "Where are we going?" she asked when he climbed into the driver's seat.

"I'm taking you home."

"Oh," she said, disappointed. "Why don't we go to a club instead? I haven't danced in forever."

He grimaced. "I have to work tomorrow."

She thought about it several moments. "I do too...I think."

"You might want to call in sick," he suggested as he started the vehicle and backed out of his parking space.

She thought she might have dozed off. It only seemed to take a few moments before he pulled to a stop before her house. "It's my house!" she said in surprise.

He laughed. "You might be a little drunker than I thought."

She smiled at him. "I feel very relaxed, though."

"I'll just bet you do. Give me your keys."

Elise looked at him in surprise. "Why?"

"So I can open your door for you."

"Oh!" She handed him her purse. She didn't feel like looking for the keys herself. "Hope the djinn's not there."

Lonnie helped her from the car, slipped an arm around her and walked her toward her door. "I think you've had enough gin for one night."

Elise giggled. "Not Gin, dummy. Djinn. But you're right! Had enough!" She tripped over the threshold, but she was pleased to see that she'd regained much of her equilibrium. She managed to catch herself without falling. "Loose board," she pointed out. No sense in letting Lonnie trip over it too.

He dropped her purse and keys on the hall table, then grasped her around the waist and pulled her close. She snuggled against him, breathing in his scent. "Mmm. You smell good!"

He tipped her chin up and covered half her face with his mouth. Panic seized her when she realized she couldn't breathe because he was blocking her nostrils. She struggled a moment, finally managed to free her nose and relaxed fractionally. His kiss was hot, wet and...not terribly pleasant. Men were such bad kissers, she reflected with a touch of irritation.

John had been good at it, though.

Raheem was very, very good at it. Just thinking about the way he'd kissed her brought her body throbbing to life and she kissed Lonnie back with more enthusiasm.

Unfortunately, it didn't last. Lonnie's kiss was nothing at all like Raheem's and she couldn't make herself believe that it was. She felt her body cooling. Concentrating, she focused on her own pleasure.

She was just beginning to actually enjoy herself when he broke the kiss and started to nibble a path down her throat. There was a wet circle of saliva all the way around her lips. Surreptitiously, she nudged her face against his shoulder. It felt better, but now one side was wet and the other dry. When he reached her breast, she turned her head on his shoulder, wiping her lips, chin and the other side of her face.

She wasn't certain why she opened her eyes. She was starting to feel a pleasant glow and it was easier to maintain it with her eyes closed, but something made her open her eyes.

Raheem was standing directly behind them, his arms crossed over his chest, his expression as dark as a thundercloud.

Chapter Seven

Elise stiffened, her eyes widening. Abruptly, her alcoholic and physical haze of euphoria withered, but it took several moments for her own anger to set in. She made a shooing motion at him. His eyes narrowed.

'Go away,' she mouthed the words.

Lonnie had noticed she didn't seem to be responding to his efforts. He looked up at her. The motion alerted her and she looked down, smiled, shooing at Raheem behind his back.

"I think I could use another drink. What about you?"

"You got beer?"

She frowned. "Uh...no, but I got the fixings to make strawberry daiquiris."

He didn't look too enthusiastic. "Sure. I'll mix. In the kitchen?"

Raheem was still standing behind him. She closed her eyes as Lonnie turned and headed for the kitchen. When nothing happened, she opened one eye a crack. Raheem was standing in the same spot as before but had turned to watch Lonnie as he headed for the kitchen. Elise looked at him in surprise. "He can't see you?" she whispered.

Raheem turned at her question, gave her a once over look. "Why have you brought this...worm here?"

Elise was first taken aback, and then angry. "Mind your own business, damn it! And go away."

"Did you say something?" Lonnie called from the kitchen.

"Did you find the mix?" she said, gritting her teeth at Raheem when he refused to vanish.

"Yeah. Did you move the mixer?"

"Appliance garage in the corner."

"He knows his way around your house," Raheem said accusingly.

"He's been here a couple--that's none of your business!"

He studied her a long moment and finally folded his arms across his chest and bowed. "As you wish."

He vanished just as Lonnie came back with two glasses. Relieved, Elise smiled at him invitingly. "Music?"

"Sure. I'll pick something out."

Elise rolled her eyes when he handed her a glass and turned toward the stereo. Halfway across the room, he tripped, sloshing his daiquiri in his face as he tried to catch himself. "Shit!"

"Oh! I'll get you a towel!" Elise said quickly as he brushed angrily at the slushy ice dripping from his face and down his shirt.

As she was returning from the bathroom with a towel, she rounded the corner toward the living room just in time to see Raheem materialize above Lonnie's shoulder. Lonnie, she saw in dismay, had set his drink down on the stereo cabinet and was bent over at the waist, holding his shirt out from his body. Raheem flicked the glass. "No!" Elise shouted, but it was too late, the glass teetered for a moment and fell, splashing ice cold daiquiri down Lonnie's back.

Lonnie let out a high pitched yelp as the slush spilled down his neck and back. Raheem sent her a cat-that-ate-the-cream smile and disappeared once more.

Elise was still glaring at the space he'd so lately occupied when Lonnie looked up at her.

"Hey! It wasn't my fault! I swear, I set that glass squarely on the shelf there. Must have bumped it with my elbow.... This shit is freezing!"

"Here. Let me help you take that shirt off," Elise said, surging forward.

Lonnie complied and took the towel from her. "Mind if I hose off? This shit is sticky as hell."

"No. Go ahead. I'll rinse this out and toss it in the dryer for you. The bathroom is just down the hall. Second door on the left."

He waggled his brows at her. "Want to join me?"

Elise smiled with an effort. She was on the point of refusing when it dawned on her that she'd forbidden Raheem the bathroom. They could have privacy.... "Sure, but I need to rinse this and get it in the dryer."

"I'll leave the door open. Don't be long," he added with a sultry smile.

Raheem was sitting cross legged on the dryer when Elise turned from rinsing the shirt out at the laundry sink. She gave him a look. "Just what do you think you're doing?"

He spread his hands wide. "As you see."

"Don't play innocent with me!" Elise said crossly. "You're...interfering with my life. You tripped him. I know it was you."

Raheem shrugged. "He is a clumsy oaf."

Elise tossed the shirt into the dryer and then leaned around him to turn it on. "He's not clumsy."

"He's a worm!"

Elise plunked her hands on her hips. "He's a stud! Everybody thinks so."

Raheem pointed in the direction of the bathroom. "That...scrawny excuse for a male?"

"Just because he's not big as an ox, like you?" Elise demanded, outraged. "He's a...desirable man. And I feel like getting laid, damn it! And it's none of your business anyway!"

His eyes narrowed. "What is this, 'getting laid'?"

Elise blushed. Obviously, there was more alcohol in her system than she'd realized. "Never mind! Suffice to say you are not welcome here...definitely not right now."

"You mean to lie with this man," Raheem snarled.

Elise's eyes narrowed. "I don't have to explain myself to you and anyway, not being human, it's not something you're likely to understand."

"My understanding is superior."

Elise drew a deep breath, turned and stalked away. She'd reached the door of the bathroom before it occurred to her that Raheem had her so pissed off, she'd lost her 'hard on'. Stopping, she muttered a few choice curses, trying to calm herself and relax.

Abruptly, the door slammed to. Elise stared at it blankly, thinking, at first, that Lonnie had slammed it.

Grasping the door knob, she discovered that it wouldn't turn at about the same moment she heard a yelp and a thud from the other side. She put her ear to the door. "Lonnie?"

A groan answered her and she turned. Raheem was standing behind her, his arms crossed, fury etched in every feature. "Open the damned door!"

His eyes narrowed. "No."

Elise stamped her foot, growling in frustration. "What did you do to Lonnie?"

"He will live. His cock will be of no use to him, however."

Elise felt her jaw go slack. "You didn't....!"

He shrugged, turned to look in the direction of the shower, as if he could see through the wall. After a moment, he looked at her again.

"He sounds like he's hurt. You could at least let me in to help him."

"He is gone. He can nurse his crooked member himself."

Frustrated and angry, Elise reached out to push him away. To her stunned surprise--since he was in the habit of vanishing when she tried to touch him--she encountered solid flesh. He didn't budge an inch. He did grab her wrists, however, his grip bruising.

She winced as pain shot through her arms and he released her immediately. Instead of moving away, however, he plunked his fists on his hips and leaned toward her until they were almost nose to nose. "You will not bring that worm here again."

More intimidated than she was willing to admit, Elise returned his angry look with one of indignation. "I'll do as I damn well please! It's *my* house...and *my* body! If I want to get laid, I will--with whomever I desire!"

She turned to move past him. In the next moment, she found herself flat on her back on the bed, Raheem above her, still rigid with anger. He made a brushing motion over her and her clothes vanished. She gaped up at him, tried to roll away. Grasping her wrists, he manacled them to the bed on either side of her head. "So be it," he growled, capturing her mouth beneath his own.

Elise stiffened, but within seconds the tension of desire overwhelmed any thought she might have had to object to his roughness. His taste and scent invaded her senses like an electric current. The pleasure was overwhelming, debilitating, devastating. The brush of her body against his with each breath made her tingle all over with need.

When he broke the kiss at last, however, she saw that anger still drove him and her own desire cooled. A knot of misery formed in her throat and she looked away from him.

He released her abruptly, angrily, and moved away. "You wanted this."

She turned to look at him. "Not like this...in anger."

He gave her a look of baffled fury. "You would have lain with that worm for nothing more than to assuage your lust."

"At least he would have felt lust for me, too!" Elise snapped, suddenly as angry as she was hurt. "He wouldn't have done it just because he was mad at me, to punish me!"

"You think I did that to punish you!" he demanded, outraged.

"Didn't you?"

He studied her a long moment. "Women! Bah! There is no pleasing them!"

Elise slung a pillow at him. "It would please me no end if you'd go back where you came from and cease to torment me!"

He caught the pillow and tossed it aside, leaping toward her like a pouncing cat and flattening her against the pillows behind her. "I will go in my own time," he growled at her. "Not because you will it, you ill tempered wench."

Before Elise could think of anything to say, he vanished. She rolled over, punching the pillows in frustration. Damn him, anyway! She shouldn't have stopped him. At least then she could've slaked her body's demands and hated him at the same time. It would've been the perfect solution to her dilemma.

She was sorely tempted to get dressed and go over to Lonnie's place.

God only knew what Raheem had done to the poor fool, though. It seemed unlikely he'd be able to do her any good, despite her childish desire to snap her fingers at Raheem and go anyway. She just hoped that whatever Raheem had done to him wasn't permanent.

As her anger dissipated, the remnants of alcohol in her system kicked in. Despite her certainty that she was too sexually frustrated to sleep, she did. She roused some time later to the brush of a warm hand across her bare belly. Caught halfway between sleep and full alertness, she relaxed, drifting in a hazy, unfocused way that convinced her she was dreaming, that liberated her from any sense of guilt. She moaned as his hand cupped her right breast, massaging it. Rolling toward the source of pleasure, she stroked her hand over his chest. He felt wonderfully familiar.

Confusion filled her when she opened her eyes and looked at him. It was John's gaze that met hers, John's face. She closed her eyes again. She hadn't dreamed of John in more than a year.

Why would she dream of him now? Why had she thought that it was Raheem who lay beside her? Raheem who caressed her?

After a moment, she dismissed her confusion. Moving closer, she lifted his hand from her breast and slipped his index finger into her mouth, sucking it. He groaned, and, inwardly, she smiled, felt desire flood through her. Releasing his finger, she guided his hand downward, over her breasts, her belly, until he cupped her sex.

She moaned when she felt his fingers slipping through her wetness, rubbing the nub of her clit. Bending her head, she nipped the flesh of his chest, tasted him with her tongue, stroking his back lovingly as she kissed her way up his throat. "I love you. Make love to me," she whispered when she reached his ear.

He stiffened. After a moment, he pulled away, flopping onto his back and staring up at the ceiling. "I am not John," he said harshly.

Elise rose up, propping on her elbow. "Why did you pretend to be?"

He looked at her, frowning. "To give you pleasure."

Elise leaned toward him, stroking his cheek. "Make love to me, Raheem."

He looked at her in surprise. "You knew I was not...John?"

Elise brushed her lips lightly across his. "I knew."

He threaded his fingers through her hair, cupping the back of her head as he opened his mouth over hers and thrust his tongue between her lips, kissing her deeply, with a hunger than sent a shaft of excitement through her. She stroked her tongue along his, sucked him as she had his finger. He groaned, rolled so that he lay atop her. Breaking the kiss, he moved over her face, down her throat, his breath harsh, labored as he blazed a trail of fire across her skin with his mouth.

Elise wrapped her arms around him, stroking his silky hair, his back. She gasped, dropping her arms to the bed and gripping the sheets tightly as he moved lower still, over her breasts, along her body, across her belly. He seemed determined to explore every inch of her body with his mouth, his hands, to stroke and taste her. When he reached her thighs, he parted them, lowering his head to taste the core of her femininity.

Elise clenched the sheets tighter as the heat of his mouth covered her, as she felt his tongue stroke and tease her. Spreading her thighs wider, she arched up to meet him as mindless pleasure thundered through her, teasing her with the possibility of release, tempting her to lie still and ride the current upwards until she reached ultimate bliss. Releasing the sheets abruptly, she clutched his shoulders. "Don't make me come. Not yet."

For a thundering heartbeat of seconds, she thought that he would ignore her, that she could not stave off the climax her body craved. At last he lifted his head and looked at her, his eyes glazed with desire.

"I want to come with you inside me," she whispered shakily.

His features tightened with desire and he moved over her, pressing his hips to her. Reaching down, she grasped his distended flesh, aligning his body with her own, feeling a fiery tide of pleasure rush through her as they joined. Her muscles clenched around him, embracing his hard cock as he sank slowly, deeply inside of her.

He paused, his face a mask of tortured pleasure, his eyes clenched tightly closed. Wrapping her arms around his neck, she lifted her head to kiss him, grinding her hips against him even as she did so. A tremor went through him. He opened his eyes to look at her. "Myska," he murmured raggedly, covering her mouth with his own as he began to move, thrusting into her deeply, drawing away slowly, almost reluctantly and then burying himself as deeply as he could inside of her once more, as if he could not reach deeply enough to satisfy him, as if he wanted to crawl inside her and become part of her.

Elise dug her heels into the mattress, arching up to meet each thrust, dragging her lips from his as she felt the muscles of her sex begin to quake as she reached her peak. Her arms tightened around his shoulders as it flooded her body with sensation, with euphoric release.

He groaned hoarsely as his own release caught him, sending tremors through him.

He did not move, even when the tremors subsided at last, he held her tightly still. Elise could hardly breathe, but she didn't object. She was scarcely conscious in any case.

Finally, Raheem rolled to his back, holding her tightly so that she went with him and lay draped limply over him. She rested her cheek on his chest, sated, content in a way she could never recall being as she listened to his heart beat in his chest, felt the caress of his hand over her head and along her back.

She didn't want to think about tomorrow, or the real world. She wanted to bask in the moment, wring the last tiny fraction of enjoyment from it that she could.

She could not keep it at bay, however. Slowly, but insidiously, reality intruded.

What they had done was forbidden. She stirred uncomfortably at the thought and Raheem's hand paused. "Are you sorry it happened?"

He tensed, pulled away, trying to see her face. After a moment, he let his breath out slowly and rolled until she lay beside him. He stroked her face with the backs of his fingers, his expression serious. "Not with my last breath," he said harshly, leaning toward her and kissing her with a hunger that belied the very satisfactory conclusion of their previous lovemaking.

Elise found, within moments, that her hunger equaled his. If possible, it was more intense than before, his caresses more fiercely possessive, their joining more desperate, their release more explosive.

Exhausted finally, sated for the moment at least, Elise drifted to sleep, her arm across Raheem's chest, her leg tangled with his, her head resting on one hard arm. She should have been far too uncomfortable to sleep, but realized she'd never been more comfortable in her life.

The phone roused her sometime later. It rang on and on, stopped briefly and began again. Finally she struggled over to the side of the bed and picked up the receiver. "'low?"

It was her boss, wanting to know if she was coming in to work. Elise was too exhausted for even the realization that she'd missed work to rouse her more than a fraction. "Sick. Tomorrow," she muttered and hung up.

Collapsing on the bed once more, she felt around for Raheem and discovered he was gone, but even that didn't prevent her from drifting off again, though it threaded a seed of doubt through her subconscious.

Chapter Eight

The sound of the ocean woke Elise. At first she thought she was dreaming it, or heard something else and was imagining it. She didn't live anywhere near the beach and, in any case, Tampa was near the gulf. The water didn't sound nearly as turbulent.

Finally, fully awake by now, she opened her eyes.

The room was filled with a soft glow of light. She didn't recognize her surroundings.

Sitting up abruptly, Elise looked around, completely disoriented.

The bed she was lying on was huge, held up by posts big enough to be porch columns. On the posts, dragons, flowering vines and birds were carved in a design that wound around them in a spiral. Gauzy hangings fluttered around the bed, caught in the tangy ocean breeze that filtered through the louvers that covered the windows nearby. The walls of the room appeared to be stone. The floor most certainly was, tiled in squares that looked like ancient, rough cut slabs of gray slate.

She was naked. After a few moments, she slid to the edge of the bed and looked around for something to put on. A gauzy, sleeveless robe that looked like a Greek toga lay across the foot of the bed. Seeing nothing else, she picked it up, studied it a moment and finally pulled it over her head.

Peeking from beneath the edge of the bed, she saw a pair of leather sandals of the sort that were little more than sole and thin straps. They looked as if they'd been made for her feet. With a shrug, she slipped her feet into them and moved around the foot of her bed, glancing at the ceiling, the walls.

She found herself face to face with a woman and jumped, gasping before she realized it was her own reflection in a mirror placed on a dressing table against the wall across from the windows.

She stared at the reflection, not recognizing herself either.

Her hair was a wild, tangled mess...small wonder when she'd spent the night before--or had she? Was it no more than an illusion? Was this?

Moving to the dressing table, she picked up the brush that lay on it's uncluttered surface, examined it and finally used it to brush the tangles from her hair. When her pale hair hung gleaming and sleek about her shoulders, she replaced the brush and looked around again.

There were two doors, one between the louvered windows, the second beside the dressing table. After a moment, she moved toward the door that seemed to lead outside. When she opened it, she saw that it led onto a balcony--which overlooked the sea.

"I see that you have awakened at last, myska."

Elise glanced quickly toward the sound of the voice. Raheem was propped against the balustrade of the balcony at one end, studying her. "Am I?"

His eyes gleamed. "Do you not know the difference?"

Elise smiled at him tentatively. "What is this place?"

"My palace...our palace by the sea."

Her heart skipped a beat when he said 'our'. Warmth suffused her. "We're in your world?"

He chuckled, lifting a hand. "No, myska. Yours."

Elise moved toward him, placed her hand in his. He pulled her against him. Elise settled her cheek against his chest, studying the waves that pounded the shoreline only a few yards away. "Why did you bring me to this place?"

He tensed. For several moments, she thought he wouldn't answer. Finally, he let out a harsh breath. "To protect you from harm."

Elise's heart skipped a beat. She looked up at him, frowning. "I...don't think I understand."

"It is not a thing that is easy to explain."

She pulled a little away from him. "You mean you don't think I can understand."

He shrugged. "The worlds...all of them and all that connects them--time, space--it is all connected, interlocking--carefully balanced, flowing, fluid, always changing but always remaining carefully measured, weighed, proportioned, equalized. We have broken the laws of the universe, myska. Misfortune will follow."

"You're certain?" Elise said, suddenly truly afraid.

He nodded. "I know this."

Anguish filled her. "Why then? It's my fault, isn't it?"

"I chose my own destiny," he said, almost harshly. "I will not allow you to accept responsibility for that which you do not control."

"But...if I hadn't bought the charm, opened it...."

"I would not have known you."

"If I hadn't tried to seduce you."

His lips quirked. "I had thought it was the other way around."

Elise's eyes widened in surprise. "You?"

"When I could contain my hunger for you no longer."

A blush rose in her cheeks. "You wanted me?" she asked, pleased.

"You did not know this?"

Elise ran a finger over his chest, tracing the swirling pattern of the tattoo that adorned his shoulders and upper chest. "I wasn't certain. I hoped. But then you said that it couldn't happen."

His expression became wry. "I should not have allowed it, but I could no more have stopped it than I could pluck the moon or stars from the sky. It was written on the tablet of fate."

Elise frowned. "What will happen now?"

"In time, fate will show us."

A shiver skated along Elise's spine and she looked away.

Raheem hooked a finger beneath her chin and forced her to look up at him. "For now I will sup from your lips the nectar that is your essence and appease the hunger that only grows stronger each time I join my body with yours."

He scooped her into his arms even as he kissed her and then strode back through the balcony door. Placing her on the bed, he followed her down, stripping the gown from her and tossing it aside. Elise reached for him as he moved over her, settling himself half atop her. Need spread through her at the look in his eyes, at his touch and, as he leaned down to kiss her hungrily, she met him, kissing him back with equal longing. As his hands moved over her in a restless caress, she allowed her fingers and palms to learn his body, to give pleasure to him as she took pleasure from the feel of his flesh against her hands.

And when he broke the kiss and moved over her body, kissing, tasting, teasing her flesh to heightened sensitivity, she writhed in mindless pleasure, touching, kissing any part of him that she could reach.

When he pushed his knee between her legs, she spread her thighs wide, opening eagerly to him, reaching down and cupping his sex, gently stroking his testicles before she slipped her hand around the distended flesh of his cock and guided him to her opening, lifting to meet him, lifting her head to watch as he sank slowly inside of her until his hips ground against her own. When she looked up at Raheem, she saw that he, too, was watching the joining of their flesh, his face tight with desire.

Gripping his shoulders, she rose up to kiss his shoulder, his throat. He wrapped his arms around her, taking her with him as he came up on his knees, impaling her more deeply than before. She locked her arms around his neck as he grasped her hips and lifted her slightly away and then pushed her down again. In his eyes, as she looked at him, she saw the reflection of her own pleasure. It multiplied as she watched it grow inside him, until she was gasping, hovering on the verge of release, and then crying out as it seized her and took her over the edge.

He gripped her tightly, burying himself deeply as his cock convulsed with his own climax, spewing his seed inside her.

Elise felt so weak in the aftermath she was certain she would have fallen if he hadn't been holding her. When he lowered her to the bed at last, she merely collapsed limply, her eyes closed as she fought to catch her breath.

Something tickled her nose. Her lips curled in a half smile as she pried her eyelids open a fraction.

"You are a lazy wench."

Elise frowned, but she couldn't summon the strength to be insulted. "Weak with hunger, more like."

Raheem's eyes gleamed. "Insatiable, too. I am not at all certain I can appease your hunger at the moment, myska."

Elise swatted at him weakly. "Food!"

He chuckled, snapped his fingers.

The door opened. Elise jerked upright, grabbing frantically for something to cover herself. A girl stood in the doorway, a tray in her hands, her head bowed politely. She looked Polynesian and Elise wondered if they were near Hawaii. She shook her head at the absurdity of it. "Magic," she muttered.

Raheem glanced at her sharply. "Nay. An islander."

Elise was taken aback. "But...she would've had to be waiting...." She trailed off, her expression horrified as it occurred to her that the girl, if real, had to have been waiting just outside the door to have heard Raheem snap his fingers, and if she'd heard that....

Raheem chuckled at her expression. "She is your maid. She will see that you have all that you need."

Elise gave him a look but waited until the girl had set the tray down on the table on the balcony outside and departed before she said anything. "I'm not used to servants. I wouldn't be comfortable."

Raheem shrugged, rolling off the bed. "You will grow accustomed," he said as he strolled outside and bent to examine the contents of the tray.

Elise wasn't certain she would. She also wasn't certain she wanted to. She hadn't spent a great deal of time considering the situation she'd found herself in, but that was, she realized, mostly because she had not accepted that any of it was real. She'd been certain it was merely an illusion that Raheem had conjured to charm her. After a moment, she located her gown and pulled it on, then followed Raheem.

He was still stark naked, lounging casually in one of the chairs, his legs crossed, his feet propped on the balcony railing. Elise dropped a cloth napkin in his lap. He glanced up at her, his eyes gleaming with suppressed laughter. "I see no reason to dress when I mean to ravish you again once you have filled your belly."

"Promises, promises," Elise chided, settling in the chair opposite him and helping herself to a selection of fruits and meat. The concoction looked exotic enough to be some island dish.

He cocked an eyebrow at her. "You believe I am jesting?"

"I believe *you're* the one that's insatiable," Elise said tartly.

Raheem popped a chunk of fruit into his mouth and chewed it thoughtfully. "I can not take you back, Elise," he finally said, his voice gentle.

Elise paused with a fork full of food halfway to her mouth. "You're not serious."

"I would not jest about something of this nature."

Placing the fork carefully back on the plate, Elise stared down at it, unseeing. "But...I have family who will worry."

"It is not safe for you now. Later, I will take you."

She looked at him finally. "There must be some way I can get in touch with them, tell them I'm alright."

He shook his head. "This island is far away from everything else. It is why I chose it."

Elise found she'd lost her appetite. "I hate to think of what they must suffer, thinking something has happened to me. If it were the other way around--if my mother or sister had suddenly gone missing--I'd be sick with worry."

Raheem frowned, but finally shook his head. "I dare not risk it now. If I could trust that I would sense the presence of another djinn, I would go, but I can not."

An uneasy feeling swept through Elise. "What do you mean?"

He stood up abruptly, snapped his fingers. Moments passed. Abruptly, the breeches he wore appeared and he was clothed. "With each day that passes I feel the chains that bind me to my own world growing weaker."

Elise stared at him in horror. "You're...becoming mortal? Human?"

He glanced at her sharply. "It matters to you?"

"Of course it matters to me!" Elise gasped, jumping to her feet. "You have to go back! Now! You can't stay here."

He turned away from her, moved to the balustrade, gripping it with his hands as he leaned against it. "You want me because of my powers, myska?"

Elise studied his back uncomprehendingly. "You don't believe that!"

He looked at her. "If I am merely a mortal, your desire for me will cool and I will be of no more interest than any other--living--mortal."

Elise paled. "I have *never* compared you to John!"

"John is dead," he said harshly. "It is hard to compete with a man who no longer exists...except in your mind. And you can not let him go, can you, Elise? This is why you have always told me to go, to leave. You will not allow anyone to even try to banish the ghost you cherish."

"That's not true...none of it! You know it's not. I only asked you to go because I don't want anything to happen to you!"

"Like losing my powers?"

Elise grew angry. "You're not mortal, weren't born in this world. Humans *born* to it have a hard time surviving and making a living! How will you adjust? Why would you want to? Just so you can grow old? Sick? Die? I can accept it because I've got no choice. You do."

"I chose," Raheem said angrily, stabbing a finger at his chest. "*I* chose. You can not make my choice for me! You can only accept what I offer to you...or not!"

"Then go! Because you don't belong in my world anymore than I belong in yours!"

He stared at her for a long moment and Elise thought he must see right through her. Abruptly, he folded his arms and vanished.

Elise felt every ounce of strength leave her. It took an effort of concentration to turn and place one foot in front of the other until she reached the chair and collapsed into it. She was afraid to cry, fearful that he might be nearby, that she would give herself away.

He could not have been more wrong about the way she felt. If he had truly known her, he would know that his doubts were unfounded. She supposed it was for the best that he didn't, although it hurt to think he believed she was like that.

She supposed, in a way, that he *had* been right about John. Deep in her heart, she would always love his memory, but she loved Raheem with far more passion that she had ever felt for John...and it didn't have a damned thing to do with him being a djinn! She loved *him*...because he was strong, and passionate, and gentle and giving. And nothing in the world like John, so how could he even think that she would compare them? Or that she would find him lacking in any way?

She wanted, desperately, to tell him, but if she had yielded to that selfish need, he wouldn't have gone.

She wasn't certain how long she sat, staring at the cresting waves blindly, but at last she noticed the sun was sinking into the sea.

With some surprise, she discovered that the maid had come and taken the tray away. Rising to her feet with an effort, she moved stiffly inside, stood for some moments looking around the empty room and finally went in search of the bathroom.

The door the maid had entered through earlier led to a dressing room, she discovered with some surprise. It was filled with her things, all arranged neatly. After a moment, she moved through the room to the door at the other end.

The bath, if possible, was even more magnificent than the bedroom. In the center was a tub big enough to accommodate three people. Along the sides, jets protruded. Pleasure flickered inside of her. Dropping the gown to the floor, she moved carefully down the steps and turned the faucets on, then lay back in the tub while she waited for it to fill.

She'd always found that water soothed her. No matter how tired, or how emotionally drained she might feel, the rush of water always relaxed, comforted, soothed frayed nerves.

When the water began to lap her chin, she sat up, reaching for the button that controlled the jets...and froze, her hand still extended mid-air.

For several thundering heartbeats, she thought that it was Raheem.

Noticing her attention, he stepped forward, a smile on his face that sent a chill of pure terror racing along Elise's spine.

"I am the djinn, Zeht."

Chapter Nine

Raheem had been racing through the stratosphere for some time before it occurred to him that he had no destination in mind, but the chill, thin air had cooled the anger from his blood.

He paused, thinking.

With a good deal of surprise, he realized that he had allowed emotion to cloud his mind and that it had prevented logical deduction. Now, very clearly, he could recall the look on Elise's face when she had sent him away. There had been no anger, no loathing. There had been pain--pain that had pulled the blood from her face until she had looked paper white. She could not have wanted to send him away if it hurt her to do it.

He had not questioned that she cared for him very deeply until she had been so shocked that he might lose his powers. When that doubt had entered his mind, others he had not allowed himself to think about had flooded into his mind, as well.

He had acknowledged the fear that must always have been in the back of his mind that she might not love him as she had John, that she might be with him and still yearn for another.

He frowned. If humans were afflicted with so many doubts, and all the emotions attendant upon them, it was small wonder their world was such a chaotic mess. Perhaps, in truth, he would have difficulty adjusting to being a mortal?

He shook that thought off. He had chosen. It had not been a true choice, because he had not been able to make another choice, but he felt no regret for it...only unaccustomed confusion.

In truth, despite his determination to try to understand these alien thoughts and emotions, in the back of his mind he could think of little beyond the urge to return to Elise.

That had been the way of it almost from the first.

Would she still be angry? Or had her temper cooled, as well?

After several moments of thought, it occurred to him that there was one way that he could ensure a welcome.

He would seek out Elise's mother and assure her that her daughter was safe. Elise would be pleased.

* * * *

The task he had set himself was not as easily accomplished as he had expected it would be. Locating her had not been the problem. He had gone to Elise's house and retrieved the image of her mother. A simple tracking spell had led him to her.

She was cleaning her kitchen when he materialized.

"Madam," he said, bowing politely. "I bring you news of your daughter, Elise."

The woman, an older, plumper version of Elise, stared at him blankly for several moments and let out the shriek of a thousand banshees. Gripping the broom she held in her hands she began to flail at him, striking him three blows before he had the presence of mind to dematerialize.

He materialized again safely out of reach, hovering near the ceiling. "Cease, woman!" he commanded her.

She gaped at him, screamed and began grabbing pots and pitching them at him.

When he materialized the third time, he was directly behind her. Grabbing her around the arms to subdue her, he tried once more to reason with her. "I mean you no harm! I am come to give you news of your daughter, Elise."

She stomped his foot that time.

Enough was enough. When he materialized the fourth time, he put a binding spell upon her.

"What have you done with my daughter, you monster!" she demanded furiously, trying to wrestle herself free of the bindings. "You'll wish for death if you've harmed one hair on her head!"

Raheem glared at the woman, planting his fists on his hips. Finally, however, he saw the fear in her eyes and his own anger dissipated. He knelt in front of the chair he had bound her to. "On my honor, I would not harm her, or allow her to be harmed, madam."

Some of the fear left the woman's eyes, but she studied him distrustfully. "Where is she? I went to her house. Most of her things are gone."

"I have taken her to a place where she will be safe. She was concerned that you would worry. I came so that she would not be fretting over you."

"Who are you?"

"Am the djinn, Raheem."

"Take me to her."

Raheem looked at her in dismay. He was willing to do most anything for Elise, but he wasn't at all certain he wanted this she-devil in his palace. On the other hand, if he simply left her, then Elise would learn of it, eventually.

"Very well, madam. But I will tolerate no more abuse from you, woman!"

"The only promise I'll make, Mister, is to cut your heart out if she isn't alright."

Raheem eyed her with some respect. It was small wonder Elise believed she could order him around when she had been spawned by this warrior female. He smiled faintly. Elise would breed fine sons for him.

"You can wipe that sappy grin off your face. I mean every word of it!"

Raheem glared at her, sorely tempted to place a spell upon her tongue. "Enough, woman! I will release you and take you to your daughter, but I give you fair warning, I will tolerate no more abuse from you...even if it does anger Elise!"

The woman looked at him in surprise. In a moment, something suspiciously akin to humor gleamed in her eyes. "I'll have to call her sister before we go, or she'll be worried about the both of us."

Raheem nodded, pointing a finger at her to remove the binding spell, waiting impatiently while she called her other daughter. When she'd hung up, she brushed past him and left the room. Puzzled, Raheem followed her and found her in a bedroom, busily packing a suitcase.

"What are you doing!"

"What does it look like? You said you'd taken her to a safe place. I assume I'll be gone a few days."

"Not if I can help it," Raheem growled.

"I assume you mean to marry her?"

Raheem looked at her as if she'd sprouted another head. "Wed?"

"You can't expect her to live with you in sin."

"She is my concubine."

The woman nodded. "I thought so. A small, quiet wedding will do."

Raheem studied her thoughtfully for several moments. "Elise would want this?"

The woman nodded, smiling faintly as she closed her suitcase. "You can just call me Carol," she said, turning with her suitcase in her hand.

Raheem studied her, frowning. "Elise has told you of me," he said flatly.

"Not everything, I'm sure...but, yes. I was afraid she'd gone off the deep end. Glad to see I was wrong...I'm ready, by the way."

Disconcerted, Raheem merely stared at her for several moments. Finally, shrugging mentally, he lifted his hand, wrapped a traveling spell around her and dematerialized.

He released her from the spell when they had entered the great hall.

Carol looked around appreciatively and set her suitcase down.

Raheem left her, striding swiftly toward the winding stairs that led up from the great hall.

The maid met him before he'd ascended more than a half dozen steps, collapsing on the stairs in front of him, weeping, muttering incoherently.

Brushing past her, Raheem took the remainder of the stairs at a sprint. When he'd checked every room he returned, furious. "Cease!" he roared, holding his hand out.

The maid turned white, but ceased weeping and babbling as abruptly as if she'd been a faucet suddenly turned off.

"Where is Elise?"

"The evil one took her!"

Raheem turned as white as the maid had been only moments before. "What evil one?"

"He said he was the djinn, Zeht. And that you must come for your woman! He said you would know where to find her."

Raheem glanced down at Elise's mother, his face grim.

"Do you know?"

He nodded. "He has taken her beyond the gateway...where no mortal being can long survive."

* * * *

The sky was golden. That alone was sufficient to convince Elise that she had been torn from her own world and whisked into another one. Below them, she saw streaks of teal, and deep blue, and gold. The blur of colors made her head swim and she closed her eyes. Unfortunately, the sense of disorientation didn't vanish when the djinn, Zeht stopped abruptly. Elise was fairly certain she would have crumpled to the ground if he had not been holding her. With an effort, she opened her eyes to look around. They were standing, she saw to her horror, on a tiny wedge of rock barely a yard square. Below them, falling away almost into forever, were other slabs of rock, each slightly larger than the next--she supposed since she could see tips of different colored rocks jutting out here and there.

Zeht released her abruptly and Elise screamed as she fell, certain she would roll off the edge. She landed with her upper body suspended over nothingness, anchored to the rock by nothing more than her lower body, unable to pull herself back from the edge.

When Zeht grasped her ankles, she thought for several terrifying moments that he meant to push her over the edge. Instead, he clamped something cold around first one ankle and then the other. Dragging her back, he grasped a fistful of hair and hauled her up onto her knees, then placed a manacle on each of her wrists. When he released her, Elise glanced around and discovered that he had chained her to a needle of rock that shot up from the rock she'd landed on. It looked solid and relief flooded through her. She was actually almost grateful to be chained to the rock. At least, if she was right and it was as solid as it looked, she didn't have to worry about falling off.

As the fear subsided, she realized her thighs, belly and breasts were stinging. Zeht had pulled her naked from the tub and had not allowed her to dress herself. When he'd dragged her back from the ledge, it had scraped her skin, she saw, leaving thin red streaks along her flesh. Curling up into a fetal position, she lay her cheek on her arm, fighting the dizziness that still plagued her. Breathing was an effort. She had no idea how high she was, but obviously too high if she had to labor so hard to breathe.

After a while, she realized that Zeht had not left. Lifting her head, she looked around for him and discovered that he was hovering, crossed legged, just beyond the rock ledge, a smile of supreme satisfaction on his face.

"Why did you bring me here?"

"You are Raheem's play thing. He will want his pretty back."

Elise stared at him a long moment, trying to think, but her head hurt, and she was nauseated, and scared and she finally realized it was virtually useless to try to think at this point. She dropped her head back onto her arm. "He won't come," she muttered.

"He will come."

She shook her head, but it only made her more dizzy. "I sent him away."

He burst out laughing. It seemed the more he laughed, the more he tickled himself, for it took him many minutes to control his laughter. He would stop, giggle and then begin to laugh all over again. "You sent...Raheem? His Royal Majesty Prince Raheem? High Magician and ruler of all Middle World?"

Elise lifted her head and looked at him. "Who?"

"The second most powerful djinn in all of the world? For I, Zeht, Ruler of the High World, am the most powerful of all!"

"Not Prince Raheem," Elise corrected. "The djinn, Raheem, Guardian of the gateway."

Zeht snickered. "Prince Raheem *is* the guardian of the gateway, for it is the gateway to his princedom, Middle World!"

With an effort, Elise pushed herself upright to study the madman who was tormenting her. "That tiny bottle?"

The amusement vanished abruptly. "You have the phial? The key?" He asked quickly, looking at her with keen interest. There was a dangerous gleam in his eyes now, though, that unnerved Elise. "Raheem must have been pleased to discover one so weak as you held it. This means he has destroyed the last of the three keys and closed the gateways mad King Yangi created eons ago and hid throughout the outer world."

Elise was more than a little inclined to think, if anyone was mad, it was Zeht. "I don't think we're working on the same page," she muttered. "I bought a tiny bottle. It was one of those things that summon a genie and then they have to grant your wishes."

Zeht's eyes narrowed. "I never cease to be amazed at the weak minds of humans. Tell them one tale and by the time they have passed it to three others, it bears no resemblance to the original! There never *was* such a thing as you describe...only the gateways, designed to allow mortals to enter our world--to steal our riches!

The mad king, Yangi, had been enchanted by a beautiful human witch and would make her queen of all the inner world. He was the most powerful of all the djinn. The djinn were forced to combine their powers to best him, and Yangi and his witch were banished from inner world for all time. The great kingdom was split into three princedoms, the Lower, Middle and High world, for no one desired that one should have so much power again.

In revenge, Yangi created the gateways, so that we could never be certain we were secure against the encroachment of the barbaric hoards."

"He created them so that humans could come here?" Elise asked curiously, wondering why any would want to.

Zeht eyed her with disfavor. "He created them so that *he* could return if he wished. We had banished him and sealed the borders against him so that he could not return--any djinn may pass, if he so pleases, save Yangi. He did it for amusement, for he claimed he had chosen to live among the mortals and had no wish to return, but we knew he had done it to prove he was still the most powerful of all and to plant a seed of doubt so that we would always have to be on guard."

Good for him! Elise thought. "Interesting, but I fail to see what any of it has to do with me. *You* brought a human here, just as Yangi did."

His eyes narrowed. "I have not brought you to make you my royal concubine, however. I have brought you...as you humans put it...as bait."

Chapter Ten

"You want to use me to get to Raheem," Elise said, a shaft of fear causing her heart to skip several beats.

Zeht laughed. "I might applaud you for your cleverness, mortal, save for the fact that I have told you as much."

Elise blushed. "I'm just trying to figure out why you needed me," she snapped. "If you're the most powerful, why not just defeat him and take what he holds? That's what this is about, right? You want the Middle World?"

"I would not be accepted as ruler," he snarled, "if I merely took it! I must make Raheem challenge me to a duel of sorcery and when I have destroyed him, I will be appointed, recognized as the most powerful."

Elise gave him a look. "So...the fact is, you're only the most powerful in your own mind? And ruler of the rocks? This is High World, right?" she said, gesturing toward the pillars of rock that could be seen in any direction.

Zeht's snarl became a roar of fury. "How *dare* you mock me, earth spawn!"

He held his hand up, like a traffic cop commanding a stop. The rock beneath Elise began to tremble, and then to shake, harder and harder, crumbling away inches at the time in dust and pebbles.

Terrified, Elise screamed, covering her head and closing her eyes, expecting momentarily to feel the tiny platform she was chained to toppling from the peak it was perched on and falling endlessly before it reached Middle World, far, far below.

The shaking stopped abruptly. When Elise peered cautiously from under her hand, she saw Zeht was wearing the self-satisfied smile once more. "Now we wait."

He left, but he didn't go nearly far enough, only to the next peak over, where he settled himself to watch her.

Sick, scared to death and tired beyond belief, Elise dozed, but she had no more than drifted off when the rock began to shimmy once more. She woke screaming. The echo of Zeht's laughter bridged the gap between them.

It didn't take a rocket scientist to figure out that he wasn't simply amusing himself. He obviously expected her terror to distract Raheem and give him an edge. With the best will in the world, however, Elise couldn't bite back a scream of fear every time he shook the rock he had chained her to.

She had no sense of time, no idea how long she lay on the rock, shivering with fear and cold. It seemed it must have been days by her body's clock, for her lips were dry from lack of water and her mouth felt as if she'd had cotton stuffed in it. She'd screamed until the only sound she could make was a hoarse croak.

She barely lifted her head when the shaking came again. As she blinked her eyes to focus, though, she saw Raheem and her heart leapt with joy. With an effort, she lifted her arms toward him.

He reached for her and the rock began to shake again. Elise screamed hoarsely, flattening herself against it to keep from being slammed against the hard surface by the shaking. Raheem let out a roar of pure rage and frustration, whirling to confront Zeht as he laughed uproariously.

"You can't break my spell! You'll pound her to death on the rocks yourself or topple it from it's precarious perch!"

Elise looked at the two men in the distance in confusion, wondering why Raheem had not come to her. Finally, Zeht's words sank in. He'd surrounded her with a spell that Raheem couldn't breach without toppling the rock. If he tried, she would die.

Hope died and desolation took its place. She had almost reached the point where she felt like throwing herself off, just so she wouldn't have to be afraid anymore. She didn't think she could take much more fear without degenerating into a blithering lunatic.

Maybe she was already crazy. If she was sane, she wouldn't be considering leaping off. But then, she couldn't, even if she reached the point of hoping for death to end the torment. Zeht had chained her to the damned rock.

Her only hope was for Raheem to break the other djinn's spell, but she had no idea how he would do that.

The sharp ring produced by the clash of metal against metal drew her from her abstraction and she glanced toward Raheem once more. He and Zeht were locked in a swordsman's dance between the two pillars of rock, moving as if there was solid ground beneath their feet. Elise's heart seemed to stop in her chest.

Zeht beat back Raheem's assault and made a flicking gesture in her direction. The rock commenced its shimmy. She hugged the ground, screaming before she thought better of it.

When Raheem whirled to look at her, Zeht attacked, swinging the wicked blade he held over his head like a whirligig before hacking at Raheem. Elise's heart leapt into her throat. She could see that, fast as he was, Raheem did not have time to parry the blow. Zeht caught him, drawing blood. Raheem whirled, moving with the force of the blow, turning a complete circle and flinging one hand out.

Zeht flew backwards like a ball shot from a cannon, colliding with the pillar he'd been perched on earlier hard enough the rocks began to tumble. Righting himself, Zeht flung an arm out and the rocks changed direction, became missiles--flying directly toward Raheem.

He dodged the first. Missing him, it shot onward, striking the column of rock beneath Elise's precarious perch. The whole pillar lurched from side to side and Elise rolled over the edge. The jolt when she reached the limit of the chains felt as if it had ripped her hands and feet from her body. Blinded by the pain, her feet and hands numb, Elise blacked out.

She came to as a gust of wind swung her upwards. With an effort, she grasped a link in the chain on the rock. Holding on for all she was worth, she rested, trying to catch her breath and throw off the dizziness, fighting the numbness in her hands. Finally, she managed to grab another handhold and hoist herself a little higher. She rested again, her hips and legs still dangling over the side. Inch by inch, she shifted herself forward until she was once more lying fully upon the slab of rock.

When she managed to look toward the combatants again, she saw that they had moved a little further away. Raheem was trying to draw Zeht away from her. Zeht, she saw, was trying to maneuver so that one of the two remained between her. If he managed to maneuver between her and Raheem, then Raheem could do nothing without risking that it would bypass Zeht and strike her. If Raheem was between her and Zeht, then he must take the brunt of whatever Zeht threw at him or risk allowing it to strike her.

The two came together again in a blinding blur of blades, hacking away at each other in fury, but, physically, they were well matched. Neither could gain the upper hand for more than a few moments. Both were bleeding from numerous cuts, though neither man seemed to have managed to land a solid blow.

Abruptly, their swords locked. They heaved against each other for several moments, each man struggling for dominance. Finally, Raheem thrust Zeht away, sent him flying backward once more against the pillar. Zeht, roaring in frustration, lifted both hands and, in each palm appeared a ball of fire. He began tossing them toward Raheem, faster and faster as Raheem parried each, flinging them back at him, but he was driving Raheem toward her.

The first fireball that whizzed past her singed her hair. Clamping a hand to her mouth, Elise flattened herself against the rock. The effort to refrain from distracting Raheem was wasted, though, for his head whipped toward her as the fireball did. The inattention cost him. Three fireballs struck him in quick succession. Elise screamed and leapt to her feet.

To her relief, Raheem merely sloughed them off, as if he were slinging water from his body. Lifting one hand, he pointed a finger at the ground and began to twirl it. Air began to swirl, elongate. It became a funnel and, at Raheem's command whipped toward Zeht. Raheem created two more, sending them to surround Zeht. The funnels closed in upon him, met and became one, with Zeht trapped inside, whirling like a top.

He summoned the fireballs once more, using the twisting momentum of the tornado to whip the fireballs out in every direction, laughing wildly because he had turned the funnel against Raheem. Ignoring the barrage of fireballs, Raheem lifted both hands like the conductor of an orchestra, pulling water up through the spout.

Zeht stopped laughing as the fireballs were extinguished, but began to hurl ice javelins in their stead.

Raheem sucked in a deep breath of air and blew it out again. As the air touched the funnel, the entire funnel began to harden. Within seconds it had become a tower of solid ice.

Raheem glared at Zeht for several moments, his hands on his hips. Then, lifting one hand, he summoned a bolt of lightening and hurled it like a spear directly at Zeht. The bolt struck the column of ice dead center, shattering it into millions of ice pebbles--shattering Zeht along with it.

Satisfied, Raheem turned and raced toward her. This time he had no trouble reaching her, for he'd destroyed Zeht's spell when he destroyed Zeht. Elise, forgetting her resolve to allow Raheem to believe she didn't care about him, threw herself at his chest when he knelt in front of her. "You're alright? You weren't hurt?"

His arms tightened around her. "Mere scratches," Raheem said dismissively, examining her carefully for injury. "It is you, myska, who are hurt. Lie still and I will take the pain away." Pushing her away, he made a brushing motion at the chains, which fell away, then took her hands, encircling each wrist with his fingers. Heat seeped into her, became fire and Elise gasped. When he removed his fingers, however, her wrists had ceased to throb in pain. She cried out when he manacled her ankles with his fingers, but, as with her wrists, the moment he removed his hands the pain was gone, as well. He scooped her into his arms and held her tightly a moment. "I must take you from this world, myska."

"Please," Elise said faintly. "Take me home, Raheem. I don't feel at all well."

* * * *

Elise wasn't aware of anything else until she opened her eyes to find her mother hovering worriedly over her. "Mama?"

Carol Vallee smiled. "I'm here, honey. You're not hallucinating."

"Here?"

"On the island. It's beautiful...like paradise. Who'd have thought there were still places like this around? Of course it's abysmally backwards, honey. No phones, no electricity, unless one happens to have a generator, which, fortunately, Raheem provided. Not that I can figure out what it runs on. There aren't any cars on the island, so I wouldn't think there'd be gasoline either. They have ships that stop here every few months or so, but otherwise it might as well be on another planet."

"Raheem's...is he here?"

Carol smiled. "Of course he's here! I banished him from the sickroom, though. I told him he wasn't doing you any good at all hovering over you. He seemed terribly perturbed when he couldn't make you instantly better. I'm sure, whatever he did do helped you a great deal." She stopped when her chin wobbled slightly. "You were as close to death...." She stopped again, cleared her throat. "But that doesn't matter, now. You're getting better by the day. I told him he'd just have to give your body time to mend itself."

Elise struggled to sit up and her mother reached to help her, propping pillows behind her back. Elise was amazed at how weak that little effort made her. She closed her eyes, fighting the urge to drift off to sleep again, listening as her mother moved about the room. When she opened her eyes again, her mother was standing over her with a brush. Settling herself on the edge of the bed, she carefully brushed Elise's hair, then leaned back and studied her. After a moment, she set the brush down and pinched Elise's cheeks. "There!" she said happily. "Just enough color to keep you from looking so pale."

She glanced up at the ceiling. "You can come in now!"

Raheem materialized near the balcony door, his arms crossed over his chest.

Carol smiled at him. "See, she's better today." Sniffing, she got up, leaned over to kiss Elise on the cheek and excused herself.

Elise was barely aware of her mother's departure, however. She was studying Raheem, trying to decide what sort of mood he was in. After a moment, she held out her hand to him, palm up. He studied her outstretched hand for several moments and finally strode forward, clasping it as he knelt beside the bed. Turning her hand palm upwards, he kissed the center. Warmth tingled along her arm and Elise curled her fingers against his cheek. "I have a terrible temper," Raheem confessed uncomfortably.

"Yes, you do. Worse than mine, even--I think," Elise said, smiling faintly.

"I would be honored if you would be my wife," he said gruffly, reddening with discomfort.

Elise stared at him, stunned. "Marry?"

Raheem threw a glance in the direction of the door her mother had disappeared through only moments before. "Your mother says it is the custom."

Elise frowned, tugging her hand free. "My mother? You mean this was her idea?"

Dismay flickered in Raheem's eyes, then irritation. "I do not know the customs of your people," he said stiffly.

"Well, marriage isn't necessarily one of them," she said tightly, struggling against the hurt she felt that Raheem so obviously felt compelled to offer something he just as obviously didn't particularly want to offer. "It's only for two people who love each other more than anyone else in the world...and vow to love no other. The ceremony is nothing, if they don't feel that way, but just another piece of paper.

In any case, I expect you'll be returning to your own world soon. I appreciate your rescuing me and bringing me home...where I belong."

Raheem stood up abruptly. "It is just as I thought, then."

Elise glared at him. "It must be wonderful always to be right," she snapped and then turned over on her side, putting her back to him.

After a moment, she heard him stride across the room and leave by way of the balcony. It surprised her until she remembered what he'd said before--the longer he was away from his own world the weaker his connection to it. He had not seemed to lack for strength when they were in his world, but she supposed that was because he had been in his own element. Here his magic dwindled daily.

He should have already gone back. All he'd needed to do was to dump her with her mother and leave...actually, all he'd really needed to do was to get her out of his world. He could've dumped her anywhere.

She was trying to decide whether she wanted to cry or throw something when her mother opened the door and peered in. "Where's Raheem?"

"Gone back to the inner world, I guess," Elise said sullenly.

"But...he didn't say anything?"

Elise glared at her, fiercely glad to have found another target. "I'll thank you not to interfere in my life, mother! How could you!"

Her mother planted her hands on her hips. "Don't you take that tone with me, Elise!"

Elise blushed, but she was too angry to heed her mother's reprimand. "I don't know what you did to convince him to offer to marry me ...."

"I didn't do anything," Carol said, turning red. "Except tell him that it wasn't acceptable for the two of you just to live together. He'd have to marry you."

Elise rolled her eyes. "Well, don't fret over it. We're not going to live together."

"You're not?" Carol asked, obviously dismayed. "Why not? You two are hot for each other, aren't you?"

"Mother!"

"Oh, I see! You just found it exciting because he was so exotic? Now that you know he's going to be just like the rest of us, it isn't nearly as exciting."

"That's not true!" Elise said furiously. "I can understand Raheem believing the worst of me, but you *know* I'm not like that!"

Carol sighed. "It's John, isn't it?"

Elise stared at her blankly. "John? That's...absurd!"

"You still love him. I thought you'd get over it after a while."

Elise fell back against her pillows, staring up at the hangings over the bed. "It's got nothing to do with John. I feel...I feel like I'm betraying his memory."

"Now you're the one being ridiculous. What's the point of loving a dead man? I can understand cherishing his memory, but he loved you, Elise. Do you honestly think he would've wanted you to be alone for the rest of your life?"

Elise shook her head, covering her face with her hands. "You misunderstood. I feel like I'm betraying John because...because I love Raheem so much more than I ever loved John! I'm a *terrible* person!"

"You're human, Elise. And I've got news for you, dear. Anybody that's capable of loving someone, can love someone else, too. The thing I don't understand is why, if you love

Raheem as much as you say you do, you're so determined to send him back!"

"Because...I don't want him to regret it. He's never had to live without magic. Don't you think giving it up would be like...like getting amputated? Like being whole and strong and suddenly discovering that you're crippled from the neck down? I can't do that to him. I'm *afraid* to let him because...I'd rather send him away and think he still cared about me than keep him here and watch him stop."

Carol let out a sigh of irritation. "That's his choice to make, Elise, not yours. And if he has regrets later, and blames it on you, then he's not the man I think he is!

You love him. He loves you. It's about time the two of you stopped behaving like complete idiots and told each other.

And, whether you decide to get married or not--naturally, it's up to the two of you--you're both idiots if you don't take the happiness you've got a chance at. Worry about tomorrow when it comes!"

Stalking across the room, Carol snatched the balcony door open. "You! Try to get it right this time! Honest to God, my yardman could've done better, and he can't even speak English!"

"Mother!" Elise cried. "You were listening!"

Carol blushed faintly. "Of course I was listening. I wanted to know what to tell the preacher. He's been cooling his heels for hours now. He's running out of patience and so am I!"

Raheem was glaring at Carol as she stalked back across the room and slammed out the door. "That woman is...."

"Don't you *dare* say anything nasty about my mother!"

Raheem planted his hands on his hips. "You are as...bossy as she is!" he snapped, glaring at her.

Elise threw a pillow at him. "And you are such a...a myska, I don't know why I love you so much!"

Raheem stared at her as if dumbfounded. After a moment, his lips twitched. A chuckle escaped him, and then another.

Elise felt blood pulsing in her cheeks. Here she'd told the man she loved him and he was laughing at her! Grinding her teeth, she gave him her back.

He landed on the bed beside her, still chuckling. Elise gave him a dagger glare and turned over. He grasped her arm and pulled her back, capturing both her wrists. "I love you, myska. Marry me."

Elise was more than a little mollified, but still miffed. "Why were you laughing?"

His eyes gleamed, but he didn't make the mistake of laughing again. "Because mi-yis-ka means 'my adored princess'."

Elise stared at him for several moments and burst out laughing. "You ass! You told me it meant 'pesky...like the fly'." She mimicked his deep voice.

He studied her a long moment, and pulled her tightly against his chest, wrapping his arms around her. "You are very gullible, beloved, but I adore you all the same."

"I love you, anyway, too," she said with a chuckle, then sighed. "Are you absolutely, positively certain that you want to give up...everything from your world and stay with me?"

Raheem looked a little uncomfortable. "I am absolutely, positively certain that I want to be with you...always."

Epilogue

Elise looked around the little house that she and John had bought when they first married. She had loved it the moment she set eyes on it. She still loved it and the memories that resided there. That was the main reason she'd decided to sell it.

She and Raheem would be living in the palace he'd built near the sea. She had been tempted to just keep her house--rent it out, maybe. She'd realized, though, that that was partly because she'd felt she needed it for security and partly because she was still reluctant to completely break the ties with the past.

The truth was, she didn't need the security blanket, and she was way past due on breaking those ties. She didn't need the house to remember her first husband, and keeping it might always make Raheem wonder if she really did still love John best.

Raheem had moved most of her belongings to the palace when he'd first taken her there, but there were still things that needed to be disposed of. She'd picked out the things she wanted to keep, invited her mother and sister to help themselves to whatever they were interested in and collected the remainder for the Salvation Army to pick up and distribute among the needy.

All she had to do now was arrange passage back to the island. It was a shame, really, that Raheem had lost his powers. It would've been a lot more convenient moving back and forth between the states and the island, especially at the moment, when she had a small truck load of household goods to be moved.

Sighing, she leaned down to pick up the last box of household goods. As she did, the sleeve of her T-shirt fell off. Elise frowned, looking at it incomprehensibly for several moments. Finally, she picked it up, studying it.

The fabric looked fine--not the least worn. While she was looking at it, she felt a tickle on her other arm and turned to discover that sleeve had fallen off, as well, slipping down the crook of her elbow.

Pulling it off, she held both sleeves in her hands for several moments, then looked up at the ceiling. "Raheem! You lied to me, you ass!" she yelled.

She had almost decided she was imagining things when the front of her T-shirt separated from the back and the rest of the T-shirt landed at her feet. She looked down at it, then looked around the room. Raheem was hovering, mid-air, as if he were sprawled out on a bed, his head propped in one hand, his other pointed at her.

She planted her hands on her hips, glaring at him.

He rotated the finger and her shorts fell off--then her bra--then her panties.

His eyes gleamed, a half smile playing around his lips.

"What am I going to do with you, husband?"

He sat up, crooking a finger at her. In the next moment, Elise found herself astride his lap. "What would you like to do with me, myska?"

Elise chuckled, then slipped her arms around his neck. Leaning toward him, she whispered in his ear.

His brows rose. "Now?"

Elise bit his ear lobe. "Right now," she murmured.

The End

GYPSY NIGHTS

By
Mandy M. Roth

Dedication:
To Shane, for all that you do to help me do what I love. Thank
you.

Chapter One

Gitana divided the mint rhizomes out carefully on the
countertop. She glanced at the parent plant and bent down to take
in a deep breath. The scent of peppermint never got old. She
concentrated on cutting the runners into the sizes needed to
replant them. She was just about to make another snip when the
bell, which signaled that a customer was in the shop, dinged.
Dusting her hands off, she gave them a quick swipe across her
smock before reaching up to adjust her falling hair.

Hours had been dedicated to trying to unlock the secrets of
keeping her unruly hair up, but after twenty-nine years, it was
still a mystery. It was hard to fight the *gift* that Mother Nature
had given her, wavy dark brown locks that seemed to grow
faster than a weed. She shrugged and gave up.

Oh, well, you can't flaunt what you don't have.

Leaving the greenhouse, she headed into her tiny herb shop. It
provided her with enough income to pay her bills and she
enjoyed it. "Be right with you," she called out, hurrying to hang
her smock on a hook and adjust her hair--again.

"Take your time," a deep male voice said, rolling over her,
through her, before finally settling in the apex of her thighs.

Gitana glanced up, and drew a deep breath in, ceasing to fidget with her smock. Every now and then she'd get a health conscious hot guy who wanted to jump on the homeopathic bandwagon, but never had she had a man as stunning as this one walk in before. The tall stranger stood smiling at her just inside the doorway. His onyx hair hung in loose curls over his shoulders and blended in with his black leather jacket.

He slid a pair of leather gloves off his pale hands. His long fingers seemed to caress the shell they'd been enclosed in. Whoever he was, he'd managed to turn the simple task of removing a glove into an erotic moment. She'd never wished to be a pair of Italian gloves before in her life, but now she did. The thought of having his long fingers sheathed inside of her was almost too much.

"Umm, hello…is there anything I can do to you…I mean for you? Can I help you?" Gitana rolled her eyes slightly, embarrassed by her slip of the tongue. A slow devilish smile crept onto his handsome face and she reddened.

Great, blush a little more, why don't you.

He took a step toward her. "*Oui*, I was told that you were the woman to see if I wanted to start my own herb garden." His voice was laced with a heavy French accent.

She gave him a sideways glance. He didn't look like the gardening type. No, he looked more like the millionaire international playboy type. Jet setting and yachts came to mind when looking at him--not herb gardens. But, if he really wanted one, she'd help. "Sure, what size garden do you have in mind…?" She didn't have a name to address him by, so she let her question just fade away.

"*Je m'appelle*," he said, stopping quick and shaking his head slightly. "*Pardon*, I did not mean to be rude. My name is Sebastian Rolle. I purchased the house across the way." He pointed out toward the woods. "I am thinking of having several gardens put in."

Yep, just as she thought, he wasn't the gardening type. He probably already had a crew of twenty men waiting for him to tell them where to dig. "You can have your landscaper call me. I'd be happy to help him out with what he needs."

His brow furrowed. "*Je ne comprends pas*--I do not understand. I have no landscaper. I will be handling all of this on my own."

She let out a tiny laugh and covered her mouth, hoping that he wouldn't notice. Much to her dismay, he did. "Do you find that amusing, *Madame...?*"

"Gitana," she said, walking out from behind her counter and extending her hand to him. "Sorry, no...I don't find it funny. It's just that you don't strike me as the type who'd want to get dirty."

"Getting *dirty* is one of my many specialties." He slid his cool hand over hers and cupped it gently. For having had gloves on, Sebastian's hands were like ice. She knew just the place to warm them, but refrained from commenting on it. Pulling away slowly, she noticed that she'd left dirt on his hand. She waited for him to try to find a place on his designer shirt to wipe it, but he just glanced down and smiled.

"Looks like I am well on my way to being an avid gardener."

Impressive, indeed, perhaps she'd underestimated him. Sebastian's shoes alone were worth more than her entire wardrobe and yet here he was in her tiny shop, wanting her assistance. The best part of it all was that he was her new neighbor. "You bought the old McGregor estate?"

Sebastian nodded. "*Oui*, it needs quite a bit of work, but what can I say? I fell in love with it." He brushed his hair back and exposed the most beautiful pair of navy blue eyes she'd ever seen. He winked at her and made her jump. A nervous laugh escaped her. "Would you mind if I use your restroom? They will not have my water on for some time yet. I attempted to find other accommodations for the night, but it seems that this quaint little town has none."

"Sure, umm, you'll have to use the one in my house. The one here in the shop has been acting up for weeks now. I've been meaning to call someone, but with spring just around the corner I've been too busy."

Chapter Two

"You are sure that I am not putting you out?" Sebastian asked as Gitana poured him a cup of tea. A piece of her chestnut-colored hair fell forward and covered one of her large brown eyes. He had to fight the urge to reach up and brush it out of the way. From the moment he'd seen those chocolate-colored eyes that were the doorway to her soul, he'd wanted to touch her and to know what it would be like to be buried deep within her while she called out his name. The very idea of filling her eyes with lust, with passion, shocked his senses, and left him shifting awkwardly to hide his erection.

He'd been surprised when she'd not only invited him in to use her restroom, but had also insisted that he stay for some tea and a bite to eat. It was clear that Gitana had no idea what he was, or she would have never bothered offering him food. Sebastian was old enough now that he could hide some of the oddities that normally betrayed his kind.

It was easy for vampires to lose their humanity if they didn't work to maintain control. His eyes would be the first thing to give him away if he didn't control them. They had a tendency to swirl with vibrant shades of navy and black whenever his emotions ran too high or too deep. The next, and generally most recognizable, trait was his teeth. He'd mastered the art of hiding his fangs when he smiled and talked, long ago. Kissing was a different situation. He'd spent centuries trying to work the kinks out, but every now and then he still drew blood. He thought of his lips on Gitana's, how tempting hers were, calling out to him, but the last thing he wanted to do was to hurt her. He'd spent too long searching for her to allow anything happen to her.

It'd taken Sebastian almost thirty years to find Gitana, but here she was. She was even more beautiful than her mother was. He hadn't even thought that possible. Her mother, even in her final moments, looked like a gift from the Goddess herself. He'd come across her mother, Tawni, during the war between the Roma (Gypsies) and the demons. Christians had long mistaken the Roma as being at one with the demons. They'd tired of this misconception and decided to banish a few well-known demons to another realm. Their power was great and they succeeded, but they also managed to bring the wrath of the entire demon community down on them. All walks of demon life attacked them and in such numbers that few tribes survived.

Sebastian cringed when he thought of the heinous acts his own kind had committed during the height of the war. Word had spread of a tiny group of healers who had come to help the victims of the war. He'd been unable to stop the others from going once they heard that the healers were Romas, so he'd followed in the shadows and did his best to save as many innocent lives as he could. The war between good and evil had been a bloody one. It still claimed victims although not in the same numbers it once did.

He could still remember how scared Tawni was when he found her pregnant and hiding in the woods. She kept calling out the word *mullo* and covering her face. Sebastian had been alive long enough to know that *mullo* meant demon in her native tongue, and that the young girl was right, that's exactly what had attacked her tribe.

Tawni went on and on about how she was pregnant with the chosen one, and that was why she and her people were attacked. He tried to tell her that it was a random act of violence, but the more he thought about it, the less random it seemed. The vampires had been ordered to seek out the Gypsies in the area and destroy them. When a master vampire ordered his people to do something, they did it without question, at least all but Sebastian did.

He carried the very pregnant Tawni to the nearest group of human soldiers and left her near their base. He'd thought that would be enough. He'd assumed that the young woman would seek help, but he was wrong. When he returned the next night, he found her bitten and on the verge of death. The *mullos* had returned and found her alone. She used what magic she had left to fight them off, but she was unable to hold them all back. Sebastian tried to pick her up and carry her all the way into the Roma base, but Tawni wouldn't allow him to touch her until he promised to make sure that her child was safe. Reluctantly, he agreed.

"You will be the one for her. It has been foreseen," she said, and with that Tawni, the tiny Roma woman, died in his arms. The actions that followed would haunt him until the end of his days. In the height of his glory as a blood drinker he would have taken great pleasure in mutilating a human, but that had changed. Sebastian had softened over the years, and forcing Tawni's child into the world was bittersweet for him. He'd aided in saving the tiny baby's life, but had been unable to save her mother. Sebastian took the baby and returned her to the survivors of the brutal attack. That night he'd been plagued by visions of Tawni and by her final words to him. The next night he tried to find the Roma tribe that he'd left the baby with, but they had vanished. He'd spent the next thirty years trying to find the child again.

Now, as Sebastian watched Gitana prepare a sandwich for him, he had a hard time believing that she was the same child he'd seen so many years ago. Gone was the tiny, purplish, screaming bundle he'd carried, wrapped tightly in his coat for miles in the pouring rain. He could still remember how loud the thunder was that night, and how severe the storm was that followed. He'd feared that the tiny baby girl would not make it, but she did. Now, Gitana was a creature of such beauty that he thought for a moment that his heart had actually started to beat. Of course, that was ridiculous, he hadn't fed today and it wouldn't beat again until he took the blood of the living into him.

"Would you like some mayonnaise?" Gitana asked, glancing at him and then the sandwich.

Sebastian wasn't sure how to respond to that because he wasn't entirely sure what *that* was. He could eat human food, but it did little in the way of sustaining him, so he tended to avoid it. Gitana wrinkled her nose up and gave him a very adorable look.

"It's okay to tell me what you do and don't like. I won't hold it against you when I help you with your herb garden."

"Very well then, no, I will pass on the may-o-nnaise. Thank you, though."

She took time to cut his sandwich and arrange it on the plate, just so. It had been ages since someone had done that for him-- over a hundred years. He sighed and thought of Tawni's last words. Could Gitana really be the life mate he'd been searching for? Could he really be the one for her? He looked around the tiny yellow kitchen for signs of a man's touch. Dried herbs and flowers hung upside down from the ceiling and lined the walls. Gitana was an excellent housekeeper, at least from what he'd seen so far, so he couldn't gauge by the number of dishes she had out. A more direct approach was in order.

"Your property is almost as large as mine. It must be hard on you caring for all of it. I am already asking myself why I bothered to buy such a large house and so much land when there is only me."

Gitana sat down at the other end of the table and looked out the window in the direction of his house. "It's not so bad. You get used to being alone. I purchased this place right out of college. My husband...."

The phone rang and she stopped talking. Sebastian felt as if his shell of a heart had been ripped from his chest. He'd been searching for centuries for that perfect someone, his one true mate, and now that he had finally found the one who was supposed to be it, she was married.

Sebastian tried to be polite and block out Gitana's conversation but his vampire hearing made it easy for him to pick up on almost any noise. He perked up when he heard an older woman's voice. The woman was talking about a man named Aaron, and about how Gitana should return his phone calls.

Gitana turned in towards the phone and tried to whisper. "Grandma, I'm not going to call him, and don't you call him either. The divorce is final and the restraining order is clear, if he sets foot on my property, I'll call the sheriff. I have to go now…yes…I'll call you in the morning."

Sebastian's blood boiled. Who was this Aaron and what had he done to *his* Gitana? If he found out that Aaron had harmed her in any way, he would personally snap his neck. Right after he drained him of his blood.

* * * *

No sooner did she hang the phone up than it rang again. Gitana picked it up expecting to find her meddlesome grandmother on the other end and felt her stomach drop out when she heard Aaron's voice. She glanced over at her guest and hoped that she didn't look as nervous as she felt.

"Gitana, don't hang up. I just want to talk to you."

"You were told not to call here. I've changed my number enough," she said, as quietly as she could.

"Come on, baby. I just want to see you, that's all. Your grandmother thinks we should try to work things out."

"She also thinks that she can communicate with the dead and read people's fortunes, still want to go with what grandma thinks?" She didn't wait for a response. "I have to go. Don't call here again."

"Don't hang up on me, Gitana, I'm warning you."

She put the phone down and shut the ringer off. Aaron could redial her number all night, and she wouldn't have to be bothered with him. She turned her attention back to Sebastian. His jaw was tight and his body language said that he was agitated.

"Is everything alright?" he asked, his gaze narrowing.

She glanced back at the phone and hoped beyond hope that he hadn't overheard her conversation. She'd had a hard enough time meeting and keeping men around due to Aaron. Her ex-husband had made it his mission in life to see that she was single. He'd once beaten up a man she'd gone out to dinner with and threatened any others that he found out about. Aaron had made it hard for her to do much of anything. He'd been possessive when they were married and he was still doing it now, two years after the divorce had become final.

Gitana gave him a slight grin and sat back down in her chair. "Yes, everything is fine. So, tell me, how do you like the house so far?"

Good girl, change the subject.

"Ah, the house is perfect. Well, it is perfect minus the lack of water, electricity, and heat. They cannot turn anything on until the contractors are done making upgrades. I apparently purchased a money pit, but after having met my new neighbor, I believe it is worth my while." He winked, and her heart fluttered.

Gitana brought her hand to her face as she smiled. If Sebastian was flirting with her, he was doing a great job. If he was only being polite, well, that was still good too.

She watched him stir his tea. He leaned forward and placed his spoon on her saucer. Her eyes bulged. One of her grandmother's specialties was reading fortunes. She could do it in just about anything: tealeaves, water, crystal balls, even candles. Sebastian's very casual discarding of his spoon was a sign of a marriage to come--at least, it was if you bought into divinations. If grandma was right, then Gitana was heading back down the aisle soon. She laughed a little at the absurdity of it all, even though part of her wanted more than anything for that to be true.

Chapter Three

It felt so wrong to him to invade Gitana's mind, but Sebastian was finding it hard to control himself around her. His rage over her ex-husband calling her had set him on the edge and he'd suddenly found himself deep within her mind, exploring her most private of thoughts. He had been pleased to find out that he'd inadvertently given her a sign of a pending marriage and was even happier to find that she hoped it was true. He wanted nothing more than to find his mate and spend eternity with her. And part of him knew that Gitana was the one.

Sebastian's only complaint about his potential mate was that she always covered her smile. He'd get her to stop doing that soon, even if he had to hold her hand away from her face while he made love to her, and he had no doubt that he *would* make love to her very soon. He would stop at nothing to see that happen. He would be a gentle lover for her, if that was what she needed, different from this Aaron fool who obviously didn't know how to treat a woman of Gitana's caliber.

He had to fight to keep a feral smile off his face when he heard Gitana thinking about his chiseled face, thick neck, and how his chest looked from the little bit she could see. He was pleased that she found him attractive, but was even more pleased by how perfect she was. In his eyes, there had never been a woman as beautiful as Gitana. Her olive skin and delicate features made him want to wrap his arms around her and protect her from the world. He had none of his normal primal urges to use a woman and discard her after he was satisfied. No, Sebastian wanted nothing more than to please Gitana.

He took a few bites of the sandwich she'd made him and tried to wash it down with the tea she'd poured him. The last thing he wanted to do was offend her, but trying to push down human food on an empty stomach was never a good idea. After he had blood, he would sometimes eat a few strawberries or have a glass of wine. He should have fed before he came to see her, but his excitement over finally finding her had clouded his better judgment. He needed to go and feed soon, or he'd be unable to control himself much longer. As much as he hated to leave her, he didn't want her to see his demon manifest itself. He rose from his chair and picked up his plate.

Gitana rushed around the table and took it from him. "Here, I'll get that."

"*Merci*, and I hope to see you again soon. I really should be getting home."

She shifted and bit at her lower lip. Instantly, his body tightened and his cock hardened. Thoughts of her lush lips wrapped around his shaft flooded him.

"Are you sure? I mean, you don't have any utilities hooked up yet and it's supposed to be cold tonight. I have a guest bedroom. You're welcome to stay in that."

He couldn't hide his shock. He never expected her to go so far as to invite him to stay the night. Sure, he'd hoped, but he never really thought that she would. Truthfully, he didn't mind sleeping in a house with no heat. His body stayed cold regardless of his surroundings, so it didn't matter. As much as he wanted to be with her, in her, the need to feed was too great. He was about to decline her polite offer when he sensed her fear of being alone. Aaron's call had unnerved her and Sebastian wanted to have a go at him if for no other reason then that. Standing slowly, he nodded.

"If you are sure that it would be no trouble, then yes. I would welcome the opportunity to not only have a warm bed, but the company of a beautiful woman as well." His comment was suggestive, just as he intended it to be. Gitana blushed and it warmed him. He wanted to touch her, hold her in his arms and feel the length of her body pressed close to his.

Suddenly, the lights flickered and then died. Gitana yelped and crashed into the corner of the table. Sebastian's vampire eyes could see perfectly in any light, and he used his speed to cover the distance between them. Touching her arm lightly, he whispered in her ear. "It is okay. A storm approaches from the west." He ran his fingers down her arm. She tipped her head back, exposing her smooth neck to him, and let out a soft, sexy sigh. "Can you smell it...the rain I mean."

Gitana took in a deep breath and held it for a moment. "Yes, I do smell it."

She turned into his arms and tightened under his touch. Her body wanted him. He could sense it. But she was unsure of what to do next. Sebastian also sensed fear in her. It was unclear if her fear was of him or for him. There was only one way to find out.

Leaning down to her, he let his lips hover just above her cheek. He wrapped his body around hers, embracing her, holding her tight. "*Ma vie*, you are shaking. Do you not like storms?"

"No, I've never liked them. I have these dreams sometimes of...." She stopped short.

He moved his head more and blew out a cool breath onto her cheek. It wasn't hard to notice the sweet smell of her nervous sweat and the soft scent of vanilla that she seemed to secrete. He wondered if her cream would taste every bit as sweet as it smelled.

Thunder boomed around them and the window lit up with the blue flashes of lightning. Gitana jumped and threw herself against Sebastian, leaving his body tightening and his cock painfully erect. He closed his eyes for a moment to try to regain his composure, but being this close to her proved to be too much.

He wanted to have her naked in his arms, to taste what wonders lay beneath her long red skirt, and to press his cock deep within her velvety folds. At least, if he'd taken blood today, he could have held his sexual urges at bay. But now he wasn't sure if blood would do much in the way of calming him while he was around Gitana, and that was a sign that she was a candidate to be his mate.

* * * *

Gitana held tight to Sebastian's shirt and took in the scent of his Dolce and Gabbana. It was one of many types of cologne that Aaron had owned. He treated his colognes the same way he treated his women. He used them quickly, changed them often, and tossed them aside. She shook her head, not wanting to associate Aaron with Sebastian any further. Something about Sebastian felt so right, and she wouldn't let her ugly past interfere.

Gitana thought about pulling away from Sebastian. She hardly knew him, and yet she had her face pressed against his hard chest. To top it off, she'd invited him to spend the night. It was a bold move on her part. She'd never done such a thing before. He'd seemed reluctant at first, but when he finally agreed to stay, she'd felt like she could fly. She wished that she'd had the nerve to ask him to stay with her in her bed, but she'd chickened out and offered him the spare room.

He moved his arms lower, leaving his hands resting on her hips. Tipping her forehead down, she let it rest on his chest. She wanted to run her hands up and through his long black curls, to feel the muscles in his neck as her fingers danced along them, and to know what it would feel like to see them straining above her as he worked his body in and out of hers. The lights flickered back on and startled her. She pulled away, brining her hand to her face as she laughed.

"*Geesh*, I'm jumpy. Sorry, I didn't mean for you…you didn't have to…" She wasn't sure how to thank him for comforting her. She'd never had a man do that before.

Aaron's temper always prevented him from being too nurturing. He liked to blame it on his "condition," but a year into their marriage she realized that was just the way he was, mean and domineering. Sebastian seemed different. He seemed to have a tender side that he wasn't afraid to let show, yet something dangerous lurked just below the surface.

Her grandmother had told her that Aaron was the one for her, her true *mullo* mate. In her language, *mullo* was a term used to describe demons like vampires and werewolves. The prophecies had told of Gitana's coming, and that one day she would mate with a *mullo*. Their union would produce a ruler that would end the fighting between the Roma and the demons, saving mankind in the process. She'd been raised to believe in demons and creatures of the night. She'd seen so many different types of things that were thought to exist only in nightmares that they no longer fazed her.

That's what had made Aaron seem perfect for her. Being a werewolf himself, he knew about how strange her life was and he understood the traditions of her people, the craft that they practiced, their vows of secrecy. Normal people just didn't get it, and letting them know that there were demons living and working among them would only cause mass chaos.

There was a loud crash and the house seemed to shake for a brief moment. The lights went out with a pop. Gitana screamed and fell backwards, tripping over the leg of the table. She waited to hit the floor, but didn't. Sebastian was suddenly there, holding her tight, protecting her. He sparked something primitive in her, something she'd never before experienced. Raw animal lust overcame her and she almost begged the stranger to take her to bed, to ravish her, to use her until their bodies were spent.

His face was so close to hers that she couldn't help herself. Leaning up, she planted her lips on his. Part of her expected him to just drop her. Another part hoped he'd reciprocate her advances. He did.

Sebastian's cool tongue slid into her slightly parted lips and inched its way around her mouth. Tiny, low moans and throaty laughs passed between them as they embraced. She shifted her legs a bit in an attempt to stop the dampness that he was creating, but only managed to stimulate her body more. Slick, wet cream lined her inner thighs now. As she slid her fingers into his silky curls, her dampened legs gave out from under her. In an instant, Sebastian had her swept up and off the floor.

It was hard to make out his face in the dark, and the sporadic flashes of lightning weren't helping much. Sebastian's pale skin looked blue as each bolt struck out. He walked with her in his arms, carrying her toward the back of the house. He was doing remarkably well for a man who had never been in her home before, especially in the pitch darkness. He stopped only once to open her bedroom door before he continued onward.

Sebastian laid her on her bed gently and moved his body over hers. His kisses came faster now but were every bit as rewarding as the first one. He was so much taller than she was that her legs stopped at just below his knee. She moved her legs out and allowed him to settle against the soft material of her long red skirt.

* * * *

Sebastian used his arms to prop himself up to keep his full weight from bearing down on Gitana. She seemed so tiny to him that he didn't want to hurt her. He'd spent too long looking for her to risk anything happening to her now. He'd thought that she would have a hard time breaking through the barrier of him being undead, but he was pleasantly surprised to find out that Gitana not only knew creatures like him existed, but had been married to a werewolf. His chest tightened as he thought of her sharing her bed with another, and he silently cursed himself for not finding her sooner.

No man but me will ever touch you again, my beautiful Gitana.

Chapter Four

She'd never taken a man she'd just met to bed before. Gitana had known Aaron for close to six months before she found herself in his arms. This was a first for her, and so far, it was wonderful. Sebastian's kisses moved down her neck. It took everything in her not to push him off her and run from the room. She had to keep reminding herself that Sebastian didn't pose the same risk to her throat and chest that Aaron had. She'd learned to be cautious about baring her neck to Aaron around the time of the full moon. He'd come close to ripping her throat out during intercourse once. Thankfully, he'd managed to stop himself before any real damage had been done.

It felt good to relax and let Sebastian's fingers and kisses run all over her. So far, he was being a gentleman. It was Gitana who finally crossed the line and pulled his shirt out of his pants. Running her fingers over his back, she felt his smooth, cool skin give way to thick raised welts. Sebastian tightened under her touch as she traced the length of the scars. His kisses slowed and he pulled back from her. He kissed the tip of her nose softly. She pulled her hands away from his back and tried to cover her mouth as she smiled. Sebastian caught hold of her wrist and pulled her hand to his lips.

"Why do you cover your mouth when you smile?"

Gitana tried to lower her face from him and pull her hand

away. She hadn't realized that she covered her mouth when she smiled, but it made sense. After years of living with Aaron she'd started to feel ugly, inferior. He made it a point to tell her daily that she was nothing like the wolf bitches he had lined up. He would go on and on about the she-wolves beauty and their knowledge behind bedroom doors. Aaron had made Gitana feel ugly, and not even divorce could erase that pain.

He bent down towards her and kissed her cheek. "Let no man tell you lies, Gitana. You are *tres jolie*, and to say otherwise is a lie."

Gitana's stomach tightened, and she had a hard time holding back her tears. Only in her wildest dreams did men say such sweet things to her. To have one here with her, whispering all the right words was a bit overwhelming. The Goddess must have sent Sebastian to her. There was no other explanation for him. He was just too perfect, but the best thing about him was that he wasn't a *mullo*--he wasn't a demon.

* * * *

Sebastian kissed Gitana's lips and tried to kiss away the salty tears on her cheeks. For the first time in over two hundred years, he felt as if he might cry as well. Some of his pain was Gitana's, but the rest was all his own. He'd been eavesdropping on her thoughts and picked up on how relieved she was that he wasn't like Aaron, that he wasn't a demon. What had Aaron done to ruin her so? How could a werewolf allow himself to harm a woman he loved? If he ever found out, he would kill him, so it was best that he not know all the details.

He wanted to take Gitana and mate with her the way it had been written long ago, but it would be a lie. She had the right to know what he was before he made love to her. If she found out that he was a vampire, she would send him away. But, he'd rather know that he'd been honest with her, than use her like she'd been used before. The Sebastian of centuries ago wouldn't have thought twice about taking advantage of Gitana, but not now.

It was so much easier then, he thought to himself as he kissed along her collarbone.

He couldn't remember the exact date of his change, but he did know that it had happened close to fifty years ago. He'd eaten his fill of human blood in a whorehouse outside of New Orleans and was ready to retire for the day. It was no different from the thousands of other pre-dawn expeditions he'd been on in his life, that was, not until he found himself on his knees with the sun pouring down on him. It'd seemed odd, at first, for the sun to be up so early, and even odder for him not to be burned by it.

Soon after his morning in the sun, Sebastian began having bizarre dreams that involved helping humans. He'd wake covered in sweat and wonder how this could be. He was a vampire, and vampires don't sweat. His tolerance for sunlight grew. He did not burst into flames as the rest of his kind did, but it would leave him drained, so he still tended to avoid the sun if at all possible. But that wasn't the strangest part of the slow change. Over time Sebastian had begun to lose the taste for the blood of the innocent victims he used to feast upon. Now, he took care to make connections at local hospitals. And if he felt the need to hunt, he'd only hunt the humans who deserved to be bled. Those were always easy to find. He could read their minds and know what they'd done. The world was a better place without killers on the street.

The only thing that mattered now was Gitana. Sebastian couldn't remember a time that he'd ever felt this way for a woman. It was hard to pull away from her when all he really wanted to do was mold their bodies into one and feel how glorious it would be to release his seed into her. She tried to pull him to her, but he kept her at bay. Her big brown eyes looked hurt, and instantly Sebastian second-guessed his decision to wait until she knew what he truly was.

I pushed too hard, moved to fast. He'll never be back, he heard her thoughts as clear as if they were his own. He wasn't sure how to comfort her without revealing that he had the power to read her mind.

He was about to say something endearing, something comforting when his vampire senses kicked in and told him that danger was near them. A tingling sensation that supernatural creatures gave off crept up Sebastian's spine. There were at least two, possible three threats. Tipping his head to the side, he took in a deep breath. Over the sweet vanilla smell of Gitana he picked up the scent of wolves. His body stiffened and his jaw tightened as he thought about Gitana's ex-husband trying to hurt her.

"Sebastian, are you okay? Did I do something wrong? I'm not normally like this. I'm sorry. You came here looking for help with a garden, and I do this…I'm sorry…I…"

"*Shh*, my sweet Gitana, you are perfect. You could never do anything wrong. I just need to...." The telltale howls of a wolf rose over the wind of the storm.

Gitana grabbed hold of his shoulders and stared up at him, a look of sheer terror on her face. "Stay here, and do *not* move," she said as she wiggled out from under him.

Rolling off her, he climbed out of the bed and watched as she smoothed her skirt down. She unpinned her hair and let it fall in dark waves down her back. She was breathtaking. "Sebastian, I'm sorry. I should've never let this happen. I need you understand...promise to stay here."

She glanced around the room and moved toward her dresser. Curious as to what she'd do next, he watched in silence as she lit several candles and took one in her hand. The soft candlelight reflected off her lovely face. He wanted to take her in his arms and kiss away the worried look that now clouded her beauty, but he had to deal with the danger lurking outside first.

Howls sounded in the darkness again. Gitana jumped and then regained herself before heading toward the door. Sebastian moved behind her and she spun around on her heels, glaring at him. Even angry she made his body burn. He wanted her now, more then ever. "I told you to wait here!"

The sound of glass breaking, followed by a loud thud filled the room. Sebastian tried to push past Gitana without hurting her, but she grabbed hold of his arm. He could have shook her off without effort, but he would never do that to her. He could never harm her. Taking her hand, he lowered it gently. "I will be back. Stay here."

She huffed and grabbed hold of him again. "Okay, rich Frenchman, I can see that you don't listen very well, so this is for your own good." She moved her hand over the candle and through the flame. It didn't harm her. Instead, the flame burned bright blue. "Spirits of the past, those beyond the grave...who no longer live today...keep the living here to stay." The candle flared, and the temperature in the room dropped as she looked up at Sebastian. "I'm sorry, I should have told you that I was a..."

"Witch, yes, but I assumed as much."

Leaning up, she kissed his cheek and he wanted to confess his secret to her then and there. He didn't. "I'm so sorry. I'll lift the spell come morning, but for now I need to know that you're safe."

Chapter Five

Gitana ran from the room. She felt horrible using her magic to imprison Sebastian, but if what she feared were true, Aaron would do far worse to him if he got the chance. She wouldn't let that happen. She'd spent hours burying crystals around her house to ward off evil and keep those intent on doing her harm out. Even though she didn't actively practice the craft anymore, she knew that she was powerful. Her grandmother had raised her to understand all the power she possessed and to respect it. It was about time that Aaron learned to do the same.

She was concerned about the amount of energy she'd used to confine Sebastian to her room. It took a great deal of her "juice" to call upon the spirits of the dead for assistance, but it was necessary for his protection. It hurt her heart to think that come morning he'd be gone. Normal, everyday people weren't used to the power of the Roma Witches and of the supernatural creatures that surrounded them. She fought back the tears that were forming in the corners of her eyes and headed toward the banging noise.

Something slammed around in her greenhouse. Aaron couldn't get into the house if his intent was harmful. What could it be? Fear gripped her as she made her way through the house, through the shop, and finally into the greenhouse. A blast of cold air hit her, reminding her of Aaron's cold heart. She shuddered.

"Aaron?"

Gitana took another step and her candle blew out, leaving her standing in the pitch-blackness of the night. Putting her hand out, she felt the edge of the long potting table that ran the length of the room. She moved down it, walking slowly to avoid tripping on any garden hoses, and listened for the sound of the wolf that she knew was near. Even with the wind blowing and the rain pounding hard against the glass enclosure, Gitana knew that a wolf was there watching her. Stalking her. Coming for her.

"Aaron, stop it! I'll talk with you, but this is ridiculous. It's too close to the full moon for you to be running around like this. You of all people know how hard the beast is to control this time of the month."

She wasn't sure why she was bothering to talk to him. He only ever heard what he wanted to hear anyway, wolf form or not.

Sliding her hand over one of her potting shovels, she picked it up and walked with it held out. It wasn't the best weapon to have, but it was silver and would inflict damage if need be.

She heard the growl a moment prior to seeing the wolf before her. Startled, she stepped backwards and raked her hand over a piece of broken glass. She grimaced. Suddenly, sound she'd heard only a few minutes before made sense. The wolf had broken into her greenhouse. She hadn't thought to surround it with crystals as well.

She debated between pulling the large shard of glass from her bleeding hand, or keeping her eye on the big white wolf that stood before her. The wolf won.

"Who are you?" She quirked an eyebrow. "You're not Aaron, he's brown."

The wolf growled, baring its teeth. She didn't run or scream. She knew better then to let it sense her fear. Werewolves fed off fear. They enjoyed it more than the kill itself. Aaron must have sent one of his pack members for her. She should have known. Aaron was, after all, alpha male for the local pack. It would make sense that he wouldn't want to get his hands dirty.

Gitana glanced down at her hand and realized how much blood she was dripping. The wolf noticed too and crouched down, ready to strike. Another bolt of lightning flashed and a swooshing noise shot past her head. The greenhouse lit up as the storm's pyrotechnics continued. Suddenly, Sebastian was there in front of her, blocking the wolf's path. He stood tall, his large muscular frame filling the aisle easily. A gust of wind blew in through the broken window, lifting Sebastian's hair and tugging on his clothing. For a second, she couldn't breath, couldn't think, couldn't move.

Protect him.

"NO! Go, Sebastian! Go!" She tried to get him to move, but was too late. The wolf lunged at him. Sebastian's hand flew up and he caught the wolf by the throat. He held it up in the air and glared into its eyes.

"Go back to your master and tell him that Gitana is under my protection now. And if he tries to harm her again, he will have me to deal with. And I am not one to be crossed." He threw the wolf out the broken window. She watched as it scrambled to get to its feet and took off for the woods. Sebastian turned to her, his face looked hard, foreign, frightening.

"Sebastian?"

He brought his hand out to touch her cheek, but she backed away. The hard edges of his face softened as he glanced at the broken window. *"S'il vous plait…ma amour* …I could not let them harm you. I wanted to tell you the truth. I never wanted you to find out this way. I am sorry. I will go once I know that you are safe."* His lip curled upwards before he turned away from her and she caught a glimpse of his fangs.

He's a vampire, a demon...a mullo.

Gitana backed up, afraid of what he might do to her next. Living with a monster for so many years gave her insight into just how ruthless they could be. She stopped when her foot hit the entrance to her shop. Sebastian had been able to cross the threshold to her home with the crystals in place. That meant that his intent had never been to harm her.

He turned his back to her and put his head down. She knew that whatever she decided next would determine her fate. If she let Sebastian walk away, then that would be one less demon to worry about in her life. Her heart raced. The thought of not seeing him again sickened her. She held firm to her spot, afraid that she'd throw herself into his arms and beg him to love her. The urge to go to him remained, did that mean he was the one that the prophecies foretold would come. Could he be her *mullo*, her mate, the future father of her child?

* * * *

Sebastian stood there struggling with the decision he'd made. It had been right. He would not have been able to go on "living" if he'd let anything happen to Gitana. But, now she knew he wasn't human, that he wasn't even alive. Her spell to keep him in the room had done nothing more than tickle when he walked out. It was only designed to hold the living captive, not the undead, like him.

"Gitana, you are hurt. You should wash that out before it gets infected." He kept his back to her, unable to face her disapproval.

"What? How'd you know...?"

"I can smell your blood. The scent of it calls to me, taunting the demon within. I can hear it, your blood, pumping through your veins. It is like a drug for my kind--you should run before you become my addiction." His words were harsh, cold. It was more for his sake than hers. He'd fallen in love with her the moment he'd laid eyes on her, maybe even before that, and he wasn't sure he could survive being cast aside.

"Well, since you're such an expert on me and my blood, come

help me clean this cut out."

Sebastian turned half-expecting to find her standing behind him with a stake. Gitana stood there holding her bleeding hand up to him with a hopeful look in her eyes. It was a remarkably brave move on her part. The Romas were well aware of vampires and the demons that they carried within, for Gitana to offer her hand up, full of fresh blood, said that she trusted him. But could she ever love him?

He took her wrist and pulled her closer to him. A six-inch piece of glass was rammed into her olive flesh. "If I pull this out, it will bleed more. We should take you to the hospital. You require stitches."

She moved closer to him and placed her other hand on his chest. "I need you. You can heal this. I've heard stories about a vampire's bite, and how your saliva can close a wound."

"I cannot take blood from you."

"Why? I'm not good enough?"

He sighed. "If only that were true."

"Then why?"

"Because, I do not want you to fear me come morning," he whispered, his eyebrow rising slightly.

"Pretty presumptuous, don't you think? What makes you think you'll be staying the night?" The idea of having his body deep in hers sounded more and more appealing.

He looked down into her dark eyes. "You invited me to sleep in the guest bedroom, remember?"

I'm such an idiot. He heard Gitana's thoughts as if they were his own. *How could I ever fear you? You make me feel safer than I've ever felt in my life.*

That was all Sebastian needed to hear. Bending down, he wrapped his arms around her tiny waist, and lifted her up and onto the long table. Her face was so close to his that he had to fight to keep from drowning her in kisses. He lifted her hand to his face and gently removed the large shard of glass. She gasped and closed her eyes. He knew that she was in pain, and he wanted to punish the person responsible.

"I will kill him if he sends anyone else here."

Gitana's warm hand touched his cheek. "Don't think about him. I just want you to think about me."

Sebastian put his lips above her bleeding hand and let the coopery smell of her blood seep into him. "Thinking of you should not be a problem." Working his tongue into her cut, he slid it around, sucking gently as he went. He could taste her power, magic, and most of all her desire for him. Visions of Tawni's last words and of Gitana talking with her grandmother hit him. In his mind, he saw a petite older woman who looked a little like Gitana smiling as she told a tiny dark-haired child of her future.

"You will love a *mullo*, he will give you the gift of a child, and the two of you will raise a future ruler," the older woman said.

The little girl smiled up at the woman. "Yes, grandma."

Sebastian's eyes flickered open, and he found that he was planting tiny kisses on Gitana's healed hand. He looked up into her dark eyes and dreaded the fact that he had to clear something up for her. Lying to her was not an option.

"I am not the *mullo* that your grandmother told you about. I can't be. Vampires cannot reproduce, at least not vampires that are as old as I am."

She put her finger to his lips. "Shh, don't worry about things we can't control. The attraction is here and it's real. Forget about prophecies and make love to me."

His cock instantly hardened. Of course, he would make love to her. He just didn't want her to have false hopes about who he was. He wondered why Twani had told him that he was the one for Gitana when she knew he was a vampire and that vampires couldn't reproduce. Gitana's slid her hands into his shirt and he stopped caring about anything other than this moment.

Gitana worked his shirt open and ran her warm fingers over his hard chest. He managed to ease her blouse off her and stood back for a moment to soak in her beauty. She was perfect, her breasts perfectly proportioned to her frame, her nipples dark and calling to him. Bending his head down, he drew one into his mouth. He rolled it around in his mouth, taking pleasure in her sweet tasting berry. Her fingers laced in his hair and then moved down his back, taking his shirt with them.

Gitana lingered over the scars on his back. Her tiny fingers worked their way over each section of raised skin. "Who did this to you?"

He didn't want to answer her, wanting only to feel her smooth skin and be allowed to take pleasure in her warm body. Gitana leaned forward and pressed her mouth to his ear. "Who would do such a thing to you, and why?"

Sebastian moved his hands up, cupping her breasts gently. Running his thumbs over her erect nipples, he took in the scent of her cream. Knowing that he was what made her wet only served as encouragement. Caught up in the moment, he gave into her questions. "My old master had me whipped for disobeying him."

"What did you do?"

"I saved an infant's life and tried to save her mother's, too."

"I hardly think that deserves punishment."

He didn't want to talk about this with her. If she had any idea what other horrible tortures he'd been subject to, she would never touch him again. The horrors in the months surrounding her birth were too painful for him to think about.

Gitana tugged at his earlobe and sent a wave of lust running through his body. "Saving an infant's life entitles you to a reward," she said in a sultry voice. Her fingers slid into the top of his pants, caressing the line of black hair that ran from his navel to his groin. She freed him from the confines of his pants, letting them slide down his body. Her warm fingers wrapped around his cool cock and he tipped his head back, savoring the moment he'd always dreamed of.

"Gitana."

"What would take the pain out of your eyes?"

Until Gitana had spoken, he'd never realized that he still carried the hurt of that night with him. The torture at the hands of his old master was secondary to the grief he felt for not staying with Tawni.

"You," he said, kissing her dark hair out of her face. "You could make it all go away." He moved her long skirt up her silky legs.

"What do you want?"

"*Je veux faire l'amour avec toi.*"

He moved his hands up and found the center of her world. His fingers glided over the tiny patch of dark curls that hid the wonders of her body. He let his finger run over her swollen mound and felt her writhe under his delicate touch. He slid his middle finger into her wet entrance and found the hot paradise that he longed to be in. She contracted around his finger, almost virgin-like from not having sex with a man in over two years. He eased her open more with a second finger. Hot juice flowed over his hand, and he used it to wet his thumb as he stimulated her clit.

* * * *

Gitana grabbed onto Sebastian's upper arms to stay upright.

Her stomach tightened as he brought her within inches of her climax. As good as it felt, she wanted more. She wanted to feel what it was like to have the length of his pale rod deep within her. She tried to get Sebastian to stop, but his fingers started to swirl, working her to the point that she could stand it no longer. Her legs shook as the orgasm swept over her. She pulled her body closer to his and watched dreamily as he pulled his finger from her pussy to his mouth, taking with him a string of her cum.

Sebastian licked his fingers clean, reached down, grasped his cock, and brought it to her entrance. The mushroom-shaped head of his shaft pushed against her but did not enter. His lips met hers, and she savored the taste of her sex on his mouth. She opened her mouth to him and, as his tongue dove in, so did he. She cried out as his girth spread her open. In one fluid movement he was sheathed deep inside her, tearing at her, pulling her to the point that pleasure and pain blurred, leaving only passion.

Tugging on her hips, he brought her body to the edge of the table, allowing him to dig even deeper. She cried out and reached for anything that would help her focus on the pleasure instead of the pain. Sebastian's hands found hers and their fingers intertwined. This simple act of holding hands was more intimate than any other level of sex, and it was just what she needed to be able to focus on him.

Sebastian brought her hands up and put them behind his head. She laced her fingers together and held tight as he rode her body. The table shook, plants tipped over and off the high countertop. Gitana didn't care. She'd give up anything to have Sebastian with her, even if that meant giving up her destiny, her *mullo*. Sebastian felt right--to hell with fate.

Looking up into his blue eyes, she watched as another flash of lightning illuminated his pale face. His rhythm slowed almost to a complete stop, and he glanced past her. She tried to follow his gaze but he caught her chin in his hand and brought her lips to his.

* * * *

Sebastian kept Gitana's mouth occupied while he looked out at the shadow that loomed in the distance, along the edge of the tree line. He could smell the scent of the wolf and sense the hatred coming from the figure. He had little doubt that the visitor was Aaron, Gitana's ex-husband.

"Bastian?" Gitana said his name, or the shortened version of it, with so much love and concern that he almost forgot about their visitor.

Glancing back up, he sensed the alpha in the man, and wanted to show him who was truly the dominant male in this situation. Sebastian concentrated on his thrusts, easing his cock in and out of her tight silk binding. She felt so good, better than he could have ever dreamt. Each movement, each connection forged an even greater bond between them. Her channel fisted him, gripping his cock tightly.

"Uhh...Se-bastian."

Gitana's body prepared to climax again. The feel of her legs tightening around him and her increased moans threatened to make him explode. He knew that he should stop making love to her, but every fiber of his being wanted to stay in her, rooted deep. In addition to that, their late-night visitor needed to know that Gitana was not only under his protection, but was also his mate.

Gitana's tossed her head back. "Do it," she said in a low sultry voice. He didn't need to ask what she meant--he could read her thoughts. She wanted him to make her into a vampire too.

He kissed her neck softly and her pussy constricted around him, milking him. A sharp pain tore through his chest and lost his rhythm, his control. His balls moved up, his cock twitched, shooting forth his seed. Shaking, he filled her with his come, his essence, his love.

"Bastian."

He looked off into the distance and saw the shadowy figure receding into the night.

* * * *

Aaron watched from the edge of the property as the vampire fucked his wife. He didn't care that the law said they were divorced. Gitana would always be his. He couldn't believe that she'd let that corpse have his way with her. His fists burned for the change, but if he let himself shift this close to the full moon, then he wouldn't be able to return to human form for several days, and he needed to be able to function to do what needed to be done.

He wanted to leap on the vampire and tear his throat out, and he would when the time was right. It was bad enough that the vampire had threatened him through one of his people, but he had taken Gitana as well.

"You will pay, vampire, and so will you, Gitana."

Chapter Six

Gitana picked up the last of the broken glass and placed it in the plastic trash bin. Glancing around her greenhouse, she smiled. Sure, she needed to get a window replaced and had smashed four flats of caraway during the night's festivities, but being with Sebastian had made it all worth it.

She scooped the tiny fern-like foliage up off the table and placed it in a small pile. She would use it in something, and at the rate she was going, she'd need it more than ever. Caraway worked great for soothing upset stomachs, and hers had been in a knot since she woke to find that Sebastian was gone. She'd been telling herself all morning that he probably had to go home before sunrise, but it seemed odd that he never said good-bye.

The bell to the shop rang. Gitana jumped to her feet and ran to the shop, expecting to find Sebastian there. She held her smile, even though it didn't quite reach her eyes when she saw one of her most loyal customers, Mrs. Mills.

"Gitana, how are you dear?"

"Fine, and you?"

"Oh, I could be better. The doctor wants to put me on 'happy pills.' Have you ever heard of such a thing?"

Gitana laughed quietly to herself. She had indeed heard of happy pills. She'd entertained asking her doctor for antidepressants during her divorce, but had managed to find some herbal remedies that had worked to lift her spirits.

Walking over to the back shelf, she pulled a box of tea down for Mrs. Mills. "Here, have look at this and see if you'd like to give it a try. It might help."

"Thank you, dear. You never did tell me why a girl with a degree in herbology and enough courses in holistic healing to qualify her as a doctor sticks around this tiny town. You could be making good money out in California, you know."

"Yes," Gitana said, laughing softly. "I suppose so, but I like it here. This place called to me and I answered. What more can I say?" She turned to head back out toward the greenhouse.

"Gitana, wait, I drink this and what will happen?"

Gitana smiled and took the tiny box of tea bags from Mrs. Mills' hands. Turning it over, she put her fingers on the ingredients. "See here, it contains Albizzia bark, it'll help improve your mood, trust me."

"Oh, I don't think a tea is going to cut it. The doctor thinks the pills will help, but I'm not too sure."

She smiled and shrugged her shoulders. "You should do what your doctor recommends and what you're comfortable with. I can't make your decision for you. I do know that within fifteen minutes of having a cup of that your mood *will* improve. Talk to your doctor first to be sure that this won't counteract with your medication and get his opinion on it. If he gives it a thumbs up then I say go for it."

"I will, and thanks, Gitana. You're a life saver."

She placed the box of tea in a brown bag and bid Mrs. Mills good-bye. She generally enjoyed seeing her, but today her thoughts were on Sebastian. Last night had been both amazing and terrifying. She'd given herself over to a vampire and expected him to love her back. She was a fool--she realized that now.

It was true, what they said about hindsight. Looking back, after they'd made love, Sebastian had seemed preoccupied, distant. He had followed her back to her room and held her in his arms. Once he thought she'd fallen asleep, he began pacing the room and watching the windows. She coaxed him back into bed with her, but knew it wasn't where he wanted to be.

It would serve me right if I never saw him again. What was I thinking, sleeping with a man I'd just met?

"Gitana?" She cringed as she heard her grandmother call out to her from the greenhouse.

Chapter Seven

"You should come in and eat. Your food is getting cold. Always playing with those plants...I tell you, in my day we did not spend all our time with our nose in a book or hand in a pot, now in my day we...."

Gitana waved at her grandmother. She meant well and Gitana knew that, but it didn't change how annoying she sometimes came across. She was tired of hearing about dead customs and ways of life, and most of all she was tired of hearing about being the chosen one. Lately, that was all her grandmother seemed to want to discuss. Gitana's thirtieth birthday was fast approaching and with it came the superstitions of old.

"You should call, Aaron. He should have dinner with us. He should come and celebrate with us."

Gitana dug down deep and cut through the mint rhizomes she'd been trying to root. "Shit!"

"Such a mouth on you. It's no wonder you don't have a husband."

"I'm not feeling very hungry." *Please don't bring up having dinner with Aaron again, please.*

"Of course you're not hungry. It's not popular for you young women to eat now. No, now you all starve yourselves trying to look like fifteen-year-old."

Turning, Gitana gave her grandmother a stern look. "I don't starve myself, and I can't help it if I'm petite. Besides, you're shorter than me, in case you haven't noticed."

"Gitana, your mother would not be pleased to know you're speaking to me this way."

She turned, wiped the mint rhizomes onto the floor, and glared at her grandmother. "I wouldn't know what my mother would think. I've never met her. I don't have the luxury of being able to communicate with the dead, Grandma…Tell me what she thinks of me now? How does she feel about me divorcing my *mullo*? Huh? Does she care? Does she even know?"

Her grandmother pulled back into the doorway slowly and clasped her hands together. "I shall ask the Goddess for forgiveness for you. You're upset about the vampire."

Gitana froze and stared at her grandmother. "What did you just say?"

The old woman shrugged, smiling sheepishly. "He came to me while I was walking home the other day in a vision. I looked down into a puddle of water and saw you in the arms of a vampire. I don't think it's wise to fall in love with a man so soon, especially not a vampire. You should be careful with him."

"Have no fear. He's gone, and I don't think that he'll be coming back."

"Hmm, that is a shame. I did want to meet him. Your mother wanted me to ask him something. It seemed important to her, but I wasn't clear on what it was." She lifted her hands in the air and dismissed the whole thing. "Oh well, I'll contact her later and find out."

Rolling her eyes, she watched as her grandmother made her way back into the house. Grandmother had been communicating with spirits ever since Gitana could remember. It used to bother her when her grandmother would pull out a pocket watch to communicate with the dead and ask it questions, waiting for it to swing to and fro signifying the answer. Over time, Gitana grew accustomed to her grandmother's theatrics and learned to ignore her. She'd even secretly practiced some of the old ways.

Chapter Eight

Sebastian sat with his head against the abandoned warehouse wall, trying to make sense of what he'd done. The last thing he remembered was making love to Gitana. A sharp pain had seized his chest while he released his seed into her. Afterwards, he took her to bed and held her warm body in his arms. He laid there for hours as the pain in his chest continued. It wasn't until he'd heard the pounding in his own ears, and felt his body warm ever so slightly, that he realized his heart was beating.

It was normal for his heart to beat during a kill, while he fed from the victim and let their warm blood flow through his veins. Sebastian hadn't fed all day. He'd had only a tiny drink from Gitana's wound, and it wasn't nearly enough to qualify as a feeding. His heart should not have started to beat again, yet it did. An overwhelming hunger had come over him. He'd spent centuries learning to control his demon, but looking at Gitana's sleeping body had nearly sent him over the edge with carnality.

He fled before she woke and did not even dare kiss her good-bye. He was blind with the raw need to hunt, to kill. He woke to find himself here, on the floor of the old warehouse with three bloody corpses at his feet. It wasn't as easy for him to read people once they were dead, but it could still be done. Two of the men had been involved in the rape and murder of at least three girls, but the third he couldn't read. That meant that he was either an innocent or a supernatural. Sebastian had no memory of tasting his blood, and that was the only way to tell if he was supernatural or not.

The thought of having killed an innocent human was tearing him apart. He'd been "clean" for close to fifty years now. Others like him had a hard time understanding how he could go cold turkey like that, and so did he. There was no logical explanation for his behavior. He had simply lost the taste for anything other than the blood of evildoers.

The afternoon sun was high and shining through the upper windows. Beams of it surrounded Sebastian as he staggered to his feet. This much direct sunlight should have knocked him out, leaving him injured. Other than feeling slightly sluggish, a bit under the weather, and hornier than hell, he was fine. Looking down at his bloodied hands, the vampire in him picked up on the pulsating vein in his wrist. His heart was still beating.

Chapter Nine

Gitana pulled the remaining weeds from her flower garden and gathered them to the side. Later, she'd add them to her compost pile, using them to fertilize next year's herbs.

"Ah, *Dicentra Formosa*," a voice said from behind her.

She looked up and had to shield her eyes from the afternoon sun. There was a tall man standing dangerously close to her. His attire screamed scholar. His tiny circular, wire-framed glasses gave his otherwise too handsome face a boyish charm. She glanced at his short brown hair and thought it complimented his green eyes well.

Smiling, he pointed at the flowers before her. "*Dicentra Formosa*," he said again, his thick British accent becoming apparent.

Gitana followed his gaze and then it clicked. "Oh, yes, I'm sorry. These are Bleeding Hearts, yes. I take it that you're a fellow plant lover?"

He flashed a smile that was so innocent it made her want to like him. "I'm William, and yes I do enjoy studying plants, among other things."

Rising to her feet, she brushed her hands on her long black skirt. The Roma in her had conditioned her to wear dresses to do most everything. For the most part, she'd severed her ties with the old ways, but still felt more comfortable in skirts. She double-checked her hand for dirt before extending it out to William.

"Hi, I'm Gitana, what can I help you with today?" She bent to pick up the pile of weeds. "I closed the shop up early today, but I'd be happy to take you in if you'd like."

Suddenly, he was behind her with his hand on her shoulder. Dropping the weeds, she spun around fast, unsure how he'd managed to move so quickly. William's green eyes began to glow, taking on a supernatural appearance. Terrified, she swung out at him and he caught her wrist with his hand. "I'm not here to hurt you. I'm here to warn you. Sebastian is a friend of mine."

Gitana stopped struggling and stared at William. "You're not a vampire?" It was more of a question than a statement.

He smiled down at her. "No, I'm not a vampire, but I'm not a completely normal human either. I posses the gifts of magic and immortality, I am also a member of the Council."

The very mention of the Council made her take a step back. The Council was in place to oversee the supernatural community, and when they paid you a visit, it normally ended in death. They were the only checks-and-balance system in place, and they'd been around for thousands of years. The thought of the Council coming for Sebastian scared her more than the thought of Aaron showing up again.

The fear must have shown on her face because William put his hands up to signify that he wasn't a threat. "I'm not here to collect anyone. I'm here to warn you and Sebastian."

"Sebastian's not here." She almost added that she didn't know where he was, but that didn't seem wise. If this man proved to be a threat then it was best he think Sebastian could show up at any moment.

"I know that Sebastian's not here." A rather knowing grin spread across his face. "I'm the one who lured him away."

"You what?"

"I lured him away. It was simple. I used my power to override his system. I imagine that he felt a hunger like he'd never felt before."

If William had indeed used magic to overload Sebastian's system, then it was amazing she was still alive. "You say that you're here to warn me about something, yet you make a powerful vampire's blood thirst border on uncontrollable. *Hmm*, doesn't sound like you're much of an ally."

He took a step toward her and she backed up. "You are right to assume that, but I am one of your *only* allies on the Council. I knew that Sebastian would never harm you. He hasn't spent all these years looking for you to let a little thirst for blood ruin his chances."

She'd only just met Sebastian. How could he have been searching for her? Opening her mouth to demand answers, she caught sight of a large green car pulling down the lane. She knew that car. It belonged to Aaron's right-hand man, Travis. Frantic, she searched for an easy escape route for William. He'd be no match for a werewolf in the woods behind them, and he'd have to cross paths with Travis to get to back to his car--that was no good either.

"Come on!" Grabbing hold of his hand, she pulled him and ran toward the greenhouse. William never protested. He simply ran behind her. They entered the greenhouse, leading him down the aisle and into the shop. She slammed the door closed behind them.

"Care to tell me what that was about?" William asked, sounding winded.

"Gitana, I know you're in there! Come on out! Aaron wants to see you," Travis called from outside. She peeked out the window and watched as the young blond walked toward her shop door. "Aaron just wants to talk to you, I promise."

The minute Travis' hand touched the door handle it was propelled off. "What the hell?"

William looked over at her and his eyebrow rose slightly. "Did you do the protection spell?"

"Yes, its only purpose is to keep anything out those is intent on doing harm to me. Looks like Travis had a little more on his mind than just talking." She laughed softly.

William made an odd noise, clearing his throat. Gitana glanced over at him, unsure what the problem was. He didn't look much like the fighting type. Maybe he was scared. "You're safe in here."

He chuckled. "I'm not concerned about my safety. I'm concerned about yours. The Council has no idea that you're a master of the craft. This will only serve to make them more intent on their mission."

Why did it matter if she could perform magic? She'd never harmed an innocent person, and rarely used her gifts. The look in William's eye told her that there was more to the council's "mission" then he was letting on. "What do they want with me?"

"That's what I came to talk to you about."

Travis tried touching the door one more time and yelped as his hand was knocked off again. "Gitana, you can't hide in there forever, neither can your vampire friend!"

The mention of Sebastian made her pulse race and her throat dry. Aaron obviously knew about him. Now, it was just a matter of time before he attacked. He'd kill Sebastian, and if she were lucky he'd kill her too. The idea of being at Aaron's mercy scared her more than the thought of ceasing to exist.

Travis climbed back into his old green car and left. He'd be back and he wouldn't be alone.

"Would you like some tea, William?" It was a ridiculous question, but it beat screaming like a mad woman out of fear, so she went with it.

Chapter Ten

"What do you mean the Council wants us dead?" Gitana choked on her tea.

William set his cup down gently and put his hand over hers. "Not both of you, they'd settle for just one. Sebastian's made many friends on the Council over the last fifty years, so they will most likely be coming after you instead."

Somehow, he wasn't making her feel any better about their situation. "So, you're telling me that they think that the prophecies about Sebastian and I are true? That's ludicrous, I mean, he's a vampire. He said it himself, he can't have children."

"Sebastian isn't a normal vampire. He's never been normal, not even when he was human. He was a clairvoyant and possessed an untapped level of magical power. The people in his village called him the boy with *clear sight*. His sire saw this in him and that's why he brought him over against his will. The 'change' affected Sebastian's powers and he wasn't able to use them in the same way he once had. Fifty years ago they began to reemerge. They're different now, as to be expected with his condition, but they are there." He took another sip of his tea and continued. "I started studying Sebastian over a hundred years ago. He wasn't the monster that the other vampires seemed to be. No, he was kind, intelligent, and he became my friend in a relatively short period. He's a good man and that's why I am here. I think, no I know, that he'd turn into the greatest threat mankind has ever seen if anything happened to you."

She sat there thinking about what William had told her. If the Council wanted someone dead, then they always got their wish. It was just a matter of time before there wish came true about her. Suddenly, her cheeks felt flushed and her stomach twisted into a knot. Pain gripped her and she let out a soft cry. Clutching her stomach, she looked at William, pleading silently for help. He jumped to his feet and came to her side. He touched her forehead and his eyes widened.

"It's as I thought." He didn't wait for her to ask anymore about it, he just picked her up and took her in his arms. She let her head lay on his chest for no other reason than it felt incredibly heavy. "You need to rest."

Nodding, she pointed him in the direction of her room. William walked her in and laid her on the bed gently. He sat next to her, taking his jacket off and tossing it aside. He rolled up his sleeve and thrust his wrist out in front of her mouth.

"Drink, your body needs it."

Stomach bile rose quickly at the suggestion of drinking someone's blood. William put his wrist closer to her mouth. "Your body temperature is lower than it should be, and I noticed your sensitivity to the sun earlier. I'm not saying you're a vampire, but I am saying that something is happening--changing you somehow. I suspected it might work this way. You and Sebastian were destined to be mates. In order for him to be able to offer you the gift of a child he needs to become more human, and in order for you to accept his seed, you need to become more like him."

Covering her mouth to keep from being sick, Gitana shook her head violently. Drinking blood was wrong and reserved only for *mullos*.

I'm not like that--I'm not a demon.

There was no way she could become more like Sebastian. She was Roma, and they were the chosen protectors of the *mullo*. Each had sworn an oath to never allow themselves to be swayed by the darkness the *mullos* presented.

It couldn't be.

Another sharp pain twisted at her gut, a hunger rivaled by no other ripped through her body. She clenched her teeth in an attempt to stave off the desire to feed. She could hear William's heart beating, his rich blood pumping through his veins. So close, so easy to taste, to touch.

She dug her fingernails into her into the palm of her. The added pain did little to help ground her. The power within her wanted to press her mouth to his wrist and sample his sweet offering.

No.

Thankfully, William pulled his wrist away slowly. Her resolve was all but gone. Whatever was happening to her, was taking control fast.

William forced a smile onto his face. "There's more than one way for a vampire to get what it needs...a vampire can feed off sex and lust as well as blood."

The mere mention of sex sent her body into a burning rage. No amount of self-mutilation could stop help bring her back now. Her gaze narrowed. She looked out from her eyes, yet was separate from it all. William inched closer and the controlling power in her set its sights on him. The curve of his jaw, and the way his tan skin held the tiniest bit of a five o'clock shadow caught held her attention. Moister collected between her legs at the thought of having William's hands run all over her body, fondling her breasts, inching over her mound, slipping in and out of her slit. She reached for him and he nearly fell off the bed trying to get away from her.

"William," she said, slowly, her voice not her own. "Let me touch you. Let me run my mouth over you and taste *every* inch of you. You know you want me to. I can see it in your eye."

"Gitana, no, I can give you my blood--not sex. Sebastian's one of my closest friends and I...."

Reaching down, she planted her hand firmly between his legs, cupping his bulge. It hardened. A clever grin spread across her face. "*Je veux faire l'amour avec toi.*" The words ran off her tongue yet she understood not what she said.

"It's Sebastian's demon coming through. You said that you want to make love to me," William tensed up. "Please, Gitana. Try to fight it. This can't happen."

The tugging in her gut encouraged her to rub the long line of his clothed erection. With her free hand, she removed his glasses, her lust filled gaze meeting his head on. Gitana cupped William in her hand, working it up and down him and licked his cheek. She'd never needed sex so bad in her life. William could deny wanting to sleep with her all night. His hard cock told her the truth.

* * * *

Sebastian climbed out of the shower, pulled a pair of black

jeans on, and towel dried his hair. He was still a little taken aback by the events of the day. Waking up surrounded by dead bodies used to be his favorite pastime. It was no longer so. He'd taken the time to dispose of the bodies, sickened by his own lack of control. His only hope was that none all of the men were evildoers. Thinking that way didn't lesson the shock of it all. He'd have spent more time searching for clues to what had happened at the warehouse, but he wanted to get back to see Gitana. He was addicted to her. For him, she was as vital as blood, maybe more so. He would have gone straight to her, and made love to her, but he'd been covered in so much blood that he was afraid he'd scare her.

Tipping his head to the side, he ran a hand through his wet hair and reached for his cologne.

Sebastian...Sebastian...its William, come quick, Gitana needs you. He heard one of his oldest friends say in his mind.

Time seemed to stand still, and his gut tightened--Gitana needed him. The vampire within took hold, allowing him to defy gravity. A normal person would have been able to cover the distance between his house and Gitana's in ten minutes it took him mere seconds. He thrust her shop door open and sniffed the air. Blood, fear, rage, sex--all assailed his supernatural senses. He licked his fangs and took a moment to breathe deeply. Now was not the time to lose hold on his demon.

"William?"

Sebastian...in the bedroom. Come quick.

Utilizing his speed, he raced to the bedroom and pushed the door open. It took a moment for the sight before him to register. William was backed up against the wall--his shirt undone, his bare chest showing, while Gitana crawled before him on her hands and knees, tugging at his pants. William had a death grip on his pants and was fighting to keep them up. Sebastian could smell William's desire to fuck Gitana in the air, and the fact that he wasn't was the only thing that saved his life. He may be an old friend, but Sebastian would kill any man that touched *his* Gitana.

"Sebastian!" William cried out, looking extremely relieved to see him.

Gitana glanced leisurely back at him and gave him a wicked smile. One that screamed sex and the promise of endless pleasures between the sheets. Gone was the beautiful smile she'd hid so many times before. No, this smile was one he'd seen on female vampires. It was a smile that said that they needed sex to quench their thirst, and that they would take it at any price.

He shook his head. "*Non*, this cannot be. I never brought her over. I never drew blood from her." As he said it, he remembered the cut on her hand. He'd lick it clean before making love to her. A vampire knew better than to draw blood from person of magic and then deposit their seed in them. He'd done this to her. By drawing her blood and then coming in her, he'd forced an exchanged of essences--of life forces.

He dropped to his knees. "NO!"

William fought Gitana off and came to his side. "I don't think you did this intentionally. I think it was meant to happen. Hell, the last case of a vampire turning someone like this was recorded over two thousand years ago. I don't think she'll change all the way, and she almost vomited when I offered her blood, so that's good. Her hunger comes in the form of sex. She's new to this and she can't control it, that's why I called you. I didn't want to have to...."

Sebastian looked up into his friend's eyes and nodded. "*Merci*, you are a good friend."

William sighed and looking forlorn. "No...I'm not a good friend, Sebastian. I was sent here to kill Gitana, and I lured you away with the intent of doing it. It was me who called your demon out and led you to slaughter the others."

Sebastian was too stunned to do anything. He fell back onto the floor and put his head down. His oldest and dearest friend had betrayed him. "*Pourquoi*--why would you do such a thing?"

"The Council fears this union. They never thought you'd find her again. In fact, they have spent years feeding you false leads to keep you away from her. They even sent a replacement here to try to fool everyone into thinking that the prophecy had been filled, but Gitana saw through him. And when they divorced the Council put extra men in the area to watch her."

"*Je ne comprends pas.*" It made no sense. To go against the Council's wishes meant death. "Why are you telling me this? Why didn't you...?" Sebastian couldn't bring himself to ask William why he hadn't carried out his orders. If he had completed his mission, Gitana would be dead right now.

William touched his shoulder. "You are the closest friend I've ever had, and when I watched Gitana tending to her flowers, I couldn't do it. I couldn't take her away from you. I can see why you love her. She's beautiful, sexy, smart and most of all powerful."

Sebastian's gaze went to Gitana and couldn't believe his eyes. She was sitting on the floor naked, tracing the edges of her breasts with one hand, while pleasuring herself with the other. He hardened instantly and he wanted to take her then and there, but they had company. Any other time, he would have stroked his cock and watched her finger herself, not now, not with an audience. "Gitana!"

William gasped. "It's not her. Somehow, the two of you morphed powers. I think she has vampire tendencies now and you...."

Sebastian touched his chest. "My *coeur*--heart beats again."

William's mouth fell open. "Then it's true, you are her *mullo*! Together the two of you will create a life that will forever change the destiny of mankind."

Gitana cried out and clawed at her face. Red welts appeared and Sebastian raced to her side. Grabbing both her wrists, he looked up at William. "I am not sure one man can satisfy her need for sex. I may need you to...you may have to stay and..." He couldn't ask another man to touch his Gitana. The thought of someone else's hands on her body infuriated him.

William touched his shoulder gently. "See what you can do, never underestimate the power of love, Sebastian. If you need me, I'll be here. I've given my word that I will protect the two of you and I'll be staying. Call me and I will come."

Sebastian didn't even wait for William to leave the room. He planted his lips firmly on Gitana's and pushed his tongue into her mouth. She bit at his lip and made his cock throb with anticipation. His fingers moved down her tight belly and found their way into her cum-soaked recesses.

"Fuck me, Sebastian."

He wasn't so sure that he liked hearing his sweet Gitana talk this way, but he had no problem obliging. He slid down her body. He wanted to taste her before he made love to her. She grabbed his wet hair and yanked his head up. Her eyes swam with flecks of blue and black. They were *his* eyes, and these were *his* vampire needs.

She pushed him backwards and he landed flat on the floor. Having his own power turned on him caught him off guard, and he felt Gitana's hands as they slid into his jeans. She peeled them from his body and crawled up his legs. A shiver ran through him as she nuzzled her face in the dark patch of hair at the base of his cock. She took one of his balls into her mouth and rolled it around gently. He tried to coax her up. She needed pleasure right now, definitely more than he did, but she wouldn't budge. She licked the length of him and took the head of his cock into her mouth. Her hot mouth swallowed him down, and he could feel himself touching the back of her throat. She varied her speed and movements, massaging his balls with her hand as she went. He thought that he'd lose it and release his seed into her throat if she didn't stop soon. As tempting as letting her suck him off was, he needed to see to her needs.

"Gitana," was all he managed to get out.

She increased her pace, her head bobbing as she took him deep in her throat. His body prepared for release, his balls drew up and his muscles tightened. "Gitana, if you do not let me give you pleasure then I will need to call William in to give it to you. Is that what you want? Would you rather have another man fuck you, or do you want me?"

She pulled away from his wet shaft and looked up at him with swirling eyes. She started to shake her head yes, but stopped. "Bastian?"

He put his arms out to her and she moved her body up and over his. "I want you so badly, what's happening to me?" She asked, straddling his waist, and sliding her body onto his. She took him into her wet opening, sheathing him, making it almost impossible not to come.

She let out a tiny gasp and continued moving her body down on him, effectively taking his entire shaft into her. He gathered her long black hair back and held it out of her face so he could watch her make love to him. It was beautiful, she was beautiful, and she belonged only to him.

"You are mine, Gitana, mine. Do you understand?"

For a moment, she just stared down at him as she rode him. He feared that she'd refuse his claim on her, and he couldn't let that happen. Pulling on her hair, he tipped her head back gently, driving his hips up as he went, and making her cry out.

"You," he thrust upwards again, driving his cock into her deeper, "are mine! You are mine, Gitana."

"Yours," she whispered.

He watched as her breasts jiggled in his face. He captured a nipple in his mouth, careful not to knick it with his fangs, and sucked gently. She rode him with the need of a hundred women, and that was putting it mildly. He knew better than anyone did just how powerful the hunger could be. Her channel tightened on him, contracting and loosening with such intensity, he had no choice but to let his come fill her womb.

Gitana screamed out and collapsed on his chest. Her body twitched slightly as she stroked his skin. "Will the hunger ever go away?"

He brushed her long hair back and caressed her soft cheek. Lying to her would be the best option. It wouldn't do her any good to know that the hunger would only grow if she didn't tend to it regularly. As long as he had breath in his body, and if she still wanted him, he would stand by her side and be there to feed the demon he'd passed on to her. If blamed him for what she'd become then he would see to it that William watched over her. No man would ever harm her.

Chapter Eleven

"How are you doing, old friend?"

Sebastian looked up to see William standing over him. He glanced down at the bed to be sure that Gitana still slept. She looked so peaceful, so clam. He couldn't bear the fact that he'd passed on part of his demon to her. He touched his chest and closed his eyes when he felt the rhythmic thumping of his once dead heart.

"She gave me so much, yet I have passed on nothing of use to her," Sebastian said, his voice full of sorrow.

"Come." William touched his shoulder lightly. "Let's talk in the other room. I do not want to wake her up either. I don't think I could say no if she begged me to touch her again. She's a temptress all unto herself. Your power only intensified that."

If it had been any man, other than William, saying these things, Sebastian would have killed him on the spot. He knew William, and he knew that he was a true friend. He would do only what he had to and never with the intent to do harm. He'd proven his loyalty when he'd refused to kill Gitana for the Council. William could never go back to his position there. They would burn him alive now that he'd disobeyed them.

Sebastian followed William out into the kitchen. William motioned toward a bowl of fruit. "You should eat."

"*Merci*, but I prefer to eat only after I have taken blood."

William turned and gave him an odd look. "Many things have changed for the both of you. I believe that you may be able to substitute many of your blood feedings with food now, and I believe that your sensitivity to light will decrease with time as well."

"The mid-day sunlight no longer burns as it once did or leaves me as drained," he said softly.

The possibility of becoming more human had never crossed his mind. He would gladly give it all up to see Gitana free of his vampiric ways. Picking up an apple, he took a bite. Normally, he would have to wash it down with water. Today it slid down his throat easily. His eyes widened as he looked at his longtime friend.

"They will not stop until they destroy us."

"No, they'll stop if they destroy her. They need you alive, Sebastian. You are a force to be reckoned with and they need you on their side in the fight against evil," William said, taking a seat at the table.

"I will kill every last one of them if they dare lay a hand on Gitana. She is my mate and will be my wife, by law as soon as I can make it official." Sebastian tossed the fruit aside. Thinking of losing Gitana made him lose his appetite.

"I know that you will. They underestimate you, Sebastian. I fear that they have also underestimated Gitana's powers as well. They've no idea that she's a master of the craft, and if they find out, they will send *legions* to see her dead."

"Where should I take her? Where will she be safe?"

William laughed methodically. "The only place safe from the council's reach is Hell itself, and I don't think you want to take her there, especially not now."

"Meaning?"

William cocked an eyebrow and shook his head. "You're a brilliant man, yet sometimes your ignorance amazes me. I believe that she's carrying your child or will be within days at the rate you two are going."

My child? Gitana might be pregnant? Non, it cannot be so.

Shocked, Sebastian moved towards the window to look out at the night sky, and collect his thoughts. Two days ago, he'd been elated finally finding Gitana after all these years. Now, his heart beat, he'd found his true mate and he might be a father. It was more than he'd ever hoped for and more than he deserved.

"Sebastian, we need to go and speak with the council. They need to understand that you and Gitana mean them no harm."

"I will not take her to them to be slaughtered," Sebastian said, surprised that William had even suggested such a thing.

"I'm not saying that we should take Gitana with us. You and I should go and plead your case. They may listen to reason if it's coming from us both."

"I cannot leave Gitana here alone. You saw her in there. Her sexual hunger would consume her and any around her. Besides, the 'decoy' your brilliant council sent is an insane alpha werewolf that has taken to stalking her." Sebastian narrowed his gaze on William. "Marvelous choice by the way."

"I only just found about Aaron and Gitana. They told me the details surrounding all of this when they assigned the duty of killing her to me. Prior to that, they kept me totally in the dark. They know that you're my friend."

Sebastian shook his head. "They know this, yet they sent you to destroy the woman I love. Do you think they suspected you would not harm her--that instead, you would confide in me?"

William cleared his throat and adjusted his glasses. "I had given that some consideration myself, but why send me with the task to kill her then? Why all the secrecy?" William shrugged. "I'm afraid, old friend, that even I can't decipher their reasoning this time. I believe that we should go to them and ask them ourselves."

"Will they answer to you or is my presence required?"

William gave him a knowing look. "Sebastian, they only just now told me that Gitana truly exists. Do you think for a moment that they would feel obligated to tell me anything further? They respect you--some even fear you. They will answer to you."

"Then I shall go," Sebastian said, his chest heavy.

"But you yourself said that we would be leading Gitana to her death," William protested.

"I shall pay the council a visit, and you shall stay and keep watch over her."

"Sebastian, *no!*" William rose to his feet. "What am I supposed to do about her newfound hunger? I could barely keep her contained for you to come from the neighboring house. What would you have me do with her while you're gone for days? Want me to tie her to a chair? She'll eat me alive, you know, and I don't mean in the cannibalistic way, either."

Sebastian stood slowly, touching his friend's shoulder lightly.

"You will do what must be done." His body hurt at the idea of another man touching his mate, but his choices were limited. He needed to assure Gitana's safety with the council members. Aaron was another matter.

* * * *

Aaron walked through the old mansion and shook his head. What in the hell would a vampire of Sebastian Rolle's status be doing in a small town like this, and how did he end up fucking his wife?

He stopped in the center of the living room and let his hand shift into a claw. He slashed the wingback sofa with one fluid motion. God, he hated vampires. He found them to be disgusting creatures that were confined to the night. His wolves were far superior. That's why the council had chosen him to stand in as Gitana's *mullo*. He'd done his best with her, but that bitch did little for him in the bedroom. She wasn't like his pack women. She didn't bow to his every need.

Who am I kidding? She was the best fuck I ever had. She gave the best head with that hot little mouth. The Council gave her to me, and now she thinks she can replace me with some walking corpse.

Aaron took one last look around Sebastian's home and growled. His people were coming, and they would find that vampire and kill him.

Chapter Twelve

Gitana stood in her greenhouse and worked the seedlings until she'd accidentally destroyed most of them. She wiped the tears that continued to flow from her cheeks and tried her best to push the thoughts of what was happening to her out of her head. How could she take on vampire characteristics, and why had the major one taken the form of sexual cravings? How could Sebastian think leaving her to visit the Council was helping her? She needed him here, not half-way around the world.

Why had fate dealt her such a hand? What had she done to deserve it? The Council now wanted her dead, Aaron had his pack after her, and as far as she knew, she could start requiring blood to survive. She let loose another sob.

Her fists burned to hit something and she scared herself with the amount of rage that now ran through her body. She tried to push it down, keep it at bay, but nothing worked. She let out a scream and threw her potting shovel at the door. The door flew open and Sebastian stood there, his blue eyes wide.

"Gitana?"

"Make it stop!" She screamed. "Make it all stop!"

Pain covered Sebastian's face. "I wish I could." He looked up at the greenhouse window and hesitated before taking another step out.

Gitana let out a small laugh. "Why would you want to make it all go away? You're able to walk in the light again and live." The burning in her loins started again, and she had to grip the edge of the potting table to keep from collapsing. She licked her lips and the taste of her own sweat made her pussy tight with need.

"Gitana, I cannot walk in the daylight as I once did, not yet, and even if I could I would not wish things to be the way they are. I did not intend for this to happen."

She ran her hand over her neck and eased it down the front of her blouse. "You've turned me into a whore. I lust after everything and everyone *all* the time. I can't control it." She touched her breast and tipped her head back. "My body craves sex, attention, anything, so much so that I feel like I'll die without it."

"I know," Sebastian said wryly. He looked up at the sun and back to her. "Gitana, come and let me hold you. My immunity to the sun's rays has increased, but I can feel it wearing away my resolve. Please come here and we will get through this-- together." He stepped back into the kitchen doorway and held his hand out to her.

"Allow me," William said, appearing from behind Sebastian. William locked eyes with her and gave a small smile. "Come on in. We need to discuss some things with you."

Gitana took a handful of seeds and threw them at William. They didn't slow him down. She grabbed another shovel and twisted to strike him with it. He put his hand out and looked at her hand. "Object of harm will be disarmed." The shovel grew instantly hot and Gitana was left no choice but to drop it.

"How?" she asked, amazed by his raw power.

"I told you that I was more than human," William said matter-of-factly. "Now, come and let us discuss several matters with you."

The closer he came to her, the more she realized just how handsome he truly was. The demonic power within her wanted to sample him. She slid her hand back into her blouse and William stopped dead in his tracks. "You want me. I can smell it on you," she said, surprised by her own sultry voice. "You've wanted to fuck me since the moment you laid eyes on me. You want it now, don't you, William? You want to bury your cock in me and have me scream out your name."

Oh, Goddess, what's happening to me?

It is my vampire lust that controls you now. I am sorry, Gitana. Fight it and come in. I will tend to your needs. Sebastian's voice answered the unspoken question in her head. She looked past William at Sebastian and he nodded, his hand still outstretched. She started toward him, but the monster that now resided within her held her in place. She struggled against it. It overtook her easily and left her crumpling to the floor.

* * * *

Sebastian watched in horror as Gitana's eyes rolled back into her head. He knew that she wasn't strong enough to fight his primal urges. She would die trying. "Grab her!" he shouted to William.

William obliged and had Gitana wrapped in his arms in one fluid movement. He raced her back into the kitchen and Sebastian took her from him. He drew in her sweet scent and could smell the mark of the vampire on her, and something else.

He took a deeper breath and recognized the magic that had once run through his veins. He'd passed that on to her as well. He dropped his head down and fought hard to remain in control of his emotions. "Forgive me."

She nipped at his jaw, her eyes swirling with the power he gave her--the curse. "Fuck me."

"You need to rest, and then we need to discuss my leaving."

"Leaving?"

Sebastian closed his eyes slowly and nodded his head. He hated the thought of leaving her even more than he hated what he'd passed on to her. The thirty years he'd spent searching for her had left his need for her so great that the idea of spending one second without her was killing him.

Gitana's brown eyes narrowed and he watched in horror as they swirled with flecks of yellow. She pushed hard on his chest, using the strength he'd given her, and freed herself from his grasp.

"Gitana!" he shouted as he lunged for her.

She dodged his grasp and ran toward the bedroom. Cold wind knocked into him and he struck the wall with such a force that he dented it. "GITANA!"

The door to her room shook. William ran up next to him, touching his arm gently. "Sebastian, are you hurt?"

"No," he said, lying. His heart was breaking, but he knew that William had only meant hurt in the literal sense of the word.

"Oh, Gods," William said, under his breath.

"What?"

His friend of more than a hundred years turned his green eyes toward him and let a tear fall down his cheek. "She's cast a desire spell, and I believe she's directed it at me."

Sebastian's brows came together. "Why?" he asked, not needing to hear William say it. He knew the demon that Gitana now carried within her. He'd spent centuries taming it. He knew that it demanded revenge for being hurt, and telling her that he had to leave to go visit the Council had hurt her beyond words. Now, the demon had taken control and would use William, his oldest friend, as retribution.

Gitana's bedroom door flew open and Sebastian's eyes widened as he took in the sight before him. His beautiful Gitana was levitating a good six inches off the ground, as wind swirled around her now naked body. Her eyes locked on him as her fingers went to the apex of her thighs. Her slender fingers darted into her silk binding, and they glistened with each stroke.

William drew in a breath and took a step forward. Sebastian grabbed his shoulder and held him steady. Green eyes of fury turned on him and he saw William's lips begin to move. He knew how powerful a sorcerer William was, and he knew if he rattled off an incantation then he'd be helpless to control the events that were about to take place. A decision had to be made, and he knew that he could not let Gitana fight this alone.

"We shall share her," Sebastian said quickly.

William tipped his head to the side. The magical influence of Gitana's spell still clouded his judgment. William peeled his clothes from his body and grabbed hold of his rigid cock. "I want to bury it in her hot little pussy. I want to feel her lips around my cock." He sounded so uncharacteristic that Sebastian did a double take.

Sebastian touched William's shoulder again. "Old friend, she is ready to conceive a child. Think about the prophecies. If you release your seed into her womb, the end will change, and the child that was once foreseen will be no more. Is that what you want?"

William licked his lower lip as he stroked his cock. "I want to fuck her. I need to fuck her."

"And you shall, but think…think about the repercussions. Think of mankind's future."

Gitana's breath came in pants as she rammed her fingers into her body repeatedly. She let out a cry and Sebastian removed his clothes quickly. "We will see you through this, *ma vie*." He reached for Gitana and she screamed out, her eyes ablaze with the power of the vampire.

"Him!" She pointed toward William.

Sebastian moved closer to her and ran his hand over her stomach. "*Ma sucré*, Gitana, fight this evil within you. I beg you. You are mine. You are my mate, and I am your *mullo*." Sebastian hoped that his words would reach her, but he knew that even if they did she was beyond any help that he alone could offer. He'd need William to satisfy her sexual craving.

Running his hand down Gitana's smooth stomach, he cupped her sex. The hand she'd been pleasuring herself with came to his lips. He drew it into his mouth, sucking her sweet cream from it. Her brown eyes locked on him as her body floated down to the floor. "Bastian?"

"I am here, *ma vie*."

"It burns," she said, softly.

"I know. Let us help you ease the pain." He motioned for William to come closer. Sharing his mate would be the hardest thing he'd ever done, but it was his curse that had created what stood before them craving sex, and he would see to it that her pain went away.

"Come, William. Let us love her as she should have always been loved."

* * * *

The scent of vampires was strong near the house. Aaron took a deep breath in and frowned in confusion. Why did it smell like there was two of the same vampire within Gitana's home?

He could smell the scent of a man as well, a human, and old magic. The little bitch had aligned herself with some powerful friends. Too bad they wouldn't be able to save her. He looked around the property and nodded to his pack. Hundreds of loyal werewolves encircled the house. There would be no escape for the occupants. If Gitana was lucky, he'd decide to keep her, even though she was damaged goods from screwing that vampire. If all else failed, he'd fuck her for old times sake before he killed her. Either way he'd force her to watch her vampire die.

Chapter Thirteen

Gitana looked at the men before her and tried to make sense of what she was seeing. Sebastian was naked and in his full glory. William was as well, and that scared her. Her body craved the touch of both men. She loved Sebastian, but wanted William's cock nestled deep in her body as well. She'd never felt so bold, so daring in her life.

Sebastian's cool fingers worked their way into her hot slit and she clutched onto his shoulder as soothing sensations shot through her legs. He pulled his fingers out slowly and licked her come from them. Her eyelids fluttered shut and she felt warm hands touching her back. She looked over her shoulder and found William standing behind her.

William caressed the small of her back and inched his way down her butt, cupping and kneading as he went. He drew in a sharp intake of breath when he parted her ass and drove a finger into her tiny rosette. Fire shot through her lower half. The mix of pain and pleasure left her clinging to Sebastian, as William's finger continued to stroke her.

Sebastian lifted her quickly and positioned himself on the bed, pulling Gitana up and over him. His rigid cock found its way into her pussy and she cried out as he filled her.

He pulled her to him, nibbling on her breasts in the process.

The weight on the bed shifted as William appeared behind her. He rubbed his shaft against her anus, gathering juice from her fucking Sebastian, and nudged himself into her ass slowly.

"More!" she screamed as she rode Sebastian harder.

Blinding hot pain shot through her body as William thrust the full length of his swollen cock into her ass. Her body clenched against him, fighting the invasion. She was too full, too stretched, too ready to explode from the heat.

Sebastian grabbed her chin and forced her to look upon his

sweet face. "Push down and relax, *princess*. Let us love you."

He pulled her nipple into his mouth and sucked gently. His fangs nicked her skin, and the minute he began to draw her blood into his mouth, her body relaxed around William's impaling cock.

She drove her body down onto Sebastian's, causing her bloodied breast to slip from his mouth. Gitana dove at his chin, licking the tiny trickle of blood that flowed from the corner of his mouth, and dug her nails into his arms as her orgasm ripped through her.

"Your ass is so bloody tight," William panted, pounding himself into her repeatedly. The odd full feeling, he gave her, made her entire body feel alive. He pumped himself into her, harder and harder, to the point that she was unable to hold her body up and her rhythm while fucking Sebastian had changed to mirror William. "Fuck, oh...oh fuck, I can't hold it much longer." His body stiffened and he flattened himself against her back as he shot his hot seed into her.

The air around them thickened, then stilled. She knew that whatever they'd just done had brought about a magic like none she'd ever seen, but she didn't care. She wanted more.

Gitana could feel William's heart pounding rapidly against her back. He stroked her arms gently as his body continued to shoot semen into her ass. He pulled out slowly, dripping onto her.

Sebastian rolled her quickly onto her back, never leaving the warmth of her womb, and pumped his body into hers. The muscles in his arms tightened as he strained to control his motions. His blue eyes locked on hers and he snarled, "Mine."

He slammed himself down on her, and she screamed out from the pain. He swiveled his hips ever so slightly and found a gentle rhythm, quickly chasing away the hurt with a pleasure such as she'd never known before. She writhed beneath him, another man's come leaking slowly from her body, while she tried to escape the supernova that threatened to claim her.

"I can't, Bastian...no more...please." The continual orgasms were sending her over the edge. She clawed at his back and he pumped into her.

"*Je t'aime*, Gitana--I love you." He said, allowing his seed to project into her body. She felt the demon within her receding, sated for the moment. He kissed her nose and she smiled. He tilted his head to the side and winked. "You did not cover your mouth."

"No, I didn't," she said, laughing softly.

She heard the shower running in the bathroom and remembered William. The shock of what she'd just done hit her and she tried desperately to get out from beneath Sebastian. He pinned her body to the bed and began kissing her neck.

"Bastian, I'm so sorry. I've never...I'm...."

"*Shhh, Ça ne fait rien*--it doesn't matter. It needed to be done and I am pleased that it was William who assisted us. I am so sorry for the curse that I have passed on to...."

"Yeah, you piece of vampire trash, you will know sorry soon enough."

Gitana stiffened at the sound of Aaron's voice. Sebastian leaned down and kissed her gently on the mouth, ignoring the intruder. His body was ripped from hers and she screamed out, trying to hold onto him.

Strong arms yanked her out of the bed and she looked into Aaron's cold, hard eyes. His lips curled and his nostrils flared. "You let this piece of rotting flesh fuck you?"

She'd seen this look in Aaron's eyes before. He would kill them all tonight, that much she was sure of.

Chapter Fourteen

Aaron took in a deep breath and growled at her. He brought his hand up and smacked her across the face. Gitana's head jerked back and for a minute, all she saw was flecks of white.

"Leave her be!" Sebastian shouted. He was pinned under a half dozen of Aaron's pack members who were being anything but gentle with him.

Aaron pulled Gitana to him and smiled wide. He let a claw extend from his finger and pressed it against her lower abdomen. Taking a deep breath in, he jerked on her. "You carry another man's child. Does the vampire know this?"

"Another man's child?" Gitana repeated the question, unclear on how she could be pregnant by anyone else. William hadn't released his seed in her womb and Sebastian was the only other man she'd had sex with since divorcing Aaron two years prior.

"You've become quite the slut, Gitana. Tell me, how many others cocks have you had? Huh? How many men have you let fuck you?" Aaron pressed his wolf claw into her flesh. Hot pain followed as he drew blood slowly. It wasn't a deep wound yet, but it would be before long. "Don't look so surprised. Tell me who else you've been screwing?"

"Me," William said, from the bathroom doorway. He held his hand out, palms up and stared at Aaron. "I suggest you leave now and never return."

The werewolves in the room laughed. They weren't scared of a naked Brit, anymore than they were scared of Gitana. Aaron took a step forward and looked William over. He glanced back at Gitana and shook his head. "Baby, I was just too good. My dick was too much for you, huh? No one could compare, so you settled on this *human*?" He said the word human like it was a disease.

Gitana brushed her hair out her face and stood tall, not caring that six other men were now seeing her naked as well. "I'll have you know that one time with William was better than all the times you were in me." Aaron spun around, letting his eyes go yellow. She knew that the wolf within him was now teetering on the edge of release.

"I'm going to fuck you so hard in front of your heroes that you'll beg me for mercy. And, when I'm done, you'll know who the real alpha is here, Bitch." He lunged at her and grabbed her around the waist. He had her on her hands and knees before she knew what hit her. He slapped her ass hard and growled, "I'll own this before the night is over."

"My good friend Sebastian is her mate, and he would greatly appreciate it if you stepped away from her," William said, taking another step into the room. Two of Aaron's men rushed him and William simply pushed his hands outward. Gitana couldn't see anything emanating from William, but something sent the two weres tumbling into the wall. The room smelled of magic, a scent she'd become accustomed to after years of living within the Roma witch community.

Sebastian tossed the remaining pack members from his body and lunged at Aaron. Aaron grabbed hold of Gitana and jerked her head back. "Take a good look at her before I gut her," he said, running a half-clawed finger down the side of her throat. Sebastian stopped in mid-motion, refusing to allow harm to come to her. "You claim she is your mate, but you let that human, with a few fancy parlor tricks, knock her up? That doesn't scream mate to me, it screams coward."

Sebastian's blue eyes swirled with black and Gitana knew that the demon within him had risen. Aaron trailed his fingers down her body, stopping at her breast and plucking her nipple. "Look, they still get hard for me, baby." His hot breath felt foreign on her ear. "Want to see how hard you still make me?"

Gitana, use the gifts that were bestowed upon you. Her grandmother's voice echoed in her head. She scanned the room with her eyes to be sure that Grandma hadn't crashed the party. As much as she wanted help, having her Grandmother show up after she'd just slept with two men wasn't her idea of a happy ending.

Aaron grabbed her ass and pulled it back toward him. Parting her cheeks, he rubbed is thumb over her anus. "Yeah, you're hot for me, I can smell it. I'm going fuck you raw, baby. It's my right, you know--you're my wife."

"Come on, Aaron. You said that you wanted to scare her and her vampire, not rape her," Travis said softly, looking a bit banged up. "She's carrying a child now, leave her be. You got her, she's scared. Let's go home."

Gitana was shocked to hear Travis, Aaron's right-hand man, stand up to him. Aaron growled, jerking her hips back against him. "I'll fuck my wife any way I see fit and then I'll kill the bastard that put that child in her."

She closed her eyes and concentrated on the air around her. Her grandmother had spent years trying to convince her that if she only listened she'd hear the spirits of the dead. Gitana hoped it was true because she needed to call upon their power to help her stop Aaron and his entire pack. She heard the whispers of the unknown. They were faint at first, but there. A low buzzing started in her head and she knew that metaphysically she'd tapped into the spirit plane. "Spirits of the dead, heed my need and...."

"Shut-up!" Aaron said slamming his body against hers. He fumbled with his pants and tried to free himself.

"Sebastian, stop her!" William shouted.

Gitana strained to hear him, but the buzzing grew louder. Her nose and throat burned. She reached up to wipe the sweat from her lip and came away with blood. She'd tried too hard, tapping into the dead's magic was too much for her body.

The room shook and Aaron's grasp on her loosened. He fell away from her and she collapsed onto the floor. Visions of a woman who looked like her, but was not, swam through her head. The woman spoke softly to her and tried to ease her pain.

* * * *

Sebastian dove at Aaron and caught his head with his hands. One quick jerk to the side and Aaron no longer resisted. Sebastian let Aaron's dead body fall from his grasp. The lycans in the room growled, and the blond one silence them.

"No more bloodshed," the blond said. "We'll take him and go."

"Travis!" Another exclaimed. Travis turned and let a low rumble escape his throat.

Sebastian knew that Travis was now the pack's Alpha male, their leader, and from his actions tonight, he would make a fine one. Stepping away from Aaron's body, he turned his attentions to Gitana.

William was on the floor next to her, pushing on her chest. Sebastian's mind raced. She couldn't be dead. His mate, his love could not leave him when he'd only just found her.

He dropped to his knees and reached for her. William touched his hand gently. "She is gone, old friend."

Sebastian screamed out, seizing hold of Gitana's tiny body. It cooled and knew that life no longer ran through it. His now beating heart felt as though it had shattered. He clutched her body to him, kissing her, rocking her back and forth gently.

"*Je t'aime,*" he whispered.

The air in the room stilled. The temperature climbed rapidly around them, but he did not care. He pulled Gitana to him, as tears fell down his face.

Gitana's body tightened, her eyes flew open, and she drew in a sharp breath. William was suddenly there--helping to support her head gently.

"Gitana?" William said, softly.

A small smile formed on her mouth as her gaze moved to Sebastian. "I love you too," she said weakly.

He dropped his lips to hers and kissed her through his tears. His body shook, partly from the shock of the Goddess giving her back to him, and partly out of the need to resist crushing her with his love.

He drew his lips back from her slowly, savoring her sweet taste. She tried to sit up, but he and William said no at the same time. She laughed. "I'm fine you two. Stop worrying about me."

"You died," William said sardonically. "How is that fine? And how exactly were we not supposed to worry?"

"I didn't die. I stepped onto the spirit plane to receive a message, that's all." She grinned mischievously.

"*Pardon?*"

Gitana touched his cheek lightly. "My mother wants to know what took you so long to find me. She said that you may be slow, but you'll make a fine father for her grandchild."

"Father?"

"Yes, Bastian, the baby is fine. I'm fine."

Epilogue

Sebastian drew in a deep breath as he watched his wife working in her greenhouse. Her hand went to her tiny belly, as it often did. At twelve weeks, Gitana's belly had the slightest curve to it. She had only begun to show and he alone had the privilege of knowing that. Though William remained with them, he had not shared their bed again. Nor would he ever. As much as he wanted to see his friend happy, he could not let it be with his wife.

"I love you," he said, as Gitana repotted a small plant.

"I love you too, sweetie, but that's not what you came out here to talk to me about."

Sebastian sighed. His wife knew him well. William had received a call from a friend informing him that the Council had pinpointed their location and were in the process of planning what their next move would be.

He and William had spent the last two days straight trying to convince Gitana to leave, to go into hiding while they hunted down all that threatened them. She refused.

"You still trying to take my granddaughter away from me?"

Sebastian turned to see Gitana's grandmother standing behind him. The old witch could sneak up on him as no one else could. She took great pleasure in getting the drop on a vampire. As much as she pretended to dislike him, he could sense that she cared for him, and he her.

"*Madame*, I think it is for the best that you all move somewhere safer."

She huffed. "We are moving boy or have you not noticed the boxes? I swear, Gitana tells me that you're a intelligent man, but

I've yet to see it."

Sebastian rolled his eyes and the old woman smacked his arm. "*Pardon moi*, I did not mean to be rude, but I had hoped to move further than the house next door."

"We all hope for a lot of things, boy. A move's a move. Besides, I've already told you that my granddaughter is safest here. Travis and the pack will aid in whatever you need, and the magic that lives in these lands will protect all of you."

"I hope you are right."

"The spirits have told me that all will be well, and I tend to listen to them. Plus, the British boy's gonna meet his mate real soon, and he can't do it if he isn't here."

The End

Be sure to check out other NCP Trade Paperback releases by
these fantastic authors!

MARIE MORIN:

The Atalantium Trilogy (Paranormal Romance)

The Fallen (Paranormal Romance Anthology, with stories by
Marie Morin, Jaide Fox, Kimberly Zant, Celeste Anwar)

MANDY M. ROTH:

Daughter of Darkness (Paranormal Romantic Suspense)

Hunters (Paranormal Romance Anthology, with stories by
Jennifer Colgan, Lyssa Hart, Mandy M. Roth)

Printed in the United States
73612LV00002B/151-153